A Marriage Made at Woodstock

ALSO BY CATHIE PELLETIER

Widow's Walk (Poems)
The Funeral Makers
Once Upon a Time on the Banks
The Weight of Winter
The Bubble Reputation

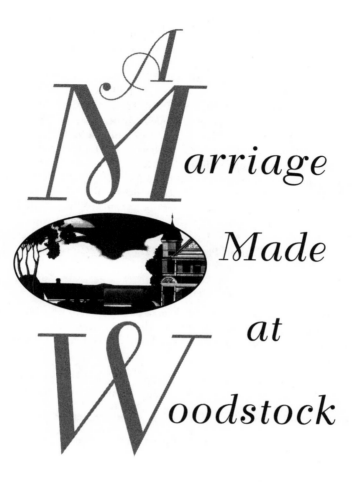

A Marriage Made at Woodstock

Cathie Pelletier

Crown Publishers, Inc.
New York

Grateful acknowledgment is made to the following for permission to reprint previously published material: Warner/Chappell Music, Inc., for permission to reprint "Lady Willpower" by Jerry Fuller. Copyright © 1968 by WARNER-TAMERLANE PUBLISHING CORP. All rights reserved. Used by permission; Warner/Chappell Music, Inc., for permission to reprint "Over You" by Jerry Fuller. Copyright © 1968 by WARNER-TAMERLANE PUBLISHING CORP. & TRACKSHOE MUSIC. All rights on behalf of TRACKSHOE MUSIC administered by WARNER-TAMERLANE PUBLISHING CORP. All rights reserved. Used by permission; Warner/Chappell Music, Inc., for permission to reprint "This Girl Is A Woman Now" by Victor Millrose and Alan Bernstein. Copyright © 1968 by CHAPPELL & CO. (Renewed) All rights reserved. Used by permission; Warner/Chappell Music, Inc., for permission to reprint "Young Girl" by Jerry Fuller. Copyright © 1968 by WARNER-TAMERLANE PUBLISHING CORP. All rights reserved. Used by permission; The Famous Music Publishing Companies for permission to reprint "Woman Woman" by Jim Glaser and Jimmy Payne. Copyright © 1967, 1972, 1973 by Ensign Music Corporation. Used by permission; New Directions's Publishing Corp. for permission to reprint "Dance Figure" from *Personae* by Ezra Pound. Copyright © 1926 by Ezra Pound. Used by permission.

Published by Crown Publishers, Inc., 201 East 50th Street, New York, New York 10022. Member of the Crown Publishing Group.

Random House, Inc. New York, Toronto, London, Sydney, Auckland

CROWN is a trademark of Crown Publishers, Inc.
Manufactured in the U.S.A.

Designed by Lauren Dong

Library of Congress Cataloging-in-Publication Data

Pelletier, Cathie.
    A marriage made at Woodstock / Cathie Pelletier.—1st ed.
      p.   cm.
    1. Marriage—Maine—Portland—Fiction. 2. Portland (Me.)—Fiction. I. Title.
PS3566.E42M37   1994
813'.54—dc20   93-38183
                                                         CIP

ISBN 0-517-59796-9

10 9 8 7 6 5 4 3 2 1

First Edition

For JIM GLASER, without whom this novel would never have been written. (It started out as an idea we were going to write together.) Jim supplied me with all the computer references I needed, and then, as usual, was my first trusted reader as each chapter was written. Thanks, Jim, for getting me permission to quote from your song, "Woman, Woman." And thanks for those seventeen years we spent together on the *Enterprise*.

And for my niece, DR. DIANA K. PELLETIER, D.V.M., for taking up the call. (I might have become a vet, too, but it's in my DNA to stay in bed until noon. Also, I keep confusing lidocaine with lanacane.)

And for all those people in the world who speak for the animals who cannot speak for themselves.

Special Thanks and Acknowledgments

Mom and Dad, as ever, and always.

To my childhood pal, buddy, and fellow terrorist, DORIS RO-BICHAUD, in memory of all those sun-bleached, pine-green, river-blue days of our childhood, a place and time we both still long for. (Strangely, we had our first reunion in years long after I'd already named Doris Bowen, in this book.)

My friend BRIAN LEBLANC, in memory of the old college years, and with great sadness that he's no longer on the earth so that he could see me turn forty years old, an event he used to claim would have earth-shattering consequences for all.

To another special niece, JAMIE DESJARDINS, in memory of red-necks, Big Al, and other crazy moments we've shared.

My brother VERNON DALE PELLETIER for the info about Jimi Hendrix's orange vest; and to my nephew-in-law, STEVE O'NEAL, for a bit of car lore.

To PAUL, SUE, and ASHLEY GAUVIN, out in Texas, simply because I *always* mention them.

A very special thanks to songwriter extraordinaire BOB MCDILL, not just for his friendship, but for giving me vital hunting information when he knew I couldn't wait to sink my literary teeth into hunters. (It's taken me five books to find the perfect spot to malign them properly.) It was Bob who told me about "The Glorious Twelfth," and "The Big Five," thus sending me to reference books. (This is why I nurture my friendships.) To all chagrined hunters who read this: Cut Bob some slack. The man has written over thirty number-one songs.

My deepest affection and appreciation to the Fates:

Rhoda Weyr, my darling agent.

Betty Prashker and Irene Prokop, my editors.

And special thanks to my publicist, Hilary Bass.

A. G. Harmon, for some legal advice.

Margery Wilson, at the University of Maine, for reasons she knows very well, which added to the weight of this book.

To Canadian novelist Eliza Clark, for being my good friend, and for helping me through my first full winter in seventeen years.

To Patsi Cox, for when her own day comes.

And to Erin Benson, for favors galore.

I often name characters, usually minor ones, after friends, if the full name or the surname seems appropriate. Thanks to the following compadres, who are nothing like their namesakes: Jennifer Kimball (Chandra Kimball-Stone) and Jennifer Kimball and Bob McDill (Jenny and Bob); Gordon Hammond; James Gordon Bennett; Janet Walsh; Cheryl Carlesimo; Patti Kelley (Patti's Poodle Parlor); Cissy Libby; Ruthie Brown; Marion Higgins; Dee Dee (Diana) Pelletier; Sharon and Randy Thompson (for the "Thompson residence"); Dr. David Horowitz; Dan Ladner; Dr. Kim Brasher, D.V.M.; Carol Lindsey, Gary Vincent, and Cathy Gurley, for the law firm of Lindsey, Vincent, & Gurley; Jim Veatch; Ed Walsh; Kathy McLain; Eliza Clark; Tomislav "Tom" Viorikic, although he hates the character for whom he was named; Glenna Smith; Alice Cary; Kathy Olmstead; Gene Nelson; Jerry Ryan; and Kristina Copkov Wiecken, for Chandra's new address.

My apologies to the people of Portland, Maine, for the fictional liberties I took with the geography of their city. Although I've spent a great deal of time in Portland, I wanted the freedom to roam the streets at will, to imagine restaurants I may have seen in Boston or Nashville, to infuse my own observations of Portland life, which may well be very different from those of the people who actually live there. Such is the magic of fiction that I can make up street names, build roads that suddenly twist along the bay, erect buildings in a flash. Some places I refer to exist, however: Demilo's floating bar, the Longfellow house, the Portland Observatory, etc. Also in existence, happily, is Will's Restaurant on Peaks Island (Peak's Island, in the book) where I once tried to extricate a stranger who was locked in the bathroom (as Chandra Kimball-Stone does) and where little blond-headed Will really does roam the premises. I thank Darrell McBreairty for taking me to Will's, and for welcoming me into his Portland home so many, many times.

To some of those readers who wrote me letters in the past year: I foolishly lost a packet containing a couple hundred of them. That's why some of you haven't heard from me. Please write again, especially the college student, in one of the Carolinas, who told me that everything she "knew and feared about the world" she read in *The Bubble Reputation!*

A Marriage Made at Woodstock

*O*ne

awn was just coming to Ellsboro Street as
Frederick Stone tiptoed across the dewy
grass for his morning paper. He stopped in
his driveway, as he always did, and surveyed the street. He felt it
arrive again, the sweet sense of satisfaction that he was the first
person to be awake for as far as his eye could see. It had not always
been that way. For two years, while the Andersons lived in the
light blue Cape across the street, their son Tommy had risen daily
at four-thirty for his paper route. Frederick Stone was glad that the
Andersons had taken their little automaton and transferred to another state. Now a bank manager and his teller wife lived in the
blue Cape. Frederick needn't worry about *their* lights coming on
before six o'clock, not unless they were embezzling. He looked
smugly at his watch. Five fifty-eight, and already he had coffee
perking, an English muffin sitting on a paper towel in the microwave. He would dawdle the two extra minutes, just for the hell of
it, just because when one gets up at five forty-five one can spare
two meager minutes. Above his head, the huge Victorian turret of
his house—an architectural oddity among the more modern
homes—pointed like a medieval steeple toward heaven. On the

lawn a plump robin was canting its head toward the soil, looking for the next available earthworm. Frederick could hear a wall of bird calls and notes rising up from all the hedges. The birds had beat him, but birds were just birds. Five fifty-nine. One more minute to wait.

He made his way through the wet grass, toward the front porch. Like the turret, the porch was a bit dated, the old-fashioned kind one sees on farmhouses in the country. But it was another reason that his wife, Chandra Kimball-Stone, had loved the house so. Frederick now had a better view of the street from the porch's top step. Thirty more seconds. He pulled his pajama sleeve down over his fist and wiped at the cast-iron mailbox, which was nailed quite firmly next to the front door. FREDERICK STONE, the small, dignified lettering announced. STONE ACCOUNTING AND CONSULTATION. Beneath this sign a tailless orange cat, no doubt another of Chandra's strays, was curled into a sleepy ball on the throw rug. Ten more seconds. The morning paper landed with a *thump* on the front porch, prompting the robin to fly off on quick wings and the orange cat to spring to life. Five seconds more and it would be six o'clock sharp. Bingo! As Frederick watched, a light burst forth from an upstairs window of the house next door.

"Aha, Walter Muller!" Frederick whispered loudly. "I beat you again!" Walter Muller, also an accountant, had once questioned Frederick's good business sense in regards to working out of his own house instead of at a downtown office. And yet here it was six o'clock and Walter was just now stirring. By the time Frederick sat down at his computer, muffin crumbs in his teeth, to begin work on a client's account, Walter Muller would be just staggering out of the shower. And by the time Walter Muller was approaching the on-ramp and morning traffic, Frederick would already have an hour's work done. He gave Walter's window an emphatic thumbs-down. He was sincerely proud that his neighbors—through chats over their backyard fences—had come to know Frederick Stone as the earliest riser on Ellsboro Street. Frederick had made slight reference to his habit, each time one of them took a break from their lawn mowing or hedge trimming to say hello. "I sure miss Tommy the paper boy," Frederick inevitably got around to mentioning. "It gets lonely, you know, when one gets up with the birds."

His wife, Chandra, felt none of this Early Bird Pride, however. "They probably think you're a lunatic, Freddy," was his wife's only remark. "An early-rising nut." But then, how could she understand his adherence to Puritan ethics? There were mornings when Frederick rose in the dark, reached a hand beneath a lamp shade, and discovered that the bulb was still radiating heat from its filament, Chandra only recently retired. One kept late hours, it seemed, when one had a degree in psychology and was concerned with matters of the mind. Frederick Stone remembered the day Chandra had abandoned teaching psychology to high-school students in order to begin a counseling service for Portland's emotionally confused. *Seminars in Human Psychology,* her new business card announced, *For Students of the Mind.* He had turned it over and over in his hands before he asked the ageless, aesthetic question: "How much money can you make?" Frederick knew that loonies desperate for a seminar in *anything,* much less an odyssey into the unchartered regions of the human brain, abounded in Portland, Maine. As long as Chandra didn't take up with any convicted murderers who may or may not be working on their autobiographies. "Oh, Freddy," Chandra had scolded. "Must you always think of money? Don't you ever think of the betterment of mankind?" Frederick had carefully considered this query from his wife. After all, they were both products of the altruistic sixties, had even met at Woodstock's famous music festival. "How much money can you make?" Frederick Stone had asked again.

It was time for his first cup of coffee, made from his specially blended beans. It had taken many months of combining the wide selection available at Full of Beans to achieve what he now considered to be the perfect coffee taste. The secret was not only his special ratio of several different Colombian varieties, but also the addition of beans from Africa's Ivory Coast. Frederick had attended a "Coffee Blender's Forum," via his computer modem, and had learned that the African beans Robusta are slightly higher in caffeine and other alkaloids than the Arabica beans from South America. This gave his morning coffee a nice little boost. He smiled again. Walter Muller probably drank Sanka.

Frederick took the cup of coffee with him to the upstairs bathroom. He could have performed his morning toiletries in the dimly lighted downstairs bath—the one Chandra referred to as *his* bath—but he preferred the upstairs mirror for facial inspections, which he did daily. It had huge lights encircling its circumference, and mirrored panels that opened for profile viewing. He lathered his face with shaving cream and then doused his razor, the Sensor, Gillette's newest triumph, in the basin of hot water. Now, here was a comfortable, close shave. He was most grateful to *Consumer Reports* for their generous tip about the razor. It had taken Gillette thirteen years before they found a way to get the twin-cartridge blade to not only swivel, but to ride on minuscule springs. Thirteen years and $200 million to perfect a razor that maneuvered like a dream and protected its owner from nicks, cuts, and pulls. Yet it cost Frederick Stone $3.50 to own it. If he shaved six times a week and averaged eleven shaves per blade, he would spend less than $25 a year to rid himself of facial hair. Such was the modern, wonderful world in which he lived. Not to mention the fact that he no longer had to listen to Chandra rant about how the disposable razor he'd been using—he tossed out forty plastic ones a year—was adding to the demise of Mother Earth. "If a million men throw out forty disposable razors a year," she'd lectured, "the plastic would fill a box twenty feet high and twenty feet wide." Who figured these things out? That's what Frederick Stone would like to know. He was about to resort to a full beard until he read about Gillette's little jewel. Chandra would simply have to suffer the disposal of his blades. Frederick had done his math and he felt quite sure that 28.4 used blades would require only the tiniest of boxes.

His shave complete, Frederick began his daily assessment. The usual whisper of gray was still entrenched at his temples, a smoky coloring he had noticed for the first time on August 5, 1981, a Tuesday that had promised to be as regular as any other morning. But Tuesday, August 5, 1981, had lied, forcing Frederick to pull up his computer calendar of important dates and list the discrepancy, next to August 5, 1977, when he had puffed sadly on his last cigarette. And lately, to Frederick's dismay, an obscene puffiness loomed about his eyes, regardless of how much sleep he got. He tipped his face seductively, searching for the cheekbones he had hoped to inherit from his father's side of the family. He sighed deeply. His genetic coding seemed more determined than ever to bequeath him the jowly-ness that had struck down his mother's face in its prime. Her brothers, his maternal uncles, had grown to look like rotund court jesters, red-cheeked, jolly, pleasing to the king. But at least they had all lived to a seasoned old age. On the other hand, all three of his paternal uncles had gone handsomely into their caskets with elongated, youthful faces. Even the funeral director had noticed. "It's like burying Gregory Peck, over and over again," he had whispered to Frederick. Frederick's father was the last to die, from a congenital heart problem. "He had the same bad heart as Jim Fixx, the runner," Frederick had heard the funeral director explaining to an employee. Yet, at the age of forty-four, Frederick was still torn between longevity and cheekbones.

He decided in an instant to ignore the puffiness, at least for the time being. No need to call up the computer's calendar one day only to find the puffiness gone the next. And why trouble The Girls—known to those ancient Greeks as the Fates, Clotho, Dumbo, and Zippo, or something like that—when they had been so kind to him thus far? True, he had no fear that The Girls would pick up their skirts and desert him over a little swelling about the eyelids, but they might be unnecessarily concerned. They were women, after all. Frederick had always prided himself in being able to prevail with the weaker sex, shuffling out that certain *je ne sais quoi* at the last moment. And The Girls were not immune to his charm. He sighed again. He wondered if Chandra was right, that his daily compulsion about aging was directly attributable to a tiny flaw in his character. "Hubris," Frederick had heard her mutter, mornings when she had risen to use the bathroom while he shaved and assessed. "Complete and total hubris, Freddy," she would caution, her words accompanied by a musical stream of pee.

At the bedroom door he paused to cant his head, his listening stance. Chandra was breathing evenly, dreaming no doubt of sound lessons in humanity for unsound minds. Frederick was reminded of the counseling she had recently given a certain Paul Jablonski, a portly butcher in his mid-sixties who was lusting heavily for his twin great-nieces, aged ten. Chandra had hypnotized the butcher and was now convinced that his pedophilic preoccupation was all because of an unfortunate incident in an earlier life, one as a nineteenth-century headmaster of a school for retarded girls. But Jablonski hadn't settled for this Karmic-

Dickensian notion. He seemed to think, good butcher that he was, that the little nieces were yearning for his big kielbasa. To Frederick it was, by God, and *finally,* a classic case of the hubris for which he himself had been accused.

Downstairs, he opened the refrigerator door in search of an apple. A sheet of typing paper caught the sudden breeze and flapped at him. It had been pinned there with two magnets—one a butterfly, the other a duck with an abnormal-looking head—and was undoubtedly one of Chandra's famous pronouncements. He poured himself a second cup of coffee before he pulled the sheet loose of its magnets and took it to the kitchen table.

"Jesus!" Frederick shouted, and jumped just enough that a trickle of hot coffee laced its way down his wrist. A sly movement in the window had startled him, but now he saw what it was, the same orange cat that had been on the front porch. Now it was stretching itself on the windowsill. Frederick ignored it. Over the rim of his cup, and through the lens of his newly acquired no-line bifocals from Gordon W. Hammond, O.D., one of his clients, Frederick read the note. *It is of earth-shattering importance that you wake me at nine. Sukie will be here at ten.* Who the hell was Sukie? *We have to drive to Augusta.* Frederick rolled the note up into a snowball and pitched it at the window. It hit exactly where he intended, into the blurry face of the orange cat, which was peering hopefully through the glass.

"Sorry, but the soup line's not open yet," Frederick said. The cat frisked back and forth on the window ledge, meowing pitifully. "Why don't you call back around nine-fifteen? Madame should be up by then." He didn't really dislike cats, but he *was* allergic to them. Yet Chandra brought strays home as though they were nothing more than doughnuts, or pencils. "Just until we find it a good home," Frederick was sick of hearing her announce. "It's all in your head anyway, Freddy. Get over it." She was right about it being all in his head. Or in his eyes and nose, to be more precise. Of course, the stray cats were easier to take than the stray humans. *Sukie.* Frederick wondered what Sukie's real name was, and if Paul Jablonski had ever served as her meatman. By the time he finished his second cup of coffee, the big orange cat had fallen asleep, like a soft field of orange poppies, spread out along the windowsill.

It was nearly eight o'clock and threatening rain when Frederick went into his office and turned on the computer. He pulled up the accounting software and began updating ledgers and entering weekly payroll information for Portland Concrete, his largest client. Having just landed a contract with the city, the company had hired a string of new people, and now Frederick added each one to the list of employees, filling in the necessary personal profile data. There were Theodores and Allans and Margarets, all straightforward and unpretentious names, names borrowed from their ancestors, most likely. There was not one Chandra or Sukie. And, thank God, there was no Paul Jablonski.

When he'd finished the lengthy data entry, Frederick pressed the keys to automatically print the payroll checks. They had to be delivered by eleven. Just as Portland Concrete's last check was sputtering out of the printer, the phone in the den rang suddenly, two loud bleats. He listened as the coda-phone clicked on. *Hello. This is Chandra,* he heard, followed by a brief message of instructions, the do's and don'ts of coda-phonology. He glanced briefly at his own phone, his separate business line, a necessity if he was to get any sensible work done. He couldn't spend hours a day prattling brainlessly to Chandra's *students of the mind,* not to mention those students of the crotch. But, out of curiosity, and in case there had been some family emergency—to Chandra's family this might mean the toaster burning up—Frederick went begrudgingly into the den and pushed the replay button. There was a call from his brother, Herbert, from the previous evening, which he'd forgotten to erase.

"Hey, Freddy!" Herbert said happily. Frederick could hear laughter in the background, mixed with music. Herbert was no doubt down at The China Boat, his favorite hangout since his wife had packed up and left him. "This is your brother, Herbert, veterinarian to the poor. I was just wondering if . . ." Frederick pushed the fast-forward button and Herbert's invitation to dinner sped past in a whir of words. The Girls were not kind to Herbert Stone these days, it was true. But then, Herbert had never been light on his feet when it came to women.

"Lorraine, it's your mother," the next voice declared. "I realize that nine-thirty is much too early for you to be up, but when you *do* turn out, call me. Joyce is quite upset that you forgot her birthday yesterday. She says strangers with mental problems are more important to you than your own sister." There was a sharp *click,* and then the blessed tone again. Chandra was going to hit the proverbial roof. Frederick smiled appreciatively. He had allies in the strangest of places. He considered taking his mother-in-law on as a client, for free, to repay her for all those years of unknowingly airing grievances for him, but her widow's mite would barely warrant his expertise. Too bad. She deserved his finding her a deduction here and there in the IRS haystack. The old battle-ax was good: *Lorraine, I realize nine-thirty is too early. . . .*

Nine-thirty? Frederick thought, and looked at his watch. Updating Portland Concrete had taken longer than he had anticipated. He groaned, remembering Chandra's declaration on the refrigerator. *It is of earth-shattering importance.* They had been married for over twenty years; *everything* in Chandra's life was of earth-shattering importance.

In the kitchen he filled a cup with hour-old coffee and headed upstairs to their bedroom. When all those blended beans went stale, they were still better than the coffee at Cain's Corner Grocery that Chandra was addicted to, although she now carried her own ceramic mug in a personal effort to speed up the demise of Styrofoam.

"Honey," Frederick said, and poked at the lump in their bed. "You'd better get up. Here's some coffee." Chandra stretched out her arms, a crucifixion figure, and yawned.

"What time is it?" she asked, reaching one hand out in search of the cup.

"A little later than you wanted to get up," Frederick admitted.

"God, this tastes good," Chandra said, and he knew she meant it. He had given up on her taste buds years ago. Just as he had given up on the stray cats. "So what time is it, really?" she asked. With a quick flash of her wrist, one slender hand rose up and, with fingers acting like a comb, she swept them through her hair several times.

"About nine-thirty," he said, though by now it was almost nine-forty. He tried to sound frivolous, as though time were a thing to be courted, perhaps, but never obeyed.

"Nine-thirty!" Chandra screamed. "Jesus Christ, I'll be late for the boycott!" She was suddenly sitting up in bed. With over twenty years of practice, he had still not grown used to how quickly she could switch like that, from being stretched out to sitting up suddenly with a new idea, from being pacifist to wishing the Shiite terrorists would get their asses kicked.

"Damn it, Freddy, I *asked* you," Chandra said. She flashed past him to the bathroom, and he followed. "I suppose you had your nose in that computer's face again." She was adjusting the knobs for her shower. "You can be pretty thoughtless sometimes," she said. He leaned against the wall.

"What boycott?" he asked.

"The National Veal Boycott, is all," Chandra said, sarcasm lacing every word. "True, there's no software offered on the subject, but out there, in the *hard wear* of the world, some important things are taking place."

"It's not even ten o'clock," Frederick said, "and already you've come up with a computer pun."

"I don't ask you to join me," Chandra said, and flopped a thick bath towel onto the floor beside the shower stall. "But I do ask you to wake me up."

"I've never understood your aversion to clocks," said Frederick, bringing up a point he'd mentioned more than once. "Almost everyone, including me, has to wake up to an alarm. That's what you call a rude awakening. But *you* get a gentle nudge in the side and a cup of coffee." He watched as she unbuttoned the top of her pajamas and tossed it past him. It landed with a soft *swish* in the hallway. Her small breasts bounced as she bent to remove the bottoms.

"Put my pj's in the hamper, would you please?" she asked as the bottoms flew past his face.

"*Excellent* coffee, I might add," he said. He watched as she pulled her hair up into a quick ponytail, some of it still brownish-blonde with youth, some of it gray with the years. It was, Frederick realized suddenly, as if an old abacus, that first computer, was busy at work, counting one hair at a time, turning it gray, numbering the days, marking the years. It was all a means of keeping track, wasn't it? *Updating humans*. Jesus, but the years were swift bastards.

"One of these days your little country with the secretive coffee beans may need our help," Chandra was saying. "And it'll be people like Sukie and me who fight to keep it going so that people like you can keep making excellent coffee."

"That little country with the secretive coffee beans happens to be a thriving democracy," Frederick said, and was thankful that the Ivory Coast was the only African country to offer beans to the Western world. Otherwise, Chandra might be right. Frederick could tune in to CNN some heartless morning to learn that half the beans of his prized blend was now in the hands of some upstart military regime. "They have a President now and can get along quite nicely without any help from you and Spooky. Incidentally," he added, "there's an orange cat on our windowsill."

"Just until I get it a good home," Chandra said. "Ignore it."

"It has no tail," Frederick said.

"*That* I can't do anything about." The shower door slammed in his face.

Back at his computer, that constant, ever-uncomplicated friend, Frederick paged down his menu of clients to James Gordon Bennett, D.D.S. As the files appeared colorfully on the screen, he heard the back door to the kitchen open with a gentle creak.

Who in hell? he thought, wondering if perhaps Joyce, maddened beyond logic, had come after Chandra with a kitchen knife, a birthday gift no doubt from someone who *cared.* But it was not Joyce. Before him he saw two women who looked as though they were editors of one of those feminist magazines, *The Lesbos Bi-Annual, The Menses Monthly,* or maybe *Sister Sappho,* circulation twenty-eight and growing. They peered at Frederick as if to ask what *he* was doing there.

"We did as the paper told us," said the shorter woman. She was dwarfish, with a long thick braid trailing down her back. Frederick accepted the paper she handed him. *Sukie. Go around to the back and let yourself in,* the note said. *The door's unlocked.* How many times had he told Chandra to lock the goddamn doors! And what good did it do for *him* to lock the things, when *she* left such notes upon them? Chandra seemed to think murders couldn't occur in Maine. Maybe she and Sukie had boycotted them there or something. And why hadn't he seen the proclamation when he went out for the morning paper? Walter Muller's upstairs light, Frederick supposed, had garnered all his attention.

"Sukie, I presume?" Frederick asked, and balled the second note that day into a perfect salvo. He looked at the windowsill for the cat, but it was gone.

"I'm Halona," the woman said. "This is Sukie." A pale, thin

creature, looking every bit as tall and anemic as *Sukie* suggested, peered at Frederick over the other woman's head.

"Chandra's just getting out of the shower," he said, and moved in front of the computer monitor to shield Dr. James Gordon Bennett's records, as though they were the dentist's exposed private parts, from the women's snoopy eyes. "Make yourselves at home," he added sarcastically.

"What's that?" asked Sukie, and pointed at the computer.

"It's a computer," Frederick replied. Good Christ. Had they stepped completely out of the crumply pages of the sixties?

"I mean, what's all the numbers for?" she plodded on.

"It's an accounting package," said Frederick.

"A *computer,*" said Halona, pushing past Sukie and staring wide-eyed. She pointed at the screen. "Is that the game where somebody steals something and you try to catch them?"

"*Game?*" asked Frederick. "This isn't a *game.* This is information on one of my clients." It would be futile, he realized, to explain his work to these flaky women. It was then that Chandra breezed into the room, still buttoning her plaid shirt.

"Sorry I'm late," she said. "Faulty alarm clock." She threw the sarcastic snippet in Frederick's direction and then disappeared into the kitchen.

"By the way," Frederick said as Chandra appeared again, a yogurt in one hand, spoon in the other. He'd been savoring the moment. "There's a message from your mother." He watched the frown curl slightly on her forehead. Sukie and Halona, trained picketers that they were, followed her obediently into the den. Frederick heard the button click, and then the curt message. *Lorraine, it's your mother.*

"Lorraine?" he heard Sukie's shrill little voice ask. He smiled, delighted.

"My name before I changed it," he heard Chandra explain. A minute later the trio was on its way, like a tiny mob, back to the computer room, and on out to the kitchen. Frederick followed them out of good-natured curiosity. "I even had a notary public involved so the name would be, you know, official. It's on my license. I mean, it's legally been my name for over twenty goddamn years, and she still leaves messages like that." Frederick shrugged his shoulders helplessly when Chandra's eyes met his.

"An emergency?" he asked, and pushed the tailless orange cat away. The visitors must have let it in, as they did themselves, and now it was twisting snakelike about his calves, marking him well with its scent. He put a foot beneath its stomach and scooted it gently aside. He could sense a major sneeze coming on.

"Emergency all right," Chandra said. "Joyce is another year along into what she calls the frightful forties. She likes for people to turn up on her birthday and pity her. Well, I'm afraid I have too many important things to do." She helped herself to an orange in the fridge and then offered the basket to Sukie and Halona. They shook their heads in harmony.

"Do you need to call her back before we leave?" Sukie asked. "We still got time."

"I *never* answer her messages when she calls me Lorraine," said Chandra. "She says Chandra, she gets called back." Frederick remembered, suddenly, the first time he'd ever heard her speak the name *Chandra,* as though it were a little song, a breeze from along some black river running through the night. *Chandra.* And he remembered *her* as she had been, her hair thick, wet with rain, smelling slightly of marijuana. "It's Sanskrit," she had told him, and he was caught up instantly in how her lips moved when she uttered syllables, as though they were coins she was offering him. "It means moonlike." And so it did. And so did she, lovely, pale, changeable thing that she was. My God, but he had fallen in love with her faster than you could format a floppy disk.

"It took her about ten years," Chandra was now saying, "but she finally caught on. If it's something important she wants, however, you'd be surprised how quickly she can remember names. By the way, my seminar this month, 'The Psychology of Names,' is in two weeks. Why don't you come?" Frederick suppressed a grimace. He imagined the house full to the rafters with Berthas and Lucilles, hoping to become Sukies and Halonas.

"My name means *fortunate,*" Halona said softly. "It's Native American Indian." Frederick stared at her, amazed. With her flaxen hair, shivery blue eyes, and buxom chest, he somehow imagined her as a kind of woman-warrior at the vanguard of some Anglo-Saxon assault upon a medieval castle. Mildred, maybe, but Native American Indian? He tried to place her on a lively pinto, her yellow braid bouncing as she followed Lewis and Clark through the raw wilderness. Somehow, he was quite sure, the expedition would have bogged down. The baffled ragamuffins that Chandra dragged home, depending on the issue of the day!

"What does *your* name mean?" Chandra was asking Sukie.

"I don't know," Sukie said, a little knot of dismay forming between her eyebrows. Her hair was thin and fine as a spider's web, her eyes those of the walking wounded. She would have made an excellent Moonie, Frederick decided.

"Where'd you get it?" asked Chandra.

"My mother gave it to me," said Sukie, backing up a bit, as though Chandra might heave the orange at her in disgust.

"But what does it mean?" asked Halona.

"I don't know," Sukie admitted, and turned even more pale. Perhaps she sensed what Frederick already knew: It was a dangerous thing when picketers turned on one another. "It just means *Sukie*, I guess."

"You need to come to my seminar for sure," said Chandra. She gave Frederick a quick kiss. "Bye, sweetie. See you after the boycott." Fine words from the woman he married. *See you after the boycott.* "Oh, and don't forget to pick up a dozen or so marigolds at Home Depot. I'll set them out tomorrow."

Chandra gathered up some posters from a corner of the kitchen. He hadn't noticed them before, but there they were, sad calf faces peering out of tiny crates at the insensitive world. He felt that pang again, the swift old kick of guilt. *Frederick the Abandoner.* He shuffled the orange cat, batting it along on the end of his foot, out onto the porch behind the three picketeers. The membranes in his nose were vibrating wildly.

"Have you found a home yet for the cat?" Sukie was asking.

"Not yet," Chandra sighed.

"Why don't *you* keep him?" Halona suggested as the cat tried to sneak back in past Frederick's legs. He shut the door promptly in its large orange face.

"We can't keep a cat," he heard Chandra say. "Frederick thinks he's allergic to them."

"Psychosomatic?" Halona wondered. Frederick felt the membranes tickling frantically, demanding his attention. He let fly a worthy sneeze, and hoped it was loud enough to alert the cynics on the front porch.

"How long have you been married?" he heard Sukie pry further.

"In October it'll be twenty-one years," Chandra said, her voice soft and lilting, hanging on to the rim of excitement. After all, she was on her way to the National Veal Boycott, no less. "We met at Woodstock," she added.

"*He* went to *Woodstock?*" Frederick heard Sukie ask in genuine shock, before he gave in to another robust sneeze.

*T*wo

ack from delivering the payroll checks to Portland Concrete, Frederick took a pad and pencil and began a systematic inventory of the house. Early in their marriage he had designated Tuesday as shopping day and had managed to maintain that schedule over the years, except for several Tuesdays that had been swallowed up by important matters. His father's funeral, for instance, had fallen on *Tui's Day,* as it was originally called, after the god of war and the sky. It had been wonderfully fitting, considering Frederick's stormy relationship with the elder Stone. He had sat stiffly throughout the services, thinking not of the wasted years that had washed between father and son, but whether or not the produce department had received the first corn of the season.

At first they had shopped together, Chandra girding her independence by wheeling her very own cart. But as the years passed, she had fallen by the wayside as a credible shopper. Frederick took the job over exclusively when he discovered that his wife bought a certain brand only if it "had nice lettering" or if she "loved the picture on the box." They had compromised. She would be sole executor of the dirty laundry, a task Frederick loathed, and he would shop.

In the upstairs bathroom he carefully checked each shelf. *Bathroom tissue, bath soap,* and *Q-Tips* went onto the list. Downstairs he inspected the canned goods, perused the fridge, the laundry room, and the closet that contained cleaning supplies and various other sundries. His inventory finished, he went to the computer and entered each item. He then instructed the machine to sort the items alphabetically. This way, it was a snap to check each one off as he deposited it into the shopping cart.

With a quick printout in one hand and his umbrella in the other, Frederick ignored the orange cat on the front porch. But he did pause to pencil *cat food* at the bottom of his sheet. He knew Chandra would only send him down to Cain's Corner Grocery for it when she returned, and Mr. Cain charged a kingly sum for a mere two-pound bag. Yet he felt a twinge of annoyance to have *cat food* glaring up at him from below *zucchini,* spoiling the poetry of his list.

At the IGA, Portland's largest grocery store, Frederick browsed up and down the familiar aisles. He had done the weekly shopping there since the giant facility opened, a year earlier. He had met the manager once, just long enough for him to brusquely refuse Frederick's pitch for Accounting and Consultation services. What had his name been? Johnson? Jacobson? He had pointed out to Frederick that the store, as a part of a major chain, already had its own computer system. Frederick considered doing his shopping at a smaller, individually owned market, one that might be more prone to becoming one of his clients. In the end, he had capitulated to the larger store's variety, convenience, and, most of all, prices.

In the fresh produce department, he spent a long time picking through the nectarines and plums, searching for the occasional dark bruise, the decaying soft spot.

"How are the cherries, Frederick?" He looked up to see Mrs. Freeman peering at him from out of her wrinkly little eyes. He tried not to sigh too loudly. They always found him first in the fresh produce department.

"Still some nice ones left," Frederick said, "but you'll have to pick through them one at a time."

"Are the oranges good this week, Frederick?" It was Janet

Walsh, who wrote articles for some woman's magazine. What had she bored him to death with last week? Oh yes, some hormonal pack which women could clamp on—Frederick imagined it would look like an unopened parachute—that would enable them to jump confidently into menopause.

"I was here first," said Mrs. Freeman. "Frederick was telling me about the cherries." Frederick suppressed a huge sigh of impatience. He *was not* telling her about the damned cherries. He had merely suggested that she pick through them for the best ones, as any sane shopper would do.

"You just need to pick through them, Mrs. Freeman," he said again, firmly. If she had her way, Mrs. Freeman would stand there and let *him* sort every blasted cherry for her, maybe even de-stem them with his teeth. And she had a magic number for cherries: thirty, never more, never less. He turned his attention to Janet Walsh.

"Yes, well, let's see," Frederick said. "I'd stay away from the prepackaged. You're better off choosing from the loose ones over there. And I think Florida has the best oranges right now."

"What about the watermelon?" Janet pressed. "You weren't here last Tuesday and I ended up buying a bad one." Frederick looked carefully at Janet's pale face. Had she forgotten to wear her infernal hormones? What was wrong with some women? Did he look like the Watermelon Fairy? Chandra had declared that his own vanity was the cause of this Bacchanalian frenzy which occurred each Tuesday at the supermarket. "You pretend to know things about produce which no mortal human knows, not even farmers," she'd accused him. "I bet you act like some Roman god of the harvest down there, Freddy. I know you. You've got those women believing you're Ralph Nader." Perhaps he had mentioned a few choice lessons from *Consumer Reports* over the months, and by doing so had possibly saved them and their entire families from being poisoned by Chilean grapes, Chicken à la Salmonella, and the like. *Consumer Reports* had been kind enough to make all this information available to PC owners via Prodigy, a computer network accessible through a modem. Frederick didn't even have to buy the magazine anymore. But he had no idea how much women talked to one another. Now, *there* was a network to be envied by even Prodigy. Rumor had spread rapidly that he was the last word on artichoke hearts, a genius with mouthwashes, a virtuoso of brown rice. But that didn't mean they could harness him every Tuesday as their own personal soothsayer, which was happening as talk of his supermarket clairvoyance increased. Chandra had been smug about it, suggesting that he learn to say three little words, *I don't know.* "But you can't do it, can you, Freddy?" she'd badgered. The more horrible truth was that Frederick Stone *did* know the answer to their piteous questions. He had done his research. Could he be faulted for that?

"By the way," Mrs. Freeman asked suspiciously. "Where *were* you last Tuesday?" Frederick thought about last Tuesday. He had actually spent the day bailing Chandra out of the Portland slammer, a tiny matter of illegal traipsing on a fur farm. But this was none of Mrs. Freeman's business, especially since she had again worn her ragged old mink to the grocery store.

"Dental appointment," Frederick lied. He tapped on the nearest melon, his hand sensing the vibrations. He leaned down and listened for that special music, a quick, resonating *plunk* that promised just enough ripeness.

"Is it playing our song, Fred?" Janet asked. He heard the women titter like a couple of Oz Munchkins. On the third melon he found it, that subtle little *bong,* the tone heavy as a bell.

"Oooh, there you are," Frederick whispered. He lifted the melon up, as though it were a plump baby, and placed it in Janet's cart.

"I think you'll find this one satisfactory," he said. He merely nodded at Janet's thank you, the way a pediatrician might nod at a grateful young mother. He wished Chandra could see him at some of his finest moments. And she might, too, if she ever picketed the meat department.

"Thanks, Frederick, you're a dear," said Janet. She tilted her head, as though listening to the same melon music, and smiled sweetly. Frederick smiled back. He wasn't sure if the recent divorce was prompting Janet to be more aggressive or if her hormonal pack was pumping overtime. It was true that grocery stores across the country had become the new meatmarket, so to speak, in which singles could bump their carts together and fall in love. Frederick had read how males loaded up with expensive gourmet items to impress the casual female shopper, the one with the nice firm ass. But he had generally been a spectator to such mate-calling, Chandra's Tampax no doubt serving as a deterrent, not to mention the fact that tofu wasn't exactly known as an aphrodisiac.

"No problem," said Frederick, and tried not to stare after Janet's retreating wiggle. Women could wiggle more easily, couldn't they, when they were leaning forward on their carts, sashaying up and down the aisles like tigresses. And his brother, Herbert, wondered why Frederick didn't mind the shopping.

"Frederick!" A stout woman was just turning down the long aisle of canned goods. Frederick listened as his name echoed around the Carnation milk, then bounced off the acoustical boxes of shredded wheat. It was Mrs. Paroni, headed for him in a maniacal hurry, coupons fluttering behind her like leaves falling.

She's going to have a heart attack one of these days, Frederick thought as he watched her legs, trussed up in tight, shiny hose, getting closer and closer. The legs looked like sausages about to burst.

"I've forgotten which you told me was better. Tomato sauce or tomato puree?" Mrs. Paroni held out two cans for his inspection. Her bleary face was red as the labels. He could hear the breath rolling around in her chest, little growls almost, her heart a tired conductor shoveling coal into the furnace. The woman needed to give up fatty foods.

"Actually, Mrs. Paroni," Frederick said patiently, "they're made by essentially the same process. You can interchange them in your recipes without tasting the difference."

"But there *was* something you said I should watch for," Mrs. Paroni insisted. She dropped her hands helplessly to her sides, a can in each.

"It's the cans themselves," said Frederick. He suppressed one of his trademark sighs. "Some are welded, some are soldered with lead. Remember I showed you how to peel the paper back a little so you can see the difference?"

"I'm supposed to get the welded ones, aren't I?" Mrs. Paroni nodded. "Maybe if I was Italian, I'd remember."

"Whether you're Italian or not," Frederick said firmly, "you shouldn't ingest any lead." He thought suddenly of *The Godfather*. Maybe the Italians *were* more conscious of lead intake than any other nationality.

"My second husband is Italian, you know, but I'm not. I'm not even part Italian. My ancestors were . . ." She paused, as if trying to remember.

"Lebanese," Frederick said. He'd heard the limbs of Mrs. Paroni's ancestral tree rattled so many times that he felt as if he knew the whole goddamn Lebanese family.

"According to my mother-in-law, I can't make spaghetti sauce," Mrs. Paroni said flatly.

"I know," said Frederick. If she didn't get the hell out of his face, he'd be in the supermarket all day.

"But if my first husband were still alive, he'd tell you that I make the best goddamn Mihshi you ever ate!" Mrs. Paroni lifted herself up on her stout little dachshund legs to announce this. Why did old ladies like to swear in his presence? And they did it in such flirting tones. "The secret is in the spice," Mrs. Paroni added, and winked hotly. "If Salvadore were alive, he could tell you lots about my cooking."

Frederick nodded as he wheeled away. How many years had poor Salvadore listened to her unrelenting jabber? Frederick had no doubt that Salvadore was sitting up in the Eternal City at that very second, praying that his ears would eventually heal.

By the time Frederick made it to the checkout counter, he had advised Cheryl Carlesimo which apple juice had fared best in the latest tests for residue of the chemical Alar. He had also paused to mention that *Consumer Reports* rated Orville Redenbacher's Gourmet Original Popcorn seventh in its ability to shear off more easily with each chew, thus not compressing excessively into the teeth.

In line behind him at the checkout was Doris Bowen, fresh from the latest Palm Beach trip, her teeth so white in her tanned face that they reminded Frederick of little banks of Maine snow surrounded by sand. She was at her coquettish best, bending over to hoist up the twelve-pack of Coors from the bottom rack of her cart, her white breasts spilling from the cups of her bra. She had the kind of dyed blonde hair that never looks as unnatural as the waitress-blonde one sees at truck stops. It was as if money could make everything look real, if you only had enough of it. And Doris Bowen was certainly rich, or at least her husband was. Frederick had heard her refer often to "power people" and social gatherings at "George and Barbara's in Kennebunkport," a place

Chandra intended to picket. It all had something to do with automatic rifles and the NRA. Frederick assumed that Doris Bowen could afford to send the housekeeper shopping. That she didn't suggested a boredom to him. After all, what can one do until the enchanting cocktail hour?

"Hello, Frederick," Doris said, the white teeth moving like ghosts behind her red lips. "Don't you have a lecture for me about the bacon?" Frederick looked at the slab of Hormel bacon which Doris held up so seductively that it could have been a dirty magazine.

"Lecture?" Frederick asked. He hoped the way in which he was canting his head, what Chandra called "birdlike," was just casual enough to be flirtatious. He didn't know what it was about Doris Bowen in her white shorts and little tops, her white summer dresses, her white slacks and sweaters, her white boots and sandals, but it was something. White had come to signal the rich, just as purple had once been worn by only royalty.

"What lecture did you have in mind?" Frederick asked coyly. He imagined Chandra behind a one-way glass, watching him like some kind of high-school principal. She'd have a good laugh, wouldn't she?

"You know," Doris Bowen drawled the words prettily. "The lecture I heard you give Mrs. Paroni one day last month about bacon." Frederick stifled a grimace, then hoped that this effort, coupled with the canting of his head, wasn't too much. He might come off to Doris Bowen as having Bell's palsy rather than a sexy aloofness. But he had been unable to suppress the thought of Chandra swooping in, waving a brochure on factory farming, one that had pictures of the sows chained to cement slabs, unable to move, eighty million of them yearly. Damn Chandra and her pictures, which *were* worth a million words. Frederick hadn't been able to enjoy pork for years, had nearly wept one morning at breakfast when he realized that he must bid good-bye to sausage patties forever. What would Doris Bowen say about that?

"Didn't you warn dear little Mrs. Paroni about the perils of eating bacon?" Doris arched one of her golden eyebrows, the eyebrows of the rich, which seem to curve naturally into a bored *What next?* question.

"Mrs. Paroni shouldn't even *smell* bacon," Frederick said.

"Didn't you tell her that it's loaded with stalactites and something else?" Doris needed to know. He smiled warmly. He did find them charming—let Chandra call him sexist—women who simply needed nothing more for the moment than for him to explain them out of some quandary.

"*Nitrates* and *nitrites*," he corrected gently. "To say nothing of the fat and cholesterol."

"I don't worry about fat," Doris Bowen said sweetly as Frederick produced his courtesy check-cashing card, and then dropped his receipt into one of the sacks. No, she probably didn't. Fat was most likely that which one liposuctions away, at the wave of a cool red fingertip.

Loading his groceries into his Chevy station wagon, Frederick couldn't help but look up, through the big plate window which advertised Van Camp's pork and beans, to see that Doris Bowen was casting blonde, shivery looks out into the parking lot of Portland, Maine's largest grocery store. Frederick considered lingering a bit, taking his time in placing the grocery sacks on the backseat, but then he saw Mrs. Paroni on her way out with a bag boy. He quickly slammed the Chevy's back door and then climbed beneath the wheel.

On the drive home Frederick remembered the soft white mounds of Doris Bowen's breasts, rolling like little hills inside her halter top. The firm, impertinent breasts of the rich. Silicone breasts. *Silicone chips!* He wondered instantly who handled the accounting for Arthur Bowen Developers, Inc. It wasn't as if Frederick didn't find Doris Bowen luscious. He had always been intrigued by women who were so openly sensuous. That was his sixties upbringing. But in the eighties, something incredible had happened. Personal computers hit the market, and it was as if Frederick had been swept away to another planet. As mountains of new material on PCs became available, he had plowed through them with infinite concentration and patience. He came to know, and then to love, the magical device. It had been a long time since his emotions had been so stirred, and the enigmatic machine, as if sensing his passion, slowly unveiled its secrets to him. This new obsession filled the lonely gaps, made up for the peace marches he had gradually dropped away from, the world problems he had come to leave to those who felt they had world answers.

There was another side effect as well. The computer gave Frederick the opportunity of making a living in his own home, of being his own boss, of keeping his own hours. As Stone Accounting and Consultation grew, Frederick began to relax. The smoky ideals of the sixties faded into the bright genius of the computer chip. His old self dwindled as his bank account increased. There was no doubt about it: The establishment had finally made Frederick Stone an offer he couldn't refuse. He had sold out. At least according to Chandra he had. But through it all Frederick and Chandra had remained together. The shades of their hair may have changed in sync, but the color of their convictions had not. It was a good thing, too, Frederick had reminded himself many times during their long marriage. After all, *computers* were putting food into their refrigerator, even if milk-fed veal wasn't among it.

At six o'clock Frederick wasn't troubled about what to fix for dinner. Later on, when he felt hungry, he would make a quick sandwich. Chandra would be eating with the rest of the boycotters in Augusta. She had already told him that there would be a discussion on factory farming at The Renaissance Teahouse after the boycott, sponsored by a group of concerned college students and professors. He expected it would be late evening before he would hear her cooing to the orange cat out on the front porch, so he mixed himself a drink and stood staring out the window. A small warm rainfall was blowing over Ellsboro Street. Frederick watched as the green leaves of the wild cherry outside his window siphoned off the raindrops. He wondered with genuine sympathy if the boycott was over. He knew the intent was to picket some restaurant still heartlessly serving milk-fed veal. He hoped that Chandra was dry, wherever she was. Frederick had done a lot of picketing himself, in his own day, and he knew the rain was a nasty thing. He knew it could turn magnificently lettered signs into wishy-washy slogans. As the cherry tree arched dramatically in a tiny wind, threw its rain far and wide, as though the drops were its own seeds, Frederick remembered one of those pickets. It had been during the countless antiwar marches, in the heart of the Vietnam era. Where, he couldn't remember, only the incessant rain, beating the marchers down, beating them back, the capitalist fists of the rain, and Chandra there beside him, her hair blonde with youth, yellow with protest, both of them in the sweetness of their lives. His sign had said WAR IS MURDER, a fine red lettering done by Chandra's own little pacifist hand. But the rain had taken the letters and splattered them like blood up and down the poster board. When Frederick looked up at them, they ran before his eyes like the blood of those soldiers, soldiers on *both* sides, like the blood of the Crusades, of all the really expensive, important wars, and all the forgotten wars. He saw on the poster the blood of all humanity in a red sea of despair, and he had felt the very first of those insights into the truth about the world that would plague him thereafter: that it was all for nothing. If the war were to stop tomorrow, then it was *time* for the war to stop. No matter that a few people voiced their displeasure, no matter how hard a few folks worked to change things, the world would continue at its own pace, and the world news would end up tucked away on reels, in tin cans on the back shelves at CBS and NBC and ABC, as if they were little lives that have already been lived and are no longer useful. It was all for *nothing,* and that's what made him cry that day, in the midst of the downpour, beneath the sign dripping its blood, the day Chandra believed to be his most emotional, *personal* protest of the war. It became a marker from then on. "That was the big march where Freddy cried so hard," he would live to hear her say, as if it were a badge of his beliefs, a medal from the battlefronts of the protest years. But Frederick remembered exactly what it was he felt. He hadn't been crying for any soldiers, for any heartless governments, for any civilians being rained down upon with napalm. He was crying for himself, for Frederick Stone, because the beginning of the end of innocence had just occurred.

It was almost ten o'clock before he finally made the sandwich. With Chandra out tilting at the rainy windmills of factory farms, he had used the entire evening to study the manual and install the latest update of his accounting package. Then he backed up the day's work on floppy disks and stored them in the safe. It was well past eleven, and a few minutes into "The Tonight Show," when Frederick snapped off the television and went to sleep. It seemed like only seconds later that he awoke enough to realize Chandra's cool body had slid into the warm bed beside him. It seemed like only seconds, but maybe it was many lifetimes, so far apart had they grown in twenty-some years.

The house was already alive with the bleeps and burps of Frederick's computer when Chandra finally awoke, a bit past noon. Frederick was deep at work, up to his neck in The Boardwalk Cafe's personal finances. He heard her footfalls above his head as she padded into the hall and down to the bathroom, then back again. He abandoned the dollar signs of Portland's oldest café and went out to the kitchen to pour Chandra her morning coffee. He sniffed it anxiously and then frowned. *He* wouldn't drink it, but then *he* had discerning taste buds.

Upstairs, the bedroom door was open, as it always was. Chandra suffered from a kind of bedroom claustrophobia, contracted no doubt from being locked up in some other, drab life.

"Hey," said Frederick. "Ready for some coffee?" He put the cup on the bedside table and then opened the blinds. "That's a beautiful day out there you're missing," he remarked. Chandra squinted the bright sun out of her eyes and then sighed deeply.

"I used to believe that a woman chooses a husband to replace her father," she said. "But I must admit, Frederick, that you sound more and more like my mother as time goes on." She reached for the coffee.

"Speaking of your family," said Frederick. "There's a little message for you, down in the den."

"There must be a God," said Chandra, "or we wouldn't have answering machines. What does she want now?"

"Joyce is threatening to kill poor Teddy," said Frederick. "The condom thing again."

"Why can't she just feel blessed that the kid is *using* condoms," said Chandra. "Who cares if he keeps them in his dresser drawer?"

"He keeps the *used* ones in his dresser drawer," Frederick reminded her. "That means he's bringing concubines home from geometry class while Joyce is at work."

"Teddy *is* sixteen now," said Chandra. "Joyce has no damn business snooping in his bedroom."

"Finding congruent angles and graphing hyperbolas right there in his own bed," Frederick added. "In Joyce's very house."

"She's just afraid of missing something."

"Well, you might call her back," said Frederick. He was leaning into Chandra's vanity mirror, inspecting the puffiness around his eyes again. He would give it one or two more days before charting it on his computer calendar as permanent damage. "She *is* your sister, after all." He began a quiet inspection of the single gray hairs on his head.

"Hubris, Freddy," said Chandra. "Unadulterated hubris." He abandoned the gray hairs and the puffiness for a later and more private audit. "Besides, when was the last time you talked to your brother, Herbert? The few times he's managed to catch you on the phone, you told him that Call Waiting had beeped and that you were expecting an important business call." Frederick pretended not to hear this, but he silently thanked The Girls for Call Waiting.

"How was the boycott?" he asked. Chandra squinted again.

"Where was the goddamn sun yesterday?"

"Did you get rained on?" Frederick leaned against the door-jamb, his head tilted, listening to the musical language coming up from the computer. He was reorganizing the hard disk in order to speed up the computer's performance. When it finished he would begin updating his newest client, Patti's Poodle Parlor. He canted his head further, catching the soft ticking music. Chandra stared at him.

"You know, you and that computer are beginning to remind me of something from the Twilight Zone. It's unnatural. It's like you speak some occult language to that thing, and it answers you."

"I believe you're jealous," said Frederick.

"One day that computer will come up the stairs with a cup of coffee, and you'll have disappeared. Just your shoes and socks left behind in your office."

"And you'll still be getting your coffee in bed," said Frederick. "The happy widow. Now tell me about the boycott."

"If you'll stop holding your head like some hawk, I'll tell you," said Chandra. She sipped more coffee. "Eighteen people turned up," she said. "And the excuses from the ones who promised to be there were the same excuses as twenty years ago. You remember those, don't you?" She sat up in bed quickly. A few more sips of coffee in that position and she would be ready to slide her legs around and make plans to stand. She had often explained to Frederick that one needed to face sunlight slowly, to pay it a kind of ritualistic homage.

"Let's see," said Frederick. "If I remember correctly, that would include sprained ankles, sick children, sudden family deaths, mysterious automobile problems such as car wrecks and flat tires, unexpected business trips, and weren't there two Hari Krishnas who claimed to hyperventilate on the interstate?"

"You can add a new one to the list," Chandra said. She was examining her toes. "Those new tennis shoes, the ones without the leather tops, have given me blisters." She pointed at the watery little hills on the tips of both big toes.

"What's the new excuse?" Frederick asked. He reached for her left foot and began to massage it evenly.

"Cissy Libby called Sukie to report that she had just gotten her hair done that morning," Chandra told him. "Got it done *for* the boycott, mind you, and as it was raining she couldn't bear to see her *do* spoiled." Frederick laughed heartily.

"How did she end up in the group in the first place?" he asked. "Doesn't sound like one of the sincere to me."

"She paid for all our printing costs," Chandra said. "Her husband owns Down East Printing Company." She slid her legs over the side of the bed.

"I wonder who does their accounting," Frederick mused. Chandra looked at him wearily.

"Must you see a potential client everywhere?" she asked.

"Well," said Frederick, suddenly defensive. "You saw her as printing costs. Why can't I see her as a client?"

"There's a difference, Freddy," said Chandra wearily. "Just don't ask me to define it."

"I take it," said Frederick, "that the boycott didn't go well?" He canted his head again, slyly, hoping Chandra wouldn't notice. It sounded as if the computer had finished the weekly rearranging of its contents, moving much of the data to areas of its electronic brain that were more quickly accessible. Frederick often wished he could do the same thing to his own brain.

"It went well enough," Chandra said, and stood up. She was in flannel pajamas.

"Aren't those hot for this time of year?" Frederick asked.

"I got chilled yesterday," Chandra said. Their eyes met. He wasn't sure, even after all these alike mornings, if the eyes were asking, *Where were you? When I was getting chilled, when I was getting sunburned, when the snow was piling up on my head, when the leaves were orange and crinkly under my feet, where, pray tell, were you?*

"The business is doing so well that I may be able to add on to the den by fall," Frederick said suddenly, and Chandra nodded. "You've been wanting a larger room for your seminars."

"That would be nice," she said. She leaned against the wall to execute some stretching exercises, the way runners work their muscles. "We walked for two hours," she explained when she noticed his look of inquiry. "As I said, the new shoes aren't very good."

"Oh, by the way," Frederick said. "I bought some more cat food, for the stray cat." Chandra smiled, a tired smile, and then leaned over to give him a little kiss.

"Thanks, Freddy," she said. "You're really good about it."

"I am allergic, remember," he added, but she ignored this.

"Just until I find it a good home," she reminded him.

"And now that I'm making a little money, you'll always, you know, have cat food, and dog food, and we can go later this afternoon and buy you some new shoes." Christ, he hated to hear himself rant on! At times like that, after each of Chandra's "civil protests," Frederick felt a little bit like Isabella financing ships for Columbus so that *he* could chance sailing out and off the flat edge of the world, while she, Isabella, remained within the pampered walls of her palace, partying no doubt. But somebody had to finance the dreamers, didn't they? How far would Columbus have gotten without the *Nina,* the *Pinta,* the goddamn *Santa Maria?* How far could Chandra walk in her next protest—saving the tropical rain forests, by the way, or so he had read between the magnets on the fridge—without new and better shoes? The backers of Great Expeditions and Important Movements are misunderstood and lonely people, Frederick thought. Then he retreated to the safety of his office.

*T*hree

*T*hey began to arrive one at a time, and then in scraggly bunches, as Frederick watched from behind the curtains of his office window: Chandra's clients, the "Psychology of Names" seminar about to fall into full swing. The last group, two women and two men, were dressed in cowboy hats, handkerchief chokers about their necks, Texas-style boots. Frederick wondered if perhaps a square dance was happening somewhere along the street and they'd missed the right address. What problem could these people have with names? he wondered. He imagined their conversation after an evening with Chandra. "Howdy, I'm Tex, formerly Norman Weingart. Meet Pecos Slim here. You remember Slim? The erstwhile Milton Sweeny?" For the second time since the first client had rung the doorbell, Frederick checked the knob to his office door. It was soundly locked. Let Chandra call him a chicken—*living on the outskirts of humanity*—as she often did. He had great suspicions about the demented souls who turned up for her Seminars of the Mind. He wished she could find an office in downtown Portland, but she had a strong argument against that: She would end up spending all her "money of the mind" on an exorbitant earthly rent. Enlarging the den was their best bet. But Frederick greatly feared that robbery might result one day, being facilitated by some burglar getting an inside look at the Stone residence, casing the joint rather than changing his Karma. And this point was finally brought home when Frederick sneaked out of his office one night for a little snack and found an abnormally tall man in his kitchen, a man bent like a question mark as he inspected the contents of the Stone refrigerator. Frederick could hardly contain himself as he'd waited for the seminar— "Psychometry as Science"—to end so that he could report the indiscretion to Chandra. He then capped it all off with a lusty little warning about rocketing crime ratios.

"I wouldn't call taking an apple from the refrigerator *stealing*," Chandra had defended her client, Joseph Peters, a man who supposedly could tell where things had been from simply touching them. "He's one of our leading psychometrists," she'd added. Well, he, Frederick Stone, might not be one of the world's *leading psychometrists*, but, by God, he knew where that apple had been before Joseph Peters had eaten it. It had been in his, Frederick Stone's, goddamn refrigerator! And he didn't even have to touch the bloody thing to know that!

Frederick looked at the clock. Seven-fifteen. That month's seminar would finish at nine. By then, everyone would know how psychologically damaging it is to grow up being called "Ernest" in a world catering to "Seans." And Chandra would be fifty dollars richer per person. *Seminars of the pocketbook.* Frederick had counted twenty sheep. If she kept that up, he might suggest she find office space somewhere more appropriate. Near a mental hospital with a handicap ramp would be a good start.

Frederick sat down at his computer and concentrated again on the letter he had started. *Mr. Arthur Bowen, of Arthur Bowen Developers, Inc. Dear Sir: As the largest real-estate developer in this part of the state, you could benefit greatly from my services and . . . and . . . and . . . I happen to know your wife, Doris.* Frederick stopped typing and stared at the words. Of course, he wasn't going to mention his and Doris's supermarket relationship. He went back and put a period after *services.* He wished there were some tactful way to mention that he did, indeed, know Mrs. Bowen, and therefore could be rescued from the dregs of anonymity. *I am a Certified Public Accountant with a degree in accounting from the University of*

Developers, making sure that he'd not mentioned Doris's breasts anywhere in it—Word Search quickly took care of that—he heard a soft rapping on his door. It was Chandra.

"A couple of us are going out for coffee," she told him. "Just a little after-the-seminar discussion." She seemed in a great hurry. Out of curiosity Frederick followed her down to the den. She looked lovely in a cotton dress with a flowing skirt, all pastel colors. Her thick hair had been swept back with combs, the better to show off her heart-shaped face. Frederick was about to suggest they have coffee alone, in front of the TV, maybe seek out an old movie on cable, something they rarely did anymore, when he saw a young man settled comfortably on the sofa.

"You *do* remember Robbie, don't you?" Chandra asked. Frederick noted the sarcasm in her voice and, in deference to it, he lied by nodding. How silly of her. Why should he remember Robbie, or any of her assembled lunatics? Nonetheless, he extended his hand in greeting and Robbie shook it, a hearty handshake. And now that Robbie was standing, Frederick saw that he was at least three inches taller than he, just over six feet. Frederick looked around for the rest of the kaffeeklatsch but saw no one else. A *couple* of us? Were the others meeting them there, maybe the cretins in the cowboy hats?

"Where are you from, Robbie?" Frederick was following them to the door. Robbie had those muscular tanned looks one sees on surfers. Frederick wanted to hear him talk, wanted to hear that effeminate slur in his words, to assure himself that this was another of the young gays so attracted to Chandra's aggressiveness. Let Chandra chide him all she wanted about there being no stereotypical gay. "Are you from the Portland area?" He saw Chandra frown her little frown, the one that began on her forehead and ended up around the corners of her mouth.

"You're kidding, right?" Robbie wanted to know, but Frederick's face remained stoical. Damn. Robbie sounded like a young Charles Bronson. Frederick now hoped that Chandra was right, that there was no stereotypical gay.

"Are you a student?" Frederick inquired. *Please say you're majoring in clothing design or interior decorating.*

"You're kidding, right?" Robbie asked again. When it came to the 158,000 words in Webster's *New World Dictionary,* Robbie was downright penurious, *see stingy.*

"Have you known Chandra long?" Frederick loped on. He felt a disturbing sensation in his temples, a thumping.

"Would you like to come along, Frederick?" Chandra asked. The sarcasm in her voice was now the kind she reserved for her mother, impatience laced with annoyance. Frederick waved his hand erratically, pooh-poohing the idea.

"You might say I'm like one of the family," Robbie answered anyway. He grinned facetiously. Frederick smiled back with what he hoped would be taken as a kind of benediction. Chandra frowned further. She had found her sweater and purse and was now waiting for him to shut up so that she could leave. Frederick knew this very well, but he pushed further.

"Have you and I met before?"

"A few times," Robbie answered. Frederick nodded, a fatherly nod.

"I try to remember Chandra's clients," he said magnanimously. "But after all, there are so many." He was being his patronizing best.

"Actually," Robbie said, but Chandra stopped him.

"We'll be at Panama Red's," she announced. Frederick considered this. Another of those renovated Yuppie restaurants that Portland was so famous for—barn boards, Boston ferns in big brass buckets, lots of seventies music on the sound system, dim lights. *Carpe diem* was rampant in a joint like that.

"Is that the place with the forty-watt bulbs?" Frederick asked, hoping to keep his tone lighthearted. Chandra gave him a tough little stare.

"Nice to see you *again*," said the well-tanned Robbie. Was there mockery in the "again"? Frederick was just about to consider this as Chandra closed the door in his face.

He went immediately to his office and looked up *couple* in the dictionary. It meant *a few; several; now often used with adjectival force, omitting the* of (*a couple cups of coffee*). He was surprised it didn't mention Panama Red's in there as he tried not to consider the next word: *coupler, a person or thing that couples*. Robbie the Coupler.

Frederick lay awake, trying not to stare at the blue-green numerals of the alarm clock. He knew without looking that it was almost midnight. All of his life he had been able to clear his mind of the day's problems and doze off quickly. It was a knack that often annoyed Chandra, but the old ability was failing him tonight. He examined the ceiling awash in the blue-green light from the clock.

"Ridiculous," he muttered. "Absolute bullshit." The jealousy was an emotion he hadn't experienced in years, hadn't thought much about. Chandra had said often that his only real contact with the world in a decade was through the keys of his computer. Had he been blind? No, he wasn't blind. He was being foolish. Chandra was still deeply affected by people, still wished greatly to help them out during their short sojourn on the planet. Sure, she took a bit of money for doing so, but most of that went into advertising, phone bills, pamphlets, and the paraphernalia that comes with protest. And she did offer a service, even if it *was* to the mentally beleaguered of the world. Robbie was probably just a young man with a big problem—that it was a heterosexual problem was a bit unfortunate, granted. And Chandra was just doing what Chandra does best: helping the idiot, the crackpot, and the imbecile.

Frederick turned on his side, determined to forget about Robbie, knowing that if he was ever going to get the monthly payroll taxes filed for his clients by tomorrow's deadline, he'd better get some sleep. He tried again to make a vast desert of his mind, but things kept popping up there, growing, hateful little things, like the get-together at the Renaissance Teahouse after the veal boycott in Augusta. "To discuss factory farming," she'd told him. And then there was the night she'd not come home at all, calling instead to say that she and Ruthie Brown would be up until dawn designing a poster for the Planet Earth exhibit, so she might as well just hole up in Ruth's spare bedroom for the night. Another time, she'd spent the night with Marion Higgins, when that quick heavy snowfall had caught her unawares on the other side of town.

"In control, in control, in control," Frederick repeated the mantra over and over. But each time he was about to float off into sleep that vague feeling overtook him, that voice from his subconscious, that finger poking out into his conscious world.

It was just past midnight when he heard Chandra's little Toyota rumble into the yard. He listened as her car door slammed and then, silence. He knew she was out there in the driveway, staring up at the stars, looking for planets, as she always did on starry nights. And it was a starry night. Frederick had gone out to his own car at ten o'clock and sat in it for a few minutes. He'd planned to drive rapidly past Panama Red's, hoping for a quick glimpse in the window, in among the Boston ferns and dimly lit bulbs. Feeling foolish, he'd gotten out of the car and stood for a few minutes looking up at Chandra's precious stars. He would tell her about this, and they would share a hearty laugh together. And then, maybe then, he could sleep. The IRS demanded that those damned payroll taxes be deposited in the bank tomorrow, and Frederick didn't relish facing the task with stinging eyes.

"Hey," he shouted out when he heard her coming softly up the stairs. "Is it a burglar? Or is it a reformed Joseph Peters bringing back my apple?" He heard her snort an appreciative little laugh. She stopped in the doorway, a silhouette there in the soft glow of the bluish-green numbers on his clock and the rosy blush of the little night-light in the bathroom.

"I'm exhausted," she said.

"But the seminar went okay?" he asked.

"Fine." He saw her lift up a hand and run it through her hair. Then she left the hand there, her arm arced, as though she carried a water pitcher on her head, something to be balanced. He remembered the first time he'd ever seen her do it, at Woodstock, the night they'd met. There had been a fine drizzle coming down and her hair was sparkling with little raindrops as she ran her white hand through it, then just let it rest there, as though she'd forgotten all about it. It reminded him of an Ezra Pound poem he'd read in college, just a month earlier. *Dark eyed, O woman of my dreams, Ivory sandaled, There is none like thee among the dancers, None with swift feet.* Those were the same feet that now had blisters from boycotting milk-fed veal. He felt a little surge of love rise up in him.

"You know what?" he asked, and saw the silhouette of arm undo itself. She put a hand on her hip and waited.

"What?"

"I got jealous tonight for the first time in almost twenty years," Frederick confessed. "Can you believe that?" Chandra said nothing. "I even went out to my car with the intentions of checking up on you," he added. "Can you *believe* that?" He chuckled good-naturedly. He had always prided himself on what he considered his self-honesty. Still, she said nothing. The silence grew like a little pond between them, broken only by the bluish-green splash of the clock. He wished that he could see her face. He pulled himself up to a sitting position in the bed. "I even wondered if you and this Robbie, this surfer muscleman, had a little thing going. Can you imagine?" He snickered, maybe a bit too much, as he waited for a response. But none came. Chandra went on standing in the doorway, in the semidarkness, the outline of his wife, the woman he knew so very well. Oh, sure, they'd drifted apart a bit and, yes, he did spend an inordinate amount of time with his computer, but twenty years means something. He and Chandra had this special relationship. At least that's what he told his brother, Herbert, so many times as Herbert was going through his divorce. "I don't remember meeting this Robbie character before," Frederick said nonchalantly. At least he hoped it was nonchalant. Chandra had often accused him of looking through people and not at them, of being too self-centered to notice the obvious. He wasn't sure why the little surge of panic was rising in his chest, but it was. If *felis catus* had been around, he would understand why his nose was suddenly vibrating. If he didn't hyperventilate, he would surely sneeze. *In control, in control, in control.* "Can you believe I thought you were having an affair?" he blurted out, his voice now a shrill whine. He hated the tone of it! He sounded like Herbert, moaning and bemoaning, all the way through the divorce lawyers, the trial, the alimony. Chandra hadn't moved, was still there in the doorway, a creature carved of stone. *Ivory sandaled, There is none like thee among the dancers.* Frederick eased himself slowly out of bed and flicked on the bedroom light. He looked into Chandra's eyes, into the place where all humanity as well as the animal kingdom lived. He looked there for an answer since none was coming out of her mouth. *Dark eyed, O woman of my dreams.* He saw her pupils growing smaller with the light, shrinking, twenty years disappearing, all those Sunday mornings in bed evaporating. He saw himself growing old alone, a crusty, ancient man, bitter to the end, *living on the outskirts of humanity,* living in a gutter somewhere, without even a laptop to keep him company.

Four

Something's wrong between us that your laughter cannot hide
And you're afraid to let your eyes meet mine
And lately when I love you, I know you're not satisfied
Woman, oh Woman, have you got cheating on your mind?

—GARY PUCKETT & THE UNION GAP

I t happened that fast, at least to Frederick, but Chandra claimed that it had been a long, slow process.

"You are so wrapped up in yourself, Freddy, and in that damn computer, that you don't even notice our lives unfolding before you," she'd accused him. "I have to introduce you to people over and over again because you can't even take the time to _remember_ them." And then, true to her nature, she would speak no more on the subject. She had spent the night in their spare bedroom and he, unable to fathom the unnecessary acreage of their king-size bed, had camped on the small settee in his office, dozing off just before daylight.

When he woke at seven o'clock, he felt an immediate pang of regret that Walter Muller had beat him out of bed on that day. He entertained for a few seconds the notion that he should record this discrepancy on his computer calendar, then decided against it. He personally couldn't help it if his wife had caused his steadfast schedule to flounder.

At eight o'clock he'd gone to work on the payroll taxes as scheduled. No need for his professional life to fall apart just because his personal one was experiencing a rumble. And besides, he

37

still didn't know the nature of the beast. Perhaps this Robbie fellow was no more than a good strong body from which to erect a picket sign, instead of something more Freudian. Although Chandra wouldn't admit it, Frederick knew that she perceived some men as nothing more than solid foundations of cemented brawn. Human billboard signs. He would wait until she let him peek into her hand, study her trump cards. He had no doubt that The Girls would stay with him on this. He was delighted to discover that he had, after all, just a morsel of the Stone family's sangfroid. He was reminded of Christmas dinners in Grandmother Stone's immense and unfriendly parlor as the Stone aunts sat on one side of the room, the Stone uncles on the other, all unsmiling, rigid in their chairs, their cheekbones wonderfully chiseled. "They look like the pieces of some great, awful chess set, don't they?" his mother had leaned over once to ask him, the sweet smell of cooking sherry on her breath. Frederick would call upon this frosty inheritance while he gathered the essential data. No need for an emotional workout until he was certain.

He felt almost smug as he lingered over a second cup of his special bean coffee. But at ten o'clock Chandra arose to begin packing—impressively early for her—and the argument commenced.

"I'm not leaving for another man," she stated. "I'm leaving for Chandra." More of her cute, cryptic poetry, her little metaphysical singsongs. Frederick wondered how *Lorraine* felt about it all. He had decided, while he was running the monthly profit-and-loss statement for Portland Concrete, to elaborate on *betrayal,* first, and then perhaps make a cutting swath or two about how marital strife could affect both their careers. This was a mere gratuity on his part, since, after all, only the loonies dallied with Chandra's seminars. A little strife was probably good for his wife's business.

"He's not a man, he's a *boy,* for heaven's sake," Frederick scoffed. He hoped to stick a pin into Chandra's own nest of hubris.

"You don't remember Robbie, for crying out loud?" she beseeched him. Why should he remember the dolts and dimwits who cavalcaded through their home? "What solar system do you live in, Freddy? What planet do you live on? What street? In which house? Surely not the same as mine!"

"You literally flaunted him beneath my nose," Frederick reminded her, and then hated his voice for declining into a low whine. And he hated what his feet seemed to be doing: following her from room to room as she packed.

"At last," Chandra noted airily, "I can flaunt something beneath your nose that doesn't make you sneeze." Then she slammed the bathroom door in his face and locked it soundly. Waiting for her to reemerge, Frederick was forced to sit upon the top stair step and listen to several minutes of shower spray, a scattering of deodorant cans, the bathroom scales announcing her weight, toiletries being noisily packed. "Damned infernal bitch" were the words that rose up in his thoughts.

"You'd better not take my Ultra-Brite," was what he announced to the solid oak door. He had researched heavily to find such an excellent product for removing tartar. Even his oral hygienist had commended him on his discerning dental-health qualities. Chandra, however, had labeled him paranoid and excessive. Well, the judge in divorce court would have no trouble telling them apart, would he? Frederick Stone would be the one *with teeth*. A rattle of bottles came back at him, most likely those silly organic perfumes she was forever collecting, *eau de cow shit* or some such, the contents of which were probably tested on politicians, Ronald McDonald, and women whose only desires were to be homemakers.

Chandra padded out past him. She had wrapped a towel about her head, engulfing her wet hair, and she bore it as though it were some great, symbolic headdress. She had always reminded him of an Egyptian queen when he saw her like this, Nefertiti maybe, who had stood firmly at her husband's side in all those Egyptian reliefs, who even followed him into a new cult—and Frederick Stone saw the computer age as a new cult—who bore future queens for him. He thought of Chandra's long swanlike neck rising up from the collar of her blouse and was instantly saddened.

"You were the one who said that people should communicate, talk to each other," Frederick said sadly. His whine seemed to have modulated upward. This was not how he had imagined, during his sojourn on the settee, that his line of attack would unfold. He had envisioned her crumbling beneath the guilt—if indeed she was guilty—flailing in the face of Stone stoicism. Bambi against Mount Rushmore. But Chandra, good Woodstockian soldier that she was, turned to meet her attacker with more zeal than Frederick had ever seen her use against Dow Chemical.

"I married an English major," Chandra reminded him. "A man who loved poetry, long walks on the beach, picnics. A man who had the same vision as I, that the world could be a better place. But I ended up with a computerized machine." Frederick Stone sighed deeply. He had, at the tender age of forty-four, become The Establishment. Heavy with this knowledge, he leaned against the foyer wall, beside the massive indoor tree which had been a birthday gift from Joyce—who had not received so much as a phone call on her own birthday—and watched helplessly as Chandra crammed candles, books, and clothing into boxes.

"I'm *not* helping you carry those out to the car," Frederick announced defiantly, and was cheered that he still retained some dignity. Through a dangling branch of the potted tree, he peered at Chandra's face, a mottled visage that had launched a thousand protests, a shadowy face that he suddenly didn't know well at all.

"Lurk in the foliage all you wish," was her only reply. This saddened him further. He knew Chandra's opinion of folks who lurked in foliage: war mongers and the manufacturers of Agent Orange. "I'll see that movers pick up the larger stuff," she added.

"Chandra," Frederick said, and wished he had a nice glass of mineral water, Perrier maybe, because it didn't have a mineral taste and was lower in sodium than other brands. Of course, he hadn't *tried* the other brands. There was no need to, with *Consumer Reports* at his fingertips. But he would drink one of those inferior products now, sodium and mineral taste be damned. His throat seemed to be stuck together when he swallowed. "Chandra, this is insane."

"You're a blind man, Freddy," she said. "Blind." She covered both her eyes for emphasis. She struck him suddenly as the monkey that saw no evil, and he was alarmed to hear a sneering laugh escape the throat that he supposed had closed down.

"You think it's funny?" she wanted to know, and he shook his head wildly. He wanted badly to tell her that it was only because she reminded him of the See No Evil monkey. But he couldn't tell a woman who was about to leave him that she looked like a monkey. *Monkey is the general name for any member of the primate order with the exception of the tree shrews,* said a voice from within him. Frederick recognized it immediately as belonging to his high-school biology teacher, Mr. Bator, who had taught evolution with a great panache. Mr. Bator had dressed as a gorilla all during finals. *Most monkeys are active during the day and many live in groups,* Mr. Bator added. Frederick looked carefully at Chandra. Had she heard Mr. Bator? She continued to secure the flap of a cardboard box with duct tape. She hadn't heard anything. Now Frederick had to wonder if he himself had heard Mr. Bator's voice. It had been so many, many years since high school. He tried to think rationally.

"Do you want to go to a movie or something?" he asked. It would be an opportunity for them to talk. Chandra always chatted through movies. She ignored him and rifled instead through their mutual stack of record albums, pulling out the occasional Pete Seeger, Joan Baez, Bob Dylan, leaving the ones that belonged to Frederick. All the CDs were his, post-sixties things that they were; she would have no problem sorting there. Frederick leaned down and picked up an album which Chandra had shuffled aside, *Greatest Hits of Gary Puckett & The Union Gap,* not exactly activists, these guys. He had bought the album at a used-record shop in 1984, the same year his father died, the same year his sister, Polly, died, a little shop piled high with teetering, used records, piled high with old memories. He had already been married to Chandra for so many years that the purchase had made him uneasy. This was not Music for the Revolution. Would Chandra think him helplessly *Establishment?* Now, as he stared down at the youthful faces looking up, a tragic realization struck him.

The Union Gap are all in their forties! he thought sadly, momentarily forgetting his wife's frantic packing.

"A blind man," he heard her say again, and he wished desperately that he could share the quick fleeting wave that was coursing through him. He was feeling the passage of *time,* he was privy to seconds disappearing, minutes, years. The Union Gap as middle-aged men. He and Chandra halfway through their lives. The years were, indeed, swift bastards. He felt Chandra press something into his hand. It was a green Post-it with a scrawled phone number.

"For emergencies," she explained. "And that word doesn't mean the same thing to Joyce as it does to me, so please don't give her this number. And, if you don't mind, I'll tell Mother about this at my own pace." A loaded box in her arms, she backed slowly out the front door, let it slam behind her. For a full minute he remained in the middle of the living-room floor listening to the pure, unblemished sounds of loneliness: a child's magical voice filtering in from off the street, a sudden squeak in the cellar of the Victorian house, the branch of the wild cherry bobbing against his office window. And he almost saw it, almost envisioned a new life for himself, as he had once envisioned a better world for all mankind, a life in which he would learn to grow old without her, in which he would rise in the morning to look at his face in the bathroom mirror and she would not be there, somewhere in the dark blue rooms of his pupils. Dreamlike, he almost beheld this new life, embraced it, realized that it waited for him, down the long twisted corridors of passing, bitter nights and days. *Almost.* But then the sound of the Toyota rumbling in the yard bounced him back to his old life. And he knew, with utter certainty, that Chandra was leaving. What he didn't know, at that moment in time, was that she would take The Girls with her. He bounded out the door and stood on the front porch, teary-eyed, still holding the youthful Union Gap. As he watched, the little Toyota cut the sharp corner of Ellsboro Street, the tailless orange cat sitting stiffly in the passenger seat, the back window filled with clothing, books, brown paper sacks full of toiletries. He hoped some of the neighbors were watching this. He felt an intense desire to muster up all the pity he could find and wear it, as though it were a good warm coat.

When he could no longer hear the metallic rattle of the Toyota's loose muffler, he went promptly to the telephone. The first person he called was Chandra's sister, Joyce. He couldn't explain it, but he needed contact, reassurance of some quirky kind, even from Joyce.

"Chandra has left me," he said, his voice unsteady, his pain obvious, he hoped. By the time Joyce—a woman he'd never really liked—finished a long sermon that sharply detailed what she'd always considered Chandra's bad points, Frederick felt just a bit better. He signed off with a promise to come to Joyce's house soon, for dinner, and hoped he wouldn't be forced to view the soggy condoms. He then gave Joyce the phone number that Chandra had left behind.

"I'll try to talk some sense into her," Joyce offered, and Frederick felt almost joyous.

"You're a good person," he told her.

Next, he called his mother-in-law and gave her a long description of events, and then the classified telephone number.

"I've no idea where it is," Frederick said sadly. "Maybe it's at his place, at *Robbie's*." He heard Lillian cluck her disapproval.

"I knew something like this would happen," she warned, "Seminars of the Mind, my foot! Lorraine needs to get her own mind straightened out and leave those lunatics to professionals."

"Lillian," he was forced to remind her. "Chandra *is* a professional." *Remember all that money you spent on psychology courses?* he was tempted to ask.

"You poor man," Lillian cooed. "Lorraine is making a grave mistake." Frederick was almost sorry he hadn't been a more appreciative son-in-law over the past two decades. He made a quick little promise to make amends in the few years Lillian had left. The emotion of the moment was so thick he even went so far as to invite Lillian to lunch the very next week. This should all serve as proof to Chandra that he, Frederick Stone, was a worthy soul if her own family endorsed his side of the argument. And families should stick together anyway. Speaking of families, what about his own? This wasn't something he could discuss with his mother, who was now residing in Florida. Physically, that is. Emotionally, she was on Mars. And even if his father was living, which he wasn't, Frederick wouldn't be able to talk to him. His father had been the coldest, most indifferent piece on the Stone chess set. His father had been the king, and Frederick had set out at an early age to capture the king's attention. But he had never succeeded. It had been the quintessential stalemate. Chandra should have lived for a time with Dr. Philip Stone, dentist to the root canals of the rich, if she thought she knew something about indifference! He called his brother, Herbert.

"I thought that you and Chandra had this great kind of relationship, one that we mere mortals could only pine after," Herbert drawled. He seemed to Frederick to be almost gloating.

"Herb, for Christ's sake," said Frederick. "I'm hurting here. I'm dying. No need to rub this in." He heard Herbert exhale cigarette smoke on the other end of the line.

"It's just that I don't remember you being real sympathetic to *me* when I went through *my* divorce," Herbert said. Divorce! Frederick wasn't even thinking of divorce. It was too soon for something like that, wasn't it? The Toyota's dust had barely settled over the new marigolds lining the driveway. Surely in a week, a month at the most, Chandra would be back, dragging her tail behind her, just like those nursery rhyme sheep, the free-range kind.

"What do you mean, I wasn't sympathetic?" Frederick demanded. "I took you to dinner, didn't I?"

"What I remember most about that dinner," Herbert said, "was you trying to talk me into buying a computer." He was almost smug.

"That's because you *should* have a computer," said Frederick. "I'm sorry, but how can anyone—let alone a veterinarian with the number of clients you have—compete in business without being computerized?" He was about to list a few statistics when he remembered the state of his artless life. Pain shot through him, a physical ache. He picked up the first photo ever taken of Chandra and him as a couple, August 1969, at Woodstock, and stared at it hopelessly. He flopped it facedown on his desk. He looked like a televangelist in that picture, what with the greasy hair and sideburns. Chandra looked like, well, a flower person.

"There I was, crying on my sleeve," Herbert machetied on, "and there you were, criticizing my business tactics. That's what *I* remember about that dinner. I just hope I'm a better brother to *you,* now in your own moment of need, which, by the way, you told me would never come."

"What is this?" Frederick said, aghast. "Some kind of contest?" He was amazed at how cold the outer world was sometimes. No wonder he had preferred to avoid it. Herbert Stone was becoming their father as he grew older.

"All right, listen," said Herbert. "Let's go to The China Boat one evening this week for dinner and a couple of drinks."

"I've got a feeling Chandra will be back in a day or two," Frederick said confidently. "This is just another one of her little protests."

"Well, just between you and me," said Herbert, "methinks the lady doth protest too goddamn much. But let's just assume that she's not back by Friday. Dinner at The China Boat?" Frederick thought about this.

"Promise you won't do the duck metaphor?" he asked, and sincerely. How many times had he been forced to sit across the table from Herbert Stone and hear him tell the waitress, "One bird with two Stones."

"I'll let you cry on my shoulder," was Herbert's answer. He sounded very big-brotherly.

"Thanks," said Frederick.

"Which is something you wouldn't let *me* do, by the way."

"Herbert!"

"Okay, okay," Herbert said. "Hey, you gonna start eating meat again, now that Chandra's out of the picture? I always thought that was her idea, you know." Frederick sighed. Even the Cancer Society was denouncing red meat, and now this spiel from a medical man.

"No," said Frederick, and sighed again, this time for Herb's benefit. "I'm not going to eat meat again. What do you think I am? A schoolkid waiting for my mom to leave so I can devour the candy?"

"Sort of," said Herbert. He was incorrigible. Frederick had always understood why the former Maggie Stone had one day just packed up and left him.

"Do you want her new number?" Frederick asked magnanimously.

"Chandra's new number?" said Herbert. "Why should I?"

"I thought you might call her or something," Frederick said honestly. "Maybe have a little talk. She always liked you, you know."

"You never called Maggie," said Herbert. "Of course, Maggie never liked *you*."

"Jesus," said Frederick.

"Well, I'm sorry, Freddy, but the truth is the truth. Did you ever call Maggie? Just answer me that."

"Jesus," Frederick said again, and hung up.

He had watched the news, had nibbled at a sandwich, and was in the process of clipping his toenails when he heard footsteps on the front porch. He smiled. He must remember not to tease her or condescend in any manner. A little civil disobedience now and then, as Thoreau knew, was good for the soul. He would encourage her instead to express herself in a more conventional manner. Maybe they could have breakfast talks, sort of like FDR's fireside chats, in which she could air her grievances. What was it she had said, earlier that morning, as she was packing? "I have to introduce you to people over and over again." Funny, but he had always considered his bad memory an asset when it came to Chandra's acquaintances. Fair enough. He would make a halfhearted effort to remember the Sukies, Halonas, and the various and assorted simpletons who filtered in and out of his wife's seminars. He paused at the kitchen door until he was certain that his smile was safely hidden beneath a mask of concern. Darn it, but he wished he had never mentioned this to Herbert, Joyce, or Lillian! He had let a spontaneous panic attack get the better of his good judgment. Well, lessons had been learned all around. So be it. He opened the door and found his brother, Herbert Stone, standing on the porch, one raised hand about to knock.

"You!" was all Frederick could say. He felt a physical change occur on his face, was aware of facial muscles rearranging themselves into a mighty frown.

"For crying out loud, Freddy," Herbert said defensively, "don't puke or anything."

"It's just that, well," said Frederick. He held his ground in the doorway. If Herbert got inside, he'd never leave. "Why didn't you call first? You know I don't like for you to drop by without calling."

"I thought maybe you could use some cheering up," said Herbert. "But now *I'm* the one who needs it." He shrugged his shoulders, dejected, but Frederick maintained his stance. Herbert peered around him and into the kitchen. "She's not back, is she? I didn't see her car outside."

"She's not back," said Frederick. "Yet," he added.

"Come on, Freddy." Herbert waved an arm. "I'll buy you dinner. Quit standing there in the door like you're about to bite someone. You look like that dog with the three heads that guards Hades."

"Cerberus," said Frederick. He felt a cool breeze wafting in. Early June evenings could be chilly. An involuntary shiver ran down his back.

"Besides, do you think I'm going to move in or something?" Herbert lit up a cigarette. "I'm having a pretty bad time myself, you know. Maggie hired Jaws as her lawyer. You remember that big movie shark? Raw meat isn't enough for this guy. He wants to see blood. They seem to think I'm making more money down at the clinic than I am."

"We don't allow smoking in the house," Frederick noted. He waved his own hand, fanning the air.

"I'm on your *porch*," said Herbert. Frederick noticed that Herbert's hair was thinner than ever, his hairline inching slowly backward. Herbert was part forerunner to him, always had been as the older brother. He hoped his own hair hadn't been shocked into retreating more quickly than nature had planned by this nasty little turn of marital events. *Certain types of shock or stress can most certainly lead to baldness, or alopecia areata,* he heard Mr. Bator say. A soft wave of regret swept over Frederick. He wondered what had ever happened to Mr. Bator. Mr. Bator had been very kind to him during the difficult years of high-school adolescence. Especially throughout that period when Frederick had greatly wanted to play football for Portland High. This was at a time when all the cheerleaders were particularly pretty, his sophomore year, especially Leslie Ann Doody, who had soft doelike eyes and a quick little bounce that shot her into the air, an inch above the other girls. "Son, you just don't have the balls for this kind of sport," the coach had pulled him off the field to say. "You gotta have a killer instinct to stay alive in football. Why don't you become editor of the school paper? Join the glee club?"

"Am I gonna hickory smoke your front door or something?" Herbert was asking.

"The smoke can go right through this screen," Frederick said vaguely. Those had been painful days, when Richard Hamel had become captain of the football team and had then gone on to pin Leslie Ann Doody. After he pinned her, he obviously nailed her because Leslie Ann had become pregnant. At least, if gossip held, that's what happened. And pretty little Leslie Ann Doody, with her large doelike eyes, had simply disappeared from the halls of Portland High, as though she'd been nothing more than a floating wisp of vapor. Frederick had turned to Mr. Bator for solace, dropping by the science lab on those afternoons when he knew

Mr. Bator would be alone. He had never mentioned a word to Dr. Philip Stone because Mr. Bator had said all the right things. "There will be plenty of other girls," he'd reminded Frederick. "And the only goals in football are the posts on each end of a rectangular field. Your goals are far greater than that, Frederick." Were they? Had his goals been righteous, far-reaching, beneficial to mankind? Would Stone Accounting rank one day with UNICEF and CARE?

"You'd better hope Chandra doesn't hire Maggie's divorce lawyer," Herbert said, and exhaled heartily. "Remember what happened to Robert Shaw in *Jaws?* I came out of my divorce trial with stubs for limbs, and they're still not happy." Frederick could almost feel the first symptoms of alopecia areata settling in. Before long, and with associates like Herbert Stone to cheer him on into loneliness and old age, he would feel nothing but wind blowing across the top of his bald pate, pure cool wind. *The human hair grows at the rate of 0.35 millimeters every single day,* Mr. Bator added. Frederick wondered how long his hair would be when Chandra finally returned to him. He was already due for a haircut. Perhaps he would let the hair grow, a little exercise to entertain himself until she tired of this latest gauntlet.

"I'm buying," Herbert added, "so shake a leg."

"Okay," said Frederick. It was almost nine o'clock, after all. Chances were that Chandra was holed up with Marion Higgins again. Or designing more posters with Ruthie Brown. "But from now on, you phone first."

"You want it all, don't you, Freddy?" Herbert asked.

When Frederick returned from dinner at The China Boat, Chandra's car was still not in the driveway. And there was no stray cat on the porch, he noted as Herbert swung his Chrysler into the yard, lighting up the catty-corner house, the sidewalk, the marigolds, the shrubs. More flowers sat in plastic containers along the front porch, waiting for Chandra to plant them into the earth near the mailbox. She had been the one with the gardening love and knowledge, as though this were a tradition passed down to her from a long line of ancient female agriculturists, those first women horticulturists. Frederick, on the other hand, kept in touch with nature by mowing the grass each Saturday during the summer, and shoveling snow from the walk as needed during the winter. His prowess at the supermarket was all the contact that a true descendant of male hunters and gatherers needed, in 1992 A.D.

He said good night to Herbert as quickly as possible, and then stood on the porch looking up at those stars still large enough to be seen in the light pollution over Ellsboro Street. In more than twenty years they had never had a major fight. He wondered now if that had been wise. And, as if to add to his emotional distress, his head was thumping just a bit about the temples, the aftermath of having had an extra scotch and water at The China Boat. But Frederick had needed that extra scotch. It was the only way he could put up with a constant stream of brotherly annoyance. And Herbert had developed a perturbing new habit since his divorce: While standing at the bar for a predinner cocktail, he spun like a top on his heel and aimed himself at every young woman who sauntered past. Early in the evening, Frederick had made a silent promise to alert NASA the very next day. It was apparent that, at the age of forty-six, Herbert's penis had evolved into some kind of heat-seeking missile. This torment aside, Herbert had gone ahead and done the duck joke, a prelude to an evening of gloating about the female pet owners he'd been examining lately.

"That's one thing you'll discover, Freddy," Herbert had lit his perpetual cigarette to announce. "Young women are going to go for you like flies to shit."

"I'm not sure I care for the metaphor," Frederick had noted.

"Ah, sweet, sweet youth," Herbert had mused. "That's the best quality of young women. Their brain cells have budded, but not yet flowered. It's that flowering part that's dangerous."

"Regardless of what Chandra's future plans might be," Frederick had reminded his older brother, "she's only forty-two years old." To this, Herbert Stone had raised his brandy snifter and declared, "Yes, but half of forty-two is *twenty-one*, Freddy. Don't forget that." That's when Frederick had had the fifth scotch and, thinking about it now, it was probably all that had prevented him from grabbing Herbert Stone by his Cave Art necktie—a thing with bisons galloping about—and dragging him into the men's room for a swift round of fisticuffs.

Frederick quietly let himself into the house and noticed that he'd left the light on in his office. Aside from that, and the small light over the kitchen sink, the house was in darkness. There were no notes on the fridge announcing a wake-up call for the next morning, and there would be no need to usher a cup of coffee up the stairs. From next door Mrs. Prather's porch light streamed into the den and silhouetted the sofa, the reclining chair, outlined the floor lamp. Frederick stood at the entrance to the den, home of past seminars, and listened to the soft sounds of the empty house unfolding around him, more little squeaks than earlier, more scratches of cherry branch against the window. Added now were snaps along the baseboard as hot water rushed through the pipes. The heating system had obviously kicked on at sixty-eight degrees. He wished intently that his wife were home with him. But the only answer to his wish, coming from that cosmic energy of the universe in which Chandra believed so firmly, arrived when Mrs. Prather flicked off her porch light and cast the den in total darkness.

Back in the lighted office, Frederick slumped into his own specially ordered computer chair. For a few long minutes he stared at the stoic face of his monitor, now his only dependable friend. Then he turned on the switch of his surge protector and smiled appreciatively as the beast burst to life. He went quickly to his menu and selected Correspondence. *My Dearest Chandra,* he typed out in sweet white letters. Then he sat patiently, waiting for the exact words to hit him. He had written her many letters in college, had plagiarized Pound, O'Neil, Eliot, Fitzgerald, other men who'd had the lion's share of crazy women. But now, after two decades of marriage, he sensed he would have to say something by *Frederick Stone* if he was to get Chandra's attention. He stared at the blank screen before him, blue as a swath of sky, and waited. After a few minutes he went back to the keyboard. He deleted the *My* and *est*—she would declare them sexist—and then inserted a capital *d. Dear Chandra.* He examined the salutation. Should he delete the *dear?* That was the wonderful thing about being computerized, something he might mention to his brother, in case Herbert felt the need to send a monosyllabic note to any of the kindergartners he'd been dating. Frederick had slaved long and hard on those college love letters, churning them out endlessly at his old IBM Selectric, retyping due to numerous mistakes. Now, with a myriad of downloadable fonts, his laser printer could spit out any type style from Baskerville Italic to Swiss Condensed. He could plead for Chandra to return to him in letters three-fourths of an inch tall, or with words small enough to look like gnats scuttling across the screen. And mistakes? What were mistakes with Spell Check right there to come in like some good motherly soul and clean up after him? Who even needed the blasted dictionary when the Thesaurus key stood at the ready? Mistakes were nothing—as he'd tried so valiantly to tell his opinionated big brother—when one was *computerized*. Frederick only wished this was something he could apply to his marriage. Maybe the Back Space key should have been used more often, the Control key less. Or perhaps he could have paid more attention to Home, Style, and particularly Save. Maybe there had even been a subtle directive in Merge Codes, had he only known how to see it. It sounded very Woodstockian, after all. He sat there wordless, unable to summon up a single thought, as he watched the anxious cursor blinking happily, *What now? What now? What now?* His eyes filled quickly with warm tears because all Frederick Stone could see, on the face of his beloved keyboard, were the words *Escape, Exit,* and *End.*

Five

or the first few days—four of them, to be exact—Frederick Stone kept busy at his computer, reconciling the latest bank statements of his largest clients and doing the weekly payrolls. Several times, on each of those days, he found himself staring dazedly into the green leaves of the cherry tree outside his window, forgetting what he was doing, forgetting where he was, forgetting even *who* he was. Then, as if a slight breeze had blown through his mind, as well as through the black cherry, he'd remember every nasty detail. His wife of twenty-plus years—a sound investment in marriage these days—had left him. And he didn't even know where she was. He had called her two days earlier, dialing the sickly digits of the number she'd left behind—it belonged to the furtive Marion Higgins—and had received a sound dressing-down rather than a plea to take her back. He'd had a little speech memorized for the latter possible event, some platitudes about forgiving and forgetting. He had nothing at all to say in response to the dressing-down.

"You gave this number to Joyce!" she had justly accused him. "And then you went ahead and told my mother, *my* mother, when

52

I'd asked you to let *me* tell her. Isn't anything sacred to you, Frederick Stone?"

"It just sort of slipped out," Frederick had lied. He'd wanted to mention that lots of things were sacred to him, plenty of things, a goddamn cornucopia of stuff, but he couldn't think of anything specific. Other than her. Other than his work. Those were pretty sacred things, weren't they?

"Try to understand what I'm going to tell you, Freddy," she'd then added. "I just can't live with you anymore. Capisce?"

Frederick bit his lip and watched the branches of the cherry dip and bob. It was a windy time of year in more ways than one. He had intended all along to summon up a good defensive front, and that's why he had said to Chandra, "You had no right to leave this house." Now even the cherry tree seemed to realize his folly. One didn't tell Chandra Kimball-Stone what her rights were or weren't. Rights were things Chandra counted at night, instead of sheep, when she couldn't sleep.

"Don't call me again," she'd curtly advised him. "I'll see that the rest of my things are out within the month."

"You'd better," Frederick found himself shouting back. "And you'd better keep *Robbie* away from this house."

"What would you do, Freddy?" Chandra then asked. "Hit him with a computer manual?" And she hung up before he could tell her just what he'd hit her friend Robbie with, if given the chance.

Several times he had come close to phoning her back, so that he might apologize, perhaps ask if they could sit over coffee somewhere, some apple strudel in a quiet café, a place where copies of Impressionist paintings hung in droves, where one had to walk through strings of plastic beads to find the john, maybe at that place with the potted ferns where she'd been spending so much time with Robbie. Panama Red's. But by the time he'd gotten to the part about Robbie, he'd be too angry to call. Besides, he felt quite sure that she'd be calling him soon. Chandra depended on him more than she realized. He and his hair—now 1.4 millimeters longer than when she left—would await this realization.

Frederick pressed his forehead against the window, let loose a tired sigh. The trouble with waiting was that he had to wait alone. He wasn't good at being alone. Never had been. Back in his college days he had even allowed a young man with extreme asthma and acne to move in as his roommate, rather than endure a quiet, peaceful solitude, void of wheezing and excessive scratching. Now the alternative to being alone in the Victorian house on Ellsboro Street was sitting at The China Boat restaurant and watching Herbert Stone tear into a duck, mandarin style. Frederick had read that there were nine classes of mandarins under the old Chinese Empire, distinguishable only by the jeweled button worn on their caps. But no one ever mixed mandarins up at The China Boat in Portland, Maine, although the menu boasted everything from mandarin buffalo wings to mandarin nachos. And none of the regulars at The China Boat appeared to be Chinese, not even the staff. The clientele ranged from fishermen to college students to over-forty baby boomers. And there seemed to be an endless supply of dead ducks down there. In the four days that his wife had been gone, Frederick had patronized The China Boat twice, for dinner and drinks with Herbert. And he had seen two such ducks expired upon plates, with slices of orange peeling nearby, tiny floral arrangements. He had seen said ducks disappear into Herbert Stone's belly, and he had seen quite enough.

What he was beginning to feel now, on this fourth day, was the first true stabs of loneliness, of what his life might be like as a single man. Surely, he was not destined to become another Herbert Stone, a thing to be pitied, a veterinarian eating ducks, eating potential patients, for Christ's sake! No, *he would not.* Frederick shook his head in defiance—a hint to The Girls—and then tapped his fingers against the glass. He would work, is what he would do. Good solid work would wipe the stupor from anyone's life. Not just the Puritans understood the need for brute exertion.

He spent the evening of the fourth day of Chandra's departure working on a cash-flow analysis for Dee Dee's Flower Emporium. Dee Dee was seeking a ten-thousand-dollar bank loan that would enable her to expand the flower shop. After running amortizations on loans of varying lengths of time, Frederick decided he would suggest she go with a two-year loan. Her payment would be steep—according to her cash flow, she could handle it—but she would pay far less interest than if she settled for a longer-term loan. He was surprised to learn, when he stopped to nibble at the sandwich he'd thrown together as a quick supper, that it was almost eleven P.M. He was exhausted. Deep sleep would be a welcomed visitor, so he'd gone up to their king-size bed, the Cadillac of marriage vehicles, and had thrown his weary body down on its expanse. Why Chandra had insisted on buying such a yacht of a bed had always plagued him. But somewhere around three o'clock in the morning, his eyes still on the soft green puddle of light thrown off by the alarm clock, it had come to him: She could keep herself at bay in such an ocean of bed. She could set up housekeeping on one corner of the Posturepedic abyss and he would never even know it. That's when he had panicked and dialed the number on the green Post-it, only to be told by a voice so impersonal it would make the Stone family aunts all sound like Mary Poppins, that Chandra was no longer living at the Higgins residence.

"I'm sorry I woke you, Marion," Frederick lied. He hung up and considered waiting for Marion to fall back asleep, then phoning again. *Sorry, Marion, but did you say Chandra had moved out?*

After loosing yet another enormous sigh—he hoped the neighbors heard—Frederick went downstairs with pillow and blanket in arms to pace the circumference of his tiny office. If this insanity kept up much longer, he would be utterly dysfunctional. That was the catchword of the decade, wasn't it? Dysfunctional mothers, fathers, husbands, wives, sisters, brothers, no one above suspicion. There were even dysfunctional pets who paid weekly visits to psychiatrists. What chance did Frederick Stone have in such a maniacal world? After all, he was only suffering from a mild case of hubris.

He fluffed his pillow behind him on the settee and arranged his blanket about his feet. He waited for that wash of drowsiness that would indicate sleep was finally on its way, but it never came. Here, then, was the synopsis of his life, the battered Cliff Notes of his existence: a middle-aged, mateless man with hair threatening to recede at any moment, sitting wide-eyed and cramped on a narrow settee at four o'clock in the morning. It wasn't a Kodak moment. So what do men do at times like this? What would Alan Alda do? A joke, Frederick supposed, as the camera panned the room. But he could find no humor in the circumstances. Instead, he imagined one of those dark tunnels that manic-depressive types liked to speak of, with no tiny circle of light wavering at the mouth. Shifting his left leg—which was now rudely asleep—he considered suicide in the Japanese sense, as a means of saving face. After all, it had been a bit embarrassing to admit his marital troubles to the likes of Joyce, Lillian, and Herbert. And by now even the mailman was asking intrusive questions, not to mention the incorrigible Walter Muller from next door. Perhaps his only recourse *was* to do himself in. He could plaster his body with feathers, climb to the top of the Portland Lighthouse Observatory, and attempt flight. He hoped Chandra would suffer intense pain just reading the headlines: MAN WITH ICARUS COMPLEX PLUMMETS INTO CASCO BAY. He could slice his wrists with Chandra's pruning shears, still hanging in the garage. Let her wade about in the ocean of guilt *that* would surely create. "Yes, Mrs. Stone," he could hear Portland's Chief of Police saying, "he took his precious life with *your* shears." But then, the shears were so rusty and corroded he'd probably have to endure not only a tetanus shot, but Herbert shuttling him down to the emergency clinic in the monstrous Chrysler. Then, if lockjaw did set in, he'd be bedridden, unable to speak, while Herbert Stone nursed him back to health, his cellular phone in one hand, a smoking cigarette in the other. The ax? He did own an ax, one he had bought to render firewood into kindling during the cold ocean winters. *The mattock was a primary agricultural tool for Neolithic and ancient peoples around the world,* he heard Mr. Bator whisper. Frederick suddenly remembered that he had gotten that answer wrong, one day in class. When called upon, he had blurted, "A mattock is hair hanging from the back legs of a horse or donkey." Ever appreciative of foibles, the class had erupted into laughter. Remembering, Frederick felt his face redden, as it had that day so many years ago. "Fetlock," Mr. Bator had said. "You're thinking of a fetlock, Mr. Stone." Bless him. He'd been a kind man. What had ever happened to Mr. Bator? And where could Frederick find a mattock in order to take his own life? Probably at Home Depot. How many Neolithic peoples had used the mattock for suicide, instead of the loosening of soil? Someone should do a study on that. The Guggenheim folks would be most interested. Surely, *The Mattock as a Deadly Weapon* was worth twenty-six-thousand-odd dollars. His head nodding forward, his knees pulled upward to accommodate himself on the settee, Frederick left off with notions of self-disposal. Remembering Mr. Bator's firm, fatherly voice, his round red cheeks and full head of hair, Frederick Stone was finally able to sleep.

It was the next morning, after a quick breakfast of coffee—nicely ground African and South American beans—that Frederick considered cruising Portland in an attempt to spot the red Toyota, perhaps in the parking lot of some restaurant. Maybe even somewhere on campus at the University of Southern Maine. Had Robbie admitted that he was a student? Portland wasn't New York City, after all. It was just possible that the laws of chance would enable Frederick to behold Chandra's car slinking about campus where it didn't belong. He would've called upon The Girls for a bit of support, but he wasn't exactly on speaking terms with them, not since they'd spun his damn wheel of fortune at such a dizzying gate. But the idea of navigating the twisting narrow streets around the university discouraged him from the act. Besides, he hated all universities these days. A self-respecting orangutan could get a Ph.D. at most of them. The "Publish or Perish" ones were bad enough, but those other ones, those "Publish? Perish the Thought!" universities were the subject of his most abrasive contempt. And why not? The halls of academia had become nothing more than subterranean tunnels into which young pedants could crawl until, one day, tenured to the gills, they emerged blinking into the sunlight, pupated into aged pedants. Only at such colleges could doddering poetasters, who lacked the athletic ability to lift the spheres of their own testicles, have football fields named after them. Besides, Frederick didn't relish being pulled over by a campus gendarme and accused of casing academic neighborhoods. Who would bail him out? Even if he *could* appeal to Chandra's sense of humanity, he had no idea where she was. And Frederick would rot in the dungeon rather than allow Herbert Stone to peer through the cell bars and ask, "Did you ever bail *me* out when I was going through *my* divorce? Just answer me that, Freddy."

To avoid all that potential embarrassment, he sat with his coffee, out on the screened-in porch, and watched the children play on Ellsboro Street, remembering the sound of his own roller skates not so many years ago, and on a street not so far away. He wondered how it was that he had moved so quickly from the sweat and laughter and tears of childhood to stout, firm middle age. Maybe they should have had a child or two. They had talked of having children, once upon a time, in those early years of their marriage. For a couple of years, when they were approaching their thirties, they had even halfheartedly tried, but something was obviously malfunctioning in one of their bodies because conception simply never happened. And after a time, they never spoke of it again, as though voicing it would necessitate tests, personal chats with doctors, extensive book reading, and then, a finger pointing at one or the other as the source of the problem. And so the urge for parenthood had slowly gone away, receded quietly in the night, as snow recedes, as hair recedes.

Out on the screened-in porch, with the sounds of a glorious summer's day unfolding all around him, Frederick thought about the time Chandra had actually become pregnant, very early in their marriage years, not from carelessness, but because of statistics. Of every one hundred women who use an inter-uterine device, one or two will conceive. Chandra Kimball-Stone was one. He had wanted no part of a child that soon. He was simply not ready, financially or emotionally. They had talked often of backpacking across Europe. How could a child fit into such massive plans? But before he had voiced his concern to Chandra, who was quite pleased with what she considered an act of fate, she had miscarried. In a great wash of irony, the inter-uterine device that had failed to protect her from pregnancy had also caused her to abort. It had been called the Copper U-7, as though a small mining operation existed in Chandra's womb. But this company, instead of churning out eggs as though they were precious metals, was there to toss the eggs out. It had been 1972. Frederick wondered if another woman had been an unlucky statistic that year, and, if so, how she had coped with the problem. There had been other ill-starred circumstances that occurred in 1972: Richard M. Nixon had been voted in a second time as President of the United States. Vietnam was still on fire with American bombs. But what Frederick now remembered most about 1972 was that it was the time in his life that he had come closest to fatherhood. And whenever he saw the numbers printed in a newspaper, or in a magazine, the first thing that flashed through his mind was the image of bright red blood smeared across white tissue paper.

Now here he was, old enough to be somebody's grandfather. That was the trouble with life. Just when you got far enough up the hill to catch a clear-eyed look back at the shitpile where you'd been wallowing, just when you knew some stuff, there was no trail to take you back there so that you could repile the shit accordingly. Frederick watched the children skateboarding past the house, the three dogs inspecting one another with glee, a bevy of sparrows flitting about in the shrubbery, the mailman clanking away at the boxes on his route. From the end of Ellsboro Street he could hear the happy excitement of the ice-cream truck, its loudspeaker blaring out, "Turkey in the Straw." These were the sights and sounds of life going on in Portland, Maine, on Ellsboro Street, on the planet Earth. And Chandra was right. He was on the outskirts of such life. It had passed him by as though he were a sad character in some Victorian novel, a poor wretch buried away in debtor's prison, because he hadn't paid any dues at all. Well, he would pay more attention to *life*. That was one reason that he had agreed to have dinner with Chandra's sister, and this was a portion of life that Miss Seminars of the Mind herself avoided. Frederick finished his coffee, waved at the children, and considered buying the dogs some chew sticks on his next shopping trip before he was finally able to walk back into a house grown so lonely.

Back at his computer, he found that it was quite impossible to concentrate on any work. Struggling to compile a financial statement for Susan E. Brown, one of Portland's newest chiropractors, he kept lapsing off, an image of Chandra coursing through his mind like some kind of cruel shock treatment. He decided that his anxiety could be traced to the fact that he had agreed to have dinner at Joyce's, eight o'clock that evening. But being with Joyce and Reginald was better than sitting home watching the wind do wild things with the cherry tree. Or watching Herbert Stone debone another bird. He left the financial statement to fix himself a sound drink. He had never been into martini lunches because he never went to lunch with anyone, not unless he had to meet Chandra downtown after some social outcry. Frederick decided instantly that if he was going to personify the Establishment to his wife—and he was quite sure that he did—he would do so with his first martini lunch.

A pitcher of martinis on the coffee table, Frederick put his feet up on the ottoman and reached for the phone, which he rested in his lap. He waited for a minute and then dialed information, only to be told that Chandra Kimball-Stone did indeed have a new phone number—oh, the speed of the nineties!—but that it was smugly unlisted.

"But I'm her doctor," Frederick insisted. "Her test results are in and, quite frankly, I think she's gonna want to know about this."

"I see," said the operator.

"So young, too," Frederick added sadly. "What a pity."

"Sir," the operator said. "I didn't get off the bus to Portland yesterday." She was far too imperious for Frederick. He suspected the day *before* yesterday as her arrival time.

"But what if she dates your son?" he was asking as the operator disconnected him. The whole damn world was disconnecting Frederick Stone, and there he was, floating away like some kind of boat person.

Frederick poured another charitable martini and sipped at it. He had never had an easy time with women, it was true. His mother had been distant and aloof—why else would she have ended up with Dentist Stone?—and Frederick remembered how she began to sleep later and later into the day as the years wore on. Afraid to wake her, he and Herbert waged silent wars with their toy soldiers, soundless canons firing, troops marching in long quiet columns, thousands of boots with ghostly footfalls, airplanes dropping muted bombs, mouths opening in hushed pain, guts spilling silently onto imaginary plains. Maybe this was why, when Walter Cronkite brought the noisy Vietnam war right into American living rooms, Frederick was ready to be a pacifist. He just couldn't stand the racket of war. He could thank his mother for that.

And he hadn't known much about his sister, Polly, except that she had grown up pale and pimply, four years younger than he. He had been told that his mother had gone to the hospital to have her tonsils removed, but she had returned three days later with a baby girl swaddled in pink. For years Frederick would get this demented urge to stand up at Sunday dinners, to fling the peas and carrots, to shout, "Liars! Liars!" at his parents. Instead, as he and Polly grew toward adulthood, he observed his sister from a distance, she with her hair rolled up tightly in brush curlers, her eyebrows plucked into thin upside-down smiles. When he thought of Polly, he thought of her in terms of *things:* a garter belt hanging over the rod of the shower curtain, the nylons still attached to it like puffy dead legs. Eyebrow tweezers lying on the back of the commode and looking very much like some miniature instrument of medieval torture. Or, once in a while, a white cotton slip with the faint outline where a bloodstain had been. He thought of her as *smells:* the cloud of Johnson and Johnson baby powder, nail polish, some brand of perfume she was always ordering from a catalog, the aroma of her winter sweaters as they lay drying on newspapers in the laundry room. One day she simply disappeared, ran off to Connecticut with an anemic-looking dental student named Percy Hillstrip, her father's apprentice, whom she had married after a quick courtship. She was seventeen years old and uninterested in college. She seemed happy enough to bear children in a suburb of Hartford, in between typing up bills to be sent to Percy's clients. When his sister left, Frederick had been in his last year of college, coming home to Portland only once a month. Thinking about it now, all he could remember about Polly's departure was that something had been different about the breakfast table. He tried vaguely to recall, with the pitcher of martinis imploding, if he had ever spoken one truly complete sentence to Polly in all those years they had shared the same house. Dentist Philip Stone had often noted that Polly was the major disappointment of his life, his two sons being minor ones. "He hates Polly," Mrs. Stone once noted, "because she's committed the sin of happiness." Each Yuletide Frederick had received pictures of Polly's kids, two boys and a girl, signed "To Uncle Fred with lots of love," and in Polly's handwriting. One Christmas the children were standing with their heads poked through a sheet with three holes in it. Around the holes, his sister had painted yellow halos. He wondered where the picture was now—Chandra saved everything—and how old that niece and those nephews must be. Polly had died in 1984 of ovarian cancer, two months after Dr. Philip Stone himself finally succumbed to the weak heart that had

claimed so many handsome male Stones. Frederick didn't worry
too much about the quality of his father's existence, but he sincerely hoped that his sister's short life had been happy, that her *sin*
had been great. Just as he had always wished that his mother could
be happy. But long before her husband died, Mrs. Stone had
slowly turned into Miss Havisham, wearing funeral black instead
of wedding white. The petunias hadn't time to root on her husband's grave before Thelma Stone carted all of the movable household items, except for some clothing and the huge family
scrapbooks, out onto the front lawn of her ranch-style home and
offered them to the public for piddling amounts. Potential buyers
were encouraged to shop inside the house as well, to browse
among the heavy pieces which a sleepy, thin widow could not
budge. This was the same house that Philip Stone, an army captain, had come home from World War II to purchase. The ranch
style itself had been new then, an architectural dream. And it was
the same ranch-style house he had brought his young bride to, the
house where he raised his family. His rare-coin collection went for
five dollars, his grandfather's solid oak desk for ten. By the time
Thelma Stone phoned up her sons and announced that she was
selling the ranch-style house for five hundred dollars—in case one
of them wished to buy it—Grandmother Stone's grand piano had
been whisked away for twenty-five dollars.

"I'm moving to a condo in Florida," Thelma Stone had told
Frederick. "The only snow I want to see from now on will be on
a Christmas card."

"Mother," Frederick had pleaded. "You can't put all our family
heirlooms in a yard sale!"

"This isn't a *yard* sale," Thelma Stone had said calmly. "It's a
life sale. If you want the house, bring cash." By the time Herbert
and Frederick had roared into the drive of the ranch-style home,
even tourists were clambering about, inspecting the silver, sniffing
at Philip Stone's custom-made suits. That was the day Herbert
Stone, with assistance from the Stone family lawyer, became executor of his mother's estate. Thelma Stone had gotten her Florida
condo, while the ranch-style home sold a year later for nearly a
quarter of a million dollars. The last time Frederick had visited his
mother, three years earlier, she was resplendent in her black re-
galia, which was topped off with enormous black sunglasses. She

was Miss Havisham in a little white condo on the beach, a finicky Pekinese perpetually on the sofa beside her. So much for family values.

Frederick was still a bit tipsy from his first martini lunch when he arrived at Joyce's house for dinner. He was wearing the one hundred percent cotton sweater Chandra had bought for him on his birthday, wool being on the outs. Joyce was still thirty pounds overweight, but she had Chandra's same little nose, those copper-colored eyes. Her husband, Reginald, was still dull. Yet they appeared genuinely glad to see him, Joyce giving him a quick kiss on the cheek and Reginald emphatically shaking his hand.

"Martini," Frederick said when Reginald gestured toward a small bar in the living room. He watched as Joyce fetched a platter of munchies, listened as Reginald shook ice in a pitcher. He felt immensely hypocritical. Hadn't he helped Chandra lambaste Joyce and her husband for years, measuring one of their handicaps against another? Reginald, who taught history at one of the local high schools, was hard of hearing. Frederick had always assumed that years of listening to Joyce's whine had eroded his brother-in-law's eardrums. Eaten them away for good. The anvil, the hammer, the eustachian tube, all turned to jelly under the bombardment of sound waves pouring out of Joyce's mouth. Now Frederick was mildly embarrassed that he had ever thought ill of Joyce. After all, she had taken him in when his own wife had thrown him to the winds. He felt a great comfort, suddenly, in being in Joyce's home, that his presence there connected him in some psychic way to Chandra. Joyce was Chandra's sister, would always be Chandra's sister, forever linked. Frederick, on the other hand, might not always be her husband. He sighed, mentally counting the Avon knickknacks which Joyce had tiered on a shelf over the sofa. In a mass-produced artwork next to the row of Avon treasures, some orphan-looking children, those little urchins with eyes like dark plums, stared at him judgmentally. They seemed to know that Chandra had dumped him.

"Lorraine was always flighty," Joyce said as she fixed herself a drink, something with butterscotch schnapps in it.

The sisters differed in personality, poundage, and the color of hair—Joyce's would probably be peppered with gray if not for the geniuses at Clairol—but watching Joyce's mouth move, heart-shaped and small, was like watching Chandra's own. "I'll be honest with you, Freddy. I'm really surprised that it lasted this long. *Really* surprised. And so is Reginald. Aren't you, honey?"

"WHAT'S THAT?" Reginald asked too loudly, as those with hearing problems often do. Joyce's question had bounced him out of his torpor, however, and he handed Frederick a fresh martini. A shock of reddish-gray hair cascaded down over one of Reginald's eyes, both of which sat beaded and blunt behind silver-rimmed glasses. He reminded Frederick of some English game-keeper who's just come in from the weekly rabbit kill, a Mellors kind of chap, sniffing at Lady Chatterly's hem, a little too close to nature for his own good.

"*Very* surprised," Joyce added.

"Are you saying you think my marriage is over?" Frederick heard a distinct panic in his voice. He felt a strange, wild terror rising in his chest. It would be so lovely just to see Chandra again, just to speak to her, touch her hair. This was cruel and unusual punishment, this abandonment, this hiding out, forcing him to seek companionship from Joyce and Reginald. Cruel and unusual. "There's counseling, after all. And who understands counseling better than Chandra? Surely, you can't think it's over?" Joyce stared at him with intense interest, studying his face closely.

"Are you suicidal?" she queried. "You can tell *me*, you know." She began gnawing on a celery stick. A grass-green bird with a yellow head and bluish tail suddenly swooped into the living room in a burst of chirps and squawks, circled the ceiling once, and then was gone.

"THERE GOES BUDGIE!" Reginald announced.

"Of course I'm not suicidal," Frederick panted. "Just because I don't want a divorce doesn't mean I'm *suicidal*. Come on, Joyce. Whatever gave you that idea?" He could feel sweat forming on his brow, his face flushing warm.

"Well, I know you're not *stupid*," said Joyce. She had graduated to a carrot and was now dipping it generously in some sour cream. "That's why I assumed that you must be suicidal."

"CAN WE EAT?" Reginald wanted to know. "LASAGNA, RIGHT?" Frederick promised himself that he would examine his own portion of lasagna most carefully, just in case Budgie had been hit with a tiny fit of diarrhea while airborne in the kitchen.

"Joyce, this isn't making me feel better," he admitted to his sister-in-law. He longed to ask: *Didn't you invite me over here to make me feel* BETTER, *you insidious troll?* He said nothing. His eyes had begun to burn.

"VEGETARIAN LASAGNA?" Reginald wondered. Above his head, the plum eyes of the urchins seemed to be growing even sadder.

"Yes, vegetarian, to accommodate Freddy's lifestyle," Joyce explained.

"I really don't think divorce is in the air at this point," Frederick said vaguely. Maybe *Budgie* was at least listening to him.

"Horsefeathers," said Joyce. She wagged a finger. "You're going through denial, mister." Frederick struggled to deliver a quick little smile, then realized that it probably came off more like a tic. What was he doing in this abominable house? With this deaf man and this insufferable woman? Chandra would be wonderfully entertained to witness this.

"TIANANMEN SQUARE WAS A NASTY MESS, WASN'T IT?" Reginald begged to know. Frederick could only shrug. Joyce ushered them all into the dining room, where English ivy seemed to be rampant. It curled about door casings, wound around lamps, encircled picture frames. It was like being in an immense terrarium. Frederick imagined Arte Johnson peering out of the foliage at any moment, his helmet green as the ivy. "Verrrry interrrresting." Any day now Reginald's family would need machetes just to find the table.

Joyce shuffled Frederick over to a chair next to a sullen young man. He had met Joyce's two sons before, at those demented family holidays, and remembered them only as rude lumps.

"We're getting Bobo a toy poodle," Joyce proclaimed as they all sat down. "For company," she added.

"It's nice to see you again, Bobo." Frederick nodded at the boy. Joyce laughed heartily. Even Reginald heard well enough to appear entertained. Something rustled in the ivy. *Budgie.*

"And you say that *my* generation is stupid," said the youth. He shook his head in disgust. "Freakin' incredible," he added.

"Bobo's our cat," Joyce revealed. Frederick heard Budgie give a low squawk.

"I see," he said. He drained the martini and nodded appreciatively as Reginald poured more from the pitcher. Joyce rattled ice in her glass, swirled it around and around. Directly above her head a huge pot of ivy cascaded down in long strands. From her position beneath the plant, Joyce had a massive head of ivy-green hair, all the leaves neat as curls. She crunched an ice cube.

"Please don't do that," snapped the young man. He looked at Frederick again, still in disgust. "Freakin' incredible," he repeated loudly.

"You *do* remember Teddy?" Joyce asked, nodding in her son's direction.

Condom Boy? Frederick wondered. He held his hand out to Teddy, who ignored it.

"We invited Robert to dinner, too," said Joyce. "But he's at that age where he doesn't want to eat with us anymore. He's in college, you know. Always protesting this and that. I had thought all that foolishness was over with the sixties." She shoved a dish of lasagna toward Frederick and he helped himself to some of the food that existed merely to *accommodate his life-style*. He was careful to inspect the bits of black olive. He didn't care a whit that Budgie was watching. As he was about to fit a bite of salad onto his fork, something came rattling down the long table toward him. Frederick jumped. His first reaction was that a crazed, jealous Bobo had gone berserk, was out to find that meddlesome toy poodle. The commotion stopped suddenly and Frederick saw before him a miniature Conestoga wagon, laden with garlic bread.

"Reginald's class is studying about the pioneers," said Joyce. Frederick stared at the loaf of French bread that protruded three inches from the wagon's back flap.

"I MAKE HISTORY COME ALIVE," Reginald admitted.

"Oh, sure," said Teddy. "That was some trouble those folks had crossing the Garlic Bread Trail." He reached over and broke a piece of bread from the loaf's tail. "And they think *my* generation is stupid."

"THOSE BABIES WERE SOMETHING," Reginald was now shouting. "PERFECT FOR HAULING HEAVY LOADS OVER BAD ROADS. AND LOOK AT THOSE BROAD WHEELS—THOSE SUCKERS COULDN'T EVEN THINK ABOUT SINKING INTO MUD. AND THAT CURVED FLOOR INSIDE KEPT THE CARGO FROM SLIDING ALL AROUND." Frederick felt as though he were sitting next to an immense helicopter, its blades rotating thunderously. He awaited what he assumed would be a great wind.

"Thank God," said Teddy. "The bread is safe." He burped loudly. This seemed to excite Budgie, who shuffled out of the ivy and lit with a small bounce on Teddy's shoulder.

"I hope you don't mind pets," Joyce said thoughtfully to Frederick.

"THEY COULD HAUL UP TO SIX TONS," Reginald added. "SOMEONE SHOULD BRING THE CONESTOGA BACK, AND YOU HEARD IT HERE FIRST." He tapped the table dramatically. Budgie did a quick little dance up into the air, then resettled on Teddy's shoulder. "WHEN WE'VE DEPLETED OUR NATURAL RESOURCES AND COMPLETELY RUINED THE OZONE, WATCH WHAT'S GONNA HAPPEN IN A BIG WAY. *CONESTOGAS.*"

"Reginald reads all those silly flyers that Robert leaves lying about," Joyce explained to Frederick. "You know, how we're all going to bake like cupcakes when the ozone disappears. I'll say it here and now, even if she *is* my sister. Lorraine is not a happy person, and I'm afraid she might get Robert arrested one day."

"Freakin' incredible," Teddy uttered. He took another hit off the garlic bread log and then stood up. Budgie retreated to the ivy jungle. Reginald gave the Conestoga a mighty push. It rolled over to Teddy's plate and bumped to a stop against it.

"HERE, SON," said Reginald. "IT'S NOT POLITE TO REACH." Teddy stomped off.

"Where are you going?" Joyce demanded. She turned her head, but her enormous green wig held fast.

"Out to deplete our natural resources and ruin the ozone," Teddy answered over his shoulder. "I'll try to have the buckboard back at midnight."

"NO, SON," Reginald protested. "THE *BUCKBOARD* IS A WHOLE DIFFERENT ANIMAL." Frederick listened as the back door slammed abruptly and then all was quiet in the kitchen. "MORE BREAD?" Reginald offered as he gave the miniature wagon another healthy push. It came rolling toward Frederick in an aromatic cloud of fresh bread, instead of the brown dust of the Oregon Trail. The Donner party would have loved this Conestoga. He tried not to think of Chandra, of how the two of them had stopped accepting dinner invitations from Joyce. He wondered if Reginald knew that he made *dinner* come alive, instead of history. He thought about Teddy, out depleting and ruining virgins, of the soggy condoms that were probably above Frederick's head at that very moment, molding, fermenting, rooting in the darkness of some dresser drawer. Unless Reginald had stowed them in the Conestoga. With the curved floor, they wouldn't slide about.

"Bobo has a urinary tract infection," Joyce informed Frederick. "He has to take a great big pill every day for a month. Don't ooh, sweet-ums?" she asked a chair over by the window. Frederick followed her gaze and was surprised to see a very large cat, its eyes stonily yellow, staring at him from atop a throw pillow. No wonder his nose had been tickling fiendishly. He had thought for one wild moment that he must be allergic to one of his hosts. Or he had caught Parrot's Fever from Budgie.

"THE CONESTOGA GAVE BIRTH TO THE PRAIRIE SCHOONER," Reginald noted. "BUT THE BUCKBOARD, WELL, THAT'S A WHOLE NEW BALL GAME." Frederick wished Chandra could see him now, wished she could witness this final decline, wished Reginald could make the *future* come to life. His eyes watered and the end of his nose vibrated. He nodded thankfully as Reginald poured more drink from the martini pitcher. He was suddenly forced to admit that Joyce was right. He was smack dab in the middle of a big pond of denial. His future held many, many dinners with Joyce and Reginald and Teddy and Bobo. He would probably end up godfather to the toy poodle. A pretend uncle. In a short time, Budgie would roost on his head. There was no doubt about it: Frederick Stone's future was dead, and he had as much chance for a comeback as did the pitiful ghost of the mighty Conestoga.

Southern Maine, as well as a degree in English from Boston University. I offer a complete computerized accounting service. He thought, suddenly, of Doris Bowen's firm brown thighs and wondered if she was lounging at that very moment in a white string bikini by the Bowen pool. *Doris.* Not really an appropriate name anymore, when he thought about it, not a name to imply a sexy image. But that's just what Doris Bowen did, with her silky blonde hair and that cute little whisper in her voice. This concept would blow Chandra's Psychology of Names philosophy right out of the water, wouldn't it? Frederick smiled appreciatively. *I would be more than eager to meet with you . . .*

"Or with Doris," he said aloud. *Or I can mail you recommendations from clients who have been thoroughly satisfied with Stone Accounting since its inception.* Could he satisfy Doris Bowen? he wondered, and then abandoned the thought. He was a married man, after all, over twenty years, something most of his friends couldn't dangle in the face of statistics. *My services would include taking care of your weekly payroll, filing monthly and quarterly taxes, and, of course, preparing state and federal income tax forms.* Frederick saw the image suddenly of Doris Bowen's white breasts as she leaned over her shopping cart. *My services could also include taking care of Doris.* Would Joseph Peters be able to tell Arthur Bowen where those breasts had been, just from holding them? Arthur would probably pay top dollar to know. Frederick considered dashing off a letter to Monsieur Peters. The man was in the wrong line of work.

By the time the last client had driven away from the house at the end of the cul-de-sac on Ellsboro Street, Frederick had put the finishing touches on his letter to Arthur Bowen. He also had enough time to run the utility software that would perform a low-level format on his hard disk. This would guard against the hard drive crashing. Frederick could not afford for any data to become irrevocably lost. Most people thought that computers were either glorified typewriters with an adding machine attached or—and Chandra was in this second group—that some completely self-sufficient form of intelligence resided inside the softly whirring CPU, waiting to spit out answers to complex questions. But Frederick knew the truth, as did his computer brothers and sisters: It took a lot of human time to keep a computer functioning efficiently.

Just as he was about to print out his letter to Arthur Bowen

"Do you want to *see* them?" Joyce suddenly leaned forward at the table to ask. Her curly green hair remained behind.

"See what?" Frederick was most cautious. He imagined Teddy's condoms elongating, crawling over themselves like large night crawlers.

"Bobo's pills," Joyce explained while Frederick stared at the butter dish and was silently relieved.

S_{ix}

t was a week after Chandra's departure that Frederick spotted the red Toyota. He was making a right turn on State Street, off Congress, when he saw her zoom by, her hair in a sweet ponytail. Frederick hit his brake pedal and made a quick turn. If he could at least follow her, maybe he could find out where she was living, talk a bit of sense into her. His stomach clenched into a fist, and he felt his heart race like some little engine. Jesus, but he had thought this kind of emotional stuff would be over after he turned thirty. Certainly by *forty*. He pulled back onto State Street in time to see the Toyota zooming through the next set of lights, which were yellow. He felt a quick flash of anger. How many times had he told her not to do that? How often had he listed the dangers in such an action? The traffic light flashed red just as Frederick pulled up to it. He could run it, couldn't he? Traffic was mild. There was even a space coming up, behind a florist truck. He watched the disappearing red Toyota as it grew smaller, as it careened away from him, on down State Street, toward new events that were taking place in his wife's life, events he knew nothing of, events that excluded him. He could rush through the red light in time to catch her. There was no police car lolling about. But Frederick sat meekly, before the round red eye of authority, and waited. He hated himself, but he waited. By the time the light flashed green, telling the wimps of the world that they could proceed like orderly sheep, he had no chance at all of catching Chandra. She had probably run the next yellow light, too. "But, Freddy, it's the chicken light," she had always protested after each of his traffic lectures. "If you don't run it, you're yellow."

Frederick Stone pulled into a 7-Eleven and went inside for a cup of coffee. He needed something to settle the cloud of distress that had formed in his stomach. He made sure to take the largest Styrofoam cup the establishment had to offer, a little protest of his own. The door to the 7-Eleven had barely closed behind him when Frederick glanced up to see the red Toyota on its way back down State Street!

She must have gone to the post office, Frederick thought. He watched as Chandra screeched to a halt at the four-way stop. He could even see the brownish-blonde of the bouncy ponytail, hear music coming from the radio. This was as close as he'd been to his wife in a week. Was that her organic perfume wafting into his nostrils? Or was it the apple turnovers sizzling on the 7-Eleven's broiler? Frederick tossed his coffee into a trash barrel by the gas pumps and bolted for his car. He heard Chandra's tires squeal as the Toyota launched out again. Frederick did his own squealing as he pulled out into the street. He only slowed for the four-way stop. He hated himself for doing this. It wasn't his turn, but there was a clear, safe opening. He barreled on through, only to hear two horns blast out angry indignation. A horn tooted in anger was as efficacious as the worst anathema. Frederick blushed instantly, but he could still see the ass-end of the Toyota as it rolled up to a red light farther down the street. He had a perfect opportunity to pull up behind Chandra until a Domino's Pizza truck shot out of its home office, blocking off the Toyota. The colorful sign on top was happily lighted. Frederick hit his brakes and jerked up behind the pickup.

"Little acned bastard," he muttered. He honked his horn angrily and saw the driver hoist his middle finger up in the rearview mirror: the language of today's generation, invented by *Frederick's* generation. Only, it had *meant something* in the sixties. It had meant *more* than what it meant now. Holding one's middle finger up at the president of some university had meant entire sentences, paragraphs, pages, books. It meant "Your policy is anti-constitutional. Racial segregation is matriculating here. Sexual discrimination is rampant. This university is investing in companies that in turn supply the war in Southeast Asia." Holding up one's middle finger in the sixties could be exhaustive. Now all it meant was "Get the fuck out of my way, mister. I got to get this pizza to Bubba within thirty minutes." Frederick thought of Chandra's presence just ahead of him on State Street and floored the accelerator pedal. The nose of his car came to within a foot of the pickup's bumper and held fast, like one dog sniffing another, a desperate play for dominance as Frederick and the Domino's Pizza boy tore down State Street. Through the windshield of the pickup before him, he could see Chandra's Toyota run the yellow light, the very one she'd ignored on her maiden voyage. He dropped back to a few feet behind the pickup, anticipating the idiot in front of him. Would the pimply youth stop for the light? Probably not. Not with a brain operating on automatic pilot for another eight to ten years. Frederick guessed right, because the Domino's Pizza truck passed through the intersection just as the light flicked from yellow to red. Now Frederick himself had two or three seconds to decide. He bit his lip—to hell with authority!—and followed his forerunner with the toasty sign announcing warm pizza. It was the Frederick of the sixties, the man Chandra had met at Woodstock and fallen deeply in love with! If only she could see him now. When he reached her, when he caught the hurtling Toyota, he would tell her. It would be his own brave testament to their love, a visual poem he'd written himself. He nursed the brake just a bit, since one foot *did* belong to his alter ego, and ignored the fanfare of angry toots that rang out around him. But out of the fanfare grew a more curious sound, something sharper than an angry horn or a serpent's tooth, a *sirenlike* sound, and Frederick was reminded of the clear, magical voices of those mythical nymphs, how Orpheus had rescued the Argonauts from them by playing so wonderfully upon his lyre. Good old Orpheus. Frederick was a little like the poor fellow, when he thought about it. Orpheus had had a heartbreaking marriage, too, hadn't he? And, like Frederick running the red light, he had descended into hell for his beloved Eurydice. Frederick's eyes teared. He would mention *this* to Chandra, too, he promised himself. That was when he saw the blue light flashing in his rearview, a siren's light, recognized the whining lilt that had lured so many sailors to their deaths, and so many drivers into traffic court. He knew immediately that there would be *two* tickets, one for speeding and one for running the red light. He sincerely hoped that there would be no citizen's arrest from any of his angry fellow men, the Argonauts he had betrayed back at the four-way stop. As he pulled over to the curb and sat waiting, Frederick Stone wondered if he should attempt to charm the policeman, as Orpheus had charmed all of Hades. But bribery was not a charge he cared to have on his now-burgeoning record. Instead, he stared off in the direction of Chandra's wake, just as Orpheus had foolishly turned, in the joy of daylight, and looked back at Eurydice, the gray of Hades still engulfing her. What had her faint final word been as she descended back into the netherworld, where he couldn't follow? "Farewell." But this was not the precious word that Frederick heard as he sat with his head bowed, his heart aching for his wild, lovely wife.

"License," the policeman demanded.

At six o'clock that evening, Frederick was pacing the floor of his office with such frenzy that, at one point, he slammed the flat palm of his hand down on his desk. He was careful not to use his fist; after all, he made a living with his hands, not unlike B. B. King, Jamie Wyeth, and others of that ilk. The slap was substantial enough, however, to topple the picture of him and Chandra taken at Woodstock, soon after they met. It was this image of her, her yellowish hair in braids, her peasant blouse puffed at the shoulders, her braless breasts outlined beneath, that sent him out into the evening shadows, sent him back to the corner of Congress and State streets, where he waited for the little red Toyota to go streaking by. Maybe, just maybe, it was an intersection that she passed often in her new life, her new part of town. If he did see her car, he wouldn't speed. He had learned his lesson earlier in the day. But he would flash his lights erratically. He would send out beacons of longing and would hope that he would not cause any great ships—the *Valdez,* in particular—to come ashore on State Street. He had committed enough traffic violations for one day.

It was almost eight o'clock when he finally gave up. He drove home slowly, taking his time, driving out of his way to find the old spots that had meant something to them as a couple: the Portland Museum, Longfellow's house, the Lighthouse Observatory, DeMilo's floating bar. Off in the distance he could see the small fuzzy lights of Peak's Island. How many times had they gone to dinner there, taking the twenty-minute ferry ride in order to dine at Will's Restaurant? Once, Frederick had even become locked in the bathroom at Will's, the doorknob refusing to turn, and he had waited fifteen minutes, sitting on the commode, a smile on his face as he listened to Chandra giving detailed orders from beyond the door, instructions to the maintenance man in the proper procedures of *jimmying*. These were the thoughts plaguing Frederick Stone as he drove back down the cul-de-sac on Ellsboro Street, to the big house with its screened-in porch, to the king-size bed that he had once shared with a woman who *used* to love him and who *still* wore peasant blouses.

Frederick was thinking heavily of a movie on television when the phone rang, a few minutes before nine. His first thought was that it was Chandra. He had heard nothing from her, nothing at all, since she'd hung up on him. Twice he'd come home to find a note taped to the door, saying that she'd stopped by to collect a few things. The call, however, was from Herb, his voice tinny but excited, calling no doubt from the bowels of The China Boat.

"Let's go to dinner," Herb offered. "My treat." Frederick was instantly happy. At least happier than he had been, sitting in the darkening living room, listening to the sounds of autos and voices along Ellsboro Street, wishing for even a stray cat to turn up in search of a hobo's meal.

"Sounds good," Frederick said honestly, pushing aside those guilty thoughts about how he had always turned down Herbert's offers to dinner before Chandra left him. The past was past. In just one week Frederick Stone had grown mightily. He was a new man. A better human being. He could be ready in a half hour, a quick shower and shave. He would wear the tan sports coat, his most comfortable.

"Ready when you are," Herbert announced. Frederick smiled. Herbert was probably on the pay phone at The China Boat. He promised himself that he wouldn't grimace once during the course of the evening, not even when Herb ordered his blasted mandarin duck.

"It'll take you at least fifteen minutes to drive over here," Frederick predicted cheerfully. "I'll be ready by then." He was about to hang up.

"I'm here now," Herb announced. Frederick heard what sounded like tires crunching the crushed rock in his driveway.

"What?" he asked.

"I'm just turning into your drive," said Herbert. Frederick felt a grimace appear on his face, and so near the promise he had made to himself. He flicked back the kitchen curtain and stared out at the headlights in his yard. He saw the silhouette of a hand flutter, his brother, Herbert, waving hello to him.

"You're *what?*"

"I'm in your driveway," Herb proclaimed. "You know, *veni, vidi, vici.* That's Roman for *grab your coat.*" Frederick felt a stab of anger tense his stomach muscles. He was more inclined to grab Herbert's *throat.*

"Herb," he said calmly, "how many times have I asked you to phone before you drop in?"

"I did phone," Herbert reminded him.

"Yes, but you're sitting in my yard."

"I can't believe you don't have one of these cellular contraptions," Herbert chided. "A man like you should look to the future."

"Herbert," Frederick began. He felt a warmth spread across his face, a fiery swath, a flushing. He had recently read that modern gadgets such as cellular phones were clogging the microwave frequency band where scientists were trying to listen for sounds of life from other worlds. "It's getting to the point where we won't be able to hear a goddamn message from other planets because of people like you, with your garage door openers and your blasted cellular phones."

"Watson, come here, I want you," Herbert whispered dramatically.

"Herbert," Frederick said again. His face was now an immense furnace. So much for promises. "People like you, Herbert, are clogging up our window on the universe with so much microwave babble that we're going to sound like a little bee buzzing its ass off, out there in space. What intelligent life form wants to visit an annoying, buzzing little insect, Herbert? Can you answer me that?"

"*I'm* visiting *you,* aren't I?" Herbert noted. Frederick saw a round orange ball glowing in the darkness of Herbert's car. Herbert was smoking again, and soon Frederick would have to breathe in the smoky entrails of Herbert's air. His nose hairs would grow heavy with debris, his lungs would shrivel, and one day he might even die from secondhand smoke. This was the fate his wife had left him to.

"Herbert?"

"Yes, Freddy?"

"Are you smoking? Are you, Herbert? Are you sitting in my yard smoking?"

"No," was Herbert's gruff reply.

"Then what's that round orange glow I see out there in the dark?" Frederick wanted to know.

"I brought my pet goldfish with me," Herbert replied, and Frederick could hear him guffaw. He prayed that he'd be on hand when the day came for Herbert Stone to die from carcinogenic misbehavior, and that he, Frederick Stone, the younger brother, would be called down to the morgue to identify the sooty remains. "Those are *his* lungs all right," he'd say, leaning over the undertaker's smelly shoulder to inspect the smoldering air sacs that had once been a pretty, healthy pink.

"One of these days I'm going to say I told you so," Frederick informed the silhouette sitting behind the wheel of the Chrysler, the outline of his brother, Herbert.

"If that's so," said Herbert, "I'll be dead and won't be able to hear you. And besides, what's wrong with lighting up in your yard? Am I gonna kill the shrubs with secondhand smoke or something?"

"There you are, a veterinarian, for crying out loud, and you're smoking two packs a day," Frederick complained. "As a professional, you should know better." He peered out into the darkening yard to see if Herbert was perhaps gesturing, although

Frederick had already received his quota of middle fingers that day.

"I don't treat many dogs with a nicotine habit, Freddy. Lighten up." Frederick saw the orange ball blaze brightly. Herbert was taking a big puff. "Now, are you going to stay on the telephone all night, or are you coming to dinner? No wonder you drove Chandra out of the house." Frederick Stone released the kitchen curtain, which he'd been twirling in his hand, and promptly hung up.

Within minutes of being seated at the usual table near the window, Herbert began to fidget. He patted his breast pocket as though in search of a pack of cigarettes. Frederick smiled sardonically. Perhaps Herbert Stone was merely in search of his stony little heart. During their previous trip to The China Boat, the two brothers had lingered in the foyer, in front of the high-blood-pressure machine and a breath-o-lizing contraption for the discerning drunk driver, while they waited for their table to be called. Frederick had inserted two quarters into the first machine, a small price to pay in order to learn if his blood pressure was excruciatingly high, another coffin nail from Chandra. But it had been abysmally normal, 120 over 80. It was then that Herbert Stone had inserted his own fifty cents, only to have the machine register nothing. "See?" Herbert Stone had pointed happily at the zeros and declared. "It's the new me, Freddy. No heart at all."

"I hope you don't intend to smoke," Frederick scolded. He glanced around at his fellow diners, all cramped into the small area of the restaurant designated as Smoking Permitted. With the nicely restored beams looming above their heads—the building had been renovated to resemble the belly of a ship—the clientele suddenly appeared before Frederick's eyes as galley slaves, their forks rising to their mouths, falling, rising. Heave-ho! And on the table before them the pepper, the salt, rich spices brought back from the Far East. He was about to share this vision with his brother, but Herbert was standing, suddenly.

"Back in a jiffy," Herbert promised. "I just spotted someone I know."

"Who?" Frederick wondered.

"Client," Herbert said abruptly. "Three-year-old cocker spaniel. Fractured tibia." He was gone. Frederick watched his departure with mild interest. The restaurant was packed with hungry
diners, and the bar area bulging with the drunken aftermath of
happy hour. A waitress dressed as a geisha appeared at the table.

"Aren't geishas supposed to be Japanese?" Frederick asked the
waitress.

"Give me a break," the geisha said. "I been on my feet all day."
She thumped a glass of water and a menu onto the table before
him. He ordered himself a Johnny Walker Black and Herbert the
house scotch—Herbert's taste buds had been eradicated by smoking, anyhow—and then sipped from his glass of water. He saw
Herbert's head bobbing in happy conversation with two young
women who were perched atop bar stools. Frederick supposed
that they were members of Herbert's flock of wide-eyed fledg-
lings, and not the owners of a cocker spaniel with a fractured tibia.
He glanced around the room, locking his attention upon a pair of
young lovers two tables away, remembering his and Chandra's
first dinner together, at a little Boston café where they listened to
a folk trio until closing, until the crowd had dispersed, until all the
chairs were legs up on the tabletops, and then only the help was
left to sweep up. It was a rainy October evening and Chandra had
taken the bus down from Portland to visit him. "It must be fate,"
Frederick had divulged when they first met, in August at Woodstock, when she'd told him that she, too, was from Portland,
Maine. It had seemed as though the cosmos had thrown them
together for that one crazy night. "I come home from BU every
single weekend," Frederick had lied, because he wanted badly to
see her again, was frightened that he might not, even when they'd
exchanged numbers and addresses at Woodstock. But he had
called, and she had called back, and they had known over the
telephone—not a cellular phone, damn it, but a *real* one—that they
would be together for all time, that they would, as "Desiderata"
instructed them, *go placidly amidst the noise and haste.* They knew,
as they listened to words winging back and forth between them
like little birds of love; they sensed, as she wrote him soul-
wrenching letters and he plagiarized good poetry, that they were,
indeed, *children of the universe,* that they had *a right to be here.* And
then, before he knew it, he was meeting her at the bus station in

Boston, in the middle of an autumn cloudburst, and she had appeared in the doorway of the bus like some vision, some mirage that thirsty men long for, some metaphor for a beautiful love poem—if only Frederick could write his own. They had gone to see *Midnight Cowboy,* even though it was months old, and she had cried in the end, when Dustin Hoffman died. Later, they had shared a bottle of Chianti, and she had called it *a basket of wine.* And he had taken her hand, kissed her fingertips, and whispered, "A loaf of bread beneath the bow, a flask of wine, a book of verse, and thou," and she had looked at him with large, believing eyes and said, "Oh, I love that. It's by Omar Khayyám." Another second, and Frederick would have claimed authorship. But that first movie, that first dinner, that first special encounter after so many weeks of separation, was a flick in time that Frederick Stone would never forget. When the owner of the café had come to their table and politely asked if they might leave so that the staff could lock up, the two of them had linked arms and walked back to Frederick's apartment, huddled against a cold steady rain that was coming in from the sea. Frederick knew then that he would always remember two things about that night. It was the last time he ever plagiarized the *Rubáiyát.* And it was the first time he ever made love to Chandra.

Chandra, Frederick thought sadly.

"Valerie," he heard someone say, and he looked away from the two lovers at The China Boat and into the beaming face of his big brother, Herbert Stone. The young women from the bar were fidgeting at Herbert's side. Frederick stood and extended his hand politely. But his knees were wobbly, so strong was the memory of that first night with Chandra, her smooth white legs wrapped about him, her thick wild hair flowing like rivers in every direction.

"Excuse me?" Frederick asked.

"I said I'd like for you to meet our dates for the evening," Herbert repeated. "This is Sarah, and this"—he pushed a tall brunette closer to the chair next to Frederick's—"this is Valerie." Frederick smiled nicely at the girls. He even helped Valerie find a place on the table for her purse, which seemed to be shaped like a lunch pail, before he motioned to Herbert that he'd like to speak with him. At first Herbert declined.

"The girls need a drink," Herbert explained, an arm in the air for the next available geisha.

"I want a piña colada," said Sarah. Frederick wondered if Sarah needed to stop and read the height requirements at underpasses and other such restricted places. He had never seen hair stand quite so tall on a human head.

"I want a Dirty Mother," said Valerie. Four tiny gold beads shone brightly from each of her ear lobes. Frederick took this as further proof of the "More is better" philosophy.

"My brother, Frederick, is a well-known criminal lawyer," Herbert proclaimed. "He was a classmate of F. Lee Bailey."

"Wow," Valerie breathed. "Didn't he shoot President Kennedy?"

"Do you handle serial killers and if so, like, who was the worst?" Sarah wanted to know.

"Hey, what's got twelve legs and still can't walk?" Valerie asked, the $64,000 question of the nineties.

"Oh, I heard *that* one," Sarah crooned. "Jeffrey Dahmer's refrigerator." The girls giggled while Herbert guffawed. Frederick excused himself politely, and this seemed to amuse the girls further.

"In the foyer, please," he said to Herbert, who lowered his arm.

"Freddy bets the horses," Herbert explained. "He needs to place a quick call. We'll be right back. You just tell the waitress what you want, okay?" The girls nodded in sync.

In the foyer of The China Boat Frederick was livid. He paced back and forth in front of the high-blood-pressure machine. It was a good thing he was without coins. God only knew what towering peaks his pressure would reveal at the moment. He finally stopped before Herbert's apologetic face.

"Just what do you think you're doing?" Frederick asked.

"Look, I'm sorry about that criminal lawyer line," Herbert offered. "But I couldn't tell them that you're an accountant. I mean, think about it, Freddy." He laughed nervously.

"I thought you invited me to dinner," Frederick said angrily. Herbert chose that moment to light up a Marlboro.

"I did invite you to dinner," Herbert said. He exhaled a thin spiral of smoke. Frederick fanned the air dramatically. "So what's wrong with some lovely company? I thought it would be fun for us to double-date."

"Double-date!" Frederick was astounded. He tried to calm himself as an elderly couple collected their jackets and went out through the front doors. "For Christ's sake, Herb, who do you think we are? Wally Cleaver and Eddie Haskell?" He had never imagined, not even in his darkest moments of puberty, that he'd end up necking in the backseat of Herbert Stone's big New Yorker at a time when he should be considering the best retirement plan.

"Are you forgetting that your wife *left* you?" Herbert wanted to know. "It's time to get a grip on things."

"Chandra's been gone for a measly week," Frederick reminded him. "Seven short days."

"That's long enough for most men," Herbert said snidely. "You're in denial. Believe me, we all go through it." Frederick remembered Joyce's diagnosis of his illness: *denial*. He suddenly envied Bobo his urinary tract infection.

"Get rid of them," said Frederick.

"Are you crazy?" Herbert implored. "Those are two quality young women—college women, I might add. They could be with men half our age right now, but they've chosen to be with us." He thumped his hand against the wall. The maître d' peered out anxiously.

"That's because men half our age can't afford to buy them piña coladas and—What was that last one? Oh yes, Dirty Mothers. Get rid of them, Herb."

"You do realize," Herbert asked, "that Valerie once turned down a dinner invite from Jack Nicholson when he was in Portland filming some movie? And I'll tell you something else, Freddy." Herbert wagged an admonishing finger. "That girl's got a test tomorrow and yet she's down here right now with us, instead of home studying, and do you show any appreciation? Noooo. You're lucky just to *get* a date with Valerie, buddy. And you can ask anybody at the bar."

"Listen to me, Herbert," Frederick said calmly. "To men who are forty-four, as I am, and to men who are older than forty-four, as you are, a *date* is that which one has written on one's calendar to remind one of a past important event, or a future important event, i.e., the birth of a loved one, or an annual checkup with one's proctologist."

"Should I have said that you were a neurosurgeon or something?" Herbert prodded. "Is that what's bothering you?"

"Get rid of them."

"Freddy, trust me," Herbert said sagaciously. He put a fatherly hand on Frederick's shoulder. "There's a wild man inside you trying to get out. That's your biggest problem. It was mine, too."

"What the hell are you talking about?" Frederick demanded. A large crowd of diners left the restaurant and assembled in the foyer, their voices rising excitedly, a club of some sort, Frederick decided. They seemed to be speaking some occult language. For a full minute, until the group finally passed through the foyer and out into the parking lot, Frederick lost all track of his brother. He was afraid Herbert might sneak back inside without settling the matter of the girls, but there he was, wresting a pack of Marlboros out of the cigarette machine.

"Well?" Frederick began, and was horrified to see his brother, Herbert, do a sudden pirouette in the middle of the foyer, then another, and another before he jumped, legs spread, arms outstretched, into Frederick's face.

"Eeeeeeeiiiiiiiiii!" Herbert screamed. "Arrrrrrgggggggg!" The maître d' came running on soft little feet.

"Mr. Stone?" the maître d' asked. Now Herbert bounced from one foot to another, a Scottish highlands dance. His Van Gogh tie—an elongated version of "Starry Night"—flew like a narrow Dutch flag.

"Oooommmmmpppph!" Herbert answered. "Lalalalalala!"

"Please," said Frederick. His ears hurt.

"Mr. Stone?" the maître d' asked again, his concern growing. Herbert waved the maître d' back into the restaurant with a reassuring gesture. He turned, smiling, to Frederick, a band of sweat shining on his forehead.

"It's the wild man in me," Herbert admitted, winded. His wild man was obviously out of shape.

"It sounded more like Big Foot," Frederick said truthfully. He was still shaken from the experience.

"Well, he *is* sort of like Big Foot," Herbert explained. Frederick wiped his own brow. He allowed Herbert to lead him back into The China Boat and steer him toward the end of the long shiny bar. Herbert signaled to the bartender for two more scotches. "What's important is that it worked," he added, and handed Frederick a drink. Dazed, Frederick stared off toward the table in the

Smoking Permitted section, to where the young lovers were now eating. The name of the little café in Boston suddenly flashed before him, The Fiddler's Cave, and he could hear Chandra's sweet voice, *a basket of wine,* and he remembered the hot, wet grasp of her legs around his body, the warm tremble in his thighs. They had had salads for dinner, huge things laden with artichoke hearts, and the trio had sung "Angel of the Morning." And then it was all gone, and he was back in The China Boat with the other galley slaves, heaving-ho, heaving-ho.

"What did you just do out there?" Frederick asked. He felt the scotch warming his stomach and realized that he could do with another one.

"Iron John," Herbert whispered, and smiled to see the puzzlement on Frederick's face. "You really do lead a hermit's life, don't you, Freddy?"

"Who's Iron John?" Frederick asked. He was still tottering from the presentation in the foyer, Herbert's song and dance to lunacy. And he was still reeling from the gossamer memories of a woman he had met twenty-three years ago, a girl so vibrant and so alive that he could actually *smell* life on her breath, in her hair, her clothing, a college girl the same age as Valerie. He had gone, in one week, from a *basket of wine* to a *Dirty Mother.* Tears formed in Frederick's eyes.

"It's a whole new movement for men," Herbert was saying. "Thanks to Robert Bly." He waved at the girls, who seemed to be ordering more drinks from the geisha waitress, and doing quite nicely without the men, wild or no. Frederick nodded sadly. He remembered Robert Bly, had even plagiarized him in one or two of his love letters to Chandra. Something about driving around in the snow trying to mail her a letter. He had usually tried to avoid the Pulitzer Prize winners and pay more attention to the obscure poets, such as the poets laureate. That had been an education in itself. He looked back at Herbert.

"You got to release the wild man from his prison, the natural man still lurking inside of Frederick Stone," Herbert whispered. He tapped at the invisible bars on Frederick's chest with a rigid finger. "What I did back there, out in the foyer, was all thanks to a suggestion by Bly. Listen to this." Herbert reached inside his jacket pocket and pulled out a raggedy sheet of paper. He unfolded it. "I carry this for quick reference," Herbert explained. "It's verbatim from the book, so listen carefully. 'When we are in a boring conversation, we could, instead of saying something boring, give a cry.' "

"What?" asked Frederick.

"Let me finish reading," Herbert said. " 'Little dances are helpful in the middle of an argument as are completely incomprehensible haikus spoken loudly while in church or while buying furniture.' " Frederick stared at him. He hoped his mouth hadn't dropped open.

"And you *believed* that?" he asked.

"What happened to our argument out in the foyer?" Herbert gloated. "Did my little presentation work or not?"

"It worked," said Frederick, "because I was afraid we'd both be arrested." He remembered, suddenly, that the trio had also played "Mrs. Robinson," and he and Chandra had sung along, their glasses of Chianti raised high. They were both wild then, wild in bed, wild on the street, wild in ideas, but so was the world, so were the sixties, so was Mrs. Robinson, so was everyone they knew.

"You've got to learn to become friends with the positive side of your sexuality," Herbert was saying, "and those two young women are the best place to start." Now Frederick remembered Chandra standing by the window of his old apartment on Baker Street, after they'd first made love, the bedsheet wrapped about her body, the rain coming at her from the other side of the pane, and he had wondered then if he could ever hold on to something so free, so ephemeral, so like the rain as this illusive, fanciful creature.

"I even gave you the smartest one," he heard the magnanimous Herbert say.

"The *smarter* one," Frederick corrected, and hoped that, indeed, there were only two of them.

Herbert ordered his mandarin duck.

"One bird with two Stones," Herbert gleefully told the waitress. "Get it?" he asked the girls, who didn't.

"You're funny," Valerie offered anyway. She tossed her hair back over her shoulders with such dynamic force that Frederick feared the Brothers Stone would not only be arrested for dining with minors, they would be sued for whiplash.

"The duck is good here," Herbert told the uninterested, "but Trudy's Palace has duckling in wine with green grapes worth killing over. And The Ocean View, over on Bay Street, has mallard with bing cherries that's out of this world."

Blah, blah, blah, blah, Frederick thought. *Quack, quack, quack, quack.* He sipped at his scotch and imagined Herbert talking with Daffy Duck's voice. It would be a mercilessly long night.

"And then Petite Maison, on the corner of Hickman," Herbert quacked on, "has *canard à l'orange* that's the best I've eaten this side of Paris, when I stopped over there on a furlough back in 1969." Valerie suppressed a soft burp. She was probably still *unborn* in 1969. She stared at Herbert as though he were talking about the Dark Ages. Sarah bit at skin from around her fingernails, if indeed they *were* fingernails. Whatever they were, they were two inches long, and purple.

Frederick finally decided on the pasta primavera, but the girls begged off. They were both on strict diets. They were also a bit drunk. Frederick wondered how many Dirty Mothers and piña coladas had gone onto the tab while Herbert was in the foyer doing an impression of Isadora Duncan on angel dust.

"We probably should be going," Valerie conceded, and Frederick was cheered to hear it. But Herbert settled back with his scotch, a rosy glow to his cheeks. He gestured importantly to Sarah.

"There were some funny things happened in vet school," Herbert began, abandoning his massive knowledge of duck cuisine. Frederick recognized this pitiful endeavor for what it was: Herbert Stone's desperate attempt to entertain the young women enough to change their minds. Herbert Stone had always believed, in the vast laboratory of his thinking, that innocent strangers longed to gather at his feet with cries of "Tell us more!" when it came to his college exploits.

"Please don't do the leg story," said Frederick, knowing it would jog his brother's memory.

"I remember the time somebody from the medical college put a human leg in the case where a horse's leg was supposed to be,"

Herbert plodded away. "But we went right along with the joke and dissected the thing anyway!" He laughed heartily. Frederick felt pure contentment as he observed the emotionless female faces before him. No matter how hard his brother tried, tales of severed limbs at vet school could never rival life on the road with Madonna. They could never rival Jeffrey Dahmer's refrigerator. The girls stared somberly.

"But I suppose you had to be there," Herbert added.

"You probably even had to be a vet student," Sarah noted, and Frederick nodded sympathetically.

"Well, listen," Valerie said. She was gathering up her lighter, cigarettes, stuffing them into her lunch-pail purse. "We better go. I got a big test tomorrow."

"What in?" Frederick asked good-naturedly. Herbert had said they were college girls, and Frederick was reminded of his old cramming days at BU.

"English history," Herbert leaned over and whispered into Frederick's ear before Valerie could answer.

"I got a test, too," said Sarah.

"Ah, come on, girls," Herbert pleaded. "The night is young." Sarah was now standing, sucking the last of her piña colada up from the bottom of her glass.

"They'd probably better go study," Frederick scolded sweetly. "After all, English history is no small task." Herbert twitched nervously in his chair.

"English history?" Sarah repeated.

"All you need to know about English history is the year 1066," Herbert declared loudly. "Before that, there was just a lot of barbarians running around killing other barbarians who were running around. As a matter of fact, it was a lot like that *after* 1066, too. So sit down. Have another piña colada. They didn't have piña coladas back then. Think about how lucky you are." He was close to raving and this intrigued Frederick. Sarah finished her sucking and put the glass down. Valerie was now twirling her long dark hair about her finger and looking generally provocative.

"But what about 1215?" Frederick suddenly wanted to know. "What about when King John signed the Magna Charta at Runnymede?" Now, *there* was an Iron John for consideration.

"What?" asked Herbert.

"Who?" asked Valerie.

"I'm just making a point that you can't dismiss English history that easily," said Frederick. "That's all." Herbert ignored him. He turned back to the girls.

"How about we go someplace that's got good music and a great big dance floor?" Herbert suggested. He winked seductively.

"What about The Hundred Years' War?" Frederick continued. Herbert turned to stare at him in astonishment.

"What are you, crazy or something?"

"It's just that we can't write off English history as easily as you suggest," Frederick replied. He looked to the college girls for support, especially to Valerie, the *smarter* of the two.

"Freddy," said Herbert, chiding. He was clearly embarrassed. "You're missing the point." Herbert bobbed his head at the girls. "These young ladies don't want to hear about wars."

"But they have a test in English history tomorrow," Frederick protested. "You girls are interested in these facts, aren't you?"

"Not really," said Valerie. She thrust out her hip. Frederick noticed that she was wearing burgundy tights beneath a short skirt. He wondered if Maid Marian had ever downed a Dirty Mother.

"We got a test on facial shapes tomorrow," Sarah said. "Cosmetology college is a lot tougher than I thought it would be." At this divulgence, Herbert spun around in his chair.

"She means *cosmology*," he whispered to Frederick. "*Spatial shapes*. So zip it, okay?"

"What about the English Civil War?" Frederick inquired. Herbert sighed loudly. He raked some fingers through his hair. He pulled at his tie. His wild man was obviously pissed.

"His wife just left him," Herbert explained to the girls. He was shaking his head erratically. "Can you understand why?"

"Well, maybe one more drink, then," said Valerie sympathetically. "I can study a half hour before class." Frederick wondered just what she'd study. The contours of anxious faces passing her window? Would she dissect the madding crowd, some of them circular, some square, some diamond-shaped? Chandra's face was an oval, a soft Japanese petal. Elliptical, like the orbit of the earth as it journeys around its burning sun. Chandra's face. Frederick raised his scotch.

"Too many scotch and sodas, for galley slaves and spices, a mandarin duck!" he sang out loudly.

"I guess maybe it *is* time to go," Sarah said cautiously.

"Thanks for the drinks," said Valerie. They waved quick good-byes and disappeared, all swaying hips, back down the long China Boat bar. Herbert watched them go, horrified.

"What the hell was that?" he turned to ask Frederick.

"That was *an incomprehensible haiku,*" Frederick told him. He downed his scotch, a toast to the wild poet still inside of him. "And it was written by none other than yours truly."

Seven

A noisy rainstorm had been battering away at the windows. Frederick woke up disoriented. He *did* used to live with Lorraine Kimball, a.k.a. Chandra Kimball-Stone, *didn't he?* Had he really spent more than two decades of his life with a woman who now seemed like a ghost, a haunting creature glimpsed on horseback at the edge of a gnarled orchard, and only at midnight? A mysterious woman clad only in black, who always disappeared when approached? Or was that in another life, maybe one he'd lived as a hostler taking care of horses at some seventeenth-century inn? But no, that would better suit Herbert Stone, veterinarian to the poor. And, besides, Chandra would have protested greatly to the Karma Board if they'd dealt her such a lowly position as a good hostler's wife.

Frederick slid his legs out of bed and sat up. Outside, a blanket of wind swept across the yard. He could hear it in the trees, against the windows, rain suddenly beating on the roof. He stared intently at his bedside clock. It was past nine. As a matter of fact, it was twenty minutes to ten. There was a time when he'd be freshly shaved, cup of coffee in hand, and at his computer by seven o'clock sharp. Now Walter Muller had been hard at work at his city desk for over an hour, and Frederick was just rising. Surely he couldn't have dropped so far away from his neatly scheduled life in less than two weeks.

"A week and six days," he muttered. It sounded like some godawful Turkish prison sentence for American tourists caught with a single marijuana joint. He ran his day's schedule about in his mind. Not only did the IRS want a complete copy of Down East Medical Group's payroll taxes for the previous year, they wanted a breakdown of Dr. David Horowitz's entertainment deductions. This meant that Frederick would have to pick through all the receipts and not just whip out a computer printout. He sighed. If Chandra chose to disrupt the course of her own life, so be it. But he would not let her disrupt his. The best thing he could do, until she returned, would be to continue with his schedule as usual, a set of rules and guidelines to keep him on a steady pace. The only thing different was that the martini lunch was now a fixture in his life. It made the day so much more agreeable. And oh, yes, he was beginning to appreciate a later lunch at Panama Red's. He had stopped by there twice that week, not because it had always been Chandra's favorite restaurant—a no-meat, no-dairy-products place—but because he, too, enjoyed the menu there. And while it was too inconsequential to even think about, it just so happened he had not seen his estranged wife there. Not that it mattered anyway, and besides, the rest of his usual schedule was virtually untouched. Except for the martinis, and sleeping on the office settee instead of in the marital bed. And the tiny little fact that the bottom of his hair, now over 4.5 millimeters longer since Chandra left, was beginning to disappear below the top of his shirt collar. Other than these minutiae, Frederick Stone was the picture of consistency. Tuesday had always been grocery shopping day and it would continue to be grocery shopping day if Frederick Stone had any say about it. And he did. Although shopping for groceries was a bit futile: He seemed destined to dine out for the rest of his life, and this for a man who'd eaten outside his own house only three times in the past year.

After Frederick had had a refreshing shower, and then some coffee for breakfast, he got out his pencil and pad and began his usual inventory of the house. It was difficult to ignore the empty spaces where Chandra's things had once been. But no need to put tampons on the list now. Besides, there were still two of the large, forty-unit boxes lounging on the bottom shelf of the linen closet, even though Frederick had learned from *Consumer Reports* that super-absorbent tampons may create a healthy environment for the bacteria that causes toxic shock syndrome. But Chandra seemed more concerned with toxins in the outer environment. Nudging the tampon boxes with his pencil, he felt a surge of anger rush through him: He hoped her period began, suddenly, in the middle of some protest march, miles from any drugstore. Let Robbie solve *that* dilemma.

Frederick eased his station wagon into an empty space in front of the grocery store. He felt his pulse quicken as he spotted Doris Bowen's little blue Mercedes sitting seductively in the next row. Why *did* the woman do her own shopping? Never mind. His unmailed letter to Arthur Bowen Developers had been lying on his desk since Chandra left. Maybe that was fate. Maybe it would be best to simply give the letter to Doris. Frederick decided to play the hand and then see what might *develop*.

Inside the store he worked his way past the fresh vegetables, putting items into his cart and checking them off his computerized list as he went. He spotted Mrs. Paroni and quickly swung down the aisle of laundry detergents, even though the only *l* on his list had been lettuce. He was in no mood for Mrs. Paroni's flirtatious prattle. Arthur Bowen's bored wife was another matter. As he rounded frozen foods and headed down through cereals, he saw her. She was dressed in her usual white, a shorts and halter outfit which emphasized a rear that had most likely done some hard time on a treadmill. Some things you can't buy. She was staring at the boxes, a little wrinkle of puzzlement between the tweezed arches of her eyebrows.

"Thinking of changing your breakfast food?" Frederick asked as he wheeled up beside her. He immediately wished he'd said something a bit more clever, sensuous even. But at least he was a step up from his brother Herbert's method. It had been just days ago, over a predinner drink at The China Boat, that Frederick had listened as Herbert asked a woman no older than twenty if he had met her before, in *Miami,* of all places! Herbert was becoming the Henny Youngman of The China Boat.

"Actually, that's just what I'm doing," Doris Bowen said. "Arthur thinks he needs a high-fiber cereal, that if he keeps his bowels moving regularly he'll stay healthy. I suppose a man his age worries about pleasing his little mistresses." She flashed Frederick a naughty smile. He did his best to appear nonchalant, pretending to read the ingredients list on a Fiber One box. But it had unnerved him to hear Arthur Bowen's dirty laundry flapping about in the wind. He cleared his throat and then threw on what he imagined was his most pensive look.

"This is one of the highest in fiber, but to be truthful," Frederick said, and they were most definitely *being truthful,* "it's a lot like eating a bowl of hay." Doris moved closer to him, looking down at the box.

"Good," she said sweetly. "I like the notion of Arthur eating hay." Her cool fingers lifted the box from his hands. He could smell her scent, a sweet, expensive fragrance that caused an involuntary tingle in his loins. The smell of *money.* "So tell me," Doris continued. "What do *you* like to eat for breakfast?" She laughed her throaty little laugh.

Frederick suddenly pictured her across the breakfast table from him, the untanned portion of her breasts showing through the gauzy material of some silky designer gown. He imagined Chandra walking in to catch him there, Doris in the act of feeding him strawberries, or maybe ringing for the butler to come and squeeze them an orange or two. Let Chandra protest *that* tidbit.

"Actually, I mix the Fiber One with this," Frederick said, hoping his voice didn't sound too shrill. He took down another box, a different brand. "I find it makes a very palatable combination. By the way," he added, "speaking of Arthur, I was wondering if you might know who does his accounting?" He felt his face flush, and hoped it wasn't turning too red. What an awful segue! Doris's smile seemed to fade a bit.

"Why?" she asked. Frederick stared idly at the number of calories in a single bowl of Oat Bran, a little thinking time. He mustn't appear too anxious.

"That's what I do for a living," he said finally, as if just remembering her there. "I'm an accountant. I wouldn't mind having your husband as a client." Doris flashed him a knowing smile.

"You sly devil. You're wanting me to put in a good word for you, aren't you?" Chagrined, Frederick fought off a second blush by staring at the sugar content in a Cap'n Crunch box, a sobering thought.

"I wrote him a letter about it," he said. "But I haven't mailed it yet. I thought maybe you'd tell me the best way to approach him."

"The best way to approach Arthur is to prove that you can save him some money," said Doris. "What did you say in your letter?" She was turning sexy again, giving him those warm eyes, leaning on her cart just enough to show a bit of cleavage. Frederick relaxed. He'd have been fine all along if it hadn't been for the blushing, a curse he'd borne since grammar school—Fred the Red—a red flush that appeared at the most inopportune times. He later learned in Mr. Bator's biology class that it was just a special aspect of skin pigmentation, a temporary enlarging of the blood vessels set off by nervousness and provoked physiologically. Chandra, however, said it was provoked by money and the talk thereof.

"I listed my credentials," he said matter-of-factly. "And clients who will recommend me, et cetera, et cetera." He saw a mischievous little smile pull at the corners of Doris Bowen's mouth. He heard Chandra, that constant goddess of his conscience, whisper her little uncertainties into his ear. He *was* doing this for the business, and only the business, wasn't he? One did have to be aggressive today, in this belligerent world. He wished Chandra would get up from her perpetual spot on his weary shoulder and go sit elsewhere—maybe in the tofu section. Besides, what business was it of hers if he flirted with Doris Bowen, now that Robbie was in the picture, now that Chandra was holed up elsewhere?

"Are you doing anything special for lunch?" Doris Bowen wondered. She arched one of her magnificent brows. Frederick felt his blasted blood vessels enlarge further.

"I got a date with my mother-in-law," he explained. He expected Doris Bowen to inquire about this. A mother-in-law, after all, suggested that one was *married*. But she seemed utterly undeterred by his divulgence. She dug down into her white purse for a card. Frederick reached for the pen in his shirt pocket—a top-rated Parker Place Vendome fountain pen, fifty bucks, which, according to *Consumer Reports,* wrote smoothly, didn't spatter, and could take some hard knocks. Doris accepted the pen and jotted down a date and time.

"Here," said Doris Bowen, wife to all those developing millions, still shopping among the hoi polloi, still interested in mortals. Frederick accepted the card. "I won't see you here next Tuesday because I'll be out of town. But I'm back the following Thursday. Give me a call. We'll have lunch. And we'll see what we can do about your problem."

"I'm a strict vegetarian," he warned.

"That can be taken care of," she told him.

"No dairy," he warned further.

"No problem," said Doris Bowen. She turned and pushed her shopping cart down the aisle. Frederick stared after her, enthralled by the sweet curve of the thighs, the provocative sound of high heels clicking like coins upon the tiled floor.

"Oh, Doris," he called out. She stopped, turned.

"Yes, Frederick?"

"Could I have my pen back?"

Panama Red's seemed to have even more brass pots with tall ferns growing out of them. Lillian was waiting for him at the front door. She looked rather energized for a dried-up prune. At least that's what Frederick had been calling her for more than twenty years.

"Frederick, dear," Lillian said, kissing the air near his left cheek. Frederick was thankful for this. As usual, Lillian's lips were brilliantly red. He had always mentioned his mother-in-law's abuse of lipstick to Chandra. "She looks like a carp that's bleeding from the mouth," was Frederick's previous description of Lillian. He had even written a little singsong: *Oh, Lill-i-an's lips are ver-mil-ion.*

"You look fresh and lovely as always, Lillian," was his newest appraisal.

They followed the hostess toward a glassed-in section of the restaurant.

"Two in the arboretum!" she proclaimed loudly, signaling a waiter. Frederick glanced about. A ficus benjamina clung to life in one corner of the room, a grassy Hawaiian-looking growth in another corner. Two scrawny ferns hung from ceiling pots. Chandra needed to get down to Panama Red's. The arboretum appeared to be in more peril than the tropical rain forest. And speaking of ficus benjaminas—he recognized the tree as such because his wife had obviously given him custody of hers, which she called Mike. *Mike, the ficus benjamina.* Frederick had decided to give Chandra another week. If she didn't come home, Mike was toothpicks. He pulled Lillian's chair out for her and waited until she hovered nicely above it.

"Thank you, dear," said Lillian, gripping the chair's seat with a sturdy grasp. Frederick wondered if she thought he might pull it away at the last minute, allowing her to flop onto the floor, a nasty little trick from the son-in-law, this carp-out-of-water routine. But she settled down with her back to the door, her view that of the busy street beyond the bulging bay window of the restaurant.

"My, my," she said, "but the lunch traffic just gets bigger and noisier." She deposited her purse on the table before them—a nice old-fashioned clasp purse, unlike the lunch bucket that Valerie had been packing—and then reached for her napkin. Frederick felt some strange reassurance in the sensible purse. And in Lillian's words. "I can remember another Portland, another time," she said wistfully. "It's all that Yuppie riffraff from out of state. Maine is such a quaint notion to them that they spoil our quaintness by moving here." Yuppie riffraff. Wondering what Lillian would call boat people, Frederick signaled for the waiter. Beads jangled dramatically as some diner sought out the restrooms. The waiter finally appeared, looking a bit impertinent that he had actually been summoned by a lowly customer. Judging by the arch of his eyebrow, one might think he had been up to his ass in neurosurgery in the kitchen. He took their order with a cool impatience. Lillian had decided immediately upon the house Chardonnay, so Frederick ordered her a glass. His mother-in-law—and this had been much to his wife's dismay—was of "the lady will have this" and "the lady will have that" generation.

When the wine arrived, Frederick raised his glass and smiled pleasantly at Lillian.

"To family," said Frederick. "It's so good to see you again, Lillian."

"Yes, well," said Lillian. "I must tell you that Joe thinks I should stay out of it. He says that you never invited me to lunch before Chandra left." Frederick nodded sadly.

"I've been remiss," he admitted. "You tell Joe that for me, okay?" He thought of his stepfather-in-law, a short-legged, short-armed dachshund of a man who still officiated at family barbecues in his skivvies, wearing a T-shirt with the suggestion BUY AMERICAN OR MOVE YOUR BUTT TO JAPAN. And smoking the most foul of cigars. "Tell Joe he's one hundred percent right," Frederick conceded.

"Now then," said Lillian. She seemed relieved to be unburdened of Joe's message as she scoured the menu. But none of the items appeared to meet with her approval. Considering the scowl on her face, she might have been selecting her own coffin. Frederick waited patiently until, finally, he pointed out that the steamed vegetables were always very good and that one could usually count on the soup du jour at Panama Red's.

"I've been having lunch here for a week," Frederick admitted.

"Oh, you poor thing," Lillian cooed. "How terribly sad. And Joe says that you're a cold fish." She tsked. Frederick stared at Lillian's vermilion lips and wondered which fish Joe had envisioned him to be. Concerning Chandra's nuclear family, carp was taken.

"Tell Joe I said hello," said Frederick.

"They don't even serve *fish*, do they?" Lillian noted, having triggered her own memories of seafood recipes. "Fish don't feel pain, do they? And no chicken?" Frederick shook his head. "Joe warned me about this very thing," Lillian admitted sternly, "when I told him where we'd be having lunch. Joe says that even vegetarians aren't what they used to be."

"The macaroni and soy cheese is good," Frederick said flatly. A visual image of Joe swept through his mind, the belly looming above the lumps of charcoal briquettes, a can of lighter fluid in one hand like some awful kind of Molotov cocktail. Frederick imagined the lighter fluid exploding in a brilliant flash, taking Joe's cigar-smoking hand and wrist with it. God, but he had always disliked—no, *loathed*—the seedy little bastard. He was not Chandra's father, anyway.

"Maybe the spinach and tofu salad will do," said Lillian, resignedly. "Bill always used to tell Lorraine that she was eating rabbit food. Remember?" Frederick nodded. Chandra's father had been comedian-in-residence at the American Legion Hall. "Bill loved his sirloins," Lillian added tearfully. Frederick nodded again. He and Chandra had been married just a year before the cholesterol backed so far up in Bill's clogged arteries that not even a Roto-Rooter could get through. Bill should have paid a bit more attention to rabbit food. But Chandra's father had still been several pegs higher up the coat rack than was Joe. And Frederick Stone saw Bill Kimball's dying young as a paltry excuse to get away from the crazy woman he had married—he was most likely three sheets in the wind—on some furlough back to the States during a slack moment in World War II. Lillian had told the story of that first meeting, of "the most handsome man to ever wear a uniform," over so many holiday toddies that Frederick could damn near see the stripes. And Bill's rank had mysteriously risen after he passed on to some greater platoon in the sky. "He's gone from a sergeant to a colonel in just two eggnogs," Frederick had remarked to Chandra one particularly dismal Christmas.

"I'll have the pita, sprout, and soy cheese sandwich," he told the waiter. He was pleased that not a single geisha was in sight. The waiters and waitresses at Panama Red's seemed content to be American.

"Ooh," Lillian shivered. "Is that as horrid as it sounds?" Instead of answering, Frederick stared at the flimsy women in the Impressionist prints that crowded the walls of Panama Red's, ghosts of women, their eyes and mouths and noses just pats of paint. Untouchable women, these wisps of smoke beneath diaphanous gowns. He was just wondering if it was possible to excuse himself from lunch, to make reference to an impatient client, an unreasonable workload, when Lillian picked up her sensible purse.

"I've got something for you," she whispered. She undid the clasp and rummaged a bit inside. Dramatically, she produced a folded piece of paper. "Joe thinks I'm a fool," said Lillian, "but I know my daughter better than he does. And Joyce tells me that you're *on the verge.*" Frederick accepted the piece of paper warily, although he sensed a gift in it, surely, a kind of endowment, a pure benefaction. A rush of appreciation swept over him, gratitude for purses that still looked as if Donna Reed owned them, respect for someone who remembered Portland as a littler, quieter town. He even felt a great love for the cracks on Lillian's face, those fissures of pancake makeup, a thankfulness for her little tan gloves, her talcum powder smell, the smear of vermilion lipstick on her white linen napkin—because he had never known these things from his own mother. He unfolded the paper. It was in Chandra's quick, off-to-some-protest scrawl. It was an address, 257 Bobbin Road. He knew where it was instantly. Bobbin Road was almost within walking distance of their house on Ellsboro Street! *When the red, red Toyota comes bob, bob, bobbin' along.* He reached for his mother-in-law's hand and grasped it. The skin moved loosely above its lattice of bones.

"Tell her anything," Lillian whispered, her face rising like a kind maternal moon above her glass of Chardonnay. "Just don't tell her where you got it."

"I won't," Frederick promised, his voice a dull whisper.

"And, Freddy?"

"Yes, Lillian?"

"Get a haircut, dear."

Herbert Stone called three times that evening, leaving informative messages, but Frederick refused to pick up the telephone. He even thought that he heard a car spin up rocks in the drive and wondered if Herbert was cruising the street, casing the joint, catching his brother in the act of not answering. Each time the phone rang, he had tiptoed to the top of the stairs, in case it was Chandra, and then back again to bed when he heard Herbert's voice. On each message Frederick could hear the excited din of The China Boat taking place over his brother's shoulder. Once, a wall of noise had risen up behind Herbert's voice—most likely a small crowd of folks filing out through the foyer—and it had sounded so much like a monstrous wave that Frederick thought of ships plowing through the waters of the Malay Archipelago, laded with cinnamon, cassia, and cardamon. Spices for southern Cathay. What had one of Chandra's seminars been, just the year before? "How Spices and Herbs Shaped the Course of History: Why Republicans Need More Red Pepper."

"Freddy, this place is crawling with nubility," Herbert announced excitedly the last time he called. "The female-to-male ratio is better down here tonight than it is at a NOW meeting." But Frederick had ignored his brother's advertisements. He had gone, instead, to lie down on the huge bed he and Chandra had bought for their life together, their marriage bed, and from that position he continued to watch the wavering light from the traffic on Ellsboro Street. Where was she right now? Was she over on Bobbin Road, curled in someone else's arms? He had driven by three times since his lunch with Lillian, and not once had he seen the Toyota in the driveway. There had been a maroon Camaro, which had caused instant pangs of jealousy—he would be ulcer-ridden before it was all over—and a sheepish-looking station wagon. But there had been no sign of the little red Toyota.

It was ten-thirty before he flicked on the bedside lamp and sat up. He found his tennis shoes—nonleather bindings—and slipped into them. The jingling car keys in his hand reminded him of wind chimes, and he thought of their first apartment, the one advertised as having a view of Casco Bay. "If you stand on this chair," Chandra had promised, "and hold on to the curtain rod this way, and crane your neck just a bit . . . See! There's the water!"

The yellow house at 257 Bobbin Road was bathed in darkness. Only a small yard light, perched on an outdoor lamppost, was still lighting up the night, the neatly trimmed hedge, the red maple, the decorative rocks lining the walkway. Frederick had turned off the car's engine and found the button for the driver's window. It whirred down. He sat there on the quiet street, his blue automobile transformed to purple beneath the streetlight, and listened, just in case, just maybe, he might hear her rhythmic breathing, might catch those tiny sighs she made in her sleep, if only he listened closely enough. And maybe he could savor a waft of her sweet breath, could at least breathe in the same air that she was breathing over here on Bobbin Road. Inhaling. Exhaling. All the tiny blood vessels in her lungs taking up the oxygen, then passing the carbon dioxide out of her blood on the exhale. She had fallen asleep without his help. Without *him*, period. *She's breathing twelve to fifteen times per minute now that she's asleep,* he heard Mr. Bator say. He wished, suddenly, that he were sitting once again in Mr. Bator's biology class, the old floor register beating and rattling away at the back of the room, the colorful charts of muscles and internal organs decorating the walls, wind and rain whipping about the corners of the school building. He had felt very safe there, in those long-ago classes, content to study about human beings while Mr. Bator's fatherly drone beat its words against the clank of the register. *The most striking difference between homo sapiens and other animals is his ability to make use of symbols such as language and writing.* What would he say to Chandra if she appeared instantly in an upper window, a gothic patina of light illuminating her like some Virgin Mary in those churchly paintings? What would he write to her, now that he was a vagabond, a bachelor bard, a traveling minstrel from another street? Would he compose Petrarchan sonnets, all addressed to *Laura, 257 Bobbin Road?* But no matter. Language and writing had been taken from him when she moved away to a place where she would not have to read or hear what he had to say. And now, instead of her sweet breathing, all Frederick Stone heard was a radio playing softly in another house, and occasional laughter seeping from a television set. Canned laughter. Something Frederick wished was on the market. He would put it, in alphabetical order, on his grocery list. And the only smells that permeated the night around 257 Bobbin Road was from the McDonald's one street over. This would not be a welcomed aroma to Chandra Kimball-Stone, and maybe that's why the windows of the house seemed so trussed up. "The United States has lost two-thirds of its topsoil, and eighty-five percent of this loss is because of livestock agriculture," he had heard her say at the seminar she gave on vegetarianism. "Sixty million people in the world wouldn't starve to death each year if livestock didn't eat eighty percent of the corn grown in this country! Don't you even care as Christians? Don't you even care that eating meat is killing you?" Frederick smiled sadly. He had never been able to explain to Chandra Kimball-Stone that most people live a life detached from nature, detached from the cruel realities of *where things come from.* And they were mindless of any distant *human* suffering. "How do you think Hitler got all those Germans, lots of nice folks, to look the other way?" he had argued with her. And yet she'd called *him* a blind man. He remembered the day she apprehended two young women—college girls who had joined her on a Save the Rain Forest march—having a Big Mac break on a park bench. "Many of those cattle were fattened in South America," Chandra had explained. "Maybe you don't care about the animal, but every quarter-pound fast-food burger that comes from one of those cows destroys fifty-five square feet of rain forest." The two picketeers had stared blankly at her. "More than half of today's destruction of the rain forest is because of raising cattle." One of the girls had promptly put her burger down. The other had remained with her hand defiantly in the air, Big Mac attached. "So?" this one had asked. "So get the fuck out of my Save the Rain Forest March!" Chandra had shouted.

Frederick buzzed his window up and started the car. He drove away from the yellow house, slowly, before flipping on his headlights. In the rearview mirror he watched the tiny beacon on the lamppost grow smaller, weaker, and then, like a lantern hung from some western outpost of the last century, like his comfortable marriage of twenty years, it disappeared entirely.

Eight

At ten o'clock on Thursday morning, Doris gave him precise directions to the Bowen home, in Portland's most elegant district. Frederick thought about her purring voice as he rinsed his Gillette Sensor and put it back into his shaving kit. Arthur Bowen was not in town, but Frederick and Doris were to have a nice casual lunch and discuss business. Or had she said, "We'll get down to business"? He imagined the two of them on the floor of Arthur Bowen's study, on all fours, taking care of business.

" 'Taking care of business,' " he sang. Bachman Turner Overdrive. Nineteen seventy-four. "All right, BTO!" He bobbed his head to his own music, just as he'd seen the young studs do on MTV, and then attempted a bit of moonwalk dance steps, shuffling his feet beneath him. Watching this action in the mirror, he was reminded of an older man trying to put out a fire on shag carpet, a trick he had perfected back in those days when marijuana seeds often fell from the tips of brightly glowing joints. He felt the cursed red blush threaten to flood his face. What would Chandra say if she saw him trying to imitate Michael Jackson? After all, moonwalking was supposed to involve *one small step for man.* Michael Jackson took a whole lot of *small steps.* What the hell was he, Frederick Stone, doing? He would be as crazed as Herbert Stone before this was over, and Herbert was so crazed that Frederick would not be surprised if his brother turned up one day with a ghetto blaster on his shoulder, talking rap. *Well, I'm Herbert Stone, and that's for sure, I'm a vet-er-narian to the poor.*

Frederick filed his fingers through his hair in slow, even strokes, the beginning act of his daily assessment. The gray hairs looked permanent, but he would be lucky if he had any hairs left at all before this latest symphony gone awry, this *Vicissitude in C Minor,* was over. He had taken the time to add to his computer calendar of important dates: *June 23, 1992. Chandra Kimball-Stone has been gone for three weeks and a day. Hair graying moderately. Wrinkles still uncertain.* He had seen Geraldo Rivera on national TV, just that morning, have some fatty tissue extracted from his buttock so that the doctor could insert it into the furrows between Geraldo's eyes. Herbert had phoned later and asked, "Did you see Geraldo get a brain transplant?" But the procedure was the most modern and natural of face-lifts, according to the doctor, better than silicone, collagen, or Retin-A, and Frederick had watched with deep interest. Joan Rivers had held up a sheet so that Geraldo could drop his pants. She had tried very hard not to peek behind the curtain. Geraldo was concerned because he had very little fat on his body, and said so. But his wife was tired of looking at his furrows and admitted it when Geraldo and the cameraman found her backstage and cornered her into a confession. His forehead would need two more injections of ass fat. Frederick leaned forward for a more precise wrinkle inspection.

"So, Doris," he said. He smiled seductively at his reflection and was dismayed to see small crow's-feet appear about his eyes. He must remember not to smile. She would think him a humorless bastard, but he would *appear young.* And he would find a doctor in Portland, Maine, qualified enough to transport parts of one's ass to one's face. "You look smashing this afternoon, Doris." Too damned British. He sounded like the butler on "Upstairs, Downstairs." Displeased, Frederick swished a mouthful of Listerine about for a few seconds and then spit it out. It tasted like shit, but the ubiquitous folks at *Consumer Reports* had promised that Listerine had a proven plaque-fighting formula. It would curb the oral bacteria that form plaque, and the last thing Frederick needed as he approached middle age and, perhaps, single status was a mouthful of gingivitis.

"You look wonderful, babe," he tried again. "A vision in white. Now can we discuss the possibilities of my handling your husband's accounts?" Too fast and glib. And—he sighed—too sexist. What was happening to him? There had been a time—*hadn't there?*—when he had been suave and sophisticated, relaxed with who he was. He had recited Ezra Pound to Chandra, that first night at Woodstock. But back then he had been in a state of complete acceptance about himself, his relationship to his fellow man, his fragile place in a changing universe. Or, on second thought, maybe he'd simply been *twenty-one.* Whatever the hell it was, it was gone. He felt silly now when he walked into stores with more than one teenaged clerk behind the counter. If they giggled, he peered anxiously over his shoulder, adjusted his clothing, feeling generally anachronistic. He rarely knew what was in style anymore. Nor did he care. He had only needed to grow old enough to see skinny ties come back in style again—this time on rock stars instead of on greasers—in order to place little significance in what fashion designers conned the consumer into purchasing. That was the first syllable of *consumer,* after all. And even that godawful eyesore his own generation had invented—probably when two potheads got in a fight over the food coloring— even *tie-dye* had crept back. Each time he saw it approaching on the back of some old hippie, or some young anti-Yuppie, the only thought that kept coursing through his mind was, *What could we have been thinking of?* No wonder everyone he knew back then, including himself, rarely took off their shades. And it wasn't ready to go away gracefully, this notion of the sixties. Sotheby's had recently auctioned off an orange vest belonging to Jimi Hendrix, for *$19,800!* And now some secondhand stores were even prompting folks to *buy* those old outfits, the bell-bottomed pants, the Made in India shirts with the groovy sleeves, the beads, the headbands, the sandals made of water buffalo that have died naturally. Frederick Stone had grown aged enough to see his former wardrobe displayed on store mannequins, could meet pants he once owned coming down the street, the new tenant a young man who had only *read* about Watergate. He thought of Chandra's flowing cotton skirt, the one she loved to march in because it was so *red,* being bought up by Valerie or Sarah, who had never heard of the secret bombings of Cambodia, who sipped Dirty Mothers, who thought Tiananmen Square was the crowded dance floor at The China Boat. He had met Chandra at Woodstock, and now Woodstock was a *goddamn movie,* like *Singing in the Rain* and *From Here to Eternity* and *On the Waterfront.* Jesus.

He decided to dress as casually as possible and, by doing so, project the "I don't give a shit" mode of fashion, a notion difficult to parade in the materialistic eighties and nineties.

"So whaddya think about this Iron John philosophy, Doris?" Frederick asked the mirror. He stepped back two steps and crossed his arms. The word *swagger* came into his mind. "A little too primal for you, Doris? Come on, let's tap-dance on the table. Let's shout haikus down the commode. Let's bake some marijuana brownies and pass them out to all those Right-to-Lifers." He patted a bit of aftershave about his face and wondered if Geraldo's own face was stinging, not to mention his ass. It wasn't just women anymore who sliced and carved and pumped and stitched their bodies in order to feel better about themselves. Geraldo said it himself, on national television, so that there could be no doubt. "I'm a jock," Geraldo confessed. "I thought face-lifts were for sissies." Well, they weren't, not anymore. Face-lifts were for everybody.

The drive up to the house seemed endless. He passed what appeared to be small groves of fruit trees, apple, he thought, and maybe some plum. He crested the hill and leveled into a driveway filled with small circular flower gardens. Enormous pots bulging with blooms rimmed the drive. The house itself seemed to begin in the front with immense, tall windows, and then expand backward, beyond more trees and arbors and what looked like a terraced pool within a stone archway. He had imagined liveried servants swarming the grounds, a veritable barricade to which he must explain his presence, but no one was about. Two cats slept in the shade of one immense flowerpot. He could hear the sounds of birds rise up from somewhere beyond the terraced pool, not the usual birdsongs and notes he might hear while walking, but *exotic* sounds. He simply pulled up in front of the house and got out of his car. If someone chose to park it elsewhere, so be it; he had left the key in the ignition.

When he pushed the brass doorbell, he heard an instant wash of music rise up inside the house, a jangling of notes and chords, more like the horrendous stuff blaring from the Ellsboro Street ice-cream truck than what he would expect from the Bowen residence. A woman with a perfectly stern visage—he assumed she was either the housekeeper or Grant Wood's model for "An American Gothic"—opened the door and beckoned for him to follow. He had been about to say, "Mrs. Bowen is expecting me," but she hadn't bothered to wonder who was expecting him or why. She led him through a hallway that was heavily mirrored. Light bounced from all angles as they walked. The sections of walls that were not mirrored seemed to be alternately covered with quilted satin and realistic paintings of plants, so real that Frederick had to look again. Hanging plants, tall narrow potted plants, little plants in dishes. None of them real. What was that "fool the eye" school of painting called? Oh yes, trompe l'oeil. Frederick had read that some Greek guy had even painted grapes so real that birds tried to eat them. But he, Frederick Stone, had never understood the concept. Why fool the birds? And couldn't the Bowens afford *real* indoor plants? They turned from the hallway into a large room filled with furniture and objects so eclectic that Frederick was certain they'd been collected over many years, from many bustling world cities, from many quaint village shops: a ceramic-tiled coffee table, a painted stool that resembled things medieval, a wine-tasting table, a hexagonal gaming table, Empire chairs, paintings that looked like honest-to-God Constables and Gainsboroughs, and probably were. What appeared to be a hand-forged chandelier dangled over the entire shebang. Massive layers of curtains hung from the walls, providing the illusion of more space, as if the Bowen mansion needed such illusions. Frederick would not be surprised to learn that Doris Bowen might be concealed behind a loud Wizard-of-Oz voice, tossing out balls of fire to frighten travelers from Kansas or Maine. Doris would be—as Geraldo had been—hiding her ass behind a curtain.

Instead, she was seated magnificently on an Empire chaise, enjoying the picture window view of a small millpond that sported several black swans. At her feet, a huge Great Dane—a descendant, no doubt, of Cerberus—lay with its massive head on its paws, its sharp intense eyes on the new visitor.

"Frederick," Doris said softly, and extended her hand. Frederick remembered Meryl Streep in *Out of Africa,* her Isak Dinesen accent. "Would you like a drink? Larry will be serving lunch in just a few minutes." Larry? Frederick glanced nervously about. Weren't male servants called Rupert and Holmes or some such?

"Martini," he said, and she rose to fix it herself. The dog turned its enormous head toward her, kept its eyes glued to her back. Frederick wondered if perhaps it had been a man in another life, a victim of courtly love, now content to lie at the feet of its mistress, waiting for the occasional stroke of a smooth white hand, the falling crumb. Doris poured herself a glass of wine.

"Arthur's in New York on business," she said. "He's really just killing time until he can kill something else, when The Glorious Twelfth arrives." Frederick raised both eyebrows. "The twelfth of August," Doris explained, "when grouse season opens in Scotland. It's been a big deal for over a hundred years." She gave him the martini.

"I see." Frederick nodded. Had Chandra ever picketed in the glens of Scotland? He could envision her now, in tweeds, thwarting Arthur Bowen's best-laid plans. *The best-laid schemes o' mice an' men gang aft agley wi' Chandra Kimball-Stone.* Doris beckoned for him to follow. The Great Dane lifted its heavy head and watched carefully.

They passed through a doorway with a corduroy valance and entered into a room with many palm trees growing up out of terra-cotta pots. Frederick studied the plants carefully. The palms were real, no more of that "fool the eye" stuff.

"As you can see," Doris announced with a swoop of her arm, "hunting is my husband's passion." Frederick followed her gesture and was surprised to behold, adorning the spacious walls, the heads of animals he'd seen only on "Wild Kingdom." He recognized an elk as such, a delicate small-faced deer, a towering moose—Bullwinkle himself, perhaps. He paused before some kind of antelope, grayish-brown, with long, twisted horns. He put a hand up to touch the tip of its soft muzzle.

"Kudu," Doris told him. "From Africa. Arthur shot it while in pursuit of the Big Five. You know, *elephant, lion, Cape buffalo, rhino,* and *leopard.*" Frederick suppressed a grimace. Good Christ, but Chandra would suffer a stroke to hear such things.

"Kudu, huh?" he heard himself reply.

"Arthur says that hunting keeps many African countries alive financially." Frederick nodded again. Tell that to Chandra Kimball-Stone. *And Negroes picking cotton kept the economy of the South alive,* she'd say. "Pretty pathetic, isn't it?" Doris added. "That's the Cape buffalo over there." She pointed. Frederick moved on into the room, toward a huge, fierce-looking head. It was black, nearly hairless, with horns joined at the base, as though the creature wore a helmet.

"I've never cared much for stuffed animals," Frederick admitted. Doris held a cautionary finger up to her lips.

"First mistake," she corrected him. "And you must remember this if you're to get Arthur's business. *Stuffed* animals are the kind you find on the beds of teenaged girls. *Mounted* animals are what you see before you."

"Thanks for the lesson," said Frederick honestly. Chandra would say he was selling out, but Chandra was gone. Chandra had sold out on their marriage, and whether or not he referred to Arthur Bowen's animal corpses as *stuffed* or *mounted* was his, Frederick Stone's, own business.

"Freud had it right all along," said Doris, "about that gun-as-penis notion. What you see before you, Frederick dear, are ejaculations, some of them quite rare, from all over the world. You see animals that have been *mounted,* and we all know what *mounted* means, don't we?" She winked alluringly. Frederick shuffled his feet. He tried not to look at the sad marble eyes of the Cape buffalo, directly above his head. His throat seemed to be constricting.

"Nice house," he said, his head bobbing erratically. Doris smiled. She reached out a cool finger and ran it about the rim of his glass. The Great Dane watched closely. Frederick wondered if perhaps it had been wired by Arthur Bowen, its eyes little cameras recording all.

"May I ask you something?" Frederick wondered. Doris nodded.

"I'm all answers," she said. She peered at him over the edge of her glass.

"Why do you do your own grocery shopping?" He waved his martini about the room. "I mean, look at this place. You could send Larry, or the housekeeper, a bunch of people. So why do you?" She laughed fully, tossing her head back, rummaging a hand in her blonde hair.

"Florence does most of the shopping," Doris admitted. "I only browse. But I think it's important to get out among real people once in a while. I was, after all, just a little housefrau when Arthur met me, a clerk at our favorite IGA." Frederick tried not to register surprise. He sipped on his martini and stared at what looked like some kind of wild goat. It had a narrow, pointed muzzle, short ears, and curving ribbed horns. It may have been Pan, for all he knew, killed by Arthur Bowen on Mount Olympus and brought back to decorate the walls of his house in Portland, Maine. *Mount* Olympus, not *Stuffed*. He leaned in to read the brass plate: *Dall Sheep,* it declared. *Alaska, 1979.* "Arthur had to crawl ten miles on his belly, over icy crags, in order to kill that," Doris informed him. "You're shocked, aren't you?"

"Well, ten miles is a long way," Frederick conceded. He personally wouldn't crawl ten miles over icy crags for great sex.

"I mean about my meeting Arthur at the IGA."

"I'm not shocked," Frederick said. He was shocked. He had imagined it all unfolding in the proper society way. When he had thought of Doris Bowen's *coming out,* he never envisioned that it would be from between the shelves of canned vegetables and fruit juices.

"Yes, you are," said Doris. "You're shocked." She reached out a slender hand to his cheek and brushed it along his jawbone. Frederick felt a tremor distort his face, and then the quick pigmentary disturbances of his blood vessels as they spewed redness about his cheeks. "You're blushing," she said. "How charming, in this day and age."

"What accounting firm represents Mr. Bowen at this time?" Frederick asked, in what he imagined was an official voice. Doris gave another throaty laugh.

"Let's have lunch," she offered.

They ate on the patio overlooking the millpond.

"Do you like the birds?" Doris asked. "Those black swans are Australian. And those birds over there are golden and silver pheasants, and somewhere around here are chukar partridges. They live in a lovely little house beyond the pool." Frederick had been trying, since his arrival, to avoid the soft whiteness of Doris's cleavage. But at the patio table she leaned forward with every other sentence, causing the cleavage to consistently rearrange itself, shift about, cool white glaciers in upheaval. Frederick watched the lazy floating swans down at the pond, the butterflies lighting on the well-groomed flowers, the Great Dane chasing a stick being thrown by a young boy. He had never before thought of her as having children.

"The housekeeper's grandson," she said as she followed his glance. "Arthur has two horrid progeny from his first marriage. Thank God they're in college. I concentrate on raising my own child, that one there." She nodded at the Great Dane. As she was about to grace him with another of her laughs, Larry plunked a fruit plate down in front of Frederick with such force that a strawberry jumped from the plate.

"Larry!" Doris scolded. Next, Larry sloshed Frederick's water, then ignored the empty martini glass. He was quick, however, to refill Doris's wineglass. "Bring Mr. Stone another martini."

"*Bring Mr. Stone another martini,*" Larry mimicked snidely.

"And stop acting like a big baby," Doris added.

"*And stop acting like a big baby,*" Larry mocked. Frederick stared at his fruit plate and wondered what Joyce and Reginald were having for lunch, almost missed Budgie.

Within minutes, Larry appeared with a fresh martini. He made no response to Frederick's thank you, but reeled on his heel instead and disappeared back inside the house. Frederick noticed that he had withheld on the olive, for symbolic purposes no doubt.

"Just ignore him," Doris laughed when she saw the quizzical look on Frederick's face. "We all have our days, don't we?" He felt her foot suddenly as it rested on his own beneath the table. He coughed uneasily.

"About Mr. Bowen's accounting firm," he said, and Doris giggled openly and sweetly, this time a pure and honest laughter.

"You're the first shy man I've met since grammar school," she said. "I thought they were all extinct, like great auks. You know, too shy to procreate." She moved her toes up his calf. He had seen this footwork before in movies and prayed that it was not foreplay to some under-the-table blow job, an oral appetizer. Larry would be furious, probably refusing to feed Frederick any salad. He tried to ease his legs back. Perhaps if he crossed them, protected his genitalia. *Castration is performed to create a sterile and more docile animal,* Mr. Bator warned suddenly, *and has even been practiced to maintain a boy's soprano voice.* Frederick imagined himself asking for a glass of water with the same rich lyrical voice of male castrati singers of the seventeenth and eighteenth centuries. Would a castrati singer be able to hail a New York City cab? Probably not. Larry suddenly appeared on the horizon with salads.

"I hope Florence remembered that this is to be a no-meat, no-dairy lunch," Doris told him. Frederick imagined Florence Henderson in the kitchen, flour on her bobbed little nose. The croutons vaulted into the air, Mexican jumping beans, as Larry placed the salad before Frederick.

"Larry!" Doris scolded. He produced a plate of cheese Napoleons and then disappeared. Doris leaned toward Frederick, showing even more soft snowy cleavage. "Larry can be so immature sometimes," she conceded. Frederick merely nodded and picked at his salad. The dressing seemed to have a red wine as its base. "Safe from dairy products," Doris said, noticing his concern. "But the cheese Napoleons are all mine. Florence refused to make them with anything but real Parmesan cheese."

"Did you know Larry before he came to work here?" Frederick asked, but Doris merely giggled. He felt the little foot again, prodding his calf, climbing slowly higher. *This little piggy went to market, this little piggy went . . .*

"Ask me no secrets and I'll tell you no lies," Doris promised. Frederick decided that that was a good deal, and accepted it, as long as Larry didn't sneak up behind him with a scalpel.

The soup was a cold cream of cucumber made from, Doris assured him, *soy* sour cream, a dollop of which still floated in each bowl, and decorated with herbs and thin slices of cucumber.

"Florence went to the health-food store at the mall," Doris told him. "She hated it, but she went." Frederick imagined the entire Brady Bunch all crowded into The Alternative Grocer, pawing over the tofu patties, sniffing the nutritional yeast, hefting the fake hot dogs.

Larry appeared with the main course, a large hollowed tomato stuffed with rice and almonds and served with cold asparagus spears.

"This looks delicious," Frederick admitted. He was trying desperately to make friends with Larry, and was also confused as to why. Wasn't Larry the *help,* for Christ's sake? Ignoring the compliment, Larry puffed up like one of the *real* cheese Napoleons and remained silent.

"When he heard about your eating habits, Larry suggested we serve you boiled beef tongue, didn't you, Larry?" Doris teased. This comment managed to wrangle a small tight smile. Frederick decided that Larry would be a perfect model for the Anal Retentive Poster Boy.

"It's perishable, fresh tongue is," Larry finally spoke, a little Mike Tyson kind of voice. "Its refrigerator life is only eight days because it's already several days old by the time it gets to our butcher."

"The tongue must be older than *that,*" Frederick wished he dare say. "Didn't the cow have it first?"

"That's why Florence was going to boil it," Larry ground on. "Then serve it up with a sweet-and-sour sauce, pearl onions, and raisins. But you *don't eat tongue!*" He spun on his heel and was gone.

"I tell you," said Doris, shaking her luscious head. "Sometimes he's even more jealous than Willy." She cut into her tomato. Frederick did the same, trying hard not to think of a huge tongue fresh from the mouth of a grazing animal, accompanied by pearl onions or no. He was almost afraid to ask, but he did.

"Who's Willy?"

"The gardener," said Doris. Larry was back with a fresh plate of fruit.

"So, as to this accounting business," Frederick said sternly. He wanted Larry and Willy to know that he was not to be considered competition of any sort. He played with the idea of mentioning Chandra, as in *My wife and I are both vegans.*

"Florence says we should serve him boiled beef *penis,*" Larry announced, to which Doris relinquished another full-bodied laugh. Even Larry smiled, with teeth so white that one might think the butler had been to the orthodontist for a round of caps. Larry's mistress must be generous. Frederick glanced up to see a hefty black woman hovering behind the glass patio door. She was toting a huge wooden spoon, which jutted from the hand she had thrust upon her hip. Had she stuck her tongue out at him? Or was she just licking her lips?

"Florence is having a bad day," Doris admitted. "They nearly tossed her out of The Alternative Grocer." Frederick wished with all his might that he could learn to go through life without food, that he would never be forced again to break bread with the loonies. Even his brother, Herbert Stone, making duck metaphors at The China Boat, was better than this. He wondered if Larry and Willy had conspired to track him down in the Bowen driveway, beat him to death with a fifty-pound bull dick. He had seen one—in reality they were ten-pounders—during an open-house visit to Herbert Stone's veterinary college. A weapon like that could probably pack quite a wallop. Frederick was beginning to feel as though he were taking part in a Clue game. *Answer: Larry the Butler, in the Conservatory, with the Bull Penis.* Larry disappeared again into the bowels of the kitchen.

"All this talk has me thinking," said Doris. She scaled his calf again with her foot. Frederick cleared his throat and waited. "Why don't we take a little walk down by the pond? Breathe in some nature?" Frederick imagined the Arthur Bowen Developers account drifting away, out into the middle of the millpond on a crisp dead leaf, disappearing forever. Now Doris was running her fork up the side of his arm, tickling him, her beautiful breasts threatening to emerge into pure sunlight at any second. "Do you know what I think about, each Tuesday, when I know I'm going to see you at the IGA?" He tried to move his arm away from the probing fork without insulting Doris, wife to those developing millions. He suddenly pitied himself, the way Chandra pitied businessmen in those notorious gray flannel suits, men who'd do anything for the almighty buck. He also felt very stimulated by Doris Bowen's advances. He imagined the two of them together, naked in the tall reeds about the immaculate millpond, her back pressed into the sweet soil, an earth goddess. He would *mount* one of the Australian swans first, in a flurry of black feathers, before he pried Doris Bowen's trim thighs apart. Zeus had *become* the swan, his *great wings beating still above the staggering girl, her thighs caressed by the dark webs, her nape caught in his bill.* Good Christ, but Yeats had been a horny bastard! Frederick wiped a beady row of sweat from his upper lip, then bounced up out of his chair.

"I gotta run," he said. "This has been a terrific lunch." His napkin fell to the floor, where Larry would curse to find it later, the rude guest gone. Frederick hoped it wouldn't end up wrapped around some voodoo doll belonging to Florence, while both Larry and Willy riddled the area below the belt with sharp pins.

Doris Bowen stretched out a beautifully tanned leg to prevent Frederick from passing. She placed a cool finger on his arm, made little circular motions. *How can those terrified vague fingers push the feathered glory from her loosening thighs?* Had Yeats pressed Maud Gonne into the rich loose soil around some Irish millpond?

"I will do two things," Doris said. Frederick wasn't sure if she had lowered her voice in order to be sexy, or to find privacy from Larry and Florence and Willy the gardener.

"What's that?" he asked, hoping to sound at least casual. He tried desperately to ignore those next passionate lines, that inescapable *shudder in the loins,* that *broken wall,* oh, especially that blessed broken wall! He knew the red on his face was spreading like some wild brushfire. He cocked his head.

"I will ask my husband, Arthur, to consider your business proposal," said Doris. *Did she put on his knowledge with his power . . .* "And I'll wait for you in my car next Tuesday, in the parking lot. I guess I don't have to worry about you eating too many oysters in the meantime."

Larry was on his way back with a pot of scalding coffee just as Frederick waved a quick good-bye and then cut through the magnificent hedge.

Nine

I would gladly teach you
If I could only reach you
And get your loving in return.
Lady Willpower, it's now or never,
Give your love to me . . .

—GARY PUCKETT & THE UNION GAP

n eyelash survives for three months and a hair of the eyebrow for three weeks, Frederick heard Mr. Bator say. It was the first month anniversary of Chandra's departure from the house on Ellsboro Street. *But the life span of hair in the human scalp is six months.* Would all his hair be brand new by the time she returned, every single strand? If so, would she recognize him with a pristine mane? Would she pass him on the street, thinking vaguely that his eyes reminded her of someone she had known once, maybe even loved? It was almost eleven o'clock. Frederick had shaved but was not through assessing. The shower drain had seemed a bit more clogged than usual that morning and he was worried that this item might need to be recorded on his computer file of important dates and facts. His own father, Dr. Philip Stone, had died before baldness had the opportunity to entrench itself. So had the other men in the Stone family tree, those Gregory Peck look-alikes. Frederick had studied the pictures in the Stone family album, one of the few things his mother had salvaged from her infamous yard sale. The males in his paternal family seemed to be thinning *and* receding just before the Grim Reaper snagged them. It was a sad legacy to leave one's sons, but it was a physical fact. *More than two thousand years ago Aristotle noted that men, not women, are usually affected by baldness,* Mr. Bator reminded him. *But baldness is not exacerbated by the wearing of hats, tight or otherwise.*

"I'll remember that the next time I get the urge to buy a tight cowboy hat," Frederick said curtly. The truth was, he was growing a little weary of Mr. Bator and wished he knew what the hell was causing him to lurk about in Frederick Stone's hippocampus. Frederick had no doubt that his old high-school teacher had set up housekeeping in there, in the dark intimate folds of his temporal lobe. He just didn't know why. Oh, he realized it wasn't the real Mr. Bator talking to him but that, under pressure, he was rifling through some old memories he hadn't bothered with for some time, was bringing them forward in his mind in order to deal with them again. To put it in computer terms, he was downloading archival data into RAM. But the sad truth was this: Remembering Mr. Bator, and those days at Portland High, and all those mornings and evenings and weekends before Chandra, before Woodstock, was a tad painful to do in the wake of his wife's leaving him. And he had never known until Mr. Bator started talking that high school had been such a place of refuge. Now it had that warm, fuzzy glow to it, a cocoon in time, a hazy launching pad before the metamorphosis. At least he assumed there had *been* a metamorphosis. So then, what had he become? In May of 1971 he had graduated from Boston University with a degree in English literature. In October of that same year he had married Lorraine Kimball, a.k.a. Chandra. But he awoke one morning in 1979 to discover that he had acquired a degree in accounting. According to most of his sixties friends—and speaking of the quintessential *metamorphosis*—this was akin to Gregor Samsa waking up as a six-foot-long cockroach. After all, people in business were the enemy. But Frederick Stone was going to represent the little businesses, wasn't he? Hadn't he said that a few times to the cabal that clustered about at wine and cheese gatherings in order to feign interest in the latest Czech poet or some dissident East German writer? What had he told Chandra's friends who pretended they were only walking the halls of academia until their novel was sold, their paintings hanging in galleries, their poetry in demand by the multitude, their papers on the Venus flytrap published? Hadn't he made vague allusions to the little businessman in Central America who could use some sound financial advice? Maybe even Southeast Asia, what with the shit having been blasted out of them with bombs and napalm and lies. He would remain concerned only for the betterment of mankind. Amid the chaffing noise and confinement of preppie business suits, he would go placidly in jeans and longish hair—that's how one could identify the Still Sincere—and maybe a gold earring bead in one ear. This sparsity of jewelry for men had of late replaced the peace symbol, hadn't it? A single earring on the male lobe meant lots of stuff. It meant *pay attention here, something really hip is taking place, someone astute is passing through.* And it was in keeping with the modest lifestyle of the sixties. Two earrings would be extravagant, but one, well, who was to criticize? And besides, who were these academic friends of his wife? Were they out discovering cures for cancer, publishing exciting papers that would enlighten the botanical world, digging up dinosaur bones, finding new planets? No, they were teaching by rote out of books written by other folks, tossing forth ideas thought up by other folks, discoveries by other folks, poems by other folks. Intelligence was supposed to be something that involved problem-solving and creativity. Not this memorizing bullshit. So much for Chandra's academic friends. They were well worth the loss. But he had lost Chandra, too. And by the time she packed up and left, in June of 1992, Frederick had no idea at all what had happened to his gold earring. He had simply cast the thing off one day, afraid its glitter might discourage an accounting client. It had probably been melted down and was now serving as the crown in Dan Quayle's back molar.

In the kitchen he took prechilled bottles from the refrigerator and mixed up a cool pitcher of martinis, ten parts gin to one part dry vermouth. He searched in vain for a cocktail stirrer and settled for a plastic ruler instead. He churned the mixture vigorously so that the dilution would make the drink smooth and delectable. There was one thing he had learned while seeking a degree in English literature, by God, and that was how to make a worthy martini. From now on he must buy his vermouth in pint bottles so that it could be replaced frequently. Let others take for granted the herb flavor that vermouth added to the tapestry. Frederick

Stone was not that foolish. He strained his first martini of the day into a prechilled cocktail glass, plopped in two olives, and then drank it instantly. His esophagus burned from the chill, and he imagined it turning frosty, like the winter windowpanes of his childhood. He let the drink settle for a minute and then poured a second. Now, now, he could think about Chandra Kimball-Stone.

He had not seen her since she left, not once, except for the day he followed her down State Street. And that had provided him with only a brief glimpse of the bouncy ponytail, the Irish nose. Twice, she had sneaked back to the house when he was away and moved out more of her belongings. Did she hate him that much? She had even taken Mike, her ficus benjamina, who did nothing—at least in Frederick's opinion—but eat plant food, drink water, and shit oxygen, all without ever leaving his pot in the corner. And while it was true that Mike had been just inches from being chucked into a fireplace blazing in Frederick's mind, Chandra could have at least given them the opportunity to say good-bye. During her last sneaky visit she had left behind a note, stating that movers would eventually retrieve her other large furniture pieces, all things she felt rightfully hers. She could have dragged the house off, as far as Frederick was concerned. And she was obviously thinking about just that. *We'll need to settle the matter of the house soon,* she had noted in a P.S. He supposed that meant paying her for half of it, or selling it outright and splitting fifty-fifty. But he still couldn't concentrate on the dollars and cents of separation, not when he longed for flesh and bone. He had truly believed, with generations of cold Stone certainty to back him up, that she would return within a few days. Now it had been thirty days. Thirty was not *a few,* and Frederick Stone was no longer certain of anything. Except that a well-made martini took the edge off marital estrangement. He decided a toast was appropriate for the special occasion.

"Here's to a month, Chandra," he said, raising his drink. "You heartless bitch." Over the top of his glass, he noticed the clock on the kitchen stove, almost eleven-fifteen. Not bad, really, considering his greatest chore that day was to run a second-quarter profit-and-loss statement for Thibodeau's Restaurant and Lounge. And oh, yes, he also had the quarterly payroll data to prepare for Bass & Tate Plumbers, Inc., but that could wait another day or two. All in all, he was holding tight to his schedule, just like a typical

Stone. Except for the martinis, sleeping on the settee in the office, rising a bit later than five forty-five A.M., letting his hair grow, appearing almost nightly with Herbert Stone at The China Boat, having lunch almost daily at Panama Red's—which he would miss today, since it was already approaching noon—life hadn't changed too much for Frederick Stone. He no longer thought each red car he saw coming at him in the opposite flow of traffic was the Toyota, and even if one of them had been, he had his own strict schedule and couldn't be chasing all over town after Japanese products. True, he had tried the parking lot of Panama Red's a few evenings before arriving at The China Boat, and then later after leaving The China Boat. And there was no harm done—after he'd delivered a client's package—to swing by the library, wait a few minutes at the four-way stop near the post office, cruise nonchalantly past The Alternative Grocer. And yes, he'd driven down Bobbin Road every single night since Lillian had given him the address, never once to see the Toyota in the drive—not that he'd even looked—but then Bobbin Road was only a few streets away from Ellsboro. He'd used it many times since they had moved to the big old Victorian house. All these things he might have done anyway, even if she hadn't left. A little driving around could cleanse the brain. No, things hadn't changed too much in the month she'd been gone, except that his hair was now 10.5 millimeters longer, almost a half inch. Added to the fact that he was in need of a haircut when she left, his hair now had to be combed back behind his ears. Two young women at The China Boat had told him he looked like Jeff Bridges, the actor. That seemed a good thing, and so it pleased him. But he was experiencing one major change in his life, the greatest change. He missed her. He missed her tousled hair sweeping over the pillow in the morning, her wet towel on the bathroom floor, her passion, her humor, her warm body in the bed next to him. Yet there hadn't been much joy between them for a long time. He could call days forward in his mind, golden days when he remembered her laughter ringing out on the Boston subway, at the Dunkin' Donuts on Commerce Street as they bought their Sunday paper, on the beach at Old Orchard where he had recited poetry to her: *Ah, love, let us be true to one another,* a poem he admired so that he didn't have the heart to steal it. And besides, it was too famous. *For the world, which*

seems to lie before us like a land of dreams . . . Frederick wondered
what had happened to the woman he met at Woodstock and fell
profoundly in love with. What had happened to her laughter? *Hath
really neither joy, nor love, nor light* . . . Was laughter like light? Did
it curve depending on magnitude? It now seemed to Frederick
Stone that the past, the twenty plus years of his life with Chandra,
had been sucked up into some faraway black hole, a place so
intensely concentrated with love and pain and joy and sadness that
not even laughter, good old malleable laughter, could escape.

"Shit," Frederick said, and poured another martini. An intense
throbbing had begun inside his body, probably cells committing
suicide. He had to do something, some physical labor perhaps, to
cure the ache, loosen the pain. Maybe a bit of gardening would
root his mind in greener pastures.

Outside in the garage he searched for the shears among cans of
nails, rolls of wallpaper, dried paintbrushes, boxes of Earth Day
fliers. He'd never been much at gardening. Having Mike the ficus
in his foster care for a month had been his major experience in
agriculture. That, and snapping a few dead leaves from off the
geranium over the kitchen sink. After all, weren't women supposed to be the first agriculturalists? Frederick had been content to
watch from behind the window in his office, sitting upon his
spongy computer chair, while Chandra clipped, snipped, up-
rooted, pruned, and got dirt beneath her fingernails. Besides,
Chandra liked that kind of work. Frederick was more interested in
configuring a database than in designing a flower bed.

When he finally found the shears, they had a spider's web entrenched between the handles, a small labyrinthine doily. Clearing
his mind of what damage he might be doing to small and helpless
worlds—he'd read far too much Zen during his pot days—Frederick wrenched the shears from their nail and made off with them
to the backyard. He began his gardening debut slowly, by picking
a dead leaf from one of Chandra's shrubs. What was the thing
called? He'd heard her refer to it a thousand times. "Freddy, water
the hydro-something," she'd say. He remembered this because of
hydro and *water. Hydrangea?* Yes, that was it. He picked a second
leaf from the hydrangea and tried to ignore Walter Muller, who
was out in his own yard, face, arms, and legs red from gardening
frenzy and sunburn.

"Yo, neighbor!" Walter shouted, waving a singed limb over his head as though it were the hideous claw of some beached crustacean. "Great day, ain't it?" Walter bobbed his head at the firmament, his tentacles at work in the shrubbery. Watching him, Frederick was reminded that Paul and Linda McCartney had just bought and freed hundreds of lobsters from English restaurant tanks, an animal-rights statement. He nodded a casual agreement at Walter Muller and then pretended to study the large green leaves of the hydrangea.

"Ain't this about the nicest day we've had this year?" Walter persisted. "Wonderful day. Couldn't ask for a better one. Just terrific." Frederick had a sudden instinct to blast the man with Chandra's garden hose. He would flatten the red-armed, red-legged, white-assed gardener (he could only assume the latter was true) with a river of cold and probably chemically impure Portland water. "It is *not* a great day," he would hiss at Walter's burned earlobe. "So don't say it again, Walter Muller." And then he would wrest Walter's shears from his Waspy little hands, would employ them to cut out Walter's thick red tongue, which he would send to Larry with a brief warning: *The refrigerator life of this tongue is only eight days.* Or maybe he'd ship it across the Atlantic, on the Concorde even, to Paul and Linda McCartney. A kind of human-rights statement: *I have freed this tongue from the terrible fate of wagging.*

Frederick abandoned the hydrangea in order to escape from Walter Muller. He edged his way around to the front yard, pretending to be fixated by some vinelike growth that was creeping about the red bricks of the house. He had no idea whatsoever if it was a *good* growth or a *bad* growth. He brought forth what he hoped would be an expression that lay between gardening terror and gardening pride. Walter Muller, if he knew what the vinelike creature was, could take his pick.

Life appeared to be more colonized in the front yard, busier, a soft buzz of activities floating in the air. Up and down the street middle-aged men were milling about in their yards like plump locusts that surface periodically, seven-day cycles, The Saturday Cicada. Frederick could see Home Depot marigolds, geraniums, pansies, and petunias in all the yards. Home Depot hammocks hung from trees like massive nests made by oversized orioles.

Home Depot shutters edged all the windows. Men with aching backs stood and proudly surveyed their three-fourths acre of land, all mown and Raided and weed-eaten to perfection, *conquered territory*. Men whose dreams swirled above their heads like small gray clouds stood and looked across the expanse of their tiny prairies, their Oregon Trails, their Northwest Passages. If Frederick were to peer into their eyes, he knew he would find the smoldering flicker of wagon trail campfires. And if he could lean into their ears, as though their ears were pink seashells, he would hear "Get Along Little Doggies" and "Oh, Susannah" and "Red River Valley." These were men whose hours are spent in real estate, in banking, in law offices, in hospitals. Men who live their entire lives in life insurance. They had probably *all* majored in English. Frederick watched as they carefully walked the circumference of their terra firma—square-foot landowners—as Home Depot children rode bikes, tossed footballs, and glided ghostlike up and down the street on neon-colored skateboards.

Jesus, he thought, a quick thickening in his chest as the vague terror of encroaching middle age engulfed him. *We're all Willy Lomans.*

It was the gardening scene that precipitated the bar scene, no doubt about it. Herbert had swung by in his big Chrysler to pick him up—Frederick no longer demanded a phone call first—and now Frederick was on his second scotch when he felt a sudden wall of pity wash down on him. It was the last place in the world he would choose as his setting: The China Boat in Portland, Maine. And these were the two last people in the world he would choose as his witnesses: Herbert D. Stone, D.V.M., Veterinarian to the Poor; and an unidentified female bartender impersonating a geisha.

"I don't think I can take it anymore," Frederick was terrified to hear himself say. His words were followed by a loud, distinctive crack, a fissure in the Stone facade, a deep and narrow cleft, most likely irreparable. Frederick Stone could almost feel air whipping about the newly made cavity.

"Well, if I were you," Herbert said consolingly, "I'd hire Maggie's lawyer before Chandra gets to him. I hate to think about what might happen to you if you don't." He hummed a few bars of the soundtrack for *Jaws*. Frederick was unable to muster up a single particle of annoyance over this remark. He wanted, instead, to explain what was happening to him, to the world he had known, to the world in which he now fretted his hour upon the stage. He wanted to point out that human beings intend, one day, to set things right with those they have once loved. He thought of his father, Dr. Philip Stone, rigid, indifferent, aloof.

We expect the day will come when everyone puts down their angst and hugs one another, Frederick thought. But he knew, long before Chandra left him, long before Mr. Bator began prodding him to remember the guts of his past, that when a coffin lid slams shut, the noise is so loud it reverberates for eternity. He had intended to make lots of changes, hadn't he? To do lots of things? He was going to reread all of the Romantic poets, the Victorians, the Edwardians, too—*someone* should dust off poor Rupert Brooke—and he was going to learn chess. Delve a little into opera, just to see what all those arias were about. He was going to get a telescope and a microscope, the better to judge a few planets, a few grains of salt. He thought he might skydive at least once, hoping to come out of the experience with both ankles intact. He had always professed a desire to write poetry seriously, not just a few gratuitous iambs on demand, a few Rod McKuenisms for Chandra, as he had done back in his college days. *If I should die, think only this of me: That there's some corner in a farmer's field that is forever Woodstock.* (No, he would write his *own* damn verse and let Rupert Brooke, the poor bugger, rest in peace!) And he truly believed that he would live for a time in Europe, write letters home from Austria, clever things about St. Stephen's Cathedral, the Hofburg, Freud's birthplace, the room where Franz Kafka had written such brilliant words. He hoped he would be international enough to remember the famed Spanish Riding School and all of those grayish-white Lippizaner stallions. He could see himself now, printing in his even hand, dipping into a plum-colored ink he had found in some dusty shop. There was no doubt in his mind that Chandra would picket the Spanish Riding School, as intentional breeding was not her cup of tea. But that aside, there were a thousand postcards in him still not written. Pictures of Irish castles, Stonehenge, St. Peter's Square, the Eiffel

Tower, the Colosseum. A thousand postcards, and each of them fluttered against his teary eyelids, huge moths, as he stared at his brother and this *geisha*.

"Here I am paying alimony meant for Donald Trump," Herbert whined, "and I've had less than thirty clients all week. Look at this." He produced a napkin from off the bar, a pen from his shirt pocket. "It's all a female code, alimony is, a secret language." On the napkin before him he drew large letters, *A L I M O N Y*. "Now watch," he said. Between the *L* and the *I* he inserted another large *L* and then an *H*. He injected an *S* between the *I* and the *M,* and then an *E* between the *N* and the *Y*. He handed the finished product to Frederick. *ALL HIS MONEY*. "See what I mean?" he prodded. "I'm telling you, it's a secret language all their own." Frederick scrunched the napkin into a tight little ball. Herbert would soon be convinced that he was being followed by Elvis. That Atlantis was somewhere in Casco Bay.

"Can I get you another drink?" the geisha asked Frederick. "Anything at all?" She was leaning on her elbows, hands under her chin. Frederick considered the invitation. Perhaps he could express himself to this stranger. She was probably the closest he would ever get to Japan. And after all, geishas were expected to be knowledgeable about the elegance of the past, as well as hip to present gossip. It *was* part of their job to entertain men in public restaurants, and there was no doubt that The China Boat had become one massive *ryori-ya* in Frederick Stone's life. He decided to chance it.

"What's your name?" he asked nicely.

"Marta," she told him.

"Marta, when my sister, Polly, was born," Frederick began, "I was informed that my mother was going to the hospital to have her tonsils removed." Marta nodded sympathetically. "I was eight years old before I realized that Polly was a permanent part of my family." He would start at the very beginning, with those adolescent angers, and work his way up to Dr. Philip Stone's cold indifference. To his mother's sleepy impassivity. He waited for the condolences that were sure to pour in.

"When I was seven my father raped me," Marta confessed. "See this?" She produced a thin white arm from out of the loose sleeve of her gown. Round ivory scars, small little craters, formed a sad latticework running along the ulna. "Cigarette burns," she explained. Frederick was stunned. He felt very foolish suddenly, for his revelation about Polly. He had not one single scar to bring forth, except the one he'd received when he cut his foot on that soda pop bottle at Willard's Pond, on a Boy Scout outing. Or the one from the mumblety-peg incident, when Richard Hamel had tossed a jackknife on Frederick's hand during a particularly vicious championship game. And Richard Hamel had *cheated* as well, insisting that the knife was not leaning too close to the earth on *fives,* and he had won. Just remembering this caused the muscles of Frederick's stomach to clench. Up until the day they graduated from high school and went their separate ways, he had hated Richard Hamel. He looked at Marta. Could he share his jackknife scar with her? Could he explain how it pains one dearly to lose a childhood championship game by defraud? He decided against it. She had probably *swallowed* jackknives in her day, could open her mouth and say, "See this?" And he would lean forward in order to look down her throat, where he would find hideous scars on her larynx, her pharynx, her palate. He would witness inflammations and swellings and excessive discharges of mucus. The palatine arches would have collapsed. My God, but she had been raped by her father at the age of seven! Frederick surreptitiously slid his hand and its tiny scar away from his drink. He removed his flawless arm from the bar, hid it somewhere below.

"Or you could hire Dan Ladner," Herbert was advising. "He'd be like *Jaws II.* Only partially effective but not so costly." Frederick's eyes grew more moist. He wanted to unburden himself of the albatross, to tell his sad story to these two wedding guests. Like the albatross, he had thought himself able to stay aloft in windy weather for a long, long time. But he had been plucked out of the matrimonial skies by his wife and, again like the bird, was now living on squid (actually tofu) and attracted to ships' garbage, namely The China Boat regulars. He wanted to remind his brother, Herbert, how loud coffin lids could be, and how their father's had closed with a rude *thunk,* the final insult, as he and Herbert stood by. Polly had not been there. She was busy with her own dying. Their mother had remained at home, sound asleep. But he found he couldn't talk about the family Stone, not even with a cold wind lashing about that opened fissure. He decided he would talk about *other* families.

"The Brady Bunch is all grown up," Frederick said idly. "Dale

Evans is eighty years old." It was true. Even Robert Young, the father that all of Frederick's generation had pined for on "Father Knows Best," had attempted suicide with a rubber hose, in his own garage, drunk. All the things you thought you could depend on, all the familiar landmarks, gone. The Union Gap were probably all grandfathers by now. "Wouldn't it be great," Frederick continued tearfully, "if Mayberry, North Carolina, was a place you could go to, and you could sit on the front porch with Andy and Barney and Floyd, and Aunt Bea would bring you a bowl of homemade peach ice cream, and Opie would be having some major math problem at school that you could help solve." It *would* be great. It would be *heroic* even, because Andy wouldn't let fathers rape their little daughters. None of the tiny Mayberrians would have a single cigarette burn. And Helen Crump would tell Opie the truth about a potential baby sister. Frederick wished he could divulge to Marta that his own father had *never* touched him, and that there had been pain in that, too. He wanted to explain how he had never come to know the meaning of *family,* had only watched from a distance, at Christmastime in department stores, from a corner table in some restaurant, at movie theaters, city parks. He had always been fascinated with how a real family seemed to work, like some great pinwheel, the children colorful vanes revolving happily around the parental stick. And, at forty-four, he wanted a pinwheel of his own. But with Chandra gone, with Polly and Dr. Stone dead, he hadn't a prayer. No wonder men like Jack Nicholson and Warren Beatty seek out, in their fifties, girls so young that a dozen children lie unborn inside them. "I just wish we could all live in Mayberry," Frederick concluded. Herbert Stone examined Frederick's face carefully, studied his brother's pupils, as if certain he would find some unusual dilation.

"Look out," he informed Marta. "I think we're witnessing the emotional breakdown of the television generation." But Frederick wasn't listening to his big brother. He was listening to another voice, one warm and assuring. A Robert Young kind of voice, before the rubber hose, before the bottle of booze that bleak night out in the exhaust-filled garage. *Time appears to be more puzzling than space,* Mr. Bator announced, *because it seems to flow or pass or else men seem to advance through it. But the passage or advance seems to be unintelligible.*

"Time," Frederick said aloud. Herbert leaned forward, as if listening for the sure noises that a nervous breakdown would emit, especially one brought on by television. "Time," Frederick said again. He knew, suddenly, what it was he had to do. He would take charge of time, not let it *pass unintelligibly*. He would, instead, advance through time like some kind of titan soldier. He would grab Cronus by those hoary, hairy balls. He stood, peered down at Herbert, who had slouched in his bar stool, a swath of genuine trepidation inching across his face.

"What?" Herbert asked fearfully.

"I need your help," Frederick told him. He stuffed a dinner roll into his shirt pocket. A little nourishment might be needed later on. Marta nodded sympathetically to Herbert.

"How long did you say the wife's been gone?" she asked.

"A month," Herbert answered. "He's experiencing his very first separation menses." He loosened his tie, one on which Toulouse-Lautrec dancers kicked up narrow, red legs. Frederick ignored his companions. He knew that some scars don't show up as round white craters. That sometimes a game of mumblety-peg was all sharp, glassy edges.

"I've got a date with destiny," Frederick stated firmly. "And destiny is currently residing at 257 Bobbin Road."

It was almost ten P.M. when they pulled up to the curb, just down the street from the yellow house, and sat there idling in Herbert's big Chrysler.

"Shut the engine off," Frederick ordered. Herbert sighed mightily but complied. Frederick surveyed the house, the narrow lawn, the veranda roof jutting out from the upper window. The red maple was full and leafy. The same lamppost blared out its warm, yellow beacon. A soft rain had begun to fall in thin threads, but Frederick refused to let Herbert use the wipers.

"That will only attract attention," he scolded. "Why would wipers be going on a parked car?"

"Why would two grown men be *sitting* in a parked car?" Herbert wanted to know. "This is crazy."

"And who was it," Frederick inquired, "who just recently

wanted *two grown men* to be sitting in a parked car with *two young cosmetologists?*" He patted about his feet for the paraphernalia he had gathered for the mission. A paper bag rustled dramatically. He pulled on his woolen ski mask, adjusted the eye holes, the nose hole, and then surveyed himself in the mirror. He would be dreadfully hot, but anonymous.

"How do I look?" he wondered.

"You look like Spider Man," Herbert complained, "who also has an identity problem. I never should have driven you home for that stuff. I'm what they call a codependant."

"You had no choice," Frederick answered. He was pulling on Chandra's gardening gloves, lavender cotton things with round yellow flowers. "You're being swept along by destiny."

"I'm being swept along by an idiot," Herbert argued. "It's apparent to even the mailman that this woman wants nothing more to do with you. So why can't you hire a good lawyer and give the hell up? Do you know what your trouble is, Freddy? You're as contrary as all the Stones before you, and you might as well admit it. You're Great-uncle William all over again. Remember the story about *him?*" Within the warm wooly interior of his ski mask, Frederick nodded sadly. He did remember. Great-uncle William had been taken prisoner during World War I. Three days later, the Germans gave him back.

"I never believed that story," Frederick said. "Now keep your eyes on the street." He didn't want to think of Stone men before him, failures in so many ways, failures except where cheekbones were concerned. He was in charge now, for the first time in a long time. Maybe for the first time ever. Perhaps it was the blasted surge of millpond adrenaline he had brought back with him from his lunch with Doris Bowen. Ponds, like happy hour at The China Boat, were teeming with life. Maybe it was everything Yeats *didn't* say about those damned shuddering loins, that torn wall—or was it *broken?*—that poor fragile neck in that impervious beak! Maybe it was Doris's own white breasts. He would *mount* the goddamn roof! Maybe it was the toasty smell of Reginald's brown Conestoga. Joyce's green hair. Lillian's vermilion lips. Valerie's maroon tights. Herbert's orange cigarette tip. Budgie's blue tail. Teddy's milky condoms. Geraldo's pink ass. These days, this was Frederick's own personal Rainbow Coalition. Maybe it was seeing the silhouettes of his neighbors, those complacent black beetles, their entire lives locked like shells about them. Yet he knew what the real problem was. It was the knowledge of having seen her wheat-colored hair lace itself with gray, her bright red protest skirt fade into a soft rose. He had even watched the tissue that lines her eyelids and runs out over the balls of those beautiful eyes—Mr. Bator would know it as the *conjunctiva*—he had seen it turn yellow as an autumn vine. He had studied this Impressionist woman, her pats and dots and short strokes of pure emotion, with the tender and discerning eye of an art critic. For twenty-three years, since he first met her in August of 1969, he had concerned himself with one single magnificent canvas. He had invested *time* with her, dammit, and it had not been time spent *unintelligibly*. Frederick found the small flashlight in his jacket pocket. Already, he was beginning to sweat extravagantly.

"If you see anyone approaching the house," he cautioned Herbert, "especially the police, be sure to honk twice." Herbert shook his head in disgust. He thumped a hand on the steering wheel.

"That's a fine line of dialogue to pass between an accountant and a veterinarian. 'If you see the police, honk twice.' What are we? Canada geese?"

"Honk twice," Frederick reminded him. "Besides, I'm not an accountant, don't you remember? I'm a top criminal lawyer. Now don't do anything to attract attention." He got out and eased the door gently shut. Herbert whirred his window down.

"Oh, heaven forbid I should attract a *client*," he snapped. "I'd hate to take advantage of this important event."

"Lay low," Frederick whispered, and was instantly gratified by the rush of adrenaline to his system. *Lay low. Swing Low, Sweet Chariot.* He moved off into the deep blanket of night, toward the yellow beacon and the leafy maple with all those magnificent limbs for an estranged husband to climb. At first he had disliked that word *estrange*. But after a bitter month of estrangement, he had changed his mind. It came from the medieval Latin *extraneare*, to treat like a stranger. It was the best word possible. He hid behind a large clump of *something*—perhaps he *should* take up gardening one day—and crouched there for a moment. All seemed quiet in the house. The downstairs was in darkness, but a light beamed from the lovely, lonely upstairs window, the one he had studied so diligently during his first visit, the Petrarchan window, Laura's window. The same maroon car was parked in the driveway, along with a small modern model. He didn't know cars anymore. Like shrubs, they all looked the same. Cars probably came from Home Depot these days, in large kits that even toddlers could assemble.

As usual, Chandra's red Toyota was nowhere to be seen. He had no doubt she'd been hiding it in the garage, hoping to discourage this very sort of invasion. He felt the coil of rope bounce against his hip. Why he'd brought a rope hooked to his belt loop, he had no idea, except that it seemed *reasonable* to bring a rope. Keeping as low to the ground as he could, he eased away from the *something* and scuttled across the lawn to *something else.* He crouched there, in the dizzying aroma of this newest shrub, and waited. The triumvirate Bitches of Fate obviously owed him a bone, for they tossed one at him by allowing the rain to stop. He made a brilliant dash to the maple. He hadn't climbed a tree since his boyhood and had no idea that he wasn't very good at it anymore. After all, wasn't climbing a tree a bit like riding a bicycle? Or sex? Didn't it come back instantaneously? *Disappearances of neurons in the nervous system make the aging person less agile than the young.*

"Fuck off, Mr. Bator," Frederick whispered. In pure defiance, he clunked his way up the maple, his tennis shoes becoming huge balls of cement at the last of it. When he reached the thick stout limb that grew out over the veranda's roof, he paused, puffing. There was the lighted window. Indeed, there was Yeats's wall waiting to be broken. Frederick sincerely hoped it would be the wall and not his neck. He would wait a moment, let his breathing resume its normal rate, before he attempted the limb. He rested his face against the smooth bark of the tree. The window was curtained, but once he was on the veranda roof he could peek into that opening he noticed, right where the two panels are supposed to join snugly together but rarely do. He was thankful that Robbie had a distaste for blinds.

Frederick carefully studied the layout before him. He knew well that the sloping roof could be treacherous, what with that smattering of light rain that had just fallen. After all, he had spent those college summers in roofing, a job he would never want again. The roof of Robbie's house was a gable style, with a slope Frederick estimated to be nine in twelve, a steep mother, too steep for do-it-yourself roofers. The roofing was new slate. This must have cost Robbie an arm and a leg and the biceps he loved to flaunt. Slate was definitely expensive and had to be installed by professionals. How could Robbie afford a slate roof? He was a goddamn kid. Slate also lasted almost a lifetime, fifty years, the way some marriages were supposed to last. And it was durable as hell, fireproof, the way some marriages should be. Frederick hoped to God—in whom he didn't believe—that someone had been careless with the chimney flashings, perhaps allowing them to join instead of overlapping. And he prayed the roofers had forgotten to install a *cricket,* so that Maine snow and spring water would build up behind the chimney and cause a myriad of leaks, preferably over the bedroom. Frederick shook his head hardily. He had to quit thinking of the dimensions and qualities of Robbie's roof. He was beginning to feel like a character in a Robbe-Grillet novel.

As he was about to crawl out the limb that would deliver him to the veranda roof, he heard a distinct buzz from down on the street, an electronic trill that pierced the quiet of Bobbin Road. Herbert's car phone.

"Hello?" he heard Herbert say. His booming voice filtered up through the wet leaves, up through the wet dark night. Frederick held his breath and waited. "Don't get on my ass, Maggie," he heard Herbert threaten. "I pay you plenty. As Paul Newman once said in *Cool Hand Luke,* DON'T FEED ON ME! And don't call me again! You got a problem? You get your Jaws to call my Minnow." Frederick cringed. He would kill Herbert Stone. He was sure of it. He waited through a few seconds of silence. Herbert must have hung up. As Frederick was about to move on, he heard him again.

"Hey, Susan? How's it going? This is Herb. Oh, fine, fine. A little skirmish with the ex-wife now and then, a little unfriendly fire, but fine. And you? You still in that photography course? Good. Good." Frederick would kill him *slowly,* savoring each drop of blood. "You coming down to The China Boat tonight? Well, if I can ever get free of my crazy brother, I'll try to catch you there. Huh? A month today. He's taking it very well, same as I did, same as Dustin Hoffman in *Kramer Versus Kramer.* Ha-ha, just kidding with you." Up in his canopy of maple leaves, Frederick decided that he would sauté each of Herbert's plucked fingernails in wine and garlic butter, and then serve them up to Maggie Stone on a silver platter. Couldn't he at least put up his blasted window? Waiting a full two minutes, enough to satisfy himself that Herbert wasn't going to phone up Charles Schwabb and invest a quarter, Frederick shimmied out the limb, mowing down maple leaves as he went. Now, to let himself drop as delicately as possible onto the roof.

No one seemed to be in the room, which was a bedroom. The bed was unmade—this caused a great emotional pain—and was scattered with an overabundance of cast-off male clothing. What was the guy? A full-blooded satyr? You could probably even *major* in Satyriasis at the University of Southern Maine. But there seemed to be no people in the untidy room. Frederick was kneeling before the window, waiting, when he heard a distinct *toot* emerge from the Chrysler, followed by a second. *If you see anyone, especially the police, honk twice.* Fear gripped him. He was already in trouble with the law over those traffic tickets. He felt his legs freeze beneath him, thaw suddenly, and then catapult him to the edge of the roof. Weren't there a zillion rules roofers were taught? Yes, there were. Two zillion, maybe, and he had learned them all well. Even squirrels probably know the biggest rule: You don't go up on any roof when it's been raining. And you certainly don't *run* on a wet roof. Tree frogs, with their excellent suction cups, probably know this rain rule. Spider Man would know it. And there were lots of other rules. Work from the top down when removing an old roof. Stay away from power lines. Keep your work area clean of debris. Wear gloves when working with metal. Plenty of safeguards. But nowhere in his collective memory of Roof Rules could Frederick recall: *Never even go near a roof if you've been driven there by Herbert D. Stone, D.V.M.*

The shrub that tried desperately to break his fall was simply not bushy enough, but it did seem to be sprouting some kind of thorn. As Frederick felt it flatten beneath his falling weight, he had to wonder why people planted such wishlike, insubstantial plants. The dinner roll he still carried in his shirt pocket had probably worked better toward breaking his fall. The shrub smelled distinctly of talcum.

"Baby powder," Frederick decided as he skidded off the bush

and bounced to the side of the house, his breath dislodging in a great *whoomph* from his lungs. As he lay there patiently waiting for new air to push beneath his ski mask, enter his nose and mouth, tippy-toe down the trachea, proceed on to the bronchi, and then have a little Welcome Home party in the lungs, his first consideration was for the gutters of the house. From his close-up viewpoint, they appeared to be copper. What was this kid's last name? Rockefeller? His second consideration was one of relief and thanks that Mr. Bator had not bothered to elaborate on the ankle—the tibia, the fibula, the astragalus—because Frederick was quite sure that his own was broken.

"Sorry," he heard Herbert whisper in the darkness. "I didn't mean to honk." Frederick knew instantly why he had brought the rope. He had brought it to hang Herbert Stone from the maple tree.

∽

The roof scene necessitated the emergency room scene. As he sat next to Herbert in the waiting room, Frederick tried hard to concentrate on things more acceptable to society than fratricide. He could call the IRS and tell them the truth about Herbert Stone's cash payments received from clients. He could offer Maggie Stone the same information. It was Herbert's own mistake that he had shared this tidbit with his brother, Frederick. Or he could sneak into the ladies' room at The China Boat and write the alliterative words: *Herbert Has Herpes, Halitosis, and Hair Lice* on the wall. (Herpes was in everyone's vocabulary, but Herbert's kindergartners would think halitosis some incurable disease, and the squeamish addition of lice would probably dissuade even prostitutes.) Or Frederick could hang a sign around some dog's neck—I USED TO BE A CAT UN-TIL DR. HERBERT STONE OPERATED ON ME—and then parade the creature up and down the street in front of Herbert's clinic. There were almost as many choices as there were rules for roof safety. Frederick was oscillating between the IRS and the dog when a curt young woman came out to announce that it would be some time before a doctor would be available to look at his swollen ankle.

"We got cases a lot more serious coming in," she confided. Frederick had no doubt that this was true. More important problems than his own abounded. Maybe Marta would turn up with her liver in her hands. Her spleen flapping about her neck. Her terrified heart throbbing in her purse. What Frederick would give for a quick case of *something dreadful*. His ankle disagreed with him by sending off a rapid volley of electrifying throbs.

"I mean, I'm really sorry," he tuned in to hear Herbert say. He had not spoken a single word to Herbert on the abysmal drive to the emergency clinic, but he had been forced to listen to the same infernal excuse over and over again. He stared at a framed murky print, pink and yellow and green watercolors, which hung on the wall over the receptionist's head. He hoped the artist was under the scalpel at that very moment. This was definitely a more serious case, this assault upon the visual senses.

"It's really easy to explain, if you'd just listen," Herbert was saying. "First I dropped my cigarette, and when I leaned forward to pick it up, I accidentally touched off the horn. Then, when I went to light up, I dropped my book of matches, and when I leaned over . . ." *The philosophy of time bears heavily on men's emotions,* Mr. Bator suddenly stated.

"Shut up!" Frederick screamed at Mr. Bator. "I'm sick of you!"

"I beg your pardon?" Herbert seemed about to cry.

"I wasn't talking to *you*," Frederick replied curtly.

"Well, who were you talking to?" Herbert wanted to know. "I think you owe me an apology."

"I wasn't talking to you," Frederick said again.

"So who were you talking to? *Her?*" Herbert pointed to the receptionist. This was when Frederick realized she'd been staring at them. "Were you, Freddy? Were you talking to *her?*" The receptionist waited.

"Please," Frederick implored her. His ankle pounded mercilessly. He mustn't anger this woman or she'd be taking cases of babies with diaper rash ahead of him. He waved his hand to emphasize. At least *it* was still functioning. "I've been under a lot of stress lately. I'm sorry if I'm causing any trouble."

"His wife dumped him," Herbert confided to the receptionist.

"Herbert, please."

"It's been a month and he still hasn't called a lawyer."

"Herbert!"

"Do you wanna know how he hurt his ankle?"

"HERBERT, SHUT THE HELL UP!"

"See?" Herbert insisted. "I *knew* you were talking to me."

"No, I wasn't!"

"Well, who else here is named Herbert?"

"I was talking to you just now," Frederick explained. "But I wasn't talking to you a minute ago."

"Don't insult my intelligence," Herbert begged facetiously. Frederick inhaled and exhaled dramatically. It was good to have the old vacuum bags sucking again.

"What intelligence?" he wondered aloud.

"That's it," Herbert said, and stood up defiantly. "I, for one, have had enough. First, I had to watch you make a fool out of yourself in front of that poor geisha. Then I'm good enough to drive you over to Bobbin Road so that you can crawl up on the roof and peer through a window, like some Patti Page dog. Next, I'm kind enough—yes, *kind*—to rush you down here to the emergency room because you stupidly fell off said roof!"

"I fell off said roof because you HONKED that the cops were coming!" Frederick shouted. The receptionist cleared her throat. "How the hell did I know you were merely TRYING TO SMOKE A CIGARETTE?!"

"Is there a full moon tonight?" he heard the receptionist ask someone.

"Will you shut up yourself?" Herbert beseeched him. "People are starting to look at you like they've just seen you on 'America's Most Wanted.' You call a cab, pal. I'm gone." He headed for the exit door.

"Good riddance!" Frederick shouted after him. "Because I DON'T CARE!" He felt the freedom, suddenly, of *not caring*. My God, but wasn't that what his whole generation had stood for, when they were packing the ends of rifles with spindly-assed daisies? Wasn't this a bona fide *do your own thing* feeling? And yet he was having his first awakening at age forty-four, like some pale confused soldier who's been hiding out in the Philippine jungle, unaware that World War II ended forty years earlier. Unaware of so many things. He'd been a virgin, hadn't he, a hymenal membrane blocking the way to his true emotions? He'd only been pretending when he grew his hair long, before the disapproving eyes of Dr. Philip Stone, and wore those flapping flare-legged pants which themselves gave so much freedom to his calf muscles. He'd never really felt the euphoria of pure freedom. It was a joyous event. Herbert pirouetted at the door and headed back.

"He really is under a lot of stress," he heard Herbert whisper to the receptionist. She seemed in the act of phoning someone. But Frederick truly didn't care. He didn't care if there might be folks in the operating room who could hear him. They could take his words with them to meet their makers. *Not only do men regret the past, they also fear the future,* Mr. Bator cautioned, *because the flow of time seems to be sweeping them toward their deaths, as swimmers are swept toward a waterfall.*

"What the hell do you know?" Frederick screamed at his old teacher. "You're a closet homosexual. That's what's wrong with *you!*" Herbert went white across his forehead, then his chin, followed by the rest of his face. A heart attack seemed to loom on Herbert Stone's horizon. For a second, Frederick again feared losing his place in line. His ankle burst forth with a new supply of pain. He wished some endorphins would kick in. So much for euphoria.

"You always thought you were a peg or two above me, didn't you?" Herbert asked, his face about to explode. "The poet. A real ladies' man. Well, let's clear the air right now, Freddy." Frederick shook his head frantically.

"Mr. Bator," he whispered, but Herbert wasn't listening.

"I'm gonna tell you what's *wrong* with me, little brother, whether you want to hear it or not. One day I was trying to figure out what it was they threw off the Tallahatchie Bridge in 'Ode to Billy Joe.' The next day I was up to my ass in mud in the Mekong Delta. You ever been up to your ass in mud, Freddy? You ever tap-dance across a mine field, Freddy? I'll tell you what's wrong with me. One day I was trying to figure out whether John was the Walrus, or Paul was the Walrus. The next day I'm dragging a dying man I've never seen before in my life out of a rice paddy, his guts trailing behind. But you never went to Vietnam, did you, Freddy? You went to *Woodstock.* That's the closest you ever came to death, isn't it? Up to your ankles in mud in upstate New York. You're probably still suffering from post-traumatic syndrome. One of the stages could've collapsed, right? You could've caught your bell-bottoms on some raspberry bushes. Someone could've sprayed something into your beer. You're probably still puking over Agent Budweiser. Woodstock was *your* big war, wasn't it, Freddy? Well, let me tell you something, you conscientious asshole. You're not the walking wounded, so don't flatter yourself. Chandra should've left you years ago." That said, Herbert trotted to the exit door and disappeared this time, just as a portal to the inner sanctum of the emergency clinic swung open.

"Mr. Stone?" a pleasant young nurse inquired. "The doctor will see you now." Hitching himself up onto his sore ankle, Frederick stood. So this was his just reward, was it, after forty-four years of minding his own business? This was what the gods would deliver him to, as a penance for his so-called hubris? He thought of Hephaestus, once married to Venus—another heartless bitch—and how he was tossed off Mount Olympus by a jealous Zeus, thus breaking his leg and leaving him crippled. Feeling a special kinship to Hephaestus, the poor bandy-legged bugger, Frederick gritted his teeth. There were worse things than a permanent limp.

"Be careful of this one, Margaret," Frederick heard the receptionist whisper as he hobbled painfully down the corridor.

T_{en}

It was almost ten o'clock when Frederick awoke to the sounds of neighborhood children playing a game of street baseball at the end of the cul-de-sac. His neck felt immeasurably cramped, his legs shriveled things. Sleeping on a settee did not offer the most advantageous positions for the body. This type of settee was commonly referred to as a *daybed*—a misnomer, the *bed* part—a thing that even Shakespeare was familiar with, for it was on just such a piece of furniture that Malvolio announces, in *Twelfth Night,* that he has "left Olivia sleeping." Frederick doubted that Olivia slept well; no wonder she was such a mournful creature. Had Shakespeare ever nodded off on a daybed? After all, the piece originated in his century. Did he rush home from plague-filled London, smelling of booze and women, only to have Anne Hathaway-Shakespeare banish him to the settee? Probably. *Extraneare.*

After replaying his messages, most of them from disgruntled clients, Frederick made a pot of coffee and stood waiting for his eyes to adjust to the magnificent sunshine coming in through the kitchen window. It had been a full week, seven godawful days, since the disastrous episodes at Bobbin Road and the emergency clinic. It had become almost impossible for him to sleep at night, what with a painful ankle, not to mention the shortcomings of the settee. As a result, he had been falling asleep at dawn, physical exhaustion winning out over mental stress. And he'd been sleeping soundly past noon. The only reason he had risen earlier this day was a message he had heard come in on his answering machine, just past ten o'clock, while he lay on the settee hoping to sleep again, but listening instead to the children shout things like "Good pitch, Sarah!" Or "Run, Jacob, run!" He had been trying to recall just when summer vacation would end in those parts, when the school bell would sound as loudly as the Pied Piper's horn and lure all the little progeny back inside those thick, sound-proof walls.

"It's me, Freddy," he had heard Herbert Stone say, his voice mirthless. "I guess it's time we had a sensible talk." This was good news, Frederick now thought as he edged two slices of bread into the toaster. He had been unable for a full week to get Herbert to speak to him. A long, limping week. Not even on the Fourth of July would Herbert answer his phone, so Frederick had watched the fireworks alone, from his front porch, before he retreated into the privacy of the house. He had even hobbled into The China Boat twice, the new addition of his cane tapping noisily upon the wooden floor—coming through the foyer, he had sounded like a peg-legged old tar—but Herbert was conspicuously absent. He had left messages with Herbert's receptionist, the one with the Chihuahua voice, but to no avail. He had managed to catch Herbert on his car phone a few times, in the early evenings, when he knew the clinic had just closed. But each time, Herbert had simply disconnected the call when he heard Frederick's voice.

The Whores of Destiny had gone out of their way to ensure that it would be a long, difficult week for Frederick Stone. Hoping to thwart their destructive plans as much as possible, he had avoided the IGA on Tuesday. The last thing he needed was to have little Mrs. Paroni run over his sore ankle with her grocery cart. Or, worse yet, to get it lodged against the ashtray in the backseat of Doris Bowen's blue Mercedes, his Fruit of the Looms dangling about his good ankle. He had really been avoiding *Doris*, the ankle being a terrific excuse. He hoped she hadn't waited too long for him in the parking lot, and couldn't help feeling a surge of masculine pride that a female had gone to such lengths on his account. And speaking of *accounts,* Frederick's eye was still firmly on Bowen Developers, so he had kindly taken the time to drop Doris a quick note on Wednesday. *Recovering from an injury. Will see you again soon.* Besides, with Chandra gone, it was no longer necessary to visit the large IGA every Tuesday. The folks at American Express were probably most happy to see his life change thusly, because lunch at Panama Red's and the token vegetarian dinner at The China Boat were now firm rituals. His stack of credit card receipts was growing daily, and faster than the average human hair. He rarely opened the refrigerator door for anything but soy milk for his coffee, or olives, gin, and vermouth for his martinis. The refrigerator was beginning to smell strongly of onion. When he ran out of bread for his late-night sandwich, he found it convenient to drop by Cain's Corner Grocery. It was nice to see Mr. Cain again, the old man who kept pictures of his grandchildren on the wall behind the cash register. Guilty at having abandoned a tiny family business—he had once planned to help businessmen in *Central America,* after all—Frederick usually went on to buy a jar of strawberry jam, an apple, the current *Newsweek,* as a measure of good faith. Perhaps, between Mr. Cain and The Alternative Grocer, he would never need to go back to the monstrous IGA, with its artificial lights and all that annoying Muzak.

It had been a bad week for Stone Accounting, too, it was true. Complaints were starting to come in from a few clients that he had not filed their monthly taxes on time. Patti's Poodle Parlor, his newest client, had gone so far as to drop him. Fury had been the prevalent emotion at Patti's when he turned up on Thursday with the payroll checks, instead of on Wednesday. If he hadn't been limping, apparently already injured by *another* unhappy client, he had no doubt that the staff would have assaulted him. How could one day make such a difference in people's lives? "This isn't some little shoestring business," Patti had spat at him. "We need someone we can depend on." Frederick had to admit that an institution that offered such important services to the world as canine toenail clipping had to be careful who handled its accounts. And he reminded himself, as he eased past irate toenail clippists and enraged fur groomists, that one or two massive accounts in the ballpark of Bowen Developers would set him up nicely. He would no longer need a myriad of shoestring—yes, Patti, *shoestring*—businesses scattered about the Portland area.

It had also been a painful week regarding his ankle, which had been sprained but was not broken. He had stretched a ligament, one of the many that connected various bones in the ankle area. There had been some swelling and tenderness, but no local bleeding. The doctor had simply strapped the ankle with an elastic bandage to relieve tension, and then sent him home with a prescription for pain pills. He had also promised to submerge the thing daily in hot water. And he was to stay off it until the tenderness had passed. All things he could have done himself, if he had only known that his ankle was not broken. And he should have realized this. After all, fate had dealt him a hand of mediocrity, a life centered squarely between Greek tragedy and the mundane. Had he been able to admit this to himself, he would have been spared the embarrassment of the emergency clinic and the horrible rift that had occurred with Herbert. A month ago, he wouldn't have given a hoot about *extraneare-ing* Herbert Stone. But he was now beginning to see Herbert as one of those vanes encircling the pinwheel. True, it was a sorry pinwheel, just Herbert and him flapping in the wind, with no central stick. But it was better than revolving in the wind all alone.

Frederick ate the toast while standing at the sink. Then he limped to the living-room sofa with his coffee and thumped down. Another few days, and the ankle would probably support his weight without too much complaint. He placed the phone in his lap and punched out the numbers to Herb's clinic. He had time to place a quick call because it was still five minutes until "Geraldo." Some damn programming genius had had the foresight to move "Sally Jessy Raphael" opposite "Geraldo," instead of letting it follow, and now Frederick had to flip back and forth from one show to the other until he decided which would be most unnerving to watch. It was always easy to switch off the movie stars who wished to tell America how drunk they'd been, how high on cocaine, how depressed. Avoiding them was an easy choice, but sometimes, when he couldn't make up his mind between Geraldo's *sisters who share the same man* and Sally's *mothers with more than one gay child,* he used the remote control to bounce back and forth. This had been another of the changes in his schedule that he hadn't really wanted known. Herbert had been the one to urge him to tune in. "I'm helplessly addicted," Herbert had admitted. "I tape 'Geraldo' and my secretary tapes 'Sally Jessy.' We exchange tapes daily. Oprah's too sensible." So he had given it a shot. For two and a half weeks he hadn't missed one show or the other. That was why he should have known, long before Marta's revelations, long before the veranda roof and the emergency clinic, that life had dealt him the aforementioned humdrum hand of cards. Jane Smith and John Doe, the average American, revealed secrets about themselves and their family members that would have caused those ancient Greek playwrights, the ones who wrote about Medea and Oedipus and Zeus and Leda, to gather up their flowing robes and run like hell for the Parthenon. He wished he could share this with Chandra, this new knowledge of the world. What had she always accused him of? Living on the outskirts of humanity. Well, things were different around the house on Ellsboro Street, that's what he'd tell her.

"I'm living right *under* the skirts of humanity now, Chandra dear," Frederick said as he waited for Herbert's secretary to answer. "I'm right between humanity's legs, looking straight up, and I'll tell you something, sweetheart. Humanity's not a pretty sight."

Herbert agreed to lunch at Panama Red's on Friday. He was still a bit gruff on the phone, but Frederick could only hope that a scotch and a spinach-avocado sandwich might toss a little oil into Herbert's rusted mechanisms. Friday would be fine. He wanted to give the ankle a few more days before he ventured out on it again.

"How's the ankle?" Herbert finally asked.

"Sprained," Frederick told him.

"That's about what I figured," Herbert conceded. Frederick sighed.

"And by that you mean?"

"I mean I figured it would end up not being too serious," said Herbert. "You overreact sometimes, Freddy, that's all." Frederick bit at the inside of his cheek. It was a good thing Herbert could not see his face just then, because a massive grimace had appeared. He would let this pass. After all, it had taken him seven days to get this far, the same amount of time required to create the Christian world, including one day for a siesta. And besides, he didn't want to be just one colored vane fluttering in a good old northeasterly.

"The doctor said I was within a hair of breaking it," Frederick lied.

"Can you drive?" Herbert wondered.

"I took a cab to The China Boat a couple times this week," said Frederick. "And I've been taking cabs to make drop-offs and pick-ups from my clients. But by Friday I should be able to drive." He wanted to give the ankle a few more days to heal, and he saw that as a precaution, not an overreaction.

Herbert had had the tofu and raisin salad along with the spinach-avocado sandwich and a second scotch before he seemed his old self again.

"I can't wait for you to meet Susie," he told Frederick. "She's one good-looking woman. And, you'll love this, she's almost twenty-seven."

"Is that in *dog* years?" Frederick inquired. The ball of brotherly banter had been tossed into the air with this remark, and Frederick had batted that ball at Herbert. He waited. Would Herbert bat it back? Could life as they once knew it go on?

"Very funny," said Herbert.

"Twenty-seven is still close to being half your age," Frederick added. He was still waiting.

"So," Herbert said, "you think she's too old for me, do you?" Frederick smiled as the ball came bouncing back into his corner. Things would be fine. He would not have to hide his grimaces in dark closets.

"Twenty-seven *is* too old for you," Frederick said. "Now that I think about it." He was amazed at how quickly they were putting the angry words behind them, how easily they were wrapping up events in the soft gauze of memory, tucking them away where they couldn't hurt anyone anymore. It was a family's job, wasn't it, to bury the dead and go on? To wipe bloodstains off the hatchets, to mop up all the messy words that have been thrown in anger?

"I'm cooking dinner for Susie tonight," Herbert said happily.

"Duck?" Frederick asked. Not even *suspecting* sarcasm so soon in their reunion, Herbert plodded on.

"You know, plums are as good with duck as oranges. Those little blue plums, freestone, and slightly acidic, are the best. Before you quit eating meat, Freddy, did you get the chance to try rhubarb duck?" Frederick felt his stomach whirl upward and then settle again.

"I must say that I missed that adventure," he told Herbert.

"Freddy?"

"Yes, Herbert?"

"What did you mean by what you said the other night?"

"What did I say?"

"Come on," said Herbert. "You know what I'm talking about." He did know. *You're a closet homosexual. That's what's wrong with you.* Frederick leaned back in his chair, clinked the salt and pepper shakers together. How could he explain?

"Do you remember Mr. Bator?" he asked. "He taught us biology in high school."

"*Master* Bator?" Herbert replied.

"Don't call him that," said Frederick.

"*Everybody* called him that," Herbert insisted.

"Well, don't *you* do it," Frederick said protectively.

"What about him?" asked Herbert. Frederick paused. *He's been talking to me, Herb,* he could hear himself saying as Herbert dialed 911. "Well?" Herbert waited. The abrasive music of forks and knives at work rose up around them.

"I've sort of been hearing his voice a lot lately," Frederick confessed. He had no other recourse, not after the remark Herbert thought was meant for *him.* "I mean, I know it's just my subconscious mind working overtime, but it sure seems real sometimes." A waitress appeared with a water pitcher, filled their glasses hurriedly, and then disappeared.

"He *talks* to you?" Herbert asked. He took the salt and pepper over for himself and began to tap them together. "What does he say?"

"Lots of things," Frederick admitted. "Sometimes it's stuff he said in class, things I memorized for tests. Other times it's stuff I read years ago and thought I'd forgotten. Sometimes it has to do with ideas about life that I guess I've always felt but didn't realize, and Mr. Bator expresses them for me."

"So he talks to you," Herbert said again. He was still waiting for an explanation.

"Well." Frederick cleared his throat. "I was at my wit's end the other night at the emergency clinic. I thought I'd see Chandra at Bobbin Road and didn't. My ankle was hurting. And Mr. Bator had been bugging me all day about how time waits for no man, and how time is essentially a meaningless idea."

"What a prick," said Herbert.

"It wasn't really Mr. Bator, of course, but I was simply fed up and, well, you remember all those stories that went around Portland High about Mr. Bator. You know, how he lived with another man and all, and how someone had seen them holding hands on the ferry to Peak's Island. I'm really ashamed of myself for calling him a closet homosexual, because those were troubled times and he was a high-school teacher. It must have been really rough on him."

"So you called *him* a closet homosexual and not *me?*" Herbert inquired. Frederick nodded. "You're losing it, Freddy. Do yourself a favor. Get a lawyer. Get divorced. Get on with your life." He gave the salt and pepper shakers back.

"I wish Mr. Bator were still around," Frederick confessed.

"Master Bator," said Herbert. "I haven't thought of him in years."

"Don't call him that," said Frederick.

"*Everybody* called him that."

"Well, don't you do it. And besides, *I* never called him that. I liked Mr. Bator. He was very kind to me."

"How kind?" Herbert asked.

"Herbert!"

"I'm just kidding you," Herbert told him. "Relax, for crying out loud." The waitress appeared with their checks and Frederick beckoned that he would take them both. He gave her his weary American Express card.

"Do you know what happened to Mr. Bator?" he asked.

"No, I don't know what happened to him," said Herbert. "I don't know what happened to Peter Lemonjello either, for that matter. And I don't care."

"I wish he were still around," Frederick said again.

"Maybe he died," Herbert thoughtfully noted. "How old was he back then? I graduated in 'sixty-four, you in 'sixty-six. We're talking over twenty-five years. I bet he's dead. Finito."

"That's the funny thing," said Frederick. "We always thought of him as being old, but I've been thinking about it a lot, and I doubt that he was as old as I am now. He's probably only in his mid-sixties."

"Master Bator," Herbert mused. "Christ, I haven't thought of him since high school." Frederick sighed. Had he really missed Herbert Stone this past week? Was it guilt or was it Memorex?

He had signed the check—Herbert needed to dash back to the clinic—and was waiting for his receipt when he happened to spot none other than Joyce, his sister-in-law, sitting at a table in the no-smoking section. He was about to wave a quick hello until he recognized one of her lunch companions. Robbie. The purloiner of wives. At first Frederick couldn't bring himself to look at the face of the third diner. He kept his eyes painfully on Robbie instead, until he could stand it no longer. It was Chandra, all right. *Dark eyed, O woman of my dreams.* He could only stare. Conversation came and went around him. Words buzzed in his ears like a horrible swarm of killer bees, but he could understand no language. Time had stopped. He felt it stop, a quick jolt to the senses, and then a dreamlike reality of floating up from his table. He heard words buzz toward him from Herbert, saw Herbert standing, his mouth moving, his eyes happy again. He even waved back, watched as Herbert disappeared into the foyer, but he had been cut afloat from the rest of the world, was bouncing somewhere just above his table at Panama Red's. And from this new position, he could see only his wife, Chandra Kimball-Stone, her face more beautiful than he had remembered, than any picture could pretend her to be. Had he noticed before the choreography that occurred when she lifted her fork to her mouth? He could write long poems about how she buttered a roll, sonnets in how she sipped from a glass of water. And her mouth! Had he even realized that when she spoke her lips moved like a red liquid over her white teeth? *The lips are two fleshy folds surrounding the cavity of the mouth,* said a familiar voice.

"But aren't they lovely folds, Mr. Bator?" Frederick whispered. *They are composed of the skin covering the outer surface, mucous membrane covering the inner portion, connective tissue, and a ring of muscular tissue and the artery that supplies blood.*

"It would be so wonderful to kiss those lips, Mr. Bator." *The functions of the lips include feeding and speech.*

"And kissing, Mr. Bator, the functions include kissing." He saw her laugh, a rich laugh that caused her to throw her head back, throat exposed, and release it, a thunderous laugh if he could only hear it. Joyce was laughing, too. Robbie was laughing. See Joyce laugh. See Chandra touch Robbie's arm. Robbie, Robbie, pudding and pie, kissed the girls and made them laugh. See Joyce touch Robbie's arm. Joyce likes Robbie. Robbie likes Joyce. Chandra likes Robbie. Chandra could do without Joyce. See Robbie smile. See Robbie smile. See Robbie smile.

"Mr. Stone," the waitress was saying, along with the usual restaurant niceties about having a good day and coming back real soon. Frederick saw before him the check he had signed and his American Express receipt. He stuffed the receipt into his shirt pocket and then staggered toward the door. At least, looking back on it, he thought he might have staggered. He hoped Chandra hadn't noticed. He would hate to disrupt her merriment, and the truth was that she was *merry*. Even with Joyce, she was merry. She hadn't been merry around him in how many years? A lot of them.

He walked, is what he did. In spite of his sore ankle, just recently workable, he walked. He left his car in a far corner of Panama Red's parking lot and went for a little stroll down along the bay. Sandpipers raced in ahead of the waves. People ambled on the beach. Dogs left their wet prints behind as they tore down the strand, becoming black bouncing dots until they finally vanished. Frederick walked. He had abandoned his shoes and socks beside a bench at the pier, and now the water and sand rode up between his toes. He wanted to talk to Mr. Bator about laughter, about why Chandra would share it with some people, not others. Not him. Laughter was a strange vehicle, really. Humans use a few muscles to laugh that would be unused otherwise. If you tickle a month-old baby, he will laugh a genuine laugh. Why does that happen? Frederick passed a volleyball game in progress, university students, judging by their T-shirts. Their own laughter followed him down the beach.

"When a human being laughs, Mr. Bator," said Frederick, "the diaphragm moves up and down and the outgoing air stimulates the larynx. The sound that this action produces is known as a *chuckle*." He heard Mr. Bator himself laugh, a resonant, ghostly laugh, as he had done one morning in class, more than twenty-five years earlier. There had been a huge chart of the human skeleton hanging at the front of the classroom, and someone had drawn a large balloon coming out of the skeleton's mouth. Inside the balloon, they'd written *Ha! Ha!* in large block letters. "Okay, class," Mr. Bator had said. "I think this is a good time to talk about the mechanisms of laughter." He had been such a good teacher, an excellent teacher. What difference did it make that he lived with another man? What injustice was there in touching the hand of someone you love, on a ferry boat ride, on a balmy summer night? "They were on the *ferry* boat, get it?" Richard Hamel had joked. God, but he had hated Richard Hamel, mumblety-peg cheat that he was.

"That was me, Mr. Bator," Frederick said aloud. "I was the one who drew the balloon on the chart." Several herring gulls floated like old dreams above his head. The organic smell of the ocean, of things living and growing, things dying and rotting, came and went on a little breeze. He thought of Chandra's larynx being stimulated by the diaphragm moving up and down, up and down, because of some little tidbit Robbie had said, up and down. *Ah, love, let us be true to one another, for the world which seems to lie before us like a land of dreams, is a world where things grow in order to die, where women like Marta look over their shoulders as a life's vocation, where fathers and mothers sometimes make big mistakes, where war comes and goes like a shower of rain.* Bouncing black dots had appeared far down the strand. He watched them race toward him, getting larger and larger until they were dogs again. In the distance a firecracker erupted, a hangover from the Fourth of July, which had passed in a panoply of fireworks, colorful pinwheels filling up the skies. Frederick walked on. Evening was coming in full force when he finally returned for his shoes and socks, to discover them gone. Why would someone want a pair of used shoes and socks? What was wrong with some people?

He went barefoot into the liquor store for the bottles of gin and vermouth, and then into Cain's Corner Grocery for the olives. He had gin and vermouth and olives at home, but he didn't want to chance running out of anything. Let Herbert say he was overreacting. There was no doubt in his mind that The Big Drunk was the next step in his life, a ceremonial rite to be observed. Many people of both sexes, nice folks who've been *extraneared* by their loved ones, had most likely been down to the liquor store, followed by a visit to Cain's Corner Grocery for the olives. One can't avoid The Big Drunk. It was probably even mentioned in some of those twelve-step manuals: *First comes Denial, then Anger, then The Big Drunk, then Acceptance.* He would be a better man—he had no doubt of this—in the morning.

By the time he unlocked the kitchen door, his bag of bottles clinking happily in his arms, he was limping again. There were two messages on his answering machine. The first was from Herbert, announcing that he'd be at The China Boat later in the evening for after-dinner drinks with the aging Susie, in case Frederick felt like dropping by. The second was from Lillian, his mother-in-law.

"Frederick, dear," Lillian's message began. "Lorraine was by today to pick up Joyce for lunch and, well, she confessed that the address she gave me, the one on Bobbin Road, was a false one. She seemed to think I'd give the real one to *you.* I'm calling, of course, because I wouldn't want you to go over there and—" He rewound the words. They passed in a vigorous whir.

"Blah, blah, blah," he said. In the kitchen, he mixed up a vicious pitcher of martinis and then hobbled with it into the living room. He found his *Greatest Hits of Gary Puckett & The Union Gap* and put in on the turntable. *Woman, woman, have you got cheating on your mind? Why am I losing sleep over you? Lady Willpower, it's now or never. Young girl, get out of my mind.* He wondered how old The Union Gap were when they had their Big Drunk. Younger than forty-four, he'd guess. Oh sure, he'd puked his guts out on prom night, but that was understandable. In those days a high-school boy drank whatever he could steal from his dad's liquor cabinet. Because Dr. Philip Stone was a teetotaler, Frederick's old school chum Nicholas Dimopoulos had agreed to bring the booze. How could Frederick know that Nick would turn up with four bottles of ouzo?

The first pitcher was a pushover. He made a second, adding a touch more gin to this batch. In his glass the olive sank to the bottom like a little green submarine. Or better yet, Alvin, the round underwater camera that nosed all through the *Titanic,* finding a bottle of wine still unbroken, bits of dishes, jewelry. The only thing Alvin didn't pick up was the melody of that last song, played as the big ship sank. Frederick had always imagined that it was down there somewhere, lingering, floating about the ballroom maybe, stealing down to the captain's quarters on lonely nights. Would he have stood and sung as the great vorticose mouth of water rose up to take him down? Or would he have donned a dress and tried to sneak into a lifeboat with the other girls? "You never went to Vietnam, did you?" Herbert had accused. "You went to *Woodstock*." Well, what of that? War was wrong. Even Herbert Stone agreed to that. But Herbert Stone hadn't wanted to go to college right away. He wanted to sow a few oats, travel about the country. What he got instead was drafted. Frederick, on the other hand, managed to stay at Boston University with a straight-A average. College material, not Vietnam fodder. Was he scared to go to Vietnam?

"You bet I was," he confessed, and raised his martini glass high. "I was scared shitless." That didn't make war any less wrong, did it? Herbert could have gone to Canada. A lot of guys they knew did that. A lot more guys they *didn't* know went to Canada, like Jesse Winchester, the singer. Look at all those songs he wrote as a result! And besides, Woodstock was a lot tougher than Herbert gave him credit for: all that rain, only the occasional sandwich, a poor sound system. Jesus H. Christ, but he had GONE TO THE WRONG HOUSE! He had knelt before the bedroom window of complete strangers, had fallen from their slate roof, had flattened their bush! He had been trying his martini best to ignore the ramifications of Chandra's using a fake address—Bobbin Road was so familiar to her, of course, she'd choose that—but he found he couldn't escape it. How cruel, that's what he kept thinking. How absolutely *cruel*.

"Mr. Bator?" Frederick cried. "Can you believe what she did? Don't you want to discuss female deception down through the ages?" A short silence followed. "Answer me, Mr. Bator, damn you!" Frederick shouted. "We can start with Eve, and then Delilah, and then Cleopatra! And don't forget what Elizabeth Taylor did to poor Eddie Fisher!" There was no reply. Mr. Bator had obviously crawled into the thick warm blankets of Frederick's temporal lobe, had locked the door, had fallen fast asleep. After all, nobody wants to listen to a drunk.

Frederick both limped and staggered into his office and flicked on the light. There was the blasted picture of Chandra and him at

Woodstock. They were kids, just fucking kids. How could they know what might lie ahead? How could they ever dream that one of the roads they would chose one day, for different purposes, would be Bobbin Road? His eyes teared significantly. He flopped into his chair and pulled open his desk drawer. Was that it? No, that was a box of staples. Ha! Ha! He laughed the same laugh he had given to the skeleton. A box of staples! Was *that* it? No, that was a stack of index cards upon which he had scribbled poem ideas for many years and had yet to computerize. There it was. He retrieved the old address book, the one with his mother's phone number in Florida. There had never been any need to computerize numbers he rarely used, and his mother's was most certainly one of them. So was the number in Connecticut, where Polly's survivors lived. His head bobbed suddenly, and it made him chuckle.

"My diaphragm just stimulated my larynx, Mr. Bator," he giggled. He focused his eyes on the index, searching for the S's. There it was. Thelma Stone, bless her heart. Bless every sleepy inch of her. He had no idea what number he dialed on his first try, but he got someone's answering machine, "the Thompson residence," a home out there somewhere in one of the fifty states. He felt an instant fondness for the Thompsons, and, at the tone, wished them all good things in life.

On his second try, he punched each digit with careful, slow deliberation. She answered drowsily on the fourth ring. At first he said nothing. He was struck by the sound of her voice, his mother's voice. Had it been the first sound he'd ever heard?

"Hello?" she said again.

"I know it wasn't your tonsils," Frederick told her sadly. His eyes teared. Why couldn't they have told him the blasted truth about Polly's birth? Didn't they know that such a monstrous lie could mess a child up for good? It was probably all connected, in some circuitous way, to why Chandra had left him.

"What?"

"Tonshills." He could almost smell her lilac scent.

"I beg your pardon?" she said angrily. Well, it was late, it was pretty fucking late to be begging his pardon.

"I know it wasn't your goddamn TONSHILLS!" he shouted, his words slurring into one another like cars on an icy freeway.

"Who the hell *is* this?" his mother demanded. Then she hung up.

Eleven

On Monday Frederick's car wouldn't start. He had left the park lights on Friday night, little beacons out in his lonely driveway. The car had been sitting there all weekend, drinking up electricity, while Frederick was inside drinking up gin. Now the engine was dead, not even a sputter when he turned the ignition key. He got out and slammed the door. The noise of it resounded inside his head, rattled his poor teeth. Gathering up a great positive sigh, he led his bicycle out of the garage—he hadn't used the thing in years—and dusted off the seat. It would hurt his ankle greatly, but he would pedal to Cain's Corner Grocery for a large bottle of Tylenol. If he didn't, he would die. He was experiencing the worst hangover of his entire forty-four years on the planet. He rued the day that his supply of prescription Percodan for his ankle had run its course. He wasn't sure which hurt more, the ankle or his head. The Big Drunk, like some insensible Mardi Gras gone awry, had spread into the next day and the next. He had spent the entire weekend in a maudlin stupor. Sunday was only a blur to him. He vaguely remembered falling asleep to the words of "Woman, Woman," waking up to the sound of the phonograph needle batting against the last ridge of the record, as though it were the last ridge in the roof of Gary Puckett's mouth, and then falling asleep again to "Lady Willpower." And speaking of Lady Willpower, to hell with Chandra Kimball-Stone—that had been his weekend philosophy. He didn't need her. He had his own friends. He had Gary Puckett and the whole goddamn Union Gap. He hadn't leaned out the bathroom window and shouted at poor Walter Muller, had he, some horrible obscenity during this period? He conjured up a mental picture of watching Walter plant a tree in his front yard, of undoing the latch of the bathroom window, of leaning far out. Please let that vague memory be a dream! He supposed he wouldn't know the truth until the next time he saw Walter Muller out in his yard.

The only positive element of the three-day stupor was that his ankle had not hurt at all. But it did now, it hurt a lot. What had he done to torture it so? Had he kept up a steady Scottish reel for three days, dancing from room to room? Had he used the sore foot to keep time to The Union Gap? Theirs wasn't exactly foot-stomping music. Whatever he did, the ankle pained him terribly.

"You take care of that ankle now," Mr. Cain cautioned him, and Frederick promised to do just that. He would nurse it back to health promptly. He then left with his Tylenol. Had anyone at the monstrous IGA ever inquired as to his health? Never. Oh, sure, if he was to have a coronary in the frozen foods, some complaining bag boy would be sent with a shopping cart to haul the body away. He was done with the IGA forever!

On the return trip, he let his good ankle do most of the work, and coasted whenever the opportunity presented itself. On a whim he turned down Bobbin Road, just to see what emotions the yellow house might stir up in him, now that he knew she had never even been there. Gliding past, he viewed it as just another yellow house, with a lamppost, a maple tree, a veranda, and at least one battered shrub. The maroon Camaro was gone from the driveway. Just another house. He watched in his bicycle mirror as it disappeared behind him.

As he coasted toward the house on Ellsboro Street, his eye caught a sudden movement, the shape of a human being peering into his den window. Frederick spun the pedal with his good foot and sped on by. Yes, it was indeed a man, a regular Peeping Tom, right there on Ellsboro Street! Frederick pulled up to the curve in front of Mrs. Prather's house and got off the bicycle. The man was now gaping into yet another window, the one to the laundry room. This was no Peeping Tom. This was a bona fide burglar. Gently, quietly, Frederick slipped the bicycle up onto its kickstand. Then, hunched over to avoid detection, he limped along the thick row of hedge that separated his yard from Mrs. Prather's. At the corner of the hedge he crouched, his head easing up above the shrubs for a view. There the man was, slithering along the house now, heading back for the screened-in front porch. He must have decided that the owners were definitely not home. He would no doubt be ready now to jimmy the lock. Frederick considered, for a few fleeting seconds, that perhaps he should slip over to Mrs. Prather's and telephone the Portland police. A few fleeting seconds. That thought was replaced by a huge surge of endorphins, mixed with some of that *hubris* Chandra was always lamenting about. How dare a perfect stranger infiltrate the privacy of Frederick Stone, not to mention rob him! He crept forward, his ankle forgetting all previous pain, his eye on the stranger's lurking form. The culprit was now peeping through the glass of the front door. Frederick accidentally crunched one of Chandra's batch of marigolds. He paused, hoping that the noise had not alerted the burglar. But the man was now rattling the doorknob. Then he knocked loudly.

"Assuring himself no one's home," Frederick decided. "The sleazy little bastard." He inched forward again and paused behind one of Chandra's larger shrubs, a thing with big white flowers. Shrub Camouflage now seemed a part of his life. He discreetly peered around a gaggle of white blossoms. The intruder had again left the screened-in front porch, the door slamming behind him with a resounding *bang*. Today's thieves were so brazen! Frederick watched him slither down the lower side of the house, stopping to squint through another window, this one a portal to Frederick's private office. Rage filled Frederick Stone. He stole forward quickly, on rickety tiptoes. He would duck behind Walter Muller's spreading lilac bush and wait for the malefactor to come back. He saw Mrs. Prather come out onto her own front porch to tend to her flower boxes. Frederick hoped the poor woman wouldn't see the battle, the excessive carnage, perhaps a showering of blood. He heard the burglar coming back. He waited, his breath pulled up into his cheekbones. An arm swung past the lilac bush and into view. Frederick lunged.

"Aha!" he screamed as he jumped onto the broad back that had appeared before him. One arm about the prowler's neck, Frederick felt them both falling through the air, earthbound. He tried to protect his ankle by thrusting his leg out from his body. They hit, face first, with a deadly thud. He could almost feel the air empty from the pervert's lungs. Good. He himself had had a bit of experience with just that problem. He himself knew that, without air, lungs were nothing more than a couple of discarded pocketbooks.

"Gaaah," he heard the man beneath him utter. He applied more pressure to the neck region, then brought his knee up to connect with the stranger's groin. "Gaaaah!" Frederick smiled. He wondered if the Three Harpies were watching this. He hoped so. He hoped to Christ so. Let them see how little he really needed them.

"Mrs. Prather!" he shouted. She lifted her head, looked up and down the street. Frederick could only hold the thief so long. When he got his air back, there would most likely be a scuffle. He needed someone to call the police. Tightening his arm more firmly around the broad neck of his victim, Frederick waved his free arm as much as he dared.

"Mrs. Prather!" She shook her head, perhaps to brush off the feeling that someone was calling her name. Then she went back to watering her flowers. Frederick rearranged himself upon the body beneath him. It had gotten that aforementioned air and was now squirming desperately. He could tell by the back of the head, the cut of the hair, the line of the shoulders that he had tackled a strong young man. A flash of pride coursed through him. He wondered when the last time was that Herbert Stone had tackled a hefty human being. Probably not since Nam, and yet he had had the gall to scream all that stuff at Frederick, that night at the emergency clinic. It was lucky for the Viet Cong, it was damn lucky, that the pacifist Frederick Stone, the biggest goddamn conscientious objector since Meathead, on "All in the Family," had not made an appearance in the Mekong Delta. Yes siree. He administered another worthy squeeze about his opponent's neck and then, suddenly, he was airborne. He'd seen professional wrestlers fly through the air after being tossed by their opponents, but he had always known it was fake. Now he flew up off the body beneath him with genuine certainty and landed with a small thud a few feet away. The burglar was now struggling to his feet. Frederick jumped up, too, not wanting to have the disadvantage. His ankle remembered that it was hurt and cried out piteously.

"Shit!" he heard the young man scream. He was shielding his testicles as though they were dainty eggs. "Are you crazy, man?" He turned to look at Frederick. Frederick was stunned, flabbergasted, astonished. It was Robbie, Purloiner of Wives. Had he come for the television set? Chandra's Super Tampax? The box of baking soda in the refrigerator perhaps? After all, Frederick Stone didn't have much left for him to purloin. But what did it matter why he'd come? It was *Robbie*. Frederick was allotted a second round of endorphins by his brain, that legal pusher—if his life didn't straighten up, he would OD on endorphins—and again his ankle numbed itself above his stomping foot. How many nights had he lain awake and watched the green numbers on the clock and wished his hands were around Robbie's stout throat? How many nightmares had he awakened from, shaken and sweating, nightmares in which he was forced to watch Chandra wrap her arms about this man, leaving Frederick out, leaving him behind. He lunged again, without a single morsel of pain.

Aware of this impending attack, Robbie fled, but Frederick blind-sided him at the front steps of the screened-in porch and let him have a sound punch up against his prominent jawbone. Robbie's legs buckled and he went down beside Chandra's hydrangea. Good. Let *him* water the damn thing. Frederick was tired of playing gardener to the *somethings* his wife had left behind.

"She's right!" Robbie screamed. "You *are* a fucking lunatic!" He attempted to escape yet again, getting to his knees and beginning a slow crawl across the yard. Winded, Frederick grabbed Robbie by the ankles and lifted his legs, creating a human wheelbarrow. He had the sensation that he was maneuvering an immense work animal. Robbie continued to crawl, his hands and arms now doing all the work. Frederick found himself being pulled helplessly along. What did Chandra see in this young bull? Surely, the brain had to have shrunk greatly in compensation for all that brawn.

"How dare you?" Frederick panted. "How absolutely dare you

come to my home?" He dug his heels into the grassy lawn. Was Mrs. Prather blind as well as deaf?

"Neighborhood Crime Watch!" he heard a voice declare loudly. It sounded like the pervasive Walter Muller. "I'm getting it all on tape for the police, Frederick, so don't you worry a bit!" Frederick twisted his head just enough to see Walter Muller, standing at the edge of his yard with a video camera. His face obscured by the body of the camcorder, Walter nonetheless waved a neighborly wave. Frederick's immediate thought was for his hair. He could feel it standing tall, bucking in all directions. His shirt was now torn. He must have dirt on his face—he had plowed his features into the lawn on that first tackle. What if this ended up on the six o'clock news? Good Christ.

"Not now, Walter," he pleaded. It would only take him a few minutes to wash up, put on a clean shirt. It would be better to catch the event for posterity—and for Chandra Kimball-Stone's own personal benefit—just as the police car roared away with the brute handcuffed in the backseat. Frederick Stone himself would be standing at the mailbox, his hair neatly combed, a stern, juris-prudent look hovering about his face. He felt Robbie buckle under him, flip over onto his back. Frederick worked at pinning the young man's arms back, but Robbie was not interested in strug-gling much at all.

"For fuck's sake, Uncle Freddy," Robbie whined. "You're making a fool of yourself." Frederick felt his grip loosen in sur-prise.

"I'm getting it all, Frederick!" a jubilant Walter Muller bel-lowed. "Lean back so I can zoom in on his face!" Frederick stared at Robbie's sour visage. *Uncle Freddy?* He felt a severe upheaval in his stomach, a sickening sense of the universe giggling at his ex-pense. As quickly as they had appeared, his endorphins disap-peared—delirium tremens was probably next—leaving behind an ankle that throbbed miserably. He could almost hear the Down East Shrews clapping their hands with glee. Robbie said nothing. A soft trickle of blood was beginning to inch down from one nostril. Frederick tried to kick a thinking mechanism into working order. *Uncle Freddy?* Could this be one of Polly's sons, one of the ones who was supposed to be living in Connecticut? He tried to remember what Polly's sons looked like, the last time he'd seen a picture of them, but no face developed in his memory. And yet Robbie was now beginning to look unnervingly familiar.

"I only came to talk to you," Robbie said. "I been feeling bad about Aunt Chandra not telling you the truth." Frederick noticed a sizable welt appearing above Robbie's left eye. He was torn between pride at having caused it and terror over a potential lawsuit. And then suddenly he saw it: his brother-in-law's face, Reginald's face, the flattish nose, the broad Neanderthal forehead, a gleam of inherited dullness in the boy's eyes. If Robbie hadn't had a crewcut, a shock of red hair would be hanging just above one eyebrow. *We've invited Robert to dinner,* Joyce had said. *But he's at that age where he doesn't want to eat with us anymore.* Yes, well so was Frederick. He tried to think further about these inherited nephews of his, a gift from Chandra. Surely he had seen Robbie before, just as he'd seen Condom Boy. But they had always remained at the periphery of the family gatherings, as teenagers will. How could Chandra expect him to remember them? Everyone under twenty-five all looked alike to him anyway. And *why* should he remember them? What could be gained from it? Frederick freed the boy's arms.

"Be careful!" he heard Walter Muller scream. He was still zooming.

"There's been a mistake, Walter," Frederick said sharply. "This is Chandra's nephew." He stood, gingerly, and brushed the grass from his jeans. Then he reached a hand down to Robbie.

"Aunt Chandra said it served you right," Robbie told him, accepting the hand. "She said it would teach you to pay more attention to people." Frederick thought about this. Well, her little lesson had backfired, hadn't it? So much for her skills as an instructress. He pulled Robbie up. The boy weighed a ton. Five percent stupidity, Frederick supposed, and ninety-five percent testosterone.

"I'm sorry," he said, and honestly. "At first I thought you were a burglar. Why were you peeping into my windows?"

"Because your car is in the driveway and you didn't answer your freakin' door," Robbie noted. "Mom says that you're on the verge, so I figured this was the day you bought the farm. You're lucky I didn't fight back. I'd have kicked your freakin' ass." He was wiping the small dribble of blood with the back of his hand. "You're a freakin' idiot, man," he added. Frederick could only nod in agreement. Over Robbie's shoulder, he saw Walter Muller, Big Brother, inching his way across the lawn, his camcorder glued to his face. He imagined a gaping well in the front yard, and Walter stepping out and into the blackness of its mouth, never to film again.

"Walter, there's been a mistake," Frederick said loudly. "Please quit filming." He held a hand before his face, the way movie stars often do with troublesome paparazzi.

"You're *both* freakin' crazy," Robbie muttered. At least Joyce's sons spoke the same language. Frederick stood helplessly, wishing he could undo the attack—Robbie hadn't even *fought back,* for Christ's sake—wishing Chandra hadn't been so devious. To let him feel all this pain for nothing! To let him be jealous of his own nephew. *Of course* he didn't know Joyce's sons. That would be like memorizing seals. He would make a civil attempt to right things.

"Well, good to meet you again, Robbie," Frederick said cheerfully, offering his hand.

"Fuck you, man," said Robbie. He stomped off toward a small black car sitting at the curb.

"What a good-looking young man," said Walter Muller, just pulling up the rear. "Look at those arms. Have you ever seen such a nice-looking kid? I tell you, I wasn't far from that physique myself, back in the college days. Football, you know. The University of Maine Bruins. Yes siree, that's one fine-looking young buck." *Walterspeak.* Robbie's car spun away from the curb in a vicious blend of rubber and fine pebbles. It roared off down the street. Frederick's ankle sang with pain. His hangover headache kicked into a higher gear, modulated. He turned slowly on his good heel. He would go inside, take a few Tylenol, and lie down for a bit. He hobbled off, his ankle sending out its complaints at every footfall, until he heard Walter Muller shout his name. Frederick sighed. He wished now that he had, indeed, leaned out the bathroom window and insulted Walter's sense of morality. He paused, turned.

"Here," said Walter Muller, catching up with him. "In case there ever is a *real* burglary." He handed Frederick a card. *Neighborhood Crime Watch,* the card stated. *Walter Muller, Camcorder Cop.*

He tried to nap, but images of Robbie's face flickered about when he closed his eyes. Joyce and Reginald's son. His nephew by marriage. How much energy and thought had he wasted these past six weeks over Robbie? How could he ever get it back? He couldn't. He was now almost thankful for his sore ankle. He needed to be reminded that he still felt things, was still in contact with the world, even if that contact was a stabbing throb. He needed to know that he was still alive, and his ankle seemed to be the only thing able to convince him. He phoned Herbert. Unlike Frederick, Herbert was having a slow and uneventful day.

"Dr. Brasher is handling things and I'm reading the newspaper," Herbert confessed.

"I'm feeling a bit under the weather," Frederick said.

"Listen to me, Freddy," said Herbert. "Women will make you feel an inch tall if you let them. You gotta keep saying to yourself over and over again, 'I'm not such a bad guy. I'm not such a bad guy.' You need to tell yourself that every night before you fall asleep. No one's gonna do it for you, buddy."

"I didn't ask you for a lecture, Herbert," Frederick reminded him. "I just felt like talking to someone."

"Tell you what," said Herbert. "I was just getting ready to go to the dry cleaners. I'll come by and get you."

Frederick had hobbled off the sofa and was waiting on the porch steps when Herbert pulled into the drive and tooted the horn.

"I see you," Frederick muttered. He was halfway down the steps when Herbert tooted again. "I'm coming, dammit!" Frederick said, loudly now. He limped toward the car. Herbert tooted a third time. "Jesus."

Frederick opened the passenger door and simply glared at his brother.

"I was just trying to cheer you up," Herbert said happily. Frederick nodded. *The dimwit, the dolt, the dunce.*

"Herbert," said Frederick patiently. "Must I remind you that my ankle is in this hellish condition because of your excessive honking?" He slid into the passenger seat and snapped on his safety belt. Smoke hovered in the air, little gray wreaths, the ghosts of cigarettes past. Frederick coughed dramatically.

"Don't start," Herbert threatened. "You're in *my* car."

"I don't think that carcinogens care who owns the car," Frederick said. He whirred his side window down as Herbert pulled out into the street and whisked them toward downtown Portland.

"You're not going to spoil my day," Herbert vowed. "I've got an interesting date tonight, and I intend to stay happy in spite of you."

"I suppose that July is too late for high-school proms," Frederick said. "So where will you be taking the young lady?" He stuck his head out the window, into the rushing summer air. The smoke in the car was stifling. He heard Herbert reply in sentences that became strings of words that melded together and were lost as wind rushed at Frederick's eardrums. He wished that he could turn the sound down on everyone. He imagined mouths opening and closing, lips moving across teeth, followed by pure, sweet silence. Was he *on the verge,* as Joyce and Robbie suspected, flitting on the cusp of a nervous breakdown?

Herbert pulled into the parking lot of Portland Cleaners and cut the engine. He reached into the backseat and retrieved a necktie, a sports jacket, and a shirt. On the necktie, a serene Mona Lisa stared out at the humanity of the twentieth century. What could she be thinking, after an evening at The China Boat, the fragrance of cooked dead duck wafting up to greet her wide nostrils? "And they call *me* enigmatic?" Frederick stared in dismay as Herbert wrapped the tie about the neck of his coat hanger. Mona Lisa's features had had to be narrowed, crunched up, in order to accommodate the slender body of the tie. Now the face of *La Gioconda* looked disturbingly like a cucumber. And her Salvador Dali eyes were staring forth as though she were some kind of guppy.

"Where, pray tell," Frederick asked, "do you get those abominable ties you wear? They're a disgrace to the art world." Herbert paused, a leg already out his open door.

"I'll tell you something, Freddy," Herbert said. "If Leonardo da Vinci were alive today, he'd be doing neckties." His clothing gathered up into a ball, Herbert slammed the car door and disappeared through the entrance to Portland Cleaners, just below a sign that announced SHIRTS 75 CENTS EACH, NO LIMIT. A tinkling noise followed as the door closed behind him and then all was quiet. Frederick sat with his window down and waited. With a medium that now offered so much freedom, maybe Leonardo *would* be putting his artwork wherever the common man could see it, in supermarkets, on underpasses, at airports, even on T-shirts. That was what it was all about, after all, reaching as many humans

as possible. An artist shouldn't touch just the people who understand and agree with him. He should reach out to capture the
people who *don't* agree with him. Frederick babied his ankle into
a more comfortable position. He eased Herbert's overflowing ashtray shut, crunching dead butts in the process. He fanned his face
a bit, the warm July air filtering in through the window. Herbert
reappeared with empty arms. Mona Lisa would soon be doused
with naphtha, or gasoline, or carbon tetrachloride.

"Maybe you're right," said Frederick as Herbert slipped back
into the driver's seat. "Maybe art should be aimed at the common
man." Herbert lit a cigarette, drew a long, steady puff. He exhaled
heartily.

"I'll tell you something, Freddy," Herbert said, and cleared his
throat. He was going to wax philosophical and Frederick knew it.
He also knew that Herbert Stone didn't just wax. He buffed and
polished. "Common men don't have personal accountants," Herbert noted. "Therefore, Freddy, you don't even *know* any common men." He drew a quick puff this time and then waited.
Frederick suspected that his brother was anticipating a rebuttal,
but how could Frederick Stone rebut? He didn't even know his
own *nephews*. "Folks like you hardly even speak to the common
man," Herbert plodded on. Frederick considered walking home,
and would have, were it not for his ankle. "But me? Veterinarian
to the poor? I see the common man every day. I've met million-
aires who would shoot a dog because it has fleas. And I've seen
millworkers who would sell the only automobile they own to
keep a dog alive on the operating table." Frederick sighed. Why
had he thought a quick ride with his older brother would cheer
him up? A ride with Herbert Stone was like going on an Iditerod
without any warm clothing. Skin diving without air tanks. Sky
diving sans parachute.

"Could we leave now?" Frederick asked. Herbert looked at his
watch.

"Another fifty-five minutes," he said. He pulled the ashtray
open again. Butts flew out and scattered about on the floor.

"What?"

"Another fifty-five minutes."

"Why are we waiting another fifty-five minutes?" Frederick felt
a small stream of perspiration tickling his upper lip.

"Because I need that stuff for my date tonight," said Herbert. "One-hour cleaning." He pointed at the sign that announced just such a service.

"Are you telling me that we're going to have to sit here for an hour?" Frederick could feel his eyes popping dramatically. He tried to remain calm. Chandra Kimball-Stone had often made mention of what she called his *frog eyes.* He would look like the Mona Lisa on Herbert's tie—the poor girl, the poor, poor lass—before this was over.

"Hey," said Herbert. "You wanted to come. *You* called *me,* remember?"

"You said we were only going to the dry cleaners," Frederick protested. The stream of sweat above his lip had overshot its tiny banks and was now cascading down into his mouth. He wiped it away with his hand.

"We *are* only going to the dry cleaners," Herbert reminded him.

"But," Frederick protested, "we're going to be here *for a fucking hour!* What a waste of valuable time!" Good Lord, his blood pressure. He could feel his veins filling up with bubbling hot blood, gushing it liberally to all parts of his face.

"You've read too much of that 'Can I part my hair, should I eat this peach?' shit while you were in college, Freddy," Herbert stated. Frederick sat, Zenlike, in the heat of the car and imagined large white numbers changing before his eyes: 130/85, 125/83, 120/80. His blood pressure going down.

"Bungie jumping without any rope," Frederick muttered.

"What?"

"Can you at least turn on the air conditioner, please?" Frederick wondered.

"If you put your window up," Herbert replied. "I get poor enough mileage as it is."

"I'll put up my window if you'll put out your cigarette," Frederick offered. He fanned the air with a *Dog World* magazine that was lying on the front seat. Maybe he should try sending some of his poetry to these folks. *She trots in beauty, like the night.*

"I don't find it warm in here," said Herbert. Smoke rose happily from his cigarette.

"Don't you have other clothes?" Frederick asked. "Why does it have to be this jacket, this shirt, this necktie?"

"Because it's my favorite outfit," Herbert insisted. "And I happen to think that Christine would like the Mona Lisa tie. We met through ties. I wore one with that big red sunrise by Manet and she went hog-wild over it."

"Monet," said Frederick.

"Manet, Monet," Herbert said mockingly. "What's the difference?" Frederick stared into the next parking space, where two sparrows were tugging at a potato chip. Even Zen, for all its peaceful attributes, for all its introspection and intuition, had abandoned him there at Portland Cleaners. A kind of anti-Zen panic overtook him. He could now imagine the numbers climbing, rising higher with his blood pressure: 140/90, 150/95, 180/110! Frederick Stone had managed all his life to keep the wings from flying off airplanes by simply *not thinking about them*. Now he was quite sure that if he didn't soon take his mind off his heart, it would explode, splatter about the Chrysler like a rotten apple. They would be at the cleaners all day having heart stains removed from Herbert's clothing.

"What happened to Susie?" he asked. Perhaps conversation would take his mind off his misery.

"Too kinky," Herbert said. "She wanted me to wear a garter belt." Frederick tried very hard not to think about this, or to picture Herbert dressed in anything but his favorite outfit. A *garter belt*? And here Frederick was, about to be thrust back into the world of dating. Numbers blinked before his eyes: 190/120, 210/ 150!

"Christine's a knockout," Herbert rattled on. Frederick sensed more streams of sweat forming now above his eyebrows, trickling down into the hairs. The wavering heat rising from the concrete lot swept at him through the open window. He stared at the ONE-HOUR CLEANING sign. "Granted, she's a couch potato," Herbert added, "but her looks make up for it. And I'll admit I wasn't thrilled to learn that she's got two children. Two little couch tater tots."

"How much longer?" asked Frederick. Herbert looked at his watch.

"Forty-two minutes." Hearing this, Frederick sighed.

"I'll put up my window if you'll at least close the ashtray," he offered. The smell of dead cigarettes was far worse than living ones.

"If I close the ashtray, I'll have to open the window to flick my cigarette," Herbert explained. "Sounds like the old rock and the hard place, doesn't it, Freddy?"

"How can you waste an hour of your life like this?" Frederick demanded angrily. Herbert shrugged.

"I do this often," he said. "It's usually quite peaceful because I'm usually alone." Frederick ignored the remark. "And I find that it's the best time to work on my writing." This last statement had come, had settled, and was almost gone in a wisp of cigarette smoke before its meaning registered in Frederick's heated brain. *Herbert's writing?*

"What writing?" he asked.

"Oh, a little book I finally finished," Herbert admitted.

"A little book?" Frederick smiled. The smell of Vanity Press permeated the stifling air in the car. He'd seen it all when it came to folks writing books. There was even one poetaster, one poor bugger who wore an earring in one ear and stood on the street in front of Panama Red's, next to a sign that said FRANCO-AMERICAN WRITER . . . WILL READ FOR FOOD. Frederick skimmed one page of the self-published pamphlet before he was certain that the man would starve to death. Had Rimbaud ever been that down on his luck? Had Baudelaire ever worn a single earring? Still wanting to help the little man, Frederick had purchased a book out of pity. It was wearisome drivel about the fellow's wearisome ancestors. But he had, after all, published it himself, in the privacy of his *maison. Merde Press.* Wasn't Frederick aiding the small business-man with his purchase? Two days later, he tossed the book into Chandra's recycling barrel, *au revoir,* where it would hopefully be made into something useful. People should know their limitations. Not everyone is a poet. Yet idiots and egos were a dime a dozen when it came to writing, but Herbert Stone? Veterinarian to the Poor?

"I finished it this spring," said Herbert. "I'd have asked you for feedback, but I figured you'd be too critical. And besides, if I had wanted to give you a winning lottery ticket, back then I'd have had to send it to you registered mail. Before Chandra left I was lucky to get you to come to the phone." Frederick thought of those antebellum days of his life, those sweet plantation days be-fore the war, of Sunday mornings in bed with Chandra, and fresh coffee, and a thriving little home business. Soon, Stone Accounting would become Merde Accounting, sister to the famous book publishing conglomerate.

"What's the book about?" He hoped Herbert wouldn't see him smirking, there in the July heat, there before the sign that announced ONE-HOUR CLEANING. Or was it ONE-HOUR PUBLISHING?

"Well," Herbert began, "it's semiautobiographical." Frederick raised a brotherly hand to stop him.

"Herbert, *everything* is semiautobiographical," said Frederick. "The flier this week at J.C. Penney's had to be written by some unfortunate bastard and it, too, is most likely *semiautobiographical.* An Oedipus complex perhaps obliged the author to dwell too long on women's lingerie." He wiped his sweaty palms. He was destined, it seemed, to explain the obvious to the oblivious.

"Well, it's all about the adventures of Kenny Perkins," Herbert went on. "Kenny is a Vietnam vet who is now a veterinarian." Frederick considered this.

"He's a *vet vet?*" Herbert smiled, nodded vigorously.

"That's his nickname at the clinic," he confessed. "And get this. He drives a *Corvette!*"

"I see," said Frederick.

"The book is a collection of Kenny Perkins stories," Herbert added. "You know, like James Herriot, the English vet? Except mine has a twist. Kenny is a vet who's been to war, so each time there's a pet emergency, he suffers a flashback from Nam." Poor Herbert. Frederick tried hard not to listen. It was bad enough that he himself had had his share of rejection slips in his lifetime, even ones from little magazines with a subscription smaller than the number of players on the Toronto Maple Leafs hockey team. He hated to see Herbert go through it. Sure, Herbert Stone had been to Vietnam, but he didn't stand a sniper's chance in book publishing. Frederick would be there, for once, finally, to console another human being. This was something he knew things about, after all, this Hades of book editors, agents, and publishers.

"Kenny Perkins?" he obliged, edging the conversation forward until he could gently explain to Herbert how high the odds were stacked against him. Why is it, would someone please tell Frederick Stone, that people who are too boring to talk to at a cocktail party decide to write books about their lives?

"Try to imagine Ernest Hemingway as an animal-rights activ-

ist," Herbert whispered, apparently fearing that someone would
steal his idea, "and you've pretty much nailed Kenny Perkins,
D.V.M."

"Herbert, it's a rough business you're trying to break into,"
Frederick began. He would start by noting the oceans of manu-
scripts mailed daily to New York by would-be writers. Of the
massive difficulties in securing the indispensable literary agent.

"I know it is," said Herbert. "That's why I need your advice."
He pulled an envelope out of his glove compartment and pecked
Frederick's arm with it. "I sent the manuscript to an agent in New
York who liked it. She sent it to an editor at Doubleday who liked
it. But what's troubling me, Freddy, is that Doubleday wants a
two-book deal and I'm not so sure that's a good idea. Here's the
contract. What do you think?" Frederick said nothing for a time.
He watched people with dirty laundry go into Portland Cleaners
and leave it, give it to someone else to clean for them. He watched
people who had already left their dirty laundry with these strangers come back and fetch it, clean again. People were strange. Life
was stranger.

"How much longer?" he finally asked Herbert.

"Twenty-eight minutes," said Herbert.

"Take me home now," Frederick said.

"But we've only got twenty-eight minutes left," Herbert told
him.

"Take me home *now*, Herbert," said Frederick, "or I'm going
to throw myself across that blasted horn which seems to both
fascinate and titillate you."

"Ouch," said Herbert, starting up the car. "I smell lame duck
cooked in sour grape sauce." They pulled out of the parking lot
for Portland Cleaners and sped toward Ellsboro Street.

"I'm not such a bad guy," Frederick whispered as the wind
whipped against his face. "I'm not such a bad guy."

Frederick was limping up his walk, vowing to never again trust
Herbert Stone as potential good company, when Walter Muller
appeared out of the bushes. Could the man simply materialize at
will? Was Scotty somewhere up above Ellsboro Street, in the
Enterprise, beaming Walter up and down?

"I have a favor to ask," Walter said beseechingly. "Mrs. Muller
can't stop laughing at the fight I taped earlier. She says it's the

funniest thing she's ever seen. Would you mind, Frederick, if we sent it to 'America's Funniest Home Videos'? Mind you, if we win, we'll split the ten thousand dollars with you."

"I'm not such a bad guy," Frederick whispered as he closed the kitchen door behind him.

*T*welve

A woman wears a certain look when she is on the move
And a man can always tell what's on her mind.

—GARY PUCKETT & THE UNION GAP

rederick had wakened Tuesday morning to the sound of a car horn bleating somewhere down the street. Maybe Robbie was still cruising the cul-de-sac, like a rat in a maze, looking for a cheesy way out. Knees arched beneath the blanket, he gingerly twisted his ankle back and forth, with little pain. It had obviously appreciated a night's rest. Still a bit sore, it was nevertheless on the mend. Just as he thought he might doze off a bit, the phone rang in his office. The answering machine clicked on. "Frederick Stone of Stone Accounting is not available," etc. etc. He listened to the business tone in his own voice with a certain amount of pride. It was the kind of assured voice to which he would trust his own personal fortune. He wriggled his toes against the horizon of blanket and waited for the caller to speak.

"Yes, I've got a message for you, Frederick Stone of Stone Accounting," an angry female voice declared. Joyce. "If you so much as *breathe* upon a child of mine again, I'll have you arrested. It's bad enough that Robbie is under Lorraine's crazy influence. I'll not have *you* assaulting him. There's a word for people like you." She hung up. Frederick sighed. Would he miss that music, that symphony of lunatics that poured forth occasionally from Chandra's family? The good thing about divorce was that each spouse was obliged to take back his or her relatives. He wondered what the *word* for him was. Chandra would say it was *hubris,* her favorite charge. Robbie would say *freakin'* hubris. Whatever Joyce's word was, Frederick felt quite sure that a little duck would drop down on a string whenever he finally uttered it, and that Herbert Stone would *eat* said duck. *You Bet Your Freakin' Life.*

It was sometime after a strong, hot shower that Frederick realized he was famished. Nothing in the fridge worth salivating over. Pickles. Olives. Gin. Vermouth. A couple of baking potatoes beginning to turn in on themselves. A shriveled lettuce. He would need to make a quick trip to Cain's Corner Grocery. He had let his run-down battery charge overnight, and now he unhooked the cables and started up the engine. It roared happily. True, it was Tuesday, his usual shopping day, but there was no need to make an extensive list of things to buy. A loaf of bread, a can of cling peaches, an apple would tide him nicely.

It was on his return journey from Cain's Corner Grocery that he became certain that someone was following him. He had tried to chalk it up to paranoia, but it was difficult not to notice that the car that seemed to make all the turns he made on the way to the grocery was now making all the turns he made on the way *back* from the grocery. He imagined the occupants of the vehicle hit men, John Gottis all, well paid by Chandra to take him out. This would avoid a messy and expensive divorce, not to mention a neat bundle of life insurance. The taped assassination might even make it to "America's Funniest Home Videos." Kenny Perkins could come upon the scene and try to revive Frederick with mouth-to-mouth exercises, resulting in a flashback and adding a new dimension to the Kenny Perkins saga. *Kenny Perkins: Vet, Vet, Paramedic.*

Frederick watched as the same brown sedan followed him down Bobbin Road. When he put his foot on the brake, it pulled off to the curb. He watched it go by again from where he had hidden, behind a bread truck at McDonald's. It was definitely following him. And now that he thought about it, he'd seen that car before, in his rearview mirror. Did Chandra think she might get him on a technicality such as adultery? He put nothing past her these days. He and Mr. Bator had decided that Chandra Kimball-Stone was ruthless. Entirely *without ruth*. Maybe he hadn't been the best husband, the most insightful friend, but he deserved more than this kind of treatment. Having him followed, indeed! Let her follow to her heart's content. He had nothing to hide.

When he arrived back home with his breakfast, a moving van was backed up to the big screened-in porch. Frederick barely took the time to shut the motor off, so quickly did he bound out from under the steering wheel and limp up the porch steps.

"She'll clean me out if I'm not careful," he muttered as he let himself in. The truth was that a strange physical tingling, one that his mental processes did not welcome, was occurring in the pit of his stomach. She might still change her mind, if only he could look her in the eye. He hated himself for even thinking about this. Surely, The Big Drunk had not been in vain. He had learned loads of stuff about himself, hadn't he? The tingling worked of its own accord and paid no attention to his intellect.

He tiptoed into the kitchen and then changed his mind about noiseless entry.

This is where I live, he thought, and slammed the door heartily. His head throbbed just to hear it. He broke into a high-pitched singing of "Woman, Woman," just to pretend that he was uninterested in the noises taking place in parts of the house, muffled voices coming down from the bedroom, furniture scraping on the ceiling overhead. *Something's wrong between us that your laughter cannot hide.* No shit. He didn't want her to think that he was singing about cheating for her benefit, so he switched to a shaky delivery of "Sittin' on the Dock of the Bay." That would be Casco Bay, he supposed, where the two of them had spent so many evenings watching the gulls, the fishing boats, the old red sun.

He had just washed three Extra-Strength Tylenol down and was putting the glass into the dishwasher when she appeared behind him in the kitchen. She seemed genuinely surprised to see him there, in his own abode. Did she expect him to have disappeared? To have disintegrated for her benefit, all his cells scattering like seeds to the wind? All his genes, all those chauvinistic Y chromosomes tossed into a trash barrel full of empty Miller Lite bottles and cigarette stubs?

"You usually take longer than this when you're grocery shopping," Chandra said flatly. She pointed to a box on the kitchen floor. One of the movers appeared from behind her shoulder, a beckoned elf, and lifted it up easily. "That's crystal," Chandra said. "Please put that box on the front seat of my car." Frederick leaned back against the stove, his hands jauntily inside his pants pockets, and waited until the mover was safely out of range before he responded to her comment.

"I don't have to pick up things for *you* anymore," he said. "No more tampons, Post-it pads, raisin bagels, cran-apple juice, Weight Watchers snack bars, a jar of pearl onions, canned artichoke hearts, cat food. Need I go on?" Let her fathom that. He'd watched a show just last week on "Geraldo" about husbands who are sexist pigs. Maybe she'd been luckier than she realized.

"You never trusted me doing the shopping," she said. "Don't you remember how that evolved? I wasn't spending hours just reading the ingredients list." He couldn't take his eyes off her hands as they carefully packed the little magnets that had been gathering dust on the refrigerator, souvenirs she'd saved since high school. "Can you believe that I'm still hanging on to these?" she asked as she plucked the last one.

"You have to be careful what you buy," he said, and sincerely.

"That's true." She looked at him. Was she thinking, And you have to be careful who you marry? She went to work separating forks, knives, and spoons.

"If I remember correctly, you bought whatever product had the prettiest packaging," he reminded her. "I didn't think we could afford to live like that." She made no response to his remarks. Knives and forks and spoons rattled and clinked.

"I thought the best thing to do with dishes and stuff like this, you know, bedding and linen," she said, "is to divide it evenly between us. I can't afford just yet to buy everything new. Is that okay with you?"

"Fine," he said. He wanted badly to move, to get away from the atmosphere in the kitchen, where the air seemed to be boiling.

"Robbie informs me that you two are officially reacquainted." Was she suppressing a smirk? He couldn't quite tell. "You're lucky he didn't kill you. He's on the college wrestling team."

"You lied to me," Frederick said.

"Oh, no I didn't," she reminded him. "Your imagination ran wild and I let it."

"Why?" he asked. "Am I such a bad guy?" Herbert would be proud to hear this.

"An excuse, I suppose," Chandra said. She hunched her shoulders. "I'd been looking for an excuse to move out for a long time."

"Were you?" He felt his heart give an alarming kick.

"I woke up last month and asked myself what the two of us had in common anymore, and do you know what the answer was, Freddy? Neither of us has ever had a broken bone. That was it."

"I see," he said. Her words stabbed him, but he forced himself to remain calm. He was tempted to tell her that, thanks to the fake address she gave Lillian, he was nearly disqualified in the broken bone category.

"You're letting your hair grow?" He nodded. "It looks good."

"Thanks." He cleared his throat. He wondered if he should ask, "Are you sure this is what you want?" But he said nothing. She kept on with her packing, rolling the silverware in sheets of newspaper.

"I'm nearly finished," she announced.

He refused to limp but walked instead into the living room. There were empty spaces all over the house, gaps where pictures had hung, where books had lounged, where furniture had crouched. She must have arrived just as he departed to have accomplished so much. Better yet, she must have been out there waiting, in her Conestoga moving van. It saddened him to know that she had taken up spying, this woman who vehemently hated the tactics of the CIA and the FBI. They had been married for almost twenty-one years and yet she would go to this trouble to avoid him. Frederick merely nodded as he looked at the empty spaces. He was surprised, and then saddened, that he couldn't remember what had been in them in the first place. He went immediately back to the kitchen and took out the bottle of gin, then the vermouth. He found what was left of the olives. It was time for lunch, and why spoil that by Chandra's sudden appearance? He carefully made up a nice pitcher of martinis. He could feel her eyes as sure as if she were touching him. He smiled, and sipped at the first glassful.

"Well, well," said Chandra. "Doesn't this interfere with your work, this nipping early in the day?" Frederick waved his hand as if to say it was nothing, a mere trifle. He imagined Kenny Perkins, D.V.M., waving in just such a debonair manner.

"Happy packing," he told her, and then fetched up the pitcher. He carried it down to the den, flicked the VCR on, rewound the tape he'd inserted that morning, and then plopped down on the sofa to watch a taping of that day's "Sally Jessy Raphael." The Ku Klux Klan had managed to find a few members with IQs as high as seventy, and had sent them forth to be viewed by the nation as their best and finest. Frederick punched at the remote-control button until their voices were barely audible. From the kitchen he heard the ruffle of newspaper as she continued packing, a gentle crinkling.

It was impossible for him to concentrate on Sally's guests. For one thing, their bad grammar stung his ears. And their pale milky faces, their pointed heads—probably from wearing those hats—their wall-eyed glares at the camera suggested to him that they should widen the community gene pool. In short, he felt as though he were watching a lineup of extras for the movie *Deliverance*. He turned off the VCR. Two more movers, like bent gnomes, shuffled down the stairs with a chest of drawers and disappeared out the front door. When they returned Chandra gave them further instructions and they came for the ottoman, upon which Frederick was resting his sore ankle. He lifted his feet and gave it to them freely.

"Sorry," the older gnome muttered, but Frederick merely gestured good-naturedly with his martini. Did Kenny Perkins drink?

"Not to worry," he told the movers. "The sofa's mine."

In his office, he flipped the button on the surge suppressor. His computer began its sweet language of clicks and then beeps as the hard drive spun toward 1,200 rpm. Had it really been four long days since he'd turned the thing on? As Herbert Stone had been freely advising him, he *needed to get a grip*. He needed to let his anger surface so that it could root. How could she wake up one morning and leave, as if twenty-one years had never happened? How could she cut him loose, without a phone call, a letter, as though he were some unwanted balloon? What had he ever done that he deserved such malignity? But these things happened. Spouses sometimes just went crazy. He knew this from his television-watching of the past five weeks—and he was not a tad embarrassed that he'd taken up television. Let Chandra think what she wished. It was no longer any of her business. Besides, Shakespeare would have watched "Geraldo." What better way to experience the dementia of these poor souls without having to visit with them in their homes? And dementia was overflowing out there in Middle America, among the current-day Desdemonas and Iagos, there was no doubt about that. Frederick had seen a veritable parade of sick and hurting humanity pass by as he sat on his own sofa and drank his martini lunch every day at eleven o'clock, his feet on *her* ottoman. He had learned about siblings abusing siblings, satanic cults raising stolen babies as members, sisters who sleep with their brothers-in-law, child pornography, husbands who cheat with their secretaries, men who bed down their mothers-in-law, parents of murdered children, children of murdered parents, folks with Lyme disease, folks with AIDS, folks with multiple personality, folks with amnesia. Frederick Stone had seen it all on television.

He looked now at another screen, the blue face of his beloved computer, blue as a Cyclops eye. Did it recognize him, with his longer hair and pale, brooding face? Did it acknowledge the cool fingertips on the keyboard as *his* fingers? He pulled up the McMurtry Landscaping account. There had been a message from Frank McMurtry just that morning that McMurtry Landscaping was forced to find another accounting firm. A little something about Stone Accounting filing taxes late *and* missing the payroll deadline. Frederick felt saddened by this, but the sadness seemed detached, floating somewhere near him, not particularly affecting his life. Frank McMurtry was a good man. He would miss him. Good-bye, Frank. Chandra appeared suddenly in the office doorway.

"This is how I imagine you, when I think of you," she told him. "Sitting just as you are, in front of your computer. Have you even moved from the thing since I've been gone?" He looked up at her and smiled. Had he moved? He had rushed speeding through a red light; he had driven up and down endless streets; he had dodged Budgie *and* a Conestoga at Joyce's; he'd been to Panama Red's and The China Boat so many times that the man who fills the cigarette machine knew his name; he had gone barefoot for olives and gin; he had tackled his own nephew from behind a lilac bush; and he had *moved* through space, as time does, *unintelligently*, his arms and legs flailing over on Bobbin Road for just a glimpse of her. Had he even moved? her majesty wondered? Yes, by crimminy, he had moved a fucking lot.

"Not much," he answered her. McMurtry Landscaping was becoming a blur in front of his eyes. Was he crying? He mustn't cry. He heard her walk away, heard the sounds of paper bags lifting. He imagined that she had just flung her purse strap over her shoulder, as he had seen her do so often. Her footfalls came back down the hall to the office, stopped.

"If I leave you my new phone number, will you promise not to give it to Joyce?" she wanted to know. Frederick looked up, seemingly surprised to find her still there.

"Whatever," he said.

"I really don't want to hear from Joyce," Chandra began. "I had lunch with her on Friday and that's enough for a while. You know how annoying she can be." Frederick waved his martini at her before she could continue. It was becoming a perfect wand.

"Listen," he said. "I've been to dinner with Joyce and Reginald and I find them to be superb people. I'll be seeing a lot more of them and, quite frankly, it makes me uncomfortable to hear you belittle them." He thought of Joyce patting Robbie's arm at Panama Red's. The nefarious witch! But then he remembered: Joyce was Robbie's mother, for crying out loud! Frederick's emotions were now like a ball of yarn that's been on the floor with a cat. His emotions were all tangled up. He didn't know who to be jealous of anymore, who to hate, who to love. The whole world was beginning to look like one big ambush.

"*The* Joyce and Reginald that *I* know?" Chandra seemed shocked. "She never mentioned this."

"Reginald and I have been talking about a little business venture together," Frederick added. "Our natural resources won't last forever, as you know only too well."

"*My* sister?" Chandra prodded in disbelief.

"A fine woman." Frederick nodded. "Makes a superb vegetarian lasagna. Reginald is one of the best history teachers this state has ever seen, and Teddy is a solid young man who practices safe sex. I feel enlightened just to be near them." Chandra watched him carefully. He could feel this, her eyes on his face, reading him;

she'd done it many times in twenty-one years. He concentrated on McMurtry Landscaping.

"Well," she concluded. "Maybe they'll change their minds about you now that you've assaulted their eldest son." Frederick merely shrugged—there was no need to bog things down with mention of Joyce's phone call. He paid attention instead to the figures before him on the screen. It had been a good month for Frank McMurtry, what with summer firmly ensconced and all. "I'll leave my number posted to the fridge. It's unlisted." She waited. He wondered what she had expected to find. An angry Frederick Stone? A Frederick Stone ready to slit his wrists in an upstairs bathtub, sticky red blood all over the tiled floor? A Frederick Stone ready to forgive and forget on any terms? Didn't she realize that there were fissures now in his psyche? Cracks large enough for one to drive through comfortably in a Mack truck? Couldn't she see that he had *grown?*

"Fine," he said. He heard her footfalls flowing down the hall and into the kitchen. Panic rose in his chest. Again, he had wanted so badly to hold her, to bury his nose into the perfumey smell of her hair, to have her face nestle into his neck. She'd been wearing those faded jeans, what she called her gardening jeans, and the old flannel shirt she seemed to have been born in. Such familiar things to him, suddenly, these items of clothing. He had wanted to release the ponytail from its elastic band, unbutton the flannel shirt, hold her cool breast in his warm hand. *The breasts are paired mammary glands on the front of the chest, composed of fatty tissues and glands.*

"Not now, Mr. Bator, for Christ's sake," Frederick snapped. "Can't you see what's going on here? Besides, where have you been for four days, when I *really* needed you?" He had wanted to promise her anything if only she'd come back. But he had seen a show just the day before that had changed his mind: Men Who Chase Women Too Much, and the Women Who Despise Them for It. Frederick couldn't remember now whose show it had been, only that he had never seen so many sniveling, whining males in his life. Two of them had even sobbed, broken down on national television, begged for their women to return. It was disgusting. Frederick thought of his own desperate attempts to find Chandra. What if he had caught the Toyota that afternoon, just weeks ago? He would have dropped to his knees on State Street, amid the seagull shit, and pleaded with her to return, wouldn't he? How many nights would he have called her, if she hadn't moved away from Marion's house, and implored her to return? The universe, the cosmos, something must have had a hand in preventing him from reaching her and becoming just another mewling wimp. He gave no credit whatsoever to The Girls, those three feminist bitches who had once been his friends. He sighed again, in pure relief.

When he heard the moving van pull away, followed by the loud muffler on the Toyota, he crept gingerly to the window and lifted the curtain. He wanted to make sure she wouldn't see him. Once, she did turn to look back at the house, sorrowfully, he thought. He watched as the big orange and white van cut the corner, Chandra following close behind, and then he went directly to the kitchen. His martini still in hand—lunch must be almost over since the pitcher was nearly empty—he found the Post-it note with the new number on it. He stared at it only briefly, afraid he may remember it otherwise.

"Don't you dare memorize it, Mr. Bator," Frederick warned. Just days ago, he would have killed for Chandra's new number. More tears weighted his eyes. He must destroy the Post-it quickly, because of those times up ahead when he would ache badly to hear her voice. He had promised himself, after watching those Men Who Chase Women, after seeing the disdain of the Women Who Despise Them for It, that he would not come begging to her. It was she who left, after all. Let her make the first moves of reconciliation. If such moves were possible.

While the martini courage coursed through his veins, Frederick found a book of matches. He struck one and watched as it flared up nicely. His eyes still teary—she had looked so damn beautiful—he dipped the corner of the green Post-It to the flame.

"I am not a *wimp,*" Frederick stated firmly. He wondered if George Bush would have the balls to burn Bar's phone number, under the same circumstances. He grimaced painfully as the fire ate into the green paper and Chandra's new number, all seven lovely digits, disappeared in its wake.

It was almost six o'clock when Frederick realized that he had not bothered to bring in that day's newspaper. He finally found the thing on the corner of lawn near Mrs. Prather's fence. Was the goddamn paper boy myopic as well as uncoordinated? Raggedy Andy could run a more orderly route. He was about to take the paper back into his house when he heard Walter Muller's car turn into the yard next door. If he walked across the lawn now, Walter would undoubtedly see him. Perhaps if he just stood, unmoving and treelike, he would go unnoticed. He froze there, paper in arms. Walter got out and slammed his car door. He spotted Frederick immediately and waved. Then he inhaled a large breath of air, released it dramatically.

"Isn't this a lovely evening, Frederick?" Walter implored. "My, my, but this is a fine time of year. A wonderful time of year. Probably my favorite time of all."

"Beam him up, *please, Scotty,*" Frederick whispered. He nodded at Walter.

"Mrs. Muller and I were talking about you just this morning, Frederick," Walter continued. He cleared his throat lustily, and then spat the result next to one of his rosebushes. "Anytime you'd like a home-cooked meal, just tap on the back door." Jesus. They'd be tying red handkerchiefs to all the bushes on Ellsboro Street before it was over. There'd be a hot meal for an honest man down on his marital luck wherever Frederick turned. And couldn't he use the *front* door?

"I'm on a diet," Frederick said, and heard what might be classified as a *neighborly tsk* in response. He waved auf Wiedersehen at Walter Muller—surely all Mullers were descended from German millers—in what he hoped was a *neighborly fashion,* although he had no idea what that was. Chandra had always accused him of waving like the Queen of England, with that little constrained gesture that the royals used—Frederick assumed they had all gone to The Royal Wave School—the hand oscillating robotically above a restricted elbow. Now, *there* was an anal retentive bunch. Larry, Doris's friend, should be butler to the House of Windsor for a time.

"I was telling Mrs. Muller just this morning," Walter bulldozed on, "that I always used to see a light burning in your office when I got up in the mornings. Nowadays, I just don't see it." Frederick was nearly speechless. How childish and competitive of Walter Muller to even notice such a thing! So what if Frederick had mentioned—and this had been eons ago—that he found working at home more advantageous than working in the city, as Walter did. How infantile of the man!

"I've been keeping my blinds closed," Frederick lied, and then pivoted on his heel, away from his neighbor.

He was about to retreat back inside the house, had his fingers safely on the knob, when he heard his name called. From out of the deepening shadows of lawn and mailbox and shrubbery, the outline of a woman emerged, Venus from her clamshell. His heart kicked against his rib cage. It was the female prerogative, according to the old saw, to change one's mind. He felt almost giddy, detached, the way he did as a child playing Kick the Can with Richard Hamel and the gang, and the opportunity to kick finally gave itself up to him. Running to the can was a slow-motion job, his arms rising softly into the evening air, falling, his knees lifting, legs thrusting outward; and there would be Richard Hamel emerging unexpectedly into the line of vision, running too, legs and arms rising and falling, too. And then, that precious moment when he felt his toe move backward inside his shoe on impact, saw the can rise and spin and shine in the moonlight. A lifetime—he knew this—had just taken place. And it was such a sweet lifetime, this lifetime of victory, that he had often wondered, as he walked home tossing the silver can up into the air over and over again, as though it were a magnificent coin, he wondered how the future could ever top it. Now he knew. This was how. Chandra had come home.

"Frederick? Is that you?" He recognized the voice a second before he saw the face: Doris Bowen. "I'm so glad that phone books list addresses," she told him, her words followed by the incessant heels, clicking like a ticker-tape machine up the paved walk. Doris Bowen. Money walking. Liquid gold.

"Doris." He nodded, then moved aside so that she could sashay past.

Frederick made them a pitcher of martinis while Doris walked about in white cotton slacks, a white cotton sweater, and surveyed all the empty spaces that Chandra had left behind. Frederick wasn't comfortable with this inspection of his barracks. He felt as though his entrails had been nailed to each blank wall, each swath of floor that had once known a stick of furniture. And now here was an outsider strutting about as though the living room was an art gallery.

Doris accepted the martini and they arranged themselves on opposite ends of the sofa.

"It was sort of like this with me and Ricky," she told him, "except I was the one to leave and, well, after all, I left for a multimillionaire. I took nothing with me. Everything I owned was too shabby." She shook her head in amusement, remembering.

"Do you miss him?" Frederick asked. "Ricky, I mean?" He waited. Somehow, her answer would pertain cosmically to him, to Frederick Stone, to his estranged relationship with Chandra. If Doris missed Ricky, then perhaps Chandra missed Frederick. Do women pine for the men they leave behind? This would make a great "Sally Jessy Raphael."

"No," Doris answered quickly. "No, quite frankly, I don't miss him." Frederick sighed.

"I mean, like on your birthday, or his birthday, or at Thanksgiving when the whole family gathers." Doris thought about this in greater depth. "Maybe you miss him when you carve the turkey?"

"No," she said. "I don't."

"Oh, come on," Frederick urged. "Surely there are times when you hear a song that used to be *your* song, yours and Ricky's, and you miss him just a little." Doris was gracious enough to give the notion even further thought.

"No," she said. "I can't say that I do."

"Let's say you're walking along the ocean and you remember how the two of you used to walk there. Or you see the snow falling just so, and you remember your first snowball fight." He felt his eyes tear up. "Or you smell strawberries on a warm summer's day and it brings back a scene from twenty years ago, a loving scene, with Ricky in it. Don't tell me that these things happen only in Ingmar Bergman films, Doris. You must miss him *once in a while*." He tipped his martini and was not surprised at how easily it slid down his throat. Goddamn women. And they were supposed to be the sentimental sex.

Doris leaned over and took his glass. She placed it beside hers on the living-room floor. The coffee table, being Chandra's, was no longer there. Then she eased her rear down the length of the sofa until she was sitting next to him.

"Do you know who I think of when I walk along the ocean?" Doris asked. She reached over and undid the top button of his shirt. "I think of you. And do you know who I'd think of if it was snowing?" She undid another button. "I'd think of you." She undid the last button. Frederick watched her lips moving, thick, full lips, the pumped-up kind that so many women were buying these days from plastic surgeons. He imagined that, one day, nursing homes in Hollywood would be full of wrinkly little women with monstrous lips. Chandra's mouth, however, had been that sweet little oval, the kind one sees painted on porcelain dolls. "And when I smell strawberries," Doris continued as she eased his arms out of his shirt, "I think of us having sugared ones for breakfast, in a huge canopied bed, with the rain coming down in torrents, and a fire snapping in the fireplace." She pulled his T-shirt over his head and tossed it onto the floor. Frederick looked down at his bare white chest. Unlike the hair on his head, the chest hairs weren't plentiful enough to recede. There were still a few straggling about in the gully on his breastplate—Death Valley— discussing whether or not they should spread out. But they'd been talking about just that sort of thing since high school and had yet to do anything about it. Doris ran a finger about his left nipple and Frederick felt it harden instantly in a rush of blood.

There goes the Bowen account, he thought, and closed his eyes as her lips descended upon his neck. It was true that he found her immensely attractive, sexy. And with all that money, well, there was another dimension that had not existed with the other women he had slept with, before Chandra. It had not existed with Chandra herself. The new element was this dimension of power, of wealth, and now Frederick trembled beside the very thought of it. He had had a lifetime of women in long faded skirts, women who couldn't wait for their hair to turn gray so that they could show the world how they refuse to dye it, who drove Volkswagens with dented fenders, who stuck candles into empty wine bottles, who used cement blocks to build bookshelves, who always bought ginger root at the market, who kept a box of Orange-Pekoe tea bags in their cupboards and far too much incense on their coffee tables. Before he married, Frederick had awakened in canopied beds where he looked up to see wind chimes circling like doves above him, prints on the walls from Picasso's Blue Period, Goya's Black Period, jeering posters from Joe McCarthy's Red Period, heaps of turquoise jewelry lying on a dresser, the soft low moans of *Abbey Road* filtering in from another room of the house, from another couple's bed. *Happiness Is a Warm Gun.* He felt Doris urging his hand beneath the cotton sweater and then up to her breast. The breast was sleek, almost slippery, and he imagined that's how store-bought breasts must feel. He tried not to concentrate on the silicone, or the fact that he was holding a handful of the stuff. It wasn't radioactive after all. Ralph Nader would be anti-tits if it was. Doris's tongue seemed to explode in his mouth, prodding here and there. Protective of his gold filling, Frederick edged his own tongue out defensively to block her move. She moaned a response as she pulled him down beside her on the sofa. But at least his filling was safe. Was this how the term *gold digger* had started? But then, Doris had enough gold to fill all the teeth in Portland, Maine. He moved his head back, away from her wildly probing tongue, which seemed to be ubiquitous. It came at his own tongue from behind molars and out of wet crevices. This had to be another slice of the "more is better" philosophy. He thought suddenly of Larry and his boiled beef tongue. This was followed by an acrobatic tumble in his stomach. He separated his lips from Doris's in a savage smack.

"Do you ever think of Ricky at *Christmas?*" he asked. Poor Ricky. Poor bastard. Doris undid the zipper on his pants and pushed them down on his hips before he realized what was happening. Did young girls practice on zippers the way young boys practiced on bra snaps? Doris slipped out of her white slacks and then the white sweater. They landed in soft clouds on the living-room floor.

"I *never* think of Ricky at Christmas," Doris whispered as she searched for the front opening of Frederick's shorts. "Why remember a Sears toaster when you're unwrapping diamonds?" She eased a warm hand inside and seemed as surprised as Frederick to find a genuine erection growing there. "Let's just put this on," he heard Doris say. She had produced a condom from thin air, this female Houdini, this Seeress of Safe Sex. Bless her. He was so rusty on matters of the boudoir that he couldn't remember the last time he'd bought a condom, only that it had cost a quarter and had ridges of some kind encircling the tip. That had been Frederick's Ridged Period. He positioned himself on his elbows as Doris helped to maneuver him inside her. This was the part he liked, the woman taking charge. He had had his share of these women from the sixties. They might have worn baggy skirts and let their hair turn gray, but they kicked ass when it came to a woman's rights. Even if they didn't want them, they still demanded them.

"Oh, Fred," said Doris, and rolled her head about on the sofa. "Oh, Fred." He was amazed at how hard he had become. It had been almost twenty-three years since he'd made love to anyone but Chandra. And Doris was sexy, yes, but he certainly didn't love her. He still loved his wife and yet he was able to engage sexually with this near-stranger. This was another separation of the sexes: Men could procreate with broken hearts, but women would die out. Men were capable of siring large families at funeral services, teetering on the very cusp of a dead wife's grave. Frederick smiled in victory, the way he had smiled when kicking the can out from under Richard Hamel's nose, all those Ingmar Bergman years ago, and now his legs felt like they were running again, his thighs on fire, his hip muscles rising and falling, rising and falling, his *great wings beating still above the staggering girl*. He heard Doris gurgle, from somewhere far away, rising and falling. Then she bit firmly on his neck. As Frederick struggled desperately to accept the metaphysics of a hickey at forty-four, Doris bit him again, much too hard this time.

"Ouch," he complained. Passion used to transform pain for him, didn't it? Elevate it to another threshold? Early on in their relationship Chandra had always bitten much harder than this, and he had loved it, had risen above the stinging in some Zenlike way, had ridden along on its crest. Now, at forty-four, he was concerned only with permanent scarring. Not to mention a severe infection. Doris bit him a third time.

"Ouch!" Frederick repeated, more forcefully. He couldn't risk another trip to the emergency clinic. They hated him down there, he was sure of it. The receptionist probably had his picture on the wall by the water fountain. *Have You Seen This Man?* But Doris seemed to have delivered her quota of nibbles for the evening. She returned to tossing her head about on the sofa and murmuring his name. Frederick forgot entirely about the smarting on his neck and concentrated instead on what he was doing. He and Chandra hadn't made love in months. He had almost forgotten the hot excitement of sexual desire. *During sexual excitement the extremely flexible tissues of the penis become engorged with blood and the usually flaccid organ assumes a rigid, enlarged position known as an erection.*

"NOT NOW, MR. BATOR!" Frederick screamed. Doris reached a hand up to caress his throat, to offer her support, but Frederick had stopped rocking, had missed the goddamn tin can altogether, had fallen on his ass from midair. He rolled onto his side.

"You call it *Mr. Bator?*" Doris giggled. "How sweet." She began stroking his back, consoling him with her encouraging touch, Earth Goddess to the Flaccid. Frederick shook his head, his breath still coming in great puffs.

"Mr. Bator's an old friend," he panted.

"I bet he is." Doris giggled again. "Can I be Mr. Bator's friend, too?" She moved her hand against the limp penis. "See you later, Mr. Bator. Not for a while, crocodile." Frederick pushed her hand away.

"Doris, please," he said. He was thinking again of Chandra, of that night at The Fiddler's Cave, of how they sang "Mrs. Robinson." He remembered now that they had toasted Joe Dimaggio, because the words of the song reminded them of how Marilyn had broken his loving heart. Poor Joltin' Joe. Poor son-of-a-gun. Then they had walked against the rain back to his apartment, full of Chianti and love and hope. That had been their first night together in bed, and it had been better than kicking a can away from Richard Hamel. It had been lots better. He had had big moments in his life, hadn't he? Great moments? He just didn't have the eyes to see them, the ears to hear them. *Every ejaculation contains several million sperm cells,* Mr. Bator said gently, *but only one of these can fertilize the female egg, resulting in a new human being.* Tears sprang again to Frederick's eyes.

"What would I know about ejaculations, Mr. Bator," he cried out, "with you sitting on my goddamn shoulder?" He swung a clenched fist at the air above his head. Doris glanced fearfully between his legs, then up to his shoulder.

"Is this like that movie *The Shining,* when the little boy talks to his finger?" Doris asked. *All the other sperm cells die in a few days,* Mr. Bator added, and now the tears were spilling from Frederick's eyes, trickling down the sides of his face. All those potential brothers and sisters, dead. What a great pinwheel they would have made! What a fireworks of a family! He was openly sobbing. Would Doris hate him for being such a wimp? He didn't care. He was a human being who had emerged one passionate night—he only supposed it was nighttime—as the result of his father's body coming together with his mother's body. Had they grown to hate each other early? Was he born of someone's teeth gritting, someone's clenched knuckles, someone's anger? Did his father's indifferent beak, like Zeus's, catch his terrified mother up in a crunching of bone? Was he, Frederick Stone, hatched from a bright blue egg, the same egg that had dropped like a tiny gum ball from Leda's body? He knew only the basic facts. His father had come home from World War II, bought a new ranch-style house, and settled down in it with his young wife. And one night Frederick had made it, from out of all those other sperm, all that sibling rivalry. He had run for the tin can and had gotten the gold instead, what with several million Richard Hamels running beside him. He had won. He was alive.

"Doris, I'm so sorry," he wept. He had images of Chandra and her jolly elves moving pieces of his life out onto the sidewalk.

"I'm not giving up yet," he heard Doris say. She was wearing her white slacks again, was fumbling about with her white cotton sweater. "You, me, and Mr. Bator are going to take a rain check. You might call it a ménage à trois." She bent and kissed the tip of his nose. From beneath her elbow, Frederick could see a long white thread dangling from her sleeve. He wondered what the Sluts of Kismet had in store for him, now that they'd stripped him of his manhood. He theorized about the thread Clotho would pull from her sewing basket, the one with his name on it, maybe the very one dangling from Doris Bowen's sweater. How long would it be? How thick? How strong? Would it represent the Bowen account? His ill-fated marriage? More important, had the Vaginas of Destiny fixed it so that he could never make love to another woman? He had read somewhere that Joe Dimaggio still sent a rose every single day to Marilyn's grave. Some women you can never forget. Was Chandra's image now glued to his wavering eyelids? It was most certainly there. The smell of her thighs was lingering like fresh Swedish strawberries in his nostrils, and the incessant beat of that old Boston rain was still sounding in his ears. He had seen so little, heard so little in his life. There had been exalted moments, seconds fit for a king, but his address had been on the outskirts of humanity, too far out for deliveries. Doris was kneeling beside him.

"I love a man who cries," she announced, wiping sweat from the meager hairs on his chest. Perhaps this pitiful watering would encourage a sprouting. "Men who cry turn me on." She blew into his ear.

"Doris, I'm really sorry," Frederick began, but she stopped him.

"Don't apologize for male sensitivity, Fred," she scolded him. "There's not a lot of it left in the world. You could ask Arthur, but he's in Scotland killing grouse. Now I gotta run." Frederick grabbed up his pants and yanked them on. At the door, he accepted Doris's little hug as genuine.

"She's been gone six weeks," he explained, "but I guess it was seeing her move out all her stuff."

On the front steps Doris surveyed the darkening neighborhood and then took a deep breath.

"I guess her stuff wasn't too shabby to take with her," she said. "Like my stuff was. But she left the most valuable thing behind." Frederick kissed her hand—a silly thing, when he thought of it later, almost too cavalier—and then she was gone, back into the neighborhood smell of marigolds and the sound of bug zappers.

He waited until the blue Mercedes pulled away from the curb and disappeared down the street before he turned out the porch light. He hoped he could find the strength to climb the stairs to the marriage bed, since it was a piece of furniture that belonged to *him*. He had decided earlier in the evening that it was time to move off the Shakespearean settee in his office and back to the comfortable field of the king-size mattress. Even eunuchs deserved a bit of sleep. And, on that perpetual advice pouring in from Herbert Stone, Frederick had to *get a grip*. That was when he heard Walter Muller's dog bark, a large volley of lusty yaps, which caused him to peer out the den window at the front yard. Was Supercop Muller lurking out there with a camcorder? A bag of doughnuts? Instead, Frederick saw the same brown car—a Chevy, he decided—pull away from the curb on Ellsboro Street and rush off into the night.

*T*hirteen

Within the prison walls of my mind
There's still a part of you left behind
And though it hurts I'll get by
Without your love and yet I
Guess there's just no getting over you.

—GARY PUCKETT & THE UNION GAP

or a full week after Chandra and her furniture left the house on Ellsboro Street, Frederick saw no one, not even the brown sedan that had been following him. At first he hadn't wanted to be alone. Shortly after Doris Bowen had pulled on her cloudy pants and skipped the white fantastic out of the seedy part of town, Frederick had experienced an immense need to be near people, even if it was the boisterous inhumanity at The China Boat. He had managed to catch the roving veterinarian, his brother, Herbert Stone, on his migratory car phone. "It didn't work out with Christine, the couch potato," Herbert Stone had announced before Frederick could mention Chandra and her elflike movers. "Foreplay was only allowed during commercials. But I got a sweltering date with a little temptress named Natalie." Frederick had said nothing about the newest crisis in his life. When Herbert surfaced again, two days later, Frederick was not interested in an evening out. He himself had a date, not with one little temptress but three: the Whores of Predestination. And he had no intention at all of wearing a condom. "I just need a few days alone," he had told Herbert.

Instead, he spent seven such days. As The China Boat was cosmopolitan enough to make deliveries, he phoned nightly for his dinner and then passed the evening sitting on the sprawling screened-in porch as neighborhood children roller-skated up and down the street. He watched lots of television. On the third day he turned the answering machine down so that he didn't have to listen as clients called in to cancel their accounts.

During the long painful nights, his hair grew silently. Unable to sleep, he lay awake and listened, hoping to hear the tiny muscles erecting the follicles, the follicles themselves secreting sebum. "Hubris, Freddy," Chandra used to tell him. "You care too much about your damn hair." Well, it was a good thing, he told himself, on those long black nights, when only the light from Mrs. Prather's porch seeped into the master bedroom. His hair was the only living thing he could draw comfort from, in the sparsely furnished house on Ellsboro Street. His hair was his only friend. Unlike Mr. Bator, it did not appear and then disappear. Unlike Herbert Stone, it was steady, unfailing, at least for the present. And he wondered if Chandra Kimball-Stone, the Queen of Humility, might resort to a speck of hubris if she herself awoke one morning to discover her hairline in remission.

Anger was becoming his friend. At least, he and anger were now acquaintances, and he felt a peculiar strength in this. With indignation as his ally, he could begin the journey back, that horrible crusade that would take him into the whirling vortex of his life. So, on each of those endless nights when Frederick Stone opened his eyes to the mottled light flickering on his ceiling, he tore away a bit of the gauze with which he'd cleverly wrapped up his past. He opened that newly formed fissure just a bit more. He reminisced, is what he did. He thought of the Christmas party Chandra had given the year before. He had excused himself early in order to explore a new spreadsheet update that had finally arrived. He was eager to see how he could improve his customers' cost projections. He imagined the updated presentations would be close to dazzling. "Promise you won't run off to that damn computer?" Chandra had asked just before the guests arrived. And he had promised. But then UPS, that chariot of the gods, had swooped up to his door with a package from Midwest Micro Peripherals. Would any computer-loving soul blame him?

And then there was her nephew's graduation from high school. Which rude lump had it been? Robbie, no doubt, because Con-

dom Boy was currently still matriculating in high school. Having
had the opportunity of late to know Robbie better, Frederick was
thankful he had missed the event. He had always hated gradua-
tions anyway, including his own, so why should he attend the
ceremony for one of Joyce's mutations? Dr. Philip Stone had not
materialized at his son Frederick's graduation. He had been invited
to be the guest speaker at an orthodontist convention in St. Louis.
Lying in the darkness of his bedroom, Frederick could remember
the class colors, green and gold, could even see all the streamers
flying like a perfect pinwheel. What had the class motto been?
Finished, Yet Beginning. Jesus. Thinking back to the problems that
his generation had faced, the brutal knives of war and poverty and
racism, it should have been *Angst Now, Angst Forever.* He wondered about the problems facing today's generation and guessed
that, at least for the underprivileged, the problems were still the
knives of war, poverty, and racism.

   Then there had been the time Chandra Kimball-Stone was presented with a humanitarian award from some subterranean group
called Curators of the Mother Soil, or some such. "What are
they?" Frederick had asked. "Earthworms?" But to hear Chandra
talk she was on her way to Stockholm to pick up a Nobel. In
reality, The Renaissance Teahouse was host to the awards ban-
quet. The event would last most of the day, beginning with
brunch, speeches, then lunch, another speech or two, more presentations, more calls for environmental change, everyone would
go to the bathroom, more speeches, a couple token presentations
for the organizers, then Chandra's presentation, then dinner, then
special thanks to the waiters and waitresses who were so kind to
spend their day carting dishes about, then everyone would go to
the bathroom again, and then everyone would finally go home. At
least this is how Frederick imagined the day would unfold. What
had he been doing that he couldn't attend? Oh yes, the Grossmire
account had presented him with an unexpected difficulty: The IRS
was investigating Grossmire Imports and Frederick was obliged to
sit down with James Grossmire and carefully inspect canceled
checks, receipts, deductions. Frederick had cautioned about those
excursions to Atlantic City, which Mr. Grossmire had insisted on
deducting as business trips because he brought his pretty young
secretary along. Frederick had also warned him about the numer-

ous business lunches and dinners, all of which seemed to occur at isolated little inns and motels, a safe marital distance from Mrs. Grossmire *and* the Portland business community. When it hit the fan, Frederick was obliged to see if he might find a way of turning off said fan and filtering through the windblown, shitty debris. James Grossmire was, after all, a heady client in terms of fees rendered to Stone Accounting. But Chandra couldn't seem to understand that. "What's one more day?" she had asked. "It's twenty-four hours," Frederick had answered. "That's a sizable amount of time when you consider that the IRS has given us only ten days to prepare. And I've got fifteen other clients whose payrolls need attending. Isn't someone going to videotape the event? We can watch it when you get home."

Those were his nights, coming at him with incident after incident from the past, nights bringing with them the knowledge that he had become his father, the man he had loathed and loved, and yet he had never even sensed it. His nights were not kind ones, but he spent his days—after a pleasant martini lunch—exploring the personality of the house, one that he never knew existed: the loose bottom step going down to the basement, the crack in the bathroom window, the spider hidden with its web beneath the fireplace mantle, the dustballs under the office settee, the peeling wallpaper over the kitchen sink, the wobbly hinge on the screen door leading to the front porch, a small print of Degas ballerinas. These were all new discoveries to him, and he was suddenly fascinated with their minute details. It had been Chandra who found and fell in love with this house. To him, it had been simply a means of shelter from extreme heat and extreme cold in a relatively safe area. Now he saw it as an interesting, kindly shell, just as his beetle neighbors had their own shells. This metaphor in mind, he perused the house as though its rooms were chambers of his own brain. The medulla, because it was located at the lowest point of the brain, would be the basement. The main floor, the one that sheltered his precious computer, would be the pituitary gland because, like a complex computer, the pituitary was the overlord of all other glands. The upstairs, where he had now returned to sleep and shower, would be the cerebellum, which spent its time thinking about body equilibrium and muscle coordination. Frederick enjoyed the idea of running from the cerebellum down to the pituitary, or stopping in now and then to see how the medulla was doing, down there in the basement. Every so often, especially in the mornings after he had just showered, he stopped in the hallway leading to the bathroom and stared up at the attic, that forbidding cerebrum. The steps leading up to the hatch door loomed before his eyes, separate lobes. Sure, he could run about in the lower parts of the house and feel comfortable. That's how he had lived most of his life, wasn't it? Or, as Chandra liked to say, that's how he had managed so cleverly to dwell on the outskirts of humanity. But the attic, the old cerebrum, Mr. Bator's pad, well, that was another thing altogether. Up there, feelings and emotions ran rampant. There were boxes of things up in the physical attic that Frederick thought he'd go his whole life without ever having to sort through. He knew there would be lots of pictures up there, scenes from his married life, because Chandra had told him she intended to leave such memorabilia behind. At least she hadn't drop-kicked everything out onto the lawn, as Thelma Stone had done, so that neighborhood children could break open their piggy banks in order to buy his rare-book collection. It wasn't so much the thought of all those pictures of his married life, of the two of them with their arms around each other, hands locked in love, eyes filled with their futures, that bothered him. But those boxes he couldn't see, the ones stacked evenly in the frontal lobes, those gave him great pause. In them were the feelings and emotions that he'd packed up years ago, like clothing that no longer fits, and put away to be forgotten. In the tangible boxes were his earliest school papers, his letters from his parents while at college, health records, yearbooks, school honors and awards, everything archaeologists would need in shaping a life for him, were they to unearth the attic in some distant millennium. In the invisible boxes were the things he had so foolishly tried to share with the geisha from The China Boat. PANDORA BOX COMPANY was stamped onto the bottoms of all *those* boxes.

A week into his hiatus Frederick was thinking that perhaps it was time to battle the attic boxes, taking with him a nice pitcher of martinis as a bodyguard, when someone rapped on the front door. He felt the nape of his neck tingle. It was a Tuesday, seven weeks since Chandra had left, if anyone was keeping track. Tuesdays used to mean grocery shopping, didn't they, in that other life he used to live? A tiny panic crept upon him. Could it be Doris Bowen again? He no longer gave a hoot about Bowen Developers or the massive account their business would mean. Doris was a pleasant, attractive woman but not one with whom Frederick cared to fraternize. Had she returned, in the grips of estrus, for her rain check? He felt his penis attempt a chin-up, then fail miserably. If Doris thinks she learned the meaning of the word *flaccid* last week, Frederick thought, a deeper education awaits her. But he opened the door to let a pale Herbert Stone into the kitchen. Frederick wasn't surprised. Herbert often surfaced from his dates with pubescent women looking as though he had the bends. And now that Herbert could boast a literary agent and an editor, heaven help the pretzel shape his psyche would end up in.

"I'd offer you a chair at the kitchen table," said Frederick, "but Chandra took the chairs *and* the table. It was a gift from her mother." Herbert leaned back against the sink, shifted about uneasily on the balls of his feet. Frederick put on a pot of coffee. "You don't look too good," he added.

"You look like hell yourself," Herbert said. "Have you been eating? You've got dark circles under your eyes. You remind me of the pet raccoon I treated last week."

"Did the raccoon's wife leave him?" Frederick asked.

"Freddy?" Herbert's restless feet seemed to be doing a little dance.

"Have you any idea how interesting the architecture of these old Victorian houses are?" Frederick probed. "So many ornate, flowery carvings." He handed Herbert a cup of black coffee, smiled genuinely. He had been instantly thankful to see Herbert Stone appear like some good omen in the kitchen door. If he hadn't, Frederick was determined to tiptoe up to the attic and open the musty boxes, the certificates, the letters, the photos, the melancholic notes of auld lang syne.

"Freddy?" Herbert said again, but Frederick didn't want to talk of things serious. And Herbert's tone indicated *things serious*. Maggie was probably hauling him back into court for some *extraneare* misdemeanor. Or perhaps he had impregnated a female who was still wearing a training bra.

"How about lunch today at Panama Red's?" Frederick asked. "We can talk about your problems then. Don't tell me, let me guess. Kevin Costner and Tom Cruise are fighting over who'll play Kenny Perkins, vet vet in a Corvette. Come on, Herb, I've been eating at home all week." He tried to pour more coffee into his brother's cup, but Herbert put out a shaky hand to stop him.

"Freddy," Herbert said. "Our mother has died."

The sun was setting over Panama City as the plane banked suddenly, causing Frederick's miniature scotch bottle to slide off the tray table and roll away on the floor below. Where were stewardesses when bottles were *empty?* He replaced the tray in the seat back and then leaned into the window to peer out. Far below he could see the magnificent white of the beach, a long dazzling shoelace. The Gulf of Mexico lay beyond the glittering sand, its shallow greens turning to a thickly blue as the water deepened. He had never liked the idea of his mother moving to Florida. She had vacationed there twice in her life, successfully, and it was this experience that convinced her to leave Maine after her husband's death. Now she had lived her own death, had swallowed enough pills to ensure her a lasting, unbroken sleep. No small sons playing war on the living-room floor, no bell on the ice cream truck, no loud pelting of rain, no lilting concerto would ever disturb her. Another lost coin in Florida's Fountain of Youth. Another streamer torn from the Stone pinwheel. But they would bring her back to Maine, her two sons, and put her into the earth there. Her only stipulation had been that she not lie next to her husband and all those other dead Stones in Woodlawn Cemetery. To assure this, she had purchased, shortly after moving to Florida, a nice little plot in another Portland cemetery, the one overlooking the clutch of pine and birch trees, the one where birdwatchers came to catch the spring warblers. So, like Hospitalers, like Knights Templar, Frederick and Herbert were coming to escort their mother home from her crusade. The following day, they would fly back to Portland, the coffin safely tucked into the belly of the plane, an embryo sleeping its fuzzy dream.

The taxi weaved so in traffic that Frederick thought he might be sick. Herbert had said little during the flight. He was her firstborn, after all. Frederick had always been a tad jealous of that unbreakable bond between Herbert and Thelma Stone. He had even imagined that the two had had a couple of relatively happy breast-feeding years until Frederick came along to create a threesome.

The condo looked the same as they had seen it last, typical, surrounded by planted flowers and shrubs. Frederick paid for the cab as Herbert patted about beneath a pink cement planter for the key.

"Here it is," Herbert said finally. "Right where Mr. Regis said it would be." Frederick felt instantly exhausted. He hoped he could find sleep in his mother's condo, a stranger's home. They had discussed it on the plane. They would flip for the guest room, and the loser would sleep on the couch. Neither was ready to plunk down on their mother's own bed. It was on this bed that the superintendent had found her. "We'll see what it's like," Herbert had offered on the flight down. "If it doesn't feel right, we'll go to a motel. Mr. Regis is meeting us for breakfast." Mr. Regis had been appointed executor of the will. Thelma Stone had not trusted either of her sons with such a delicate chore.

When they opened the door, the faintest smell of perfume hovered in the air, a scent of lilacs, and Frederick was reminded of his mother's lavender sachets. She had always hung them in closets, stuffed them beneath pillows, put them on laundry shelves, dangled them from nails in the basement. "Why are you trying to make the world smell good?" Dr. Philip Stone would ask. "Because the world stinks," Thelma Stone always assured him.

" 'When lilacs last in dooryard bloomed,' " Frederick said. Herbert hadn't moved. He stood looking about the room with the face of a child lost in a department store. *What's the matter, little boy? You lose your mother?* Frederick could see a glistening in his brother's eyes. He patted Herbert's arm. Herbert cleared his throat, shook off whatever memory was plaguing him.

"What a crazy thing for her to do," Herbert said, and Frederick nodded. He nodded, but he had been thinking about all kinds of ways to do himself in since Chandra left. Now, faced with the real McCoy, he realized that he'd been only playing martini games with himself. It was 1992, after all. You could buy a book to help you measure out the right pills, remind you to tighten the plastic bag over your head, make the best arrangements for your loved ones. Frederick believed in that book, but obviously his mother did not. According to Mr. Regis, she had left nothing behind as way of explanation, not even a tiny lavender sachet. But Frederick knew she had said it all the day she held her famous yard sale. "This is a *life* sale," she'd said.

"At least she left her little piece of the world smelling better," said Frederick. He kicked his foot at a single black shoe, lying on its side by the sofa. There were the usual houseplants, a few books, scattered dog toys. They had agreed to let Mr. Regis's daughter have the poodle. It seemed that Mr. Regis's daughter *loved* the poodle. The poodle *loved* Mr. Regis's daughter. A great sin would be committed in separating the two. And the poodle was neither son's idea of inherited treasure.

"It's funny," said Herbert, "but I thought about Mother a lot after Maggie and I got divorced. Wondered what she was doing, if she ever missed us, the old days, Polly, Dad." Frederick simply nodded. "I phoned her once a month, you know." Frederick nodded again. He did know. He had phoned her himself, several days earlier, in order to clear up an early mother-son conflict. *The tonshills are masses of spongy lymphoid tissue situated at the sides of the throat,* Mr. Bator whispered respectfully. A car pulled up to the condo next door and excited voices rose into the air, car doors slammed, then all was silent.

"I thought those monthly calls depressed you," Frederick said.

"They did," Herbert admitted. "She rarely wanted to talk. Usually answered my questions with yes or no. Sometimes she just hung up after a few minutes."

"She was sick," Frederick reminded him. She *was* sick, tormented by the same dark depression that had lived for so many generations in her family's genetic makeup. But there had been pills. She had felt better—at least Mr. Regis said so. When her bothersome sons left her alone, she even found a bit of pleasure in walks along the ocean, the poodle, in picture puzzles.

"I've just been thinking about the last time we saw her," Herbert said. Frederick didn't bother to nod this time. How could either he or Herbert forget the Mother's Day visit they had paid Thelma Stone? They hadn't seen her in almost four years. The trip was Herbert's idea. "She'll be glad we came, you wait and see," he'd told Frederick. Thelma had spent most of the afternoon out on the beach with her poodle, coddling it, allowing it to empty its bladder, chase a rawhide bone, bark at the laughing gulls. Her sons had waited inside, watching through the condo's bay window. It was the last time they would see her alive.

"Look at all these pictures," Herbert said now as they moved forward into the room. Frederick had just noticed them, too, and they overwhelmed him. Everywhere he looked were photos of their dead sister Polly: Polly on her first bicycle, Polly with her first dog, Polly on the way to her eighth-grade prom, Polly about to blow out sixteen candles, Polly as a cheerleader, Polly at her wedding, Polly, Polly, Polly.

"I didn't think they even liked each other," Frederick whispered hoarsely.

"Women stick together, even in death," Herbert replied. Frederick knew that his brother, Herbert Stone, had spent far too much time in divorce court. But Frederick himself wanted to know what had happened to all those snaps of the male Stones, nearly fifty years of photos, barrels of pictures.

"There isn't a single picture of any of us men in here," Frederick protested, pointing erratically around the room. "None of Father, none of us, none of the uncles, not even of her grandsons. Where could all those photos have gone?"

"She probably piled them on the beach," Herbert said, rubbing his finger across a dusty picture frame. Beneath the glass, and as though it were a transparent sepulcher, Polly was holding her baby daughter. "She probably sent a picture out each time a wave came in," Herbert added sadly. "We're all gone now. Gone to sea."

"Let's get a motel room," Frederick suggested.

⁀⁀

It would take them two days to make the preparations to bring Thelma Stone back to Maine. On the second day, one of the sunniest that even Florida could conjure up, they watched the coffin being loaded into the stomach of the plane. Frederick had bought sunglasses at an airport shop, rickety things that cost him twenty dollars. Standing there in his shades, with Herbert beside him, two aging men with dark rings of sweat under their arms, Frederick had felt almost foolish, as though he were in a scene from *Casablanca* that had wound up on the cutting-room floor.

"I'm the oldest in the family now," Herbert whispered as the empty hearse made a dramatic U-turn away from the plane and sped off. Frederick said nothing. He wasn't just next in line. He was *the only one* in line. He and Herbert shook Mr. Regis's hand in farewell and then went on a desperate search for the nearest lounge. Herbert's hands were trembling, and there was still time for a quick shot before the flight.

Just south of Boston they hit a tremendous rainstorm, which sincerely rocked the plane. Water raced across the windows in quick little streaks. Off in the distance, Frederick could see lightning erupt in magnificent veins, all sheer power and force, indifferent as to whether it blew the plane into fragments, indifferent as to whether everyone aboard would die. In the mind of the storm, all the passengers sitting up above in comfortable seats were no different from the passenger who rode below, in the coffin her sons had chosen for her, in her last, long, drowsy sleep. Frederick thought about Chandra Kimball-Stone, down there on the ground somewhere in Portland, Maine, scurrying about in her new life, unaware that he rode above the clouds in a fury of wind and rain. More turbulence struck the plane and a woman sitting somewhere behind them screamed. Frederick closed his eyes. They would be on the ground in twenty minutes, and it would all be over. He felt something cool touching his hand, seeking out his fingers. He opened his eyes and looked down. It was Herbert's hand, his big brother's hand.

"Damn it, Freddy," Herbert was saying as Frederick grasped the damp hand up into his own and squeezed it tightly. "She was only sixty-six years old."

When Frederick finally stood before his own door, at the Victorian house on Ellsboro Street, a special letter was waiting for him in his mailbox. He sniffed at it first, wondering if he would smell lilac seeping out from under the flap. It was a business envelope and had Chandra Kimball-Stone's name typed in the return corner. The address she listed was in care of the Portland Law firm of Lindsey, Vincent, & Gurley. *Dear Frederick,* she began. Well, that was friendly enough. He perused the letter quickly. She had obviously gotten all her linen put away, all her furniture arranged in the proper places, all the souvenir magnets attached to her new refrigerator, because now she was ready for the divorce. *I hate to have to do it this way, but I feel that it's best.* Along with her letter Frederick found a document politely referred to as "marital dissolution papers." He would only have to sign his signature, agreeing to split things evenly, fifty–fifty. That sounded fair to him. His overnight bag in one hand, he stuffed the letter into his shirt pocket with the other.

"Hasta la vista, O woman of my dreams," he mumbled as he let himself into the darkened house.

Fourteen

he funeral services could have been mistaken for a golf foursome, so tiny was the gathering: Frederick, Herbert, the priest, and old Mrs. Cary, who had lived next to the family Stone all those years of their growing up.

"I still use that lovely silver tea service I got from your mother's yard sale," Mrs. Cary confessed happily. She had puffed her way up the grassy hill to Thelma Stone's gravesite. Frederick had thought Mrs. Cary might also be among the dead, but he had looked in the phone book anyway, and there she was. He decided it was only fitting to let her know about Thelma Stone. After all, they had been friends for years. In fact, she had been Thelma Stone's *only* friend. And he felt good, now, to see her in attendance. Her son, Mrs. Cary announced with pride, was waiting for her in a car by the front gate.

Then Maggie Stone appeared, creating a fivesome. She looked good for a woman who spent every second of her day harassing Herbert, plotting outrages against him. At least this was Herbert's assessment of how Maggie passed her hours. She gave Frederick a quick little hug, which surprised him. "Maggie never liked you," Herbert had confessed. She had cut her hair short, and now it was frosted a soft blonde. She wore a neat cotton suit, the skirt quite short, at least for Maggie. She looked good, darn good, just as Chandra had looked good. Was this what a few weeks away from Stone men could do for one's constitution? Frederick sighed greatly, then hugged Maggie back.

"Is Chandra coming?" Maggie whispered, but Frederick shook his head. He had for a fleeting moment considered phoning Lillian and asking that she pass the sad news on to Chandra, but he had changed his mind. And he doubted that Chandra read the Portland obituaries. She was too busy reading marriage dissolution papers these days.

"Freddy's gonna say a few words," Herbert told the priest who had come at Herbert's bidding. Thelma Stone had been a Catholic the last time anyone could remember her going to church. The priest nodded. He appeared relieved. It was the first time Frederick had heard anything about his delivering a eulogy.

"Herb," he said. "I didn't prepare anything."

"That's okay," said Herbert. "Just wing it." Frederick thought about this. It was his mother's funeral. *Wing it? Wing it,* for Christ's sake?

"I don't know what to say," he protested. "Why didn't you tell me about this earlier?"

"Just say a poem," Herbert suggested. Frederick stared at his brother. He had a sudden urge to push Herbert into the gaping grave before them and cover him up with six feet of dirt. He would make sure that the blasted cellular phone did not get buried with him. He imagined irritating, late-night phone calls from Herbert. *You better get down here, Freddy. This place is crawling with nubility.*

"That's so like him," Maggie leaned toward Frederick and whispered. "I know, believe me."

Frederick looked down at the coffin before him. What could he say? "This is a life sale?" The aroma of the flowers sent over by Herbert's clinic rose up to meet him, and he imagined the smell of lilac. Could he say, "She was one who tried to make the world smell better, because the world stinks"? He took a deep breath, ran through the index file in his head of poems he had loved. This was not a time for Yeats's shuddering wall, so he decided upon something from the early work, although he could not remember the title or the entire poem. He remembered only the refrain, and that became his mother's eulogy.

" 'Come away, O human child,' " Frederick said, " 'To the waters and the wild, with a fairy hand in hand, for the world's more full of weeping than you can understand.' " His legs swayed suddenly beneath him and he felt as though he were standing on stilts. He heard Herbert sob, Maggie consoling her ex-husband. He wished he had called Chandra. But how could he have known it would be this difficult? How could he have known he was still not ready to let her go, this sleepy woman who wanted nothing more than that her sons be seen, not heard, and preferably neither. Now Maggie was comforting him, her hand warm on his arm, the soft sweet touch of a woman. He had missed this nurturing element, which Chandra had once provided, even if it was only to allow him, in bed, to hold her sleeping body. This kind of nourishment couldn't be supplied by Doris Bowen's touch, or her money, or her cool white pants that never seemed to dirty. Frederick took Maggie's hand in his, brought it up to his face, held its warmth against his cheek as though the hand were a pulsating little bird. He saw tears rush into Maggie Stone's eyes.

"Forgive me," Frederick whispered. Maggie was puzzled.

"For what?"

"For all those years of ignoring you," he answered. He remembered family gatherings when he may not have spoken more than a single word to her, a quick hello. He had never imagined that she possessed a mind he could find interesting. Now he saw in the cut of her hair, the style of the new cotton suit, a woman determined to change old patterns, get on with new patterns. He saw someone *strong,* and strong is what he himself wanted so desperately to be.

"Let's go for coffee," Maggie suggested. Herbert had dried his eyes on the tissue she had given him, and was now staring off at other graves, other human children who have gone to the waters and the wild.

"You two go," Frederick told them. "I have to clean the attic today."

He watched as they weaved their way among the gravestones, the priest in the lead and old Mrs. Cary bringing up the rear, their four heads disappearing finally below the horizon of headstone and hill. Vanishing, it seemed, into the very earth. On the opposite edge of the cemetery, a blue pickup sat waiting, sunlight glinting from its rearview mirror. Frederick could see cigarette smoke wafting from a side glass. The gravediggers were waiting for him to leave so that they could finish their job. He looked down at the huge hole near his feet, a bigger hole than she would ever need, the casket towering above it.

"Come away, O human child," Frederick said again. He kicked his toe at the ridge of the grave, and a small rivulet of ground and pebbles rolled down into the abyss. "For the world's more full of weeping than you can understand."

He had left the gravesite and was almost home when another wave, a perfect swell of loneliness, gripped him. He felt left out, abandoned, the way he had felt for every football game that Portland High ever played, with guys like Richard Hamel sweating and virile and envied in their grass-soiled uniforms, the cheerleaders going wild, their hormones tossing them farther into the air than they'd ever imagined, pure leaps and bounds of estrogen. And afterward, at the Casco Diner, the jukebox would bleat out songs like "This Diamond Ring," by Gary Lewis and the Playboys, or "It Hurts to Be in Love," by Gene Pitney, or "Yesterday," by the Beatles, or "The House of the Rising Sun," by the Animals. And it was all so wonderful because it *did,* it did *hurt* to be in love with Leslie Ann Doody, the head cheerleader. It hurt like hell to watch Richard Hamel leaning jauntily against the jukebox, like some soldier home from the war, still in his battle-soiled uniform, the protective cup beneath his pants subtly suggesting to the giggling cheerleaders who had gathered around him that the greatest mystery of their lives was still to unfold. As Frederick and the other Portland High *Bugle* staff sat off to the side in one of the less popular booths, the booths farthest from the jukebox and nearest the restrooms smelling of pee, he would find himself hypnotized by the display of Richard Hamel's engorged protective cup, those secretive laurels of war hiding beneath it, that special equipment that had outfitted Richard for the rigors of combat, yet had given Frederick Stone the kind of prowess it would take to edit the Portland High *Bugle,* to write unfinished love poems for

Leslie Ann. "Son, you just don't have the balls to stay alive in this sport," the coach had told him. "You don't have the killer instinct. Why don't you write for the paper? Join the glee club?" With a different mechanism in their genes, in their very Fruit of the Looms, Frederick and the other bugle boys had watched from their booth with its cracked red Naugahyde, had ogled the luscious cheerleaders, had assured themselves that they didn't care a whit, because the day would come when they would be publishers of magazines, famous poets and novelists, world-class journalists. And where would the Richard Hamels be? Where, pray tell, would the Richard Hamels be?

At the traffic light on State Street, the very place where he had chased after his wife, Chandra Kimball-Stone, Frederick turned the car around. Gulls rose and fell over the turquoise waters of Casco Bay. Sailboats were busy sailing. Tourists blended as well they could along the stretch of beach. A whole world was taking place without him. Frederick turned left, away from the ocean, climbed to the top of State, leveled, and then drove on down Ocean Drive, toward Cemetery Road. You had to bring a lot of bodies down a road, a lot of corpses, before it could be remembered as *Cemetery Road,* before a map finally listed it as such. A lot of dead people. That was just one more aspect of cartography, as well as of life.

At the cemetery, he saw their heads bobbing up and down like birds feeding, heard the crisp bite of their spades shoveling earth. They were no older than he, Frederick decided, maybe even younger. Had these two men dreamed, once, from a cracked Naugahyde booth, that they would head major newspapers, would write the best war novel, would have only the loveliest of women strung about their arms? Surely they hadn't longed, as children, to grow toward the day when they would bury the dead for the living. Had Burke and Hare dreamed, as small Irish schoolboys, of growing up to supply medical schools with murdered corpses? Where did a person's dream twist and coil backward on them? Where did a dream go wrong?

He had intended to sit in his car and watch, maybe even listen to the sounds of gravel being flung onto the casket, but he found himself graveside. Not even he knew anymore what he might do. Life had become one big mystery. The workers didn't hear him approaching, his footfalls lost upon the soft padding of graveyard grass.

"I only paid eight hundred bucks for it," one was saying, his words punctuated with a jab of the spade. "All it needs is a good tune-up."

"It'd look real good with chrome wheels," the other said. Frederick stood behind them, peering into what was left of the hole. The mixed aroma of fresh gladioli, of fresh earth, of fresh summer air was almost invigorating to him. Only bits of the casket could still be seen, a gray wood peeping through the earth here and there. When they turned to see him standing graveside, the shovelers stopped their work instantly. They leaned on their shovels, uneasy looks on their faces, men who expected to be caught for things they'd done years ago, jailed for childhood misdemeanors. Such is the terror of the underclass.

"We was told to finish up here," the one wearing a Red Sox cap said apologetically. Frederick wanted to put them at ease, to be friends with the men who had not only dug his mother's grave, but were now filling it up. He looked from one to the other. What could he say to them? *Come away, O Human Child?* Or *How about those Red Sox, huh?* He needn't tell these men that the world's more full of weeping than people like George Bush and Dan Quayle can understand. He needn't tell these men anything. He merely nodded. Then he reached a hand out, offering to shake, but the hatless man misread his intent. The hatless man, instead of shaking, passed Frederick his spade.

"Are you sure, man?" he asked Frederick warily.

For a second Frederick considered handing the spade back, explaining. But in his hands, the tool felt suddenly like a marvelous wand. He could sense a power in just gripping it, a secret that his ancestors had probably learned about a hard day's toil. *The mattock was a primary agricultural tool for Neolithic and ancient peoples around the world,* Mr. Bator reminded him. *It was used for the loosening of soil.* Frederick nodded at the hatless man. Men were meant to work with their hands, to use them in some kind of labor. Now he was no longer a bystander in his mother's death. He was included. He would not need to sit in the Naugahyde front seat of his car, as though it were a smelly booth at the Casco Diner, and watch this turn of events. He would participate.

He took off his suit jacket and tossed it onto the grass beside a flower arrangement. *Dearest Friend,* the banner read. It must have come from old Mrs. Cary. Frederick was glad that Mrs. Cary had grabbed up the silver tea service from the yard sale. What good was a silver tea service in the wash of a lifetime? He had read about Anglo-Saxon tribes who took all the belongings of a dead man, seized them from his widow, and piled them on the outskirts of town. Then the men mounted their horses and raced toward the booty, the winner taking all. That had been a kind of primitive yard sale, that dispersal of a man's life. Frederick understood, now, his mother's statement. "This is a life sale." Sometimes the two were interchangeable.

The hatless man sat back on the little hillside, wiped his brow, and then popped a cigarette out of its packet. He lit up. Smoke curled into the blue air, a sweet soft smell of tobacco, the way it must have smelled to those first settlers of Virginia, when tobacco was still considered a nice thing. With each spadeful of earth that he ladled up, Frederick silently offered a little mantra, a litany of good-byes to his mother. The man in the Red Sox cap went back to work, his spade biting the loose ground next to Frederick's, the *splat* of his earth sounding in harmony behind Frederick's own *splat* on the coffin's lid. They labored side by side, two sweating men. Two men getting a job done. Frederick wished that he was bilingual enough to speak the Language of the Male. They could chat about chrome wheels, and tune-ups, and the Red Sox. Could the three of them sit together over Budweisers, like real men do in those beer commercials, and toss back a cold one? Would it be a Kodak moment? Frederick could see himself peering into the black eye of the camera: *You know what I like to do once I've buried my mother?* he'd ask, and then the sound of a beer top popping, a slow fizzing noise. *I like to sit back and enjoy a cold Bud with my buddies.*

How could he know that this would be the place where it would occur? How could he ever guess that the bulwark of stored-up pain would crumble when it did, while he was hovering over his mother's grave? But it did. They had finished the covering, had patted the ground snugly into a nice mound. He had handed the spade back to the hatless man, and they had shook hands.

"I sure am sorry, man," the hatless one said. The other man tapped Frederick on the back, as though he were knocking at the door of some strange house.

"Hang in there, buddy," the Red Sox hat said. "I lost someone I loved, too. It ain't easy, brother, but you gotta do it." Frederick hated to see them go. In their words, in their quick little touches, had been the camaraderie of the sixties, that sense that he was part of the Family of Man. They had patted his back. They had shook his hand. They had called him *brother.*

As the pickup disappeared from the cemetery in a soft spray of pebbles, Frederick dropped to his knees beside the mound. When he cried, he cried about *loss,* the loss of his mumblety-peg championship, the loss of Leslie Ann Doody, the loss of his family members, the loss of his wife, the loss of a childhood, because he had, very young, taken upon himself the burden of the adults in his life. He had set out to make his mother happy, his father less angry. It had been his job, his youthful calling, and he had failed miserably.

He might have stayed there, on the mossy little knoll, except that a new batch of mourners was making its way into the grave-yard, ahead of a long procession of cars that had most likely inched down Cemetery Road, where once wagons had rolled, maybe even a few of Reginald's Conestogas. Does a long line of shiny cars really mean something? Does it mean that the guest of honor, the newly dead, must have leaned, once, against a jukebox sur-rounded by adoring fans? And does that shorter line hint that the dead once sat at the outskirts, in cracked Naugahyde booths, wait-ing. How could one tell? But now that new mourners had come into the cemetery with their own grief, with their own freshly dead, Frederick would leave them to it. His only other alternative was to jump feet first into that other opened maw, lift an imagi-nary skull up in his hands, and moan, "Poor Yorick, I knew him well, Horatio." He got to his feet, wiped his swollen eyes, straightened his tie. The marigold sun had begun its descent into the west as Frederick put on his suit jacket and went home.

A nice cool pitcher of martinis before him, Frederick unfolded the Dear John letter from his soon-to-be former wife, Chandra Kimball-Stone. *Marital Dissolution Papers,* a little poem, really. In some ways, he was almost relieved that an answer to his estrange-ment problem had finally arrived. But in those other ways, those ways that speak of time spent, of books shared, of movies watched, of breakfasts eaten, of mornings awakened to, the news was devastating. For three days, ever since his mother's funeral, Frederick had eaten nothing. Food had lost its pleasure for him. He found himself thinking of fasting, of cleansing himself of all those old Stone impurities. He thought of Gandhi, using up all his fat reserves, growing lean yet moving closer to the day when he would be shot by a Hindu fanatic. Had Gandhi dreamed of sugarplums, round and juicy and sweet? Or did he dream of the gun, waiting up ahead with time, unintelligently, the bullet lingering in limbo?

It was his brother, Herbert Stone, who broke the three-day fast in which Frederick inadvertently found himself partaking.

"Remember," Herbert advised, "that this, too, shall pass." He had stopped by on his way to the clinic, without phoning—niceties meant nothing now to Frederick—and insisted on popping two slices of bread into the toaster. Then he pried a frozen can of orange juice from a mound of ice in the freezer. Frederick listened to the spoon clinking about in the glass pitcher as Herbert stirred, wondered what it would have been like if his mother had done such a thing. But meals at the Stone residence had not been large happy gatherings, the way one might imagine the Kennedys at dinner, world events being tossed about while one passed the peas. Dr. Stone had hired a housekeeper, who also cooked the family dinners. Sometimes they ate together. Mostly, they ate when they thought of it. Frederick's brightest memory of the immense dining-room table was a picture of Dr. Stone, sitting alone before his dinner plate, reading the evening paper.

"If I have to start eating again," said Frederick, "how about dinner tonight at The China Boat?" Herbert shook his head, a funny little smile appearing on his face.

"I've got a hot date," he announced. Frederick wasn't surprised.

"Natalie, the temptress?" he asked. Herbert shook his head again, the smile expanding, puffing out his cheeks. "Is she of legal age?"

"She's forty-four," said Herbert. "She's your age." Frederick considered this. Suddenly he knew.

"You're kidding!" he exclaimed.

"Maggie, my ex-wife," Herbert said happily. "We're going to

dinner at the Kimberly Inn. They've got a great rotisserie duck basted in Chinese bead molasses, sherry, soy sauce, and garlic." Frederick found himself immensely delighted to hear this news. Not about the duck, about the date. They could begin the pinwheel again, slowly. Herbert and Maggie and Frederick were at least a start. Their mother had left them a kind of legacy after all. It was her funeral that had reunited them.

"Good for you," said Frederick. "Good for you, Herb. I don't know what you did wrong last time, I just know that it was *you* who did it. So don't do it again, okay?" Herbert smiled.

"We'll see," he said.

In the tiny attic a deep smell of summer and heat and mold rose up together. Frederick poked about the boxes, lifting a top here and there, reading the scribblings Chandra had written on the sides, the contents revealed. He found the heavy box that held his medical books and flopped down on the attic floor before it. His father had wanted him to be a doctor, and for a time Frederick even believed that he wanted it, too. Mr. Bator had been such a wonderful teacher, had such a great influence upon him, that Frederick imagined for a time that his whole life could be spent in medicine. Biology, as Mr. Bator taught it, had been Frederick's greatest subject all through high school. He could toss off medical definitions as easily as his peers could name popular rock songs. But, to Dr. Stone's parental dismay, he hadn't gone to medical school. It began with a squabble between father and son, just after his highschool graduation, and ended with Frederick moving out of the family house. He had spent his first year out of high school at work in the roofing business, rather than at college. The problem had been Vietnam. Dr. Philip Stone, an army dentist, had always envisioned that his sons would go eagerly to war. "The army will be your greatest education," the doctor had prophesied. "You'll be ready for college after two years in the military." This was 1966, before Vietnam had burst into a full bloodbath. At odds with his father, Frederick had been forced to put off his education, for he had no tuition money to pay for it. It was the year in roofing that enabled him to finally begin his studies, but by that time medical school had lost all its interest for him. He had already bought his first bell-bottoms, was wearing a headband decorated with peace symbols, had taken that first historic toke from somebody's glowing joint, had let his hair grow to his shoulders. How could he tell some kid today, some punky little Axl Rose, what long hair had meant in the sixties, how it had separated kids from their parents and grandparents, got them expelled from colleges and universities, assured them that they would be glared at in restaurants, denied at banks, eyed suspiciously by the police and airport personnel. Dr. Philip Stone had told his son never to come home again until he *looked respectable*. "I'd rather you turned out a queer," his father had said of the flowing hair. "At least that's something the neighbors can't see." Feeling like a perpetual orphan, he had been welcomed in by the huge wide arms of the sixties, to a family that accepted him for what he was, that embraced his triumphs, rued his failures. He even lived for a time in a big rambling house where *everybody* touched *everybody,* a commune full of folks who needed families, who all sat around the table eating dinner, then singing songs by Dylan and Baez. *The times they are a'changin'.* They sure as hell were. They were changing a lot. More than a hundred and fifty American cities had caught on fire, literally, with the same bright orange flames that were turning up on television sets, in those film clips from Vietnam. And in those photographs in *Life* magazine, the billowing orange fire of bombs being dropped on peasants: the fire of war. In Detroit and Watts, the fire was the color of racism and poverty, a black and white fire, because only the rich had color television sets. And through it all, Lyndon Johnson was peering helplessly out of the windows of the White House, afraid to be the first American President to lose a war. To Frederick Stone, it had seemed as if the whole world was on fire. He and his father hadn't spoken for an entire year. By 1967, when Frederick was accepted at Boston University, a half million American soldiers were firmly ensconced in Vietnam. It was, for Frederick and his peers, the Summer of Love; yet General Westmoreland would be crying out for a hundred thousand more young men, and Frederick didn't want to be one of them. Herbert Stone, however, did. Always the son who wanted to please, Herbert had abandoned his studies at vet school and gone off to fight the undeclared war. Frederick had never doubted his brother's motives. He had never, once, believed that the apolitical Herbert Stone had gone to the jungles of Southeast Asia to stop Communist aggression. Herbert was only interested in fulfilling his father's notion of war, that of a young Rupert Brooke donning khaki and walking boldly away from the cricket field. As long as Herbert could come home alive, with his precious life intact, maybe he would then get a little attention from Dr. Stone. And he needn't even come back whole. Surely, a leg blown to smithereens, an amputated arm, a severe limp would all be good fodder for some after-dinner attention in the Stone parlor. Frederick, on the other hand, had chosen to protest the same undeclared war while working weekends to put new roofs on Portland houses.

But he made enough money in roofing to pay for his college education. After his first year at Boston University, he spent his next three summers at Down East Roofers, Inc., in order to pay for the next year, and the next. And he had graduated with a degree in English literature all on his own. Dr. Philip Stone was unable to make it to the commencement services. Frederick could no longer remember the reason, just that, unlike high school, he no longer cared that his father was not in the audience of happy faces on graduation night.

Frederick put the lid back on the box of old medical books and pushed it into a corner. He should give them to the local library, except that they were now outdated. A lot can happen in twenty-odd years in the medical world. He opened the next box, old photos of his early marriage: Chandra at the ocean in her rose skirt, Frederick hovering over a cake for his twenty-fifth birthday, Chandra and Frederick and the Fosters, all with their arms around one another. They were going to be friends forever, weren't they? Then the Fosters moved to New Jersey and in a short time the two couples had lost touch. He looked at Karen Foster's pretty, young face. Jim Foster's thick mustache. They were the hippiest of all their friends, the Fosters were. Jim had a knack for fixing up old houses. He had done so for a half dozen friends, and had never accepted a penny payment for any of it. Such was the atmosphere in which they all lived. Karen had a way of sowing cosmos and dill and lots of chrysanthemums in among the marijuana plants in her immense garden. Frederick wondered if they were still the free spirits they professed to be eternally. Somehow, he felt quite sure, Jim Foster was the owner of a renovating firm these days, and Karen was operating her own landscaping business. She would have cut her long flowing hair into the short style that was so popular among women of the nineties, Maggie's new style. And Jim's mustache would be considerably tamer, his own hair cropped to a business respectability. Lots of their other friends had gone on to teach school, become parents. Some had even disappeared like moles into banking and the law, which would have been the ultimate cop-out back when they were listening to the Jefferson Airplane, Iron Butterfly, and the Grateful Dead. This was just the opposite of what Timothy Leary had meant when he encouraged everyone, especially junior and senior executives, to *turn on, tune in,* and *drop out.* But now Timothy Leary was involved in something to do with space migration and had stated that drugs are stupid.

There were photos of other faces, the old college crowd, even friends they'd made at Woodstock and then lost somewhere down the years.

Kids, thought Frederick as he stared down at the faces. *We were just kids.* And yet he had experienced such a rush back then, a pure electrifying shot of *life,* the kind of adrenaline flood that never happened anymore. It was all ahead of him then, his future a fluttering butterfly, events waiting to explode any which way he wanted them to. *Because he didn't know any better.* And now that he *did* know better, all he had to look forward to was the end of it all. *Come away, O human child, for the world's more full of weeping than you can understand.* When had it happened that he had grown away from being that young man who captured Chandra Kimball's heart at Woodstock? When had his youth receded, escaped into old memories and photographs? He still didn't feel *grown up.* And he suspected that most of his generation were in the same halfway house, an emotional teetering between becoming their children and becoming their parents. But their playground had been the sixties! The worst of times, the best of times, the craziest of times. Frederick could remember college professors who were wearing crewcuts one day and talking about the Monroe Doctrine. The next day they'd be tripping about campus in bell-bottoms and headbands, saying things like "Groovy." You could be certain of nothing. And now, with this distance from his youth, the way historians distance themselves from wars, Frederick had come to the conclusion that baby boomers didn't want to grow up. And, to make matters worse, they had raised up a new generation of brats. The fashion world, always the first to identify and exploit mass mental illness, was catching on. Oscar de la Renta was now designing shorts that would resemble a baby's diaper. People were beginning to wear pacifiers about their necks, symbols of a less complicated time: *I suck, therefore I am.* Yuppies—thanks to the sincere religion of Mutual Funds—were able to buy their pacifiers in sterling silver for a hundred and fifty bucks a shot. *Infantilism,* or so the pop sociologists were calling the trend. So what was a basically self-centered and egotistical guy like Frederick Stone to do, in the face of such debauchery? Such unabashed excess? Such extravagant self-indulgence? Good God, but even the Romans had had the common decency to regurgitate in private. But then, the Romans hadn't had "Geraldo." The Romans had been light-years away from television, that back-talking box that could convert light rays into electronic signals, that could bring the face of Rush Limbaugh, that roly-poly, pasty-faced Baby Hughey of the air-waves, the undisputed King of Infantilism, spitting and gurgling forth, and all without a bib. Public tantrums. And then there was the other side of infantilism. Eleven- and twelve-year-old girls were staring out from the covers of magazines, their eyes heavily made up, their flat cleavages pushed up into a premature bloom. "Try me," their eyes suggested to male buyers. "If my mommy scares you, I promise I won't."

Frederick put the pictures back into the box. There were hordes more, but he didn't want to look at them. He heard the wind start up about the eaves of the house, the sound of a shingle flapping up and down. He shut his eyes, and he was Kim suddenly, in the old Kipling book, resting at the top of the world. He longed for his boyhood with such intensity that he feared he might hyperventilate. His heart beat fiercely. What if he died, there at the top of the world? Who would find him? Would Walter Muller come looking for him, a chocolate cake in one hand, a pan of fudge in the other? Why did people think that food could mend a broken heart, especially if one was a man? Wasn't that sexist in some culinary way? Frederick opened his eyes, almost expecting to see Chandra appear before him, so intensely had he tried to conjure her up. But all he saw through the round attic window were the tops of the outdoor trees swaying back and forth, back and forth. All he heard were the drops of rain that had started a steady beating upon the roof.

His composure regained, and the image of Chandra diminished, the next box he opened said *Christmas cards*. There they all were, souvenirs from holidays gone by. Why she had saved them, he'd never know. Especially since it had turned out that she didn't even want them anymore. He found the last card Polly had ever sent, in 1983, the Christmas before she died. Inside, there were three school pictures. Polly had written on the backs of each: *Vanessa, age 6; Jason, age 7; Charles, age 10*. Frederick looked at the faces of his nephews and his niece. When was the last time he'd seen them? This was Christmas of 1983. They'd be nine years older now, young adults. How had they managed without Polly? Had Percy Hillstrip ever remarried? He slipped the three pictures out of the card and fitted them into his wallet.

The other holiday cards were from more ancient friends who one year sent a final Christmas card to Frederick and Chandra Stone, that couple they used to know up in Portland, Maine. He wondered if Chandra had sent cards back, with pictures inside of the two of them, aging, a pair of bright balloons deflating with time. He had not been good at things like occasion cards, considering them a business venture that benefited only Hallmark and its ilk. A lot of men were like that, though. His father never signed a card. That had always been his mother's job. And Frederick remembered cards from aunts and uncles, years of greetings, always in the aunts' handwriting: *Best of luck from Aunt Minnie and Uncle Bob; Happy Birthday from Aunt Trudy and Uncle Stan*. Could his uncles even write? Had they perhaps been expelled from kindergarten—little Stone boys that they were, little rocks—never learning to take pen to paper? Had Chandra, and Aunt Minnie, and Aunt Trudy, and Thelma Stone minded this sole job of communication? Well, what now did it matter if Frederick had been damned excellent at it? Where had it gotten Chandra? How had it elevated Karen Foster? Was the whole world singing Aunt Minnie's praises these days? Canonizing Aunt Trudy?

He opened the cardboard box that had *College Correspondence* written on the lid. Inside were the letters from his father, addressed to Frederick at his Boston address. Dr. Stone *had* written letters, perhaps afraid that Mrs. Stone would make them too friendly, if this task were left to her. No need to send the boy a lilac-scented envelope, a heartwarming platitude scribbled at the bottom of a note. The letters had averaged about six a year for the four years he was at college. None were more than a paragraph long. Some contained an occasional clipping, a neighbor's son becoming a hero in Vietnam, another winning a medical scholarship, one studying at the Sorbonne, successes blossoming up and down the street. Looking through the letters quickly, Frederick saw that they all read much alike, with a brief line that Thelma was finding the weather a bit too warm or too cold, then a general reminder to keep one's nose to the university grindstone. Unlike the letters from home received by his classmates, there was never a twenty-dollar bill clinging to the stationery. Well, so what? It had taught him cool, firm independence, an ability to stand on one's own two feet. It had taught him all of that, indeed, and it was perhaps that very lesson that had cost him his marriage.

He dug deeper into the box in order to find the love letters from Chandra. *I can't wait for the wedding,* she'd written in the first letter he opened. *Joyce told Mom that our plans are crazy and Mom seems to feel cheated out of the church thing, but Jenny and Bob think it's the coolest thing they've ever heard.* They had stopped off at the courthouse to get married, just the two of them. Then they'd taken the Bluenose ferry from Portland to Yarmouth, Nova Scotia, had spent the night at a tiny motel in Yarmouth, and then taken the eight-hour ferry back the next morning. It had been a perfectly sixties notion of the ideal honeymoon. Or had it been? Had the honeymoon night meant as much to Chandra as it had to him? He had felt swelled with pride—a near physical sensation—that she was suddenly his wife. It wasn't that they hadn't made love before. It's that they had promised to join their lives together forever and, because of that, the lovemaking had been even more charged. He wondered now what that honeymoon night had meant to Chandra, and wished that he could ask her. Had she closed her eyes and thought of Woodstock? Who the hell were Jenny and Bob? *Dear Sweetie, Rain coming down here today, reminding me of you and how much I love you and always will,* the next letter declared. He couldn't read on. She had been writing from Portland on a rainy day, and now, all these years later, he was in Portland reading the letter again on a rainy day. He had known that time was a prankster. He just had no idea how unintelligently vicious time could be.

He brought the huge bundle of letters, most of them in baby-blue envelopes, down from the attic. It would take another pitcher of martinis, but he would read them all. He would remember how much she had loved him. Maybe he could find a clue in the letters as to what went wrong. But the letters were written before they were married, in those days when *nothing* was wrong. What was wrong in the present had to do with gin. He was out. Well, that's why the gods had invented liquor stores. And as long as the Hormonal Harpies were not working down there as clerks, Frederick imagined he would be able to replenish his stock.

He had just turned off the car's engine and gotten out when he noticed the ubiquitous brown car pull up beside his own in the liquor store parking lot. The passenger door opened and a man got out, a man about Frederick's own age and height, but a stranger to him. A second stranger, this one wearing a red and green tam, leaned over from behind the steering wheel and peered out at him.

"Frederick Stone?" the first man asked. Frederick suffered a wild impulse to deny his own identity, but he could feel his head nodding an affirmative. This was unfolding like a scene out of *Goodfellas.* He imagined being whisked out to a patch of thick woods in the trunk of the brown sedan, never to see Chandra again, never to see Portland again, never to resurrect Stone Accounting. He considered for a reckless moment petitioning The Girls. But then, he'd been less than polite, a male chauvinist pig to them lately. What had he called them, aloud, just that morning? Oh yes, The Goddesses of PMS. He decided to forget about them. He glanced, instead, toward the large glass window of the liquor store. If he waved his arms frantically, would the clerk see him? Probably not, considering that, from his present view of her, she was swathed in cigarette smoke.

"Mind taking a little ride?" the stranger now asked. Terror and indignation teamed up in Frederick Stone's emotions. *How dare this person infiltrate his right to come to a liquor store and purchase gin? Oh, good God, he was doing to die!*

"Do I know you?" he heard his voice finally ask.

"You know my boss." His *boss,* as in *godfather?* Frederick knew then that he had made a grievous mistake in dropping James Grossmire of Grossmire Imports just because the IRS and U.S. Customs had discovered—much to Frederick Stone's chagrin—that many of those said imports were stuffed with a variety of illegal sundries, some of it white as snow. "Arthur Bowen," the alien added, and Frederick felt his feet rattling beneath him, taking him toward the brown sedan, propelling him inside the door that had suddenly opened to the backseat. Arthur Bowen, like some thinner, richer version of Jabba the Hut, was lolling in the backseat with a bowl of macadamia nuts on his lap.

They were almost to the end of Jefferson Street before Arthur Bowen uttered a single word.

"Macadamia?" he asked, extending his arm so that the bowl of nuts rode before Frederick's face. Frederick refused with a shake of his head. What did Arthur Bowen want? The best that could happen would be if Doris had finally put in that good word for Stone Accounting after all. Now Frederick was thankful that he had let Doris see him cry. Any large firm could do with a sensitive accountant. Maybe Frederick Stone would evolve into a kind of social conscience for Bowen Developers, steering them away from acts of environmental assault, fulfilling his sixties heritage. How can one go wrong with Alan Alda keeping an eye on the company books? But before he had time to further consider the best that could happen, Frederick was hit with the worst.

"Have you been fucking my wife?" Arthur asked. He continued to crunch on macadamias. Frederick felt his heart slip out of his rib cage and flutter beneath his shirt, trying desperately to escape the chest of such a stupid, imprudent man. The warm flushing of his face told him that his blood vessels had enlarged again, in a great pigmentary disturbance. He wished he had the opportunity to tell Chandra Kimball-Stone, and finally, that she was wrong in thinking that the talk of money caused his blushing. Talk of fucking a rich man's wife could also do it. Especially if the rich man himself initiated the conversation.

Frederick floundered for a few seconds, uttering such things as "Ah" and "Ahhhh" as he struggled for the best answer. The truth, pure and simple—and he could thank Mr. Bator for this—was that he had not actually consummated the act. Or had he? Was ejaculation necessary these days to constitute adultery? What would

Judge Wapner say about that? What would Dr. Ruth say? Would Joyce's son, the Condom King, know the ramifications? No matter how Frederick personally looked at the incident, he felt quite certain that Arthur Bowen, Doris's husband, would not view penetration as *politically correct.*

"No," Frederick said, and quite firmly, he thought. "I haven't. I *have not.* Your wife and I shop at the same supermarket. You might say we're acquaintances." He was delightfully satisfied with the business tone with which he was addressing one of the richest men in all of New England. His heart flopped back into its natural place and the little drum in his temple stopped its drumming. "I've enlisted her help in offering my accounting services to you, however," he added. "I *am* guilty of *that.*" Arthur Bowen was nodding agreeably, and this compliance urged Frederick's denial further. "It was merely a business venture," he tossed in as Arthur Bowen reached for a brown envelope at his feet and opened it. "Mrs. Bowen was kind enough to listen to my proposal that Stone Accounting represent Bowen Developers." Arthur Bowen was now rifling through a stack of papers and what looked like the occasional photograph. "And she was patient enough to let me pester her about it. At the IGA, of all places," he added. He offered up a tiny chuckle, but his diaphragm obviously didn't move up and down sufficiently enough to stimulate the larynx, and what emerged was a light squawk. "However, I'll be doing my grocery shopping at Cain's Corner Grocery from now on." *Why don't you just shut up?* he heard Mr. Bator suggest. "The IGA has seen the last of me," Frederick went on to announce, slapping this knee good-naturedly. Maybe this promise would appease Arthur Bowen, who seemed to have found the documents he was looking for. "Mr. Cain is a very nice old gentleman who is competing with such a large conglomerate that I've decided to give him my business." This was what was known as *prattling,* and Frederick knew it. Couldn't he shut up, as Mr. Bator had suggested? Couldn't he just keep his lips closed tightly together, the fate he'd wished on Walter Muller all these years of living next door to him? He couldn't. His face knew better. Fiery red now, his face knew that no way in hell did Arthur Bowen believe him. His whole body seemed to comprehend this, and told him so by shaking noticeably. What did King Arthur have in those blasted documents? Frederick knew now how poor Sir Lancelot probably felt, when cornered about Guinevere. He accepted the photo that Arthur had finally selected. In it, he was on his front steps kissing Doris Bowen's pale white hand.

"Ah," said Frederick. "Ahhhh." He knitted his brows into a puzzling look, as if to say, "Yes, now let's see. What was *that* all about?" Arthur Bowen waited, amid the sound of macadamia nuts being crushed. Frederick crossed his legs, the metaphor painfully apparent. He tried to pass the photograph back to its owner, but his hand wouldn't work. It dropped to his lap, the hand of a rag doll. The hand of a ghost, maybe, nothing of substance to it, just a wisp of smoke. The faint trill of radio music drifted in from the front seat. The man in the red and green tam turned occasionally to glance back, assuring himself that "the boss" was okay. One of his eyebrows seemed to be missing, the other disappearing in wild wiry hairs under the corner of his tam. He looked like some kind of Scottish pervert. His buddy, riding shotgun, was eating something from a crinkly wrap. The smell of ground beef hung in the air.

The car suddenly swung into the parking lot of the Portland Greyhound station. Frederick imagined Arthur Bowen putting him on a bus to Peoria or someplace hellish, banning him from the Casco Bay area forever. But Mr. Tam pulled the vehicle into an empty space and then turned the engine off. No one moved at first, and then the sound of crinkling paper rose up again from the front seat, and Mr. Tam burped softly, and the radio kept up its faint strain.

"She *did* come to my house," Frederick finally admitted in a sweeping exhalation of breath. "But that was all." What else could he say? The photograph was so clear that he could see Walter Muller's hideous lilac bush pushing its smelly purple face into the corner of the frame. Why hadn't he just waved? Why did he have to kiss her damned hand? Chandra had said it, hadn't she, a thousand times? "Hubris, Freddy," his soon-to-be ex had noted. "You go the extra inch every time your vanity is involved. I've seen you try to impress electric-eye doors."

"You're very photogenic," Arthur Bowen conceded.

"Thank you," said Frederick, able now to hand the photo back to Doris Bowen's husband. He waited. The last macadamia nut fell beneath the power of Arthur Bowen's molars and then all was quiet for a few meaningful seconds. Then more paper rustled in the front seat. Mr. Tam had pushed *scan* on the radio panel because short blurps of song came and went. The *scan button:* Now, there was an invention that boosted mankind ahead to the future. Thanks to some genius at Sony, the human thumb would probably atrophy somewhere down the evolutionary road and eventually disappear, the important index finger becoming the opposable digit.

"I merely kissed Mrs. Bowen's hand," Frederick heard some liar say, and realized that he was blabbing again, his vocal chords vibrating with words. But why not attempt it? What proof did Arthur Bowen have that anything more occurred? Proof arrived— and just as Frederick was finishing up this thought—in the form of another photo selected by Arthur Bowen. Again, it was of Frederick Stone, from the Frederick Stone portfolio, although it might have been a work left over from a Robert Mapplethorpe exhibit. Frederick stared at a most uncomplimentary shot of his own buttocks, which were beaming above the naked body of an insatiable Doris Bowen. Judging from the angle, it had been taken from outside his living-room window, at his Victorian house on Ellsboro Street. And, judging from the look of rapture on Doris's face, the architecture of the house was the only thing Victorian. The focus was excellent. Where did people find such cameras? Under the sunniest of circumstances, and with his subjects as still as statues, Frederick had never taken such a professional-looking photo. He canted his head as he studied the composition. Was that a mole of some sort on his left buttock?

"You need to get yourself a tan," Arthur Bowen said. He whirred the back window down. "You're too pale." He whirred the window up. "Or maybe it's because my wife is so brown that you look so white."

"Ahhhhh," said Frederick. He closed his eyes. Had it been just a few weeks ago that he was living a one-dimensional, cardboard life that bordered on the comatose? Yes, it was. A small breeze could have blown his flimsy life away.

"Maybe you should start fucking pale women," he heard Arthur Bowen suggest, followed by the sound of the back window whirring down again and then up, down and then up, Arthur Bowen's artificial diaphragm, up and down. Anxiety in motion.

"Maybe you should start fucking albinos," Arthur counseled further. Frederick heard Mr. Tam snort out a brief little laugh from the front seat, a pig squealing. He remembered, irrationally, that he even *knew* an albino, the woman who wore those dark glasses at the library and handled delinquent books. His frightened mind raced unreasonably, images of milky, anemic women filing past, their eyes radiating pink light. *Fair-complexioned persons must be extremely wary because their skin absorbs more of the sun's rays than the skin of darker persons.* Frederick was elated that Mr. Bator was along for the ride. At least there would be someone there to whom he could whisper the last, historic words: "Tell Chandra Kimball-Stone to feel no guilt. I die glad that I knew her at all."

"Recognize this guy?" he heard Arthur Bowen inquire. The sharp corner of another picture pecked against Frederick's hand. He opened his eyes. The face before him did, indeed, look familiar. It was Ronnie, the bag boy who'd worked at the IGA last summer before he went off to grad school in search of a Ph.D. in psychology. Frederick had been unimpressed with Ronnie. After all, what was a doctorate in psychology, or education, or any of the pseudo sciences compared with genuine doctorates? Ambitious monkeys were capable of such degrees. What had Ronnie declared his thesis would be? Oh yes, "First at the Sale: How Personality Determines Aggression in American Shoppers." The next picture was of Preston, another pregrad student with a bad attitude, or so Frederick had thought. Apparently his attitude had suited Doris Bowen just fine. In the picture, she was standing behind her raised trunk as Preston loaded groceries into the Mercedes, a huge smile transfiguring his face. Arthur handed over another photo, same scene, this time with Preston's arm encircling Doris's neck as he kissed her. The other hand was busy kneading her firm ass. All this behind the raised trunk of the car Arthur Bowen had probably bought her as a birthday gift. Why *does* the woman do her own shopping? Frederick had often wondered. He was shocked to see Billy Lawford, a current bag person, smiling up at him from Doris Bowen's résumé. Billy Lawford was, in Frederick's opinion, several bricks short of the proverbial load. As a matter of fact, Billy didn't even have wheels on the brick wagon. And there in another photo—good God!—was the manager of the IGA, coming out of a motel room while Doris wavered in the door, her hair looking like something out of Ronnie's thesis: "First at the Sale: Sexual Aggression as a Hindrance to Haute Coiffures." Frederick hadn't felt quite so foolish since Mr. Veatch, the security officer at Portland High, had yanked open the gym closet door and found him inside, his hands thrust up under Maria Pritchard's blouse, a place well-traveled. It was sickening.

"Recognize these guys?" Arthur wondered. The pictures were of Larry, the butler, and another thin-faced man with straggly hair. Could it be Willy, the gardener? "Oh, but you never met Willy, did you?" Arthur acknowledged. "Doris found these guys at Foodline, in the Portland mall, but you might say they work for me now." Frederick handed the group of pictures back to Arthur Bowen.

"Jimmy Swaggart isn't among these, is he?" Frederick asked. Arthur Bowen laughed heartily.

"I like you," Arthur confessed. Well, that was a start. "Let's go, Sammy," he added.

Mr. Tam, *Sammy*, backed the car out of its parking space and once again they rode. Frederick watched out his window as street signs flew by. He waited. He expected that his just punishment, at least in Arthur Bowen's eyes, would be a good sound beating by the two gentlemen in the front seat. He assumed that they would represent Bowen Developers much like the dueling champions of yore. So be it. Let them slap him in the face with Arthur Bowen's glove and demand that he choose his weapon. He wished they would allow him to choose *spelling,* since it had been one of his best subjects since grammar school. But the intellect was not at war here, Frederick knew. Very well. He would choose bare fists, and he would take his medicine like a man. In advance, he tried to imagine his lips as puffed-up, impossible things, a missing front tooth, a broken rib or two, several nasty scrapes and bruises, a grape of an eye sealed shut. He would heal. As long as he lived, he would mend. Worse things had happened to people. He could even learn to limp permanently, if he must. He had limped for a week, after all, and had managed just fine. He wondered if the two men in the front seat were waiting for *him* to initiate the confrontation. Was that how these things were officially handled?

Frederick had just decided that, once the car stopped, it would be politically correct for him to lean forward and place a good sound wallop on the back of Mr. Tam's head, when Arthur Bowen spoke.

"You're not worth beating up, if that's what you're worried about," Arthur Bowen said. Frederick couldn't possibly agree more, unless that meant that he was worth killing. But surely they wouldn't kill him with witnesses about. And after all, signs indicating his neighborhood, his home turf, had begun to emerge. They weren't taking him to some lonely limestone quarry. Cain's Corner Grocery appeared in a blurb of lights and then disappeared. Bobbin Road flashed by, and then the car turned down Ellsboro Street. Frederick was about to mention that he had left his automobile at the liquor store, then refrained. If his only punishment was walking back down there to get it, he would be lucky, although Watergate politicians had suffered less. And Ollie North hadn't paid such a price. Ollie North didn't have to limp anywhere.

"I'm a law-abiding man, Mr. Stone," Arthur Bowen admitted. "Let's keep it that way. Stay away from my wife. And stay away from my home. Florence doesn't just cook. She keeps her eyes open. All three of them." Frederick nodded, remembering Florence's wild, voodoo gaze.

"Tell me something, Mr. Bowen," he asked meekly. He couldn't help it. He needed to know. "Why do you do it? Why do you allow it to keep happening?" Arthur Bowen smiled, his cheeks puffing greatly.

"It's all in the hunt," he said finally. Frederick nodded. He had no doubt that this was true. Arthur Bowen had, after all, crawled ten miles on his belly, through the Rocky Mountains, over sharp icy crags, in order to kill a two-hundred-pound sheep. If you can't put human heads up on your wall, *mounted* heads, well, what's wrong with a little collection of photos? *Head shots?*

The car pulled quietly up to the curve in front of the Victorian house. Frederick sat there patiently until it occurred to him that he was to get out. He opened his door and stepped out onto the sidewalk. He saw Arthur Bowen move forward in the darkness of the car, saw his body slide over to where Frederick had been sitting. A tremor of fear rushed up Frederick's back, tingled at the nape of his neck. He sensed a hideous trick floating about. After all, you can penetrate the CIA. You can penetrate the KKK. But there are some things you just can't penetrate and get away with. And Doris Bowen was surely one of them. His just fate would probably be worse than that of the Big Five: *the elephant, the Cape buffalo, the rhino, the antelope, and the leopard.* Those guys had been *innocent.* His eyes closed, Frederick waited for the sound of a gun going off, but nothing. Then he waited for a cap pistol to pop, frightening him unreasonably. Nothing. He opened one eye. Perhaps a cold stream of water shot from a water gun. *Anything.* But nothing happened. That was it? That was all? He'd had another blind date with mediocrity? The rush of adrenaline he had called forth—as a buffer to the pain he was sure would come—ran rampant in his body. His gut contracted in anticipation of nothing, his head ached, his heart throbbed. His endorphins were really pissed. He peered down at Arthur Bowen.

"I could have been a contender," he said in his best Brando mimic.

"You've seen too many movies, Mr. Stone," Arthur Bowen said. He appeared amused by it all.

"May I ask you something else?" Frederick wondered. Arthur Bowen nodded magnanimously. "Why does a guy with all your money drive around in a brown Chevrolet?" Arthur Bowen smiled again, his teeth perfect as Greek pillars, Doric columns.

"Because guys like you would notice a Rolls." The window whirred up. Mr. Tam applied a speck too much foot to the accelerator pedal and the brown Chevy tore off into the night.

"I noticed your goddamn Chevy, too!" Frederick yelled at the taillights. He shook his head in astonishment. Did all estranged men suffer vicissitudes such as these? No wonder the talk-show circuit was buzzing with tales of woe and horror.

"Oh, Frederick." He felt his nostrils contract in fear. But no, it couldn't be Doris, not unless she'd had a few shots of testosterone at the local clinic, because it was a man's voice. Walter Muller materialized from out of the lilac bush.

"Mrs. Muller sent this over," he proclaimed happily, lifting wax paper from a cookie sheet and exposing doughnuts, a pair of brownies, a slab of pie. "I was just about to leave them on the steps for you." Frederick wanted to stir up a bit of ire. He wanted to cry out, "For Christ's sake, man, can't an extraneared person find any peace from you do-gooders? Can't you see that I've just returned from the brink of death?" And he would have said that, every word of it, had his mouth not watered extravagantly at the sight of such pastries thrust beneath his nose. The truth had been that he was starving, that he'd had no dinner, that he'd wanted some of Arthur Bowen's damned nuts all along but was just too frightened to bite into one. The luxurious smell of brownie, a sweet thick chocolate, rose up into the evening air.

"How neighborly of her," Frederick said, slipping a cool hand under the warm tray. "Many thanks to Mrs. Muller."

*F*ifteen

*I*t was a week later, over a peanut butter sandwich on the screened-in porch, that he saw Chandra's picture in the *Casco Bay Daily,* her face swimming out from a group of faces: the Animal Rights Coalition. He stared longingly at her eyes, those light and dark dots of newspaper ink that formed her cheek-bones, the tip of her nose, the lay of her lips, before he went on to read about the animal-rights march gearing up against Radnor Laboratory, a facility still experimenting on any species that could not protect itself. There had already been a stir-up the day before, when a few People First advocates had pitched tents in the park across from Radnor and had started giving interviews to the press. The anti-Radnor march would be a candlelight vigil, a walking parade beginning at eight o'clock in The Alternative Grocer parking lot and ending on the sidewalk in front of Radnor Laboratory. Everyone wishing to take part was encouraged to bring a box of emergency candles so that the procession would be well-lighted.

Frederick read the article with interest. The People First advocates were preparing, they declared, for an all-out battle with this element who wanted to spare animals from the horrors of the lab. "If I had the choice of my wife dying," someone named

Reginald Steen was printed as saying, "or some damn baboon, you'd better believe it'd be the baboon." Frederick wondered if Reginald's wife would chose the baboon over her husband. He had no doubt at all whose side the baboon would be on. He read on, knowing that Chandra would have to be quoted somewhere. Since the inception of the Animal Rights Coalition several years earlier, she had been at the group's vanguard. So he was *not* surprised when she was identified as their spokesperson. What *did* surprise him, however, was that she had gone back to using her maiden name. "We've spent over two billion tax dollars and more than thirty years on animal tests," a certain Chandra Kimball had told the reporter covering the story. "And we're still no closer to a cure for cancer, our number-one killer. Nor are we any closer to eradicating any other major disease because tests on one species cannot be accurately applied to another species." She was wearing a small locket, heart-shaped, lying there in the picture against her bare skin. Frederick recognized it as one he had bought her, for one of her birthdays, early on in their marriage. She had put a picture of him in one of the heart-shaped sides, a picture of her father in the other. He wondered, now, what pictures were hiding in that locket, what clues to her future. "Why do you think the recipients of these baboon hearts are dying?" the paper had gone on to report Ms. Kimball as asking. "And this is not to mention the animals who are blinded, maimed, tortured, and killed by Radnor Laboratory in order to test household cleansers and cosmetics." Frederick studied her beautiful face carefully. She and several other activists in the shot were holding up a picture of Britches, the little monkey whose eyes had been sewn shut for studies in light deprivation at the University of California at Riverside. In the picture, Britches looked like Lamb Chop, the famous Shari Lewis puppet.

Chandra was in her usual fine form. Even reading her words, Frederick could hear the soft lilt behind them, the way she liked to pause after a particularly vivid description, letting the picture of it settle into her listener's mind. Thankful that he could finally learn a bit about Chandra's personal life, if even from the strangers who print up newspapers—was this how Pierre Trudeau had kept tabs on Margaret, during her wildest romps—he read on with great interest. Demonstrators on both sides had been warned by law enforcement officials that anyone breaking the law could expect a visit to the local jail.

Frederick folded the paper and tossed it aside. A small wind suddenly appeared and quickly flicked the pages over to the latest food coupons being offered by the Portland IGA. He breathed a breath of relief that her image was finally taken from him, for he hadn't the heart to turn the page himself. He sat staring at the street, listening to the sounds of local children involved in some argument over chewing gum. He tried not to call her face up before his eyes, but there it was, shimmering, gossamer, the face of an angel. It had been nice, damn nice, to see a current picture of Ms. Kimball, but Frederick wished that the *Casco Bay Daily* had not used a photo of the round-faced Reginald Steen, the People First spokesman. It was just possible that Reginald was walking, talking proof of the world's first baboon *head* transplant.

Frederick scooped up the newspaper again, crinkling it into a fine ball to be pitched into the waste basket. So she'd gone back to using her maiden name, had she? Well, he couldn't be too surprised, could he? That she had taken his name in the first place, even all those years ago when she still loved him, was surprise enough. But she had done it, by her own testimony, because she never liked the name Kimball. Blood must be thicker than water, for in her middle age she'd found the heart to endorse her paternal roots. And it certainly wasn't a *baboon's* heart. He now wondered what had happened to the poor little hyphen that had glued their names together for over twenty years: Chandra Kimball-Stone. Or was it now Chandra Kimball-. . . He had always thought of that hyphen, used by so-called *liberated* women, as a kind of trailer hitch. If he went to divorce court, would he get custody of the hyphen? Did the hyphen eventually end up in the word *ex-husband?* Was that its fate?

Frederick sat at his computer and stared at the form letter that he'd begun just that morning. *Dear Blank.* He would merge the letter with the file of his clients' names and addresses later so that each would receive a personally typed letter. Publishers Clearinghouse did it. Why not Stone Accounting? *This is to sadly inform you that Stone Accounting and Consultation will no longer be in business as of September 1, 1992, due to personal reasons. I wish to thank all of you for the trust you once placed in Stone Accounting and Consultation, and to assure you that if this company resumes business, you shall be notified immediately. I also wish to apologize for any inconvenience you may have experienced during the past few weeks.* He stared at the letter, thought about the content of the words. Did anyone really care that his wife had left him, if he should suddenly find himself telling them all the truth? *To be honest with you, O Trusted Client, my wife, Chandra Stone, a.k.a. Chandra Kimball, moved out of our house, out of the blue, caught me with my emotions down and, so help me, try as I may, I can't seem to get a grip on things, as my brother, Herbert Stone (who has no grip himself), assures me I must do. I'm asking, for the sake of humanity, as a member of the human race to other members, hang in there with me, brother, cut me some slack, float with me until I can see dry land. I've just lost my marriage, and I don't want to lose my business, too. So, whaddya say, old bean? Is the world more full of weeping than I can understand?* Frederick sighed as he signed his original letter with a *Sincerely yours, Frederick Stone, President, Stone Accounting and Consultation.* If he sent the personal letter, the letter of entreaty, his clients would be roasting his testicles for lunch, a new Yuppie appetizer to accompany the buffalo wings and chicken nuggets: *Accountant's Balls with Horseradish.*

Stone Accounting was dead, no doubt of that. Only a handful of clients were left, and that was simply because they hadn't the time yet to find a new service. His best clients had abandoned ship at the first sign of floundering, the first news of rats on board, a madcap women-and-children-first dash to the lifeboats. Well, he had learned from all of it, hadn't he? *Hadn't he?* Wasn't that what people could expect of bad situations, that a little useful knowledge had been shoveled up among the shit and, therefore, not all was lost? But, dammit it, all he had learned was that people were capricious fly-by-nights, disloyal to the last man or woman. And he had known that *before* his downfall. It had been another of life's reruns. He needed a drink.

The happy-hour crowd was dour as usual. Frederick said hello to Amanda, a forty-eight-year-old divorced nurse whose slogan was "Honey, you're looking at the World's Greatest Female Survivor." Herbert Stone had contended that all Amanda wanted was for a man to ask her out. "She'll go back to being the World's Biggest Female Pushover in a second," he'd predicted. Eddy Walsh was there, a real-estate person who drank too much tequila and wore a mood ring. Frederick had been surprised to see such an adornment still in use. He would have bet good dollars that the only place one could view a mood ring in 1992 would be the Smithsonian Institute, in some godawful Twentieth-Century Pop Art collection, probably next to Andy Warhol's soup can. But Eddy Walsh obviously took good care of his jewelry. Frederick could see that the ring seemed, currently, to be a deep green. *Anger.*

"Goddamn buyers these days," Eddy was saying as Frederick found his usual stool unoccupied. "They see a crack in the ceiling, they go crazy." Kathy McLain, the hairstylist, was at *her* regular station, the stool near the cash register and the free bowl of fish-shaped crackers. He had heard Kathy McLain elaborate many times, during the quieter moments of *l'heure heureux,* that she and those of her ilk had *educated the public.* Frederick had been relieved to learn that this schooling all had to do with shampoos and cream rinses, not history and art.

"I see that Kathy the Hair Scientist is here," said Herbert as he slid up to the bar next to Frederick. He had agreed earlier, when Frederick phoned the clinic, that a smooth scotch might be the best way to end a busy day. "The unskilled all want titles these days," Herbert added, nodding at a new geisha bartender.

Frederick was trying not to look at the clock over the plastic leaves of the fake plant behind the bar. Down in the belly of The China Boat, where there were no portholes, it was difficult to keep track of the time of day. Frederick had hoped that would happen, and that he'd have several scotches before he finally glanced at his watch to find out that it was, say, midnight, and the Animal Coalition protest would be long over. The time was eight o'clock. He hated himself for looking, but there was the big hand, resting jauntily on the twelve, the little hand on the eight.

They must be in the throes of lining up, he thought, lighting their candles, arranging their signs. He could almost see Chandra, her thick hair swept back from her oval face, the small gold beads shining from her earlobes, her tiny mouth resigned as she issued orders to the group. And then they would march, like a string of worshipers in some Down East Candlemas, their voices Gregorian chants rising above the purr of traffic, they would move in a flickering wave of light down State Street. They would inch along like processionary caterpillars, with strings of silk dropping behind them, Radnor Laboratory their food source. How he envied them, envied the fiery, luminous pinwheel that the group embodied, the Animal *Coalition,* that family of men and women joined in a single purpose. Frederick decided he would not think of Chandra again, nor would he look at the clock. He ordered a second scotch.

"You haven't asked me about Maggie," Herbert noted.

"That's because it's none of my business," said Frederick.

"Well," said Herbert. "I just want you to know, I mean in case Maggie and I do get back together, that she likes you. I mean, you should just forget what I said when I told you she didn't. I was angry, talking off the top of my head. She likes you. She really does." Frederick smiled. Talk of getting back together with Maggie. What next would he hear from Herbert Stone's lips? He could feel the clock's hands pulling at his eyes like elongated magnets. Had they reached the corner of Market Place, where the little flower shop stood? Was the candlelight illuminating her face, tracing those magnificent cheekbones? Should he even care, at this point in their separation, if the Domino's Pizza boy careened out into the street and knocked her down? He would care. He would care very much, and this was what bothered him so. When would it end? Was he destined to chase her forever, the way Arthur Bowen, one of the richest men in New England, was forever spying on his own crazy wife?

"Maggie even told me last night that she thinks you've changed a lot since your separation," Herbert was still apologizing. Frederick reached for a bowl of the fish-shaped crackers and popped a handful into his mouth. The cracker bodies broke easily between his teeth, skeletal remains, fragile bones. He washed the gooey mouthful down with scotch and then pushed the bowl away. Why did they have to shape crackers like fish, for Christ's sake? Who thought these things up?

"Maggie likes you a lot," Herbert was still insisting, a record going round and round, repeating itself, unable to stop. He wished he'd never phoned Herbert. It was a time to be alone, at the park maybe, where visitors fed the seagulls and then sat upon benches that look out over the sea.

"Maggie had every right to dislike me," Frederick finally answered. "So quit with the apologies, okay, Herb? And watch yourself this time around. Don't make the same mistakes you made last time. Maggie's a good woman."

"I don't know," said Herbert, scratching at his receding hairline. "Sometimes I'm glad to have a second chance with Maggie. Other times I think about the Valeries out there in the world, all those firm thighs walking past me. Sometimes I'm satisfied with my life at the clinic. Other times I can't wait for my Kenny Perkins series to take off so that I can sell the damn place and never look back. There are days when I wish I had children. Other days I realize how much freer I am that I don't. What do you think, Freddy? Am I suffering from multiple personality or something?" Frederick thought about this deeply.

"No, Herbert," he finally answered. "I think you're suffering from *no* personality." Was that the clock he could hear ticking? Or was it his heart beating, his own broken heart bleating out? Could it be that Eddy Walsh was wearing a pacemaker? Eddy had already spoken long and in medical depth, at previous happy hours in the past, about the two heart attacks that had kept him out of the Million Sales Club. And he blamed it all on today's home buyer. Eight-thirty. They must certainly be in front of Radnor by this time. She would be floating before the crowd like a radiant Joan of Arc, her hair in a wild frenzy, her hand raised in leadership. What was she wearing? Had that awful man, the one who wanted to give his wife a baboon's heart if she ever needed it—*Here, honey, a little something for Mother's Day*—had he shouted angry words at Chandra? Thrown an animal-rights flier in her face? Was she in any danger from the madding crowd?

"I ran into an old acquaintance of mine the other day," Herbert was saying, his words deadened by the crunch of fish crackers. "Remember Tommy Viorikic? We graduated from high school together."

"I remember Tommy," said Frederick. He had been one of the popular kids, always dating the prettiest girls, always being voted president of this and that. "He was engaged to that little brunette cheerleader. What was her name?" Herbert shrugged.

"Whoever she was, they're divorced." Herbert ate another fistful of crackers. "He married two more times after that. Both divorces. He drives a bus for the city now. He asked me to stop by his house. He had something he wanted to show me. Know what it was?" Frederick shook his head. Herbert sounded like he had a mouth full of static electricity.

"Please quit eating those crackers, Herb," he said. "The noise is driving me crazy."

"Remember that bright green Chevy he used to cruise in?" Herbert asked. Frederick remembered. The brunette's name emerged suddenly, out of the past, appeared before him in a flash of sleek green car, the sound of a souped-up engine, *Eliza Clark,* her blackish-brown hair flying about her face as she and Tommy roared into the high-school parking lot. So they were divorced now. *Eliza Clark-Hyphen,* unless she had remarried.

"Listen to this," Herbert crunched on. "Tommy's got the Chevy set up in his living room now, the entire goddamn car, in the middle of the room! And he entertains all his dates *in the backseat!*" Herbert grinned widely. "That old radio plays just like a gem. He keeps it tuned to the oldies-but-goodies station. Nights he can't sleep, he gets behind the wheel and pretends he's cruising the old haunts. The man just never grew up." Herbert banged the empty crackers basket on the bar, signaling the geisha. "Can I have some more fishy-wishies?" he begged. Then to Frederick: "Tommy and I have made plans to double-date. Think Maggie will go for it?"

"Jesus," said Frederick. He'd been wondering how lives could get so twisted in such a relatively short time. Were there people out there now who were trying to remember his name? Were there people saying things like "Oh, yes, now I remember Frederick Stone. He was editor of the school newspaper and he married some girl he'd met at Woodstock who went to Central High. He was kind of cute, but very shy. He's divorced, you say? An accountant? I'll be darned. I would've thought he'd be publishing novels by now, maybe editing a major magazine. What? You say his brother, Herbert Stone, the class clown, is now the author?"

Frederick could stand it no longer. He dug cash out of his pocket and tossed a twenty onto the bar. A credit card would take too much time. Besides, what gallant lover of times past had stood and waited for a receipt when his mistress might be in peril? Perhaps practitioners of courtly love had time to wait for such things, but Frederick Stone was no longer content to watch from the sidelines, hidden in the bushes beneath some woman's bedroom balcony, sending her anonymous love poems. He was getting into the game of life again.

"Hey," said Herbert. "You haven't finished your scotch. Where are you going? You got that crazy look in your eye."

"There's something I gotta do," said Frederick. He accepted change from the bartender and then left her a generous tip. Herbert stood, too, the last of his own drink disappearing in a quick swallow. He plunked the empty glass onto the bar.

"You don't have someone's roof in mind, do you, Freddy?" he asked. "Because, with that crazy look in your eye, I gotta come with you."

"You boys leaving?" asked the geisha. *Boys*. Didn't geishas know any better? Where were all the talk shows where men complained about how *they* feel to be condescended to? If Frederick called her a *girl*, she'd probably drop-kick him into the men's room. He waved a quick good-bye. Eddy Walsh turned on his stool as Frederick and Herbert passed.

"Whaddya say, fellas?" asked Eddy. "If you were to see water trickling—*trickling*, mind you—into the basement of a sharp-looking house, wouldn't you still buy it? What's wrong with people these days?" His mood ring was a grassy snarling green. Kathy McLain was wearing her favorite T-shirt. On the front it warned: I DON'T FETCH COFFEE, I DON'T DO WINDOWS. On the back was the paramount declaration: AND I DON'T FAKE ORGASMS. Frederick shivered, as he did every time he read the back of Kathy McLain's T-shirt. He shivered in memory of all those young women he had known pre-Chandra, women who shook and trembled and tossed their heads beneath him. Women who had bitten his earlobe and murmured, "Yes, Freddy, oh yes." Had they all been actresses, little thespian liars?

"You need a haircut, sweetheart!" Kathy McLain shouted at Frederick. If he called *her* sweetheart, some wagon would pull up to his door late at night, with one of those Nazi sirens whirring, and uniformed soldiers would take him away to a lonely field. Frederick waved good-bye, not bothering to stop for restitution. He had an animal-rights march to attend.

"Are you *sure* you don't do windows?" he heard Herbert ask.

The street in front of Radnor Laboratory was littered with picket signs waving above bodies as Herbert edged the big Chrysler up to the curb and shut the engine off. Frederick could hear the ruckus without getting out of the car. But out on the sidewalk, it was deafening. The People First advocates were not even putting people in their own group first. None of them seemed willing to let any individual speak. Their angry faces blended into a swirl. Frederick had seen this anger, from his days of watching Sally and Oprah and Geraldo. He'd seen the KKK twist their faces in ignorance and hatred. He'd seen advocates of war shaking their fists above their heads and demanding that the USA blast the hell out of Iraq, the cradle of civilization, a country they couldn't even find on the map. Even Charlton Heston, Moses himself, had not been able to name Iraq's bordering countries when pressed to do so on a television show. Flustered, he had blurted out Bahrain, an island. Frederick had watched as Mr. Heston tried to hide his notes, from which he was quoting George Santayana. *Charlton Heston* advising the country about war! *Charlton Heston* advising the country to bomb the hell out of innocent men, women, and children. A half million people would eventually die. The man had been to too many NRA meetings. What was it Chandra called the NRA? *Nitwits, Racists,* and *Assholes.* But this was more evidence of what Frederick Stone had been saying all along to Chandra. "You can't get people to feel emotion for animals when they don't even feel it for other human beings."

The animal-rights group was now chanting in unison.

"Animals have feelings, too! Animals have feelings, too! Animals have feelings, too!" He saw Chandra suddenly appear on the gray steps of Radnor Laboratory, a natural podium. She raised an arm and the Animal Coalition, forming a protective wall around her, grew quiet so that she could speak. Behind Frederick, the People First crowd grew antsy. They moved forward, pushing, stomping one another's feet.

"It wasn't so long ago," Chandra Kimball shouted, "that fifteen thousand babies were born severely deformed because Thalidomide was thought to be a safe drug, due to animal testing." The

Animal Coalition roared in support, their candles hoisted dramatically over their heads.

"Would you rather your kid died?" a thin woman yelled from Frederick's right. She seemed very tired. "Instead of a rat?" The People First group burst into a loud wave of approval. Frederick was astounded. Was this what Chandra had been telling him about what she called "The Idiot Segment of Society"? There was no common sense in that statement. It was like saying "Would you rather your iron quit working or the moon?" The woman was smiling now, her thin face expanding with the comfort of her comrades, their praise rising up around her.

"Why don't you people move to the jungle," someone else yelled, "if you like animals so much?" A thunderous ocean of applause followed this suggestion. Frederick bulldozed his way closer to the front, hoping to get away from the People First gang so that he could hear what Chandra was now saying. Across the tops of a hundred heads he could see her beautiful face, aglow with the moment, that Impressionist face, flushed with its second in time.

"We have alternatives to this cruelty," he heard her proclaim. "We have highly developed mathematical and computer models, cell and tissue cultures, already in existence." A murmur of displeasure swept over her detractors, a furious billowing wave. For a moment, Frederick was frightened that he'd be swept under, drowned in the vicious sentiment. He had no heart for protest anymore, did he? No wonder he'd gradually grown away from it as the years of his married life passed. He'd never had any heart for it to begin with. He just wasn't a contender. Even Arthur Bowen knew that. And now he felt the guilt, his old *compadre,* flood his senses.

"If your husband was dying because he needed a heart transplant from a monkey, you'd be the first to do it!" This latest declaration came from a woman at Frederick's right elbow. He tried to imagine himself with a monkey's heart. Would he crave bananas? Would he consider lice a culinary gift? He tapped the woman's arm, just above her elbow, just enough to get her attention in that mad sea of humans.

"What?" she wanted to know, eyeing him suspiciously.

"She wouldn't want her husband to get a monkey's heart,"

Frederick stated. "Believe me, I know. I'm her husband." Chandra might even deny him an artificial Jarvak's heart, considering that she seemed to hate him these days. He felt his own arm being tapped roughly and turned. Herbert.

"This is no place for us, Freddy," said Herbert. "You told me we were going to do happy hour."

"Going 'to do' happy hour?" Frederick asked. "You're starting to sound like you're from the West Coast, Herb." That's what a literary agent could do to some people. That's what a cellular phone could do.

The crowd bent forward, taking all bodies with it, and then, just as suddenly, bent back again, a tall, thick reed swaying.

"Jesus," said Herbert. "This is no place for a man thinking of reconciliation with his wife."

"It is if *that's* your wife," said Frederick, bobbing his chin at Chandra. She had managed to quiet her own group, her hands waving gently, the hands of a lithe conductor. The evening had drawn inward, the sun having already sunk toward some happier longitude. Candles now bounced and flickered like insane lightning bugs, dots of fire strung upon the night.

"Each year tens of millions of animals are burned, shocked, poisoned, and killed in repetitious experiments that are conducted for unnecessary research data, just so that a few people can earn their Ph.D.s, or in the hopes that they'll be able to get grant funding." The Animal Coalition broke into an inferno of applause as the People First supporters swelled forward again in anger. It was with difficulty that Frederick maintained his balance. He felt Herbert's hand grasp his arm.

"You got your training for this at Woodstock," Herbert whined, "but I have none at all."

When Frederick was able to right himself, Chandra was gone. The steps where she had stood were now swarming with people from both groups, signs were being flung down in anger, and a generic mayhem seemed to be the mood of the moment.

"I've got to find her, Herb," Frederick said. "You go on back to The China Boat." He saw Herbert's face form a protest of its own, his mouth about to speak words, his eyes disapproving, and then Herbert was swept backward into the crowd, Jonah being sucked into the belly of the whale. Frederick was propelled forward, toward the edge of the crowd, its outskirts. He would feel right at home there. *You live on the outskirts of humanity, Freddy.* He needed to think like Chandra, like a Seminars of the Mind person. What would she do next? She had given her speech to the crowd, but he knew that that wouldn't satiate her. He'd bailed her out before for trespassing, once during an attempt to sabotage a deer hunt, once at a Fur Free Society protest when she'd managed to sneak inside the Portland Fur Boutique and spray the walls with a bloody red paint. He felt quite sure, somehow, that Chandra was hoping to infiltrate the halls of Radnor Laboratory. Pushing forward through the undulating crowd was rather like being on an inner tube in a wave pool. But he finally crested the last mass of bodies at the edge and then rode out into a serene pool of folks hovering near the front steps. "Hello, Mr. Stone," he heard someone say. Halona. Behind her, Sukie. They still held lighted candles. Sukie looked like a tall, thin rendition of the Little Match Girl. And then Robbie's face suddenly appeared, a pristine visage, not a single bump or bruise on it. He was carrying a picket sign, the way Frederick had once carried picket signs, a lifetime ago, with Chandra's little pleas to humanity scrawled on each of them. Frederick smiled weakly. Robbie graced him with the middle finger of his right hand and then disappeared back into the crowd. *Hasta la Vista, little nephew.*

"Where's Chandra?" he asked the two women. He had been unaware until he spoke just how winded he was from the job of weaving in and out among the protestors. Halona hunched her shoulders and Sukie had already disappeared toward the front of the building.

"She just seemed to vanish," Halona said. "She was here a minute ago." The back door, or entrance, Frederick decided. If he was going to think like his wife, that's what his choice would be. A private route into the bowels of Radnor Laboratory while all eyes were on the crowd out front. She had always been the Queen of Distraction. He made his way, discreetly, down the side of the building. Both groups had turned their attention to the newest speaker, a tall man with a beard who spoke of sharing the planet with all living things. The People First group had turned its full attention on drowning out his words.

"Human beings first!" their rant declared. "Human beings first!"

At the rear of the building, Frederick found the lifted window and smiled. She had always had a way of bribing people, either with money or charm. Would a janitor have left it open for her, for that perfect oval face? An infiltrator from the Animal Coalition, perhaps? No matter who did the job, she was someone to be reckoned with, his wife, Chandra Kimball, was. She would have seen to it that the Watergate conspirators remembered to take that guilty strip of tape from off the jimmied door.

A red plastic milk crate sat outside the window. Frederick hesitated only a second before he stepped up onto it and then lifted himself across the waiting sill. He inched down the dark hallway, his eyes struggling with the dim light, toward the soft murmur of voices, which rose and fell quietly. Whispering. Excited levels and tones. He recognized Chandra's voice almost immediately. There was too much of the song in it, even in the midst of her murmurs. He crouched along the wall, hurrying now toward the voices.

"Oh, God," he heard Chandra say, her words louder now. He identified the room from which they were seeping, grasped the door handle, and turned the knob quietly. A light had been switched on in the room. There she was, kneeling on the floor before one of the cages, an animal of some sort in her lap. He could hear quiet curses now coming from his wife, and around the room other voices suddenly filtered up to him, other people kneeling before open cages.

"Shut that door!" someone whispered loudly. "They might see the light!" He realized for the first time that he was in a room with no windows. Of course, it would be a room with no windows. The unspeakable could occur in rooms with no windows. He recognized several members of the Animal Coalition.

"Tim, you and Elaine get those cats over there," Chandra was directing. He could hear the sobs she was fighting back. She stood, a cat in her arms. Frederick saw that its head had been shaved bald, several red pinpoints the only indications of where the wires had been. All around him now, he saw eyes staring out of the metal cages, frightened eyes, eyes filled with pain. Cats, monkeys, rabbits, some thin and dying, others waiting for what might come next. He felt his stomach heave with a bout of nausea. A small chorus of meows had begun, with cats pushing against their cages in the hopes of being freed, dogs barking now with desperate

abandon. Chandra turned with the cat in her arms, and they stood
face to face. He wanted to say so much to her, wished to speak all
the things that one can utter in a few desperate seconds, words to
last a lifetime. Her eyes were filled with tears, the cat in her arms
looking now with cautious curiosity at Frederick, as though he
might be one of the white-coat people. He reached his arms out to
her, not to hold her, not to touch her, but to take the animal, to
do his share. She gave the cat to him, its body curling quickly into
the crook of his arm, its purring beginning instantly. He tried not
to think of the bald head, the holes made by the wires—what the
hell had they been doing? Instead he listened to the rhythmic purr,
an animal ready to forgive this new human for what the last one
had done.

"I'll get another one," Chandra said, and forced a smile.
"There's a van just around the corner, to the right of the window.
You'd better hurry, though. They can keep them busy out front
just so long."

"I'm allergic, you'll remember," Frederick noted. But she was
already busy with the cages where the monkeys pressed their thin
faces up to the bars, eyes full of more intelligence than Frederick
had ever seen during happy hours at The China Boat. He couldn't
do this, not after this one rescue. He didn't have the heart for it.
And suddenly, he was full of love and compassion and thankfulness for those who *could* do it. He looked around the room at this
moving pinwheel of people, strangers bonded together in a common need, men and women rocking animals in their arms as they
unlatched cages. He recognized a few faces from past meetings in
his living room. But he had never paid much attention before to
Chandra's coalition members. He knew only what he had read
in that day's paper, that the leaders of the group consisted mostly
of professionals—a dentist, a librarian, a veterinarian, a writer, a
history teacher, a classical musician. Hardly a crew of demented
radicals. What Frederick found most unusual was that the animals
seemed to know: *These are not the humans with the needles and the
wires and the pain. These are new people.* His own eyes were blur-
ring. He was, after all, allergic. Chandra passed him again, a
monkey in her arms. She was still softly issuing orders.

"You can bring them to my house," Frederick heard himself
say. "You can bring the sick ones to Herbert. It'll be okay." She

smiled at him, a sweet genuine smile. It had been a long time since he had witnessed such a thing.

"Thanks, Freddy," she said. "But we've got it all planned out. There's a vet in our group, so we have a clinic." Of course they would have a plan, two plans, ten plans. It was just that he suddenly wanted to be included, a quiet streamer on the pinwheel he saw twirling before his eyes. They were all moving about with such forethought that, even though he held a cat of his own, he still felt like an observer.

Outside, he handed the animal over to the woman who seemed to be in charge of van duty. She quickly deposited the cat in a cardboard box.

"It's got a nice blanket in there," she whispered. "We just need to keep it as quiet as we can. These animals have been through enough." Frederick nodded. He felt good, having only transported the cat out of the building. He wished he could do more, but he knew that he couldn't. He dug down into his pocket again and came up with two twenties. He gave it to the woman.

"Put this toward some food, litter, that sort of thing," he told her. She gave his hand a little squeeze as she took the money.

"You're Chandra's ex-husband, aren't you?" she asked, and he nodded. Her *ex-husband*. Everybody in Portland seemed to know that he had been *extraneared*. Everyone in Portland had seemed able to go on with their own lives as though this event were not at all important. He realized that the time had come to hoist his jacket collar up about his neck, hang his head in poetic remorse, and amble off toward a new life. But it seemed that he needed his old life to slap him one more time in the face. As he stood by the door, waiting for her to appear, he felt suddenly like an old boxer, getting back up on shaky feet only to be knocked down again and again, long after the crowd has lost its taste for blood, even with the crowd yelling, "Stay down! Stay down!" He watched as they all filed out, the vet, the lawyer, the librarian, the musician: *rich man, poor man, beggar man, thief.* He would not be surprised to see Kenny Perkins there, doing his serial share. They filled the van with fragile animals. Chandra appeared finally, the last one out, a blanketed bundle in her arms. Her face was the color of white flour, the color of something soft but pale, linen, maybe. At the doorway, she reached out a hand to steady herself before she saw him waiting, there in the lurch of his life.

"Chandra," he said, but he could tell by her eyes that they wouldn't talk, not then, not of things disconnected to the suffering that was taking place right at that moment. She lifted the blanket away from the bundle and Frederick felt his facial muscles tense, a little gasp escape him. It had once been a cat. He could tell this by the shape of its head, its body, its blank oval eyes. But the body itself was furless, a pinkish white carcass breathing up and down, up and down, the same motions that would produce a chuckle in the human being.

"Dr. Olmstead says that it's been treated with chloroprene," Chandra told him. Her voice was tinny, a tremble behind her words. "They're searching for a cure for baldness. They've been doing these very same tests for years now, with the very same results." Frederick reached out a hand to touch the cat, its skin as hard as rubber now. It lifted its head and looked at him with a deep inquisitiveness. It was something not real to him, suddenly, an invention in a Spielberg movie, an *ET* creature, perhaps. *Phone home. Chandra, please, phone home.*

"Jesus," he said. "Jesus." He closed his eyes, wishing that he would forget, minutes from now, that he had ever seen such a thing, that he would never think of it again, not on any of those numerous sunny days that he would be driving past the dark windows of Radnor Laboratory, as he lived out the rest of his life, days when he would be hurrying to the post office, the laundry, the library, he never wanted to remember what would be taking place inside those pearly gray walls, inside where so few people would ever see. He was not made for truth such as this. He was not cut from Chandra's magnanimous cloth. He could forget the ugly facts about the world while he was forced to live in it.

"Look at the positive side," Chandra said, and he opened his eyes again to what was taking place. She had covered the cat once more with the blanket. All Frederick could see now was the round pink head, a baby being born, the big yellow eyes of his conscience staring back at him. "You'll never be allergic to this one," Chandra added. "Its hair follicles have been destroyed forever." She put the bundle in the van woman's arms, the last one to be loaded.

"Let's get out of here," Chandra said. Frederick touched her arm. He couldn't stop himself. He even knew the ramifications of doing such a thing. She would think, Even in the midst of this grief, both animal and human, he is thinking of himself. And that would be true. For he was. He had even stepped over the horrid picture of the bald cat in order to present his case.

"Chan," he said. It had been years since he'd called her that. He'd stopped doing it because, quite frankly, it evoked memories of the Chinese detective Charlie.

Chandra had crawled into the back of the van and was about to pull the door shut, but this stopped her. She turned toward him, her pale face tensing.

"I can't seem to shake this thing," he told her. "I can't seem to go on. I still love you, is why."

"But *I* don't love *you*," she said.

"I'm sorry for the animals and all," Frederick admitted. He didn't want to listen to what she'd just said. It was the first time she'd actually told him this, his greatest fear. "But is there some way we can talk about this, maybe later tonight?"

She shook her head, her resigned expression telling him that she was not at all surprised.

"Hubris, Freddy," was all she said. "Complete and unadulterated *hubris*."

As the van pulled out of the parking lot and disappeared down the street, Frederick could hear the angry confrontation still roaring at the front of the building. He decided that his brother, Herbert Stone, could take care of himself. He had no intentions of fighting through the bulging belly of that crowd again. He stood in the back lot of Radnor Laboratory feeling very much like a person left behind in an old place, while everyone else rushed off to a new place. The Animal Coalition had left him behind as if he was some kind of bad penny. But then, he'd never turned up to help them out before, had he? He'd never even offered a bit of encouragement.

Lights had begun to burst on, one at a time, in the back rooms of the laboratory, and Frederick knew that it was only a matter of seconds before the *theft* would be discovered. The last place that he, as Chandra Kimball's soon-to-be-ex-husband, needed to be found was in the aftermath of her illegal activities. He put his hands into his pants pockets and ambled off toward Ellsboro Street, four miles away, with what remained of his dignity. A good long walk would give him plenty of time to sort through the remnants of his old life, to consider the life that lay ahead, a life in which he would forever be labeled *a divorced person.* There would be much news about the removal of the animals, he was certain. Chandra and the others would be labeled extremists, and maybe they were. But still, he saw their actions commendable in some sort of heroic way. He admired their unwavering notion of the world as a place that can be changed, because it was a belief he wished he held, but didn't. How could he think of world peace, about a brotherhood for all mankind, when the remnants of his own family were lying like exploded shrapnel on the battlefields of the sixties? He wanted to tell this to Chandra. He wanted to say, "Hey, Chan, listen to this. I'm not such a bad guy." But there was that mountain of a fact rising before his face. There was the truth, like some groundhog sticking its head up out of a hole and seeing its shadow. "But *I* don't love *you,*" she'd said. His eyes watered quickly, tears of sympathy for himself, for the task which lay ahead, for the transition, the obstacle, the hurdle placed there in his middle age by his wife. If it had been another man, if it had been a *Robbie,* there would still be hope. Frederick would pronounce it an infatuation and wait as calmly as he could until it passed. But it wasn't an infatuation. "I don't love you."

At the park he paused to stare out over the water, listen to the waves nipping at the strand. He felt, suddenly, as though he were in the ending to a novel, one where the protagonist is left standing with a satchel in his hand, Kenny Perkins signaling to the reader that there will be a sequel. But this was no novel. This was real life. As real as the lights that were shimmering on Peak's Island, electricity coursing from one home to another, electrical families tied together with a single invention. He thought about a warm dinner at Will's Restaurant, an inch of some VSOP cognac to put enough fire into him for the ferry ride back. Maybe some pale woman would be on the boat, a tourist, her purse strap slung over her shoulder, the ocean wind lifting the wide skirt of her dress, lifting her hair, lifting his spirits. An extremely pale woman, in the light of Arthur Bowen's advice about His and Her tans. And they would lock eyes, knowing that they'd been thrown together for the sheer sake of circumstance, knowing that their meeting would be as meaningless but necessary as pollination. He would invite her to dinner at Will's. "It's named for their son," he'd tell her, an air of importance in his knowing this. "A little blond boy. I have no children myself." A woman on the ferry boat. What had ever happened to Richard Hamel? *They were on the ferry boat, get it? Master Bator and his boyfriend, holding hands, honest to Christ, I think they might have even kissed.* And on the return ride he would take this pale woman up into his arms, this woman with the warm dinner in her belly, with a trickle of cognac in her veins, and he would shelter her from the breezes, shelter himself in the smell of her breath, the soft bounce of her *real* breasts, the sweet slack curve of her pale thighs.

He went on home to find a note taped to the screen door of his Victorian house. It was from Doris Bowen. *Please don't try to contact me,* the note pleaded. *It's over between us.* She had signed it *Mrs. Arthur Bowen.*

"You flatter yourself, Doris," Frederick said, letting himself into the dark kitchen. There had not even been a single cookie left on his front steps, manna from Mrs. Muller, to soften the blows of a tough day.

He slept a deep sleep that night, waking only once before dawn and then returning to the thick blanket of dreams that had wrapped itself around him. Faces came and went. Even Chandra's stepfather, Joe, turned up in his soiled apron to say hello, a can of charcoal lighter fluid clutched in one hand, a platter of steaks leaking blood in the other. Lillian's red lips pounced out of dark corners, the corners of Radnor Laboratory, the lips of authority. "Get a haircut, dear," the lips told him. He saw Mr. Bator's cherubic face peering out of the teachers' room at Portland High. "The toe bone connected to the foot bone," Mr. Bator sang, snapping his fingers. "The foot bone connected to the ankle bone." Joyce appeared, her finger wagging like a dog's tail, oscillating. "You're in denial, mister." She disappeared, followed by Reginald's Conestoga, rolling toward some lesson in history, a loaf of garlic bread protruding from its flap. Doris Bowen suddenly emerged from the montage. "Ask me no secrets and I'll tell you no lies," Doris promised again. And now came the old faces, the faces of pain: "The world stinks," said his mother, scattering lavender petals to the winds. His father, austere and solemn, cleared his throat. "You missed a free education in Vietnam, Frederick. And do you know why? Because you're spineless." And then Mr. Bator again, always Mr. Bator, following in the angry aftermath of Dr. Philip Stone's words, sweeping up the carnage, as he had done for Frederick all through high school. "Invertebrates are animals without a backbone or a spinal column," Mr. Bator said. "Invertebrates are spineless, but you, Freddy, you are an excellent example of a *vertebrate.*" And Polly, lastly, Polly. It pained him instantly to see her again, full-flesh, vital, because he had never really known her in life, had only considered the outline of her, the contour, the silhouette. Now here she was, her face glowing and pink, her eyes alive. "I was never college material, Freddy," his sister told him. "Why can't Daddy understand that? I have a life now. I have a husband. I have my children." Had she ever talked to him about such things? At some family function? He couldn't remember. And if she did, what had he replied? "We're all fodder to The Great Man, dear sister. What *kind* of fodder doesn't matter." Had he said anything at all to Polly in her time of need? Probably not. They had been a tongueless, earless, eyeless family. *Invertebrates,* those soft-bodied animals with hard outer skeletons, bumping against one another in the dark.

It seemed as though he waited weeks for her to appear. But in dreams, time is even more the prankster. They say it all happens in a second. And you believe that. And then some further study is done on sleep, and the experts change their minds and declare that a dream takes as long to occur as it takes the dreamer to dream the events. It didn't matter, because it seemed he waited weeks for Chandra Kimball to slip into the drama, to claim her own pound of his flesh. But she didn't show. She was obviously off somewhere, involved in the betterment of mankind. Of animalkind. She was simply not there. It was as if some naughty computer elf had gone into the hard disk of his mind and wiped out everything in the file titled *Chandra.* She herself did not appear, but she was kind enough to send a proxy: the bald, bleached cat, its round head straining upward for a stroking hand, its piteous meows pummeling his ears, its incessant tongue lolling about in its wet mouth.

"Put it out of its misery," Frederick murmured. "It's dying anyway." He awoke in a burst of sweat: sweat on his forehead, his neck, his chest, sweat swimming in his eyes. His hand reached out toward the green puddle of light, toward the clock humming away in the darkness. It was four-thirty. He sank back into the pillows. It occurred to him that he had no reason to get out of bed early, to get out of bed at ten o'clock, to get out of bed at all. No reason. Oh, yes, he had promised himself to return Mrs. Muller's cookie sheet that very day, but otherwise he may as well stay put. He sighed deeply, his body now basking in the coolness that comes with perspired sweat, the sickly odor of panic. One didn't have to be a poet to catch the metaphorical message of the dream. It occurred to him—although he had never smoked a cigarette, give or take one or two in boyhood—that he would like a lovely puff off someone's Marlboro. At least he assumed it was a cigarette urge he was feeling, a little tug of anxiety in his stomach, his hands restless for some kind of job, his lips working in what appeared to be hysterical inhaling.

"Put it out of its misery," he said to the soaked pillow, to the clock, to the green numbers that were recording the unintelligible passage of time. "Put it out of its misery."

ixteen

utumn came quickly to southern Maine, or so it seemed to Frederick Stone. But perhaps that was only because the universe had finally gotten his attention. The universe had taught him to pay heed. The Fates themselves had kneed him in the genitals numerous times, blackened both his eyes, stomped upon his toes. He regarded them with great respect these days, usually referring to them as Ms. Clotho, Ms. Atropos, Ms. Lachesis. If they had been real women, he would never, *never,* open a door for them. He would never order for them in a restaurant. Providence help him if one of them should catch him ogling her retreating ass. He was a new man. He knew some important stuff. He knew that The Fates were three tough broads. The Fates were Jimmy Hoffa, Norman H. Schwarzkopf, and Pat Buchanan in drag.

His hair now grown long enough that he could put it in a ponytail, Frederick sat out on the steps of the house on Ellsboro Street and watched the burgundy leaves of the red maple scuttle across the lawn in little bursts of wind. The For Sale sign had tilted during the night, but no matter. The young couple who came by the week before with Eddy Walsh had made an acceptable offer and was now awaiting approval on their loan from the bank. Now the smell of harvest rose up into the bluing sky. The squirrels on Ellsboro Street were looking bushier, their fur fluffing itself, thickening for the winter cold. The birds had begun their journey equatorward, some flying by night across the spectacle of moon, some looking to the sun for orientation. They had built up enormous fat reserves to fuel them, and now the birds were skipping town. Once, from the window of his car, he had noticed the sky black with migrating hawks. At least he thought they were hawks. Whatever they were, they were going somewhere he wasn't.

He looked at his watch. It was nine-thirty. He would need to be at Cain's Corner Grocery by ten o'clock. Mr. Cain had had the Help Wanted sign in the window only ten minutes, or so he claimed, when Frederick ambled in a month earlier, looking for a jar of olives. It seemed a perfect opportunity to put to work what Frederick had always considered his enormous marketing talent. So he himself pulled the sign down, tape ripping away dramatically, and began his duties by urging the archaic Mr. Cain to order soy milk, tofu hot dogs, fat-free cookies, a few items that would interest the Yuppie homeowners in the area. And already it was working. In just one week Frederick had jotted down several other products that shoppers had inquired about—the Sunday New York Times, veggie egg rolls, fat-free baked beans, Perrier, couscous— all sales boosters for a tiny corner grocery. During his second week, he and Mr. Cain had leaned upon the counter, two men hovering above their elbows, and discussed the expansion of the store to include a small café, a few round tables, a handful of chairs. They would offer several varieties of coffee bean, the brews of which could be sampled depending upon the special of the day. "It'll be a good place for folks to come and read the newspaper," Frederick had noted. "A perfect gathering place for a morning cup of coffee." By the end of his third week, he had convinced Mr. Cain to expand the tiny selection of wines. The growth of the store meant more than just dollars for Mr. Cain's coffers, or a paycheck raise for Frederick. He saw himself as a kind of affable proprietor, waving from the storefront window to passersby, listening with a patient nod of his head to family problems, setting a fine example for neighborhood youngsters. He would be the

Andy Taylor of Portland, solving problems daily with his home-spun advice. He wanted, in his loneliness, to gather people about him as though there would be a safety in their numbers. He wanted a thick, breathing blanket of warm-blooded mammals, verte-brates, to serve as a buffer to the cold, as the squirrels were thick-ening their own coats for winter. True, Chandra would have said that it was his notion of himself as some kind of all-knowing god, his full larder of *hubris* that motivated him. And maybe she would be right. But then, she was out rescuing rain forests, and animals, and badly named human beings. Was his job any less heroic? It was, after all, the job he had set out to achieve early on, the day he found an accounting degree in his hand instead of his first pub-lished book of poems. It was what he had told the artsy crowd who hung out at those university wine-and-cheese clusters. He, Frederick Stone, would help the small-business man. Now, in his forties, he realized he didn't have to go to Asia, or Central Amer-ica, or more than four blocks from his house in order to resuscitate the dream. Cain's Corner Grocery was a modest beginning, but at least he now knew that the vision of the sixties was still alive.

He waved a good morning to Mrs. Muller, who was backing her little Datsun out of her driveway. She had turned out to be a good neighbor, and an even better cook. Frederick had had fresh pastries all month. It was from Mrs. Muller that he got the idea for home-baked pastries at Cain's Corner Grocery. And Mr. Cain had been only too pleased to employ one of the locals in such a man-ner. Mrs. Muller tooted affectionately, a little *blep* of horn.

"I'm just off to Cain's with a batch of blueberry muffins and four fruit pies," she announced happily from her car window. Frederick licked his lips dramatically, rubbed his belly. One was no longer living on the outskirts of humanity if one was employed at a neigh-borhood grocery. If one was in culinary contact with one's neigh-bors. Perhaps he was destined to wander around the country, bringing goodwill and cheer to all he encountered. Like David Janssen in "The Fugitive," he would come into a town, set things straight in the lives of a few people, and then leave for another town. He wondered if Chandra would applaud the addition of Mrs. Muller's pastries—and may the Fates know that Mrs. Muller herself told him to call her *Mrs.* Muller, and not *Ms.* Muller.

"I consider it an educational degree," Mrs. Muller had announced. "It's not a Ph.D., it's an M.R.S." Chandra would probably declare that Walter's wife needed to take a seminar: "From Housefrau to Entrepreneur: Cleaving the Bonds of Marriage."

Frederick flung the last of his coffee, that half-inch in the bottom of his cup that had grown cold, out toward the dried marigolds lining the drive, the marigolds of spring, Chandra's flowers. He had, weeks ago, given up on the martini lunch. He decided that excessive gin was responsible for his receding hairline, the threadlike wrinkles highlighting his eyes, and certainly the middle-aged paunch which he awoke one morning horrified to discover growing like moss around his middle. He had made the mistake of mentioning this ignominy to his brother, Herbert. "You know what's happening to these bodies of ours, don't you, Freddy?" Herbert had beseeched him. "Oxidation." Frederick had merely stared at his brother, waiting. "That's the old age process, buddy," Herbert had gone on. "Get used to it. We're *rusting*." Frederick's computer calendar of important corporeal dates had been busy *that* morning, until, tired of charting and coursing his own demise, he called up the calendar and deleted the entire shebang. Maybe he could beat the passage of time by simply ignoring it, by avoiding mirrors, the reflections in store windows. Not that he didn't think himself still attractive. He did. But the threat of old age had perched like a buzzard on his shoulder. He felt the weight of the thing daily, felt it breathe, eat, and shit. Daily, it was waiting for his corpse to finally drop. Good Christ. He was *rusting*.

As he had done for the past month, Frederick left his car sitting in the drive and walked the four blocks to work. A man his age, a man old enough to have been to Woodstock, needed daily exercise. From the top of Ellsboro Street, he had a brief view of the water. It seemed as if Casco Bay had turned indigo with autumn. It lay still and cool in the distance. The anxious cries of the gulls rose up, mingled with the buzz of traffic. He saw a small red car cut the corner of Ellsboro and rush toward him. For a second, his heart raced wildly, and did so without permission from his mind, *wildly*. But it was a newer-model car than Chandra's, with a younger woman driving, a different man she'd no doubt come to visit.

At Cain's Corner Grocery he paused before the storefront window and read the computer-generated signs he had taped there

over the past month. SUNDAY *NEW YORK TIMES* NOW AVAILABLE.
CAIN'S CORNER GROCERY IS HAPPY TO HANDLE SPECIAL ORDERS. COM-
ING SOON: CAIN'S CAFÉ! SPECIAL COFFEE BLENDS. His favorite was a
personal announcement for the clientele: WE AT CAIN'S CORNER
GROCERY WISH OUR FRIENDS A VERY PLEASANT AUTUMN. To make
this sign he had thumbed through his file of clip art and had chosen
a cornucopia to decorate the upper right-hand corner.

He clocked in by writing out the time in pen. A time-card
system would be too extravagant for Cain's at this point. But,
with Frederick in-house as a kind of entrepreneurial adviser, he
imagined that the store's growth might one day demand the time
card in order to keep track of the flock of employees. But then,
Cain's would no longer be a corner grocery. It would be another
goddamn IGA, with its Muzak, and its bright overhead lights, and
its horny bag boys. Rather than turn the neighborhood grocery
into a multimillion-dollar business and old Mr. Cain into a bitter
and unhappy man, Frederick Stone knew he would probably have
to mosey off into the sunset one day, taking his immense marketing skills with him. He just had no idea how soon he would be
moseying.

It had seemed like any other day. He had waited for certain
deliveries, had chatted up the customers. He had been enormously
surprised at how many of the old high-school gang still lived in
Portland. In his month at Cain's he had run into Jerry Ryan, who
had been in Mr. Bator's biology class. "I have no idea what happened to him," Jerry had said when Frederick asked about the
biology teacher. "Didn't you go to BU or something?" Jerry had
ended the conversation, looking a bit embarrassed. Funny, but
Frederick didn't feel embarrassed at all. What was wrong with an
honest day's work? Jerry Ryan must've turned into a George Bush
boy, his fingers white and pale and unused. Law could do that to
a fellow. Then he'd almost not recognized Gene Nelson, from
Boy Scouts. "Freddy!" Gene had shouted, beating him about the
shoulders and upon the back. "How the hell's it been hanging?"
At first, Frederick thought surely this man must've meant the
inflated Budweiser bottle, three feet long, which he'd hung just
minutes ago from the ceiling over the cooler. But then Gene had
said, "It's Gene. Gene Nelson. Remember that Boy Scout picnic
at Willard's Pond when you cut your foot?" And Frederick had

been instantly cheered to see someone from the past, someone from the yellow days of childhood, someone who could give him meaning, who knew him B.C. *Before Chandra*. And then Gene had gone on to describe what had become of several of the boys. Nick Dimopoulos had married an Italian woman who shot him in the scrotum when she caught him cheating on her. Frederick grimaced. *Arrivederci, testicales*. But Nicky had married again, and now owned a car sales business in Kansas, but no, no children. "Why didn't you come to the reunion last year?" Gene had wanted to know. "Twenty-five fucking years. Can you believe that?" Frederick had merely shrugged. Why *hadn't* he gone to the reunion? He could almost recall the invitation arriving in the mail. He wondered if Nicky Dimopoulos remembered prom night, when they had drunk four bottles of ouzo. "And Richard Hamel?" Frederick had asked. Jesus, but he had hated Richard Hamel. "Dead," Gene had said. "Vietnam. The class of 'sixty-six lost ten boys to Nam. Can you imagine that? I went down to D.C. last summer and traced their names off the wall so I could put them up for the reunion. Why did you say you didn't come, Freddy?" And then they'd said good-bye, and Gene was gone, back into the old high-school yearbook, maybe, back to where he was the last time Frederick had seen his face. Richard Hamel, dead in Vietnam. Dead all these years that Frederick had hated him, had planned to look him up in order to tell him what a mumblety-peg cheat he was. Dead. Richard Hamel should have been Dr. Philip Stone's son.

Frederick was looking down at the newspaper in front of him, thinking about Nicky Dimopoulos dodging well-aimed bullets, and trying to keep his thoughts away from Richard Hamel, a war hero according to Gene Nelson, when he heard customers come in. How could he know, with the past already rushing through him like liquid smoke, that Chandra would walk into the store, out of a blue-bright ocean day, to leave him even more shaken, to rattle his confidence again? He couldn't know.

He gave only a casual glance up from his paper to see a bearded man in the doorway, his arm extended behind him, a woman's arm reaching forward as he led her inside, their hands clasped. All Frederick noticed was that the man was wearing a scarf about his neck, and it reminded him again how quickly winter was coming.

His view of the woman was blocked by the burly gentleman, but Frederick saw red sneakers, white anklets, the hem of a denim skirt. As they disappeared down the wine aisle, he quickly folded his newspaper and tossed it aside. From his first minute of employment he had decided to become the customers' best friend, to ingratiate himself, to share with them his vision of the future of Cain's Corner Grocery. It would be a Norman Rockwell place for Yuppies when Frederick was finished. That's what Yuppies flocked to Maine for in the first place, and the locals, after all, shouldn't disappoint them. By the time he straightened the sacks of potato chips and slid a bag of peanuts back onto its proper rod—customers could be so sloppy—the couple was standing in front of the small wine selection. He could see the back of the gentleman's head, full hair laced with a stately gray. He would inform them that the wine selection would be growing in leaps and bounds, in case they found it unsatisfactory on this day.

"Within the month we'll have a wider selection of French and California bottles in here," Frederick announced as he turned down their aisle. From this angle all he could see was the man's back, his massive arms wrapped about the woman, his head tilted forward. They were kissing. Frederick smiled after the first rush of sadness, maybe even jealousy, flashed through him. The sight of a couple in love could still leave him shaken. He was about to turn back, to give strangers their moment of love in a corner grocery store, when he heard the distinct laugh, a trill almost, a girlish giggle. *Chandra. The Ghost of Woodstock Past.* He felt his legs disappear beneath him. He was walking on air, walking above ghost legs, all sensation gone. And the sound of his voice must have finally caught up with her, too, for her face emerged instantly from behind the man's back. They stared.

"Freddy," she said. He saw her swallow, saw her eyes flutter as she raised a hand to her mouth. There hadn't been many times in his life when he'd seen her speechless. And as for him, wouldn't it have been great if he had taken advantage of the moment, had tilted his head in some John Wayne gesture? *Howdy, pilgrim,* he might've said. Or he could have nodded sweetly, the poet in him rising, finally, to the ultimate occasion. *And speaking of pilgrims, I was one who loved the pilgrim soul in you.* He did none of that.

"Chandra," he answered. His blood vessels enlarged in what

would be the greatest pigmentary disturbance of his life. Had someone attached a commode handle to his ear? It felt as if his face had been flushed. Blood raced throughout his veins, tingling, spreading a warmth so intense, a fire so sincere, that he feared he would accidentally thaw the blasted frozen-veggie egg rolls.

"You're *working* here?" she asked. The gentleman regarded him with what Frederick recognized as a territorial gaze, a tacit threat. *She's mine,* his eyes said. The smell of testosterone filled the aisle before he seemed to recognize the situation.

"Oh, so *you're* Frederick," he apologized, holding a massive hand out to be shook. "I somehow thought you were an accountant."

"I somehow thought so, too," Chandra said, her perfect little lips barely moving.

"We'll have an improved selection by next week," Frederick told them, ignoring the hand that had been offered up to him. "Chile, Australia, Germany. Much improved." That said, he retreated to the back of the store, pretending to fetch something in the stockroom. Instead, he leaned against the wall, his eyes shut, his heart thumping up and down in a manic frenzy. When he finally emerged, two minutes later, they were gone. *Put it out of its misery.*

Twenty minutes passed, twenty minutes in which he simply stared out the storefront window or rang up the few sales items that were given him, as though he were an automaton, as though he had dreamed the visit. Then she called him, there at Cain's Corner Grocery, and that was good of her, big of her, really, it was. Chandra called and apologized for the embarrassment she had just caused him.

"Ted is someone I met last month," she explained. "He works for the EPA." Where else?

"He seems like a nice guy," Frederick told her. What could he say? It was the truth. The son of a bitch, the bastard, the odious prick did seem like a decent fellow. And he had such thick hair, the kind of hair that wouldn't recede even if it was attached to pulleys.

"Are you going to be okay, Freddy?" she asked. He thought about that. She had left him in June, moved her stuff out of their home, avoided him as though he were covered with buboes, given out a wrong address so that he couldn't find her, hung the phone up on him, and, ultimately, divorced him. Now, here in September, here just days before the autumnal equinox would bring a night that would be as long as the day—his longest night to suffer through yet—she wondered if he was *okay*. And she had had the nerve, all these years, to accuse *him* of excessive pride.

"Of course," he replied. He hoped his light tone assured her that he was deliriously happy, and he went on to remind her that the wine selection would grow and grow and not to be a stranger to Cain's Corner Grocery just because he was employed there. He, *ha-ha*, needed all the business he could get. *Ha-ha*. He hung up the phone and went to pieces.

For almost twenty-four hours he shook. Mr. Cain, taking pity on the mess his employee was in, had sent him home immediately. Once there, Frederick took to his bed. Covered from neck to foot in blankets, he shivered all night and into the dawn, until he finally let the heat of his morning shower beat some sense into him. He shook *physically, uncontrollably,* as though love were some awful malaria, a parasite in the bloodstream, a thing to be gotten over after excessive chills, a high fever, a bit of vomiting. But he had stepped from the warm shower, shivering, his feet cold upon the tiles of the bathroom floor, and he had known, finally, that it was over. It was *over*.

At first, he was struck with the knowledge of time wasted, all those letters he had written her, and the letters he had read in return, her fragile name scrawled on the upper corner of the envelope. He considered the minutes he had lost to standing before Hallmark displays, agonizing over the right card for Christmas, her birthday, a get-well message. The hours squandered in picking out the perfect gift. He considered all the family gatherings he had been forced to sit through, *her* family gatherings. He thought of mornings across the breakfast table when they had discussed plans to travel in their old age, nights in bed before sleep when the discussion turned to the proper course each should take if the other were to die first. He thought of all those stolen words that had spilled foolishly from his mouth. This waste of a perfectly good life was his first thought, those twenty-some years frittered away.

His second thought was that it would have to begin all over again with someone new—the cards, the gifts, the mornings and nights in bed—unless he was to live the rest of his life alone. But how could he unpack it all again, dig his zest for life out of the attic, where the rest of his idle youth had been boxed up and stored? And even though he was now utterly subservient to the Three Chairpersons of the Board, the Fabulous Fate Sisters, how could he trust them to treat him fairly a second time around?

At six o'clock that evening Herbert phoned. He and Maggie would be having dinner at eight. Would Frederick care to join them? Frederick was pleased to discover that he felt only gratification in hearing that Herbert and Maggie would be dining together yet again. He was thankful to learn that jealousy, even envy, were not among his emotions. Good for them. And good for him, too.

"Maggie's got a friend, Glenna, who's dying to meet you," Herbert added. "So what do you say to dinner at DiMaggio's? They serve Long Island duckling in a nice little port. Besides, it's the perfect place for the over-forty crowd." Frederick smiled. Perfect place, his foot. The last thing Herbert Stone needed in the first stages of his reconciliation was to run into hordes of young women such as Valerie and Sarah, all beseeching him to buy them Dirty Mothers, or Sex on the Beach, or Screaming Orgasms. What would Maggie Stone think of such extracurricular activity?

"Why not The China Boat?" Frederick asked. He was pleased that he could still detach himself from his own personal grief in order to badger Herbert just a bit. His sense of humor would save him, buoy him up over the waves of remorse that were beating him against the rocks.

"To tell the truth," said Herbert, lying, "I'm a little tired of the atmosphere at The China Boat." Frederick heard him exhale what must have been a silver stream of cigarette smoke. "So what about it? You up to meeting Maggie's friend?"

"Maybe another time, Herb," said Frederick. How could he explain to anyone that he needed to live alone first, to learn to function by himself before he looked for another relationship? After all, it wasn't like buying a car, or a house, or even a computer. It took time. And he was no different from the women he'd been listening to on talk shows, women who wanted to get to know themselves as adults, to learn to live alone before they hooked their lives up again to another human being. That's just how Frederick felt. He had been passed from Thelma Stone to

Chandra Kimball in one fell swoop, as though they were exchanging cake recipes—and may the Fates forgive him the sexist metaphor.

"You're going to go out and wander lonely as a cloud, or something stupid like that, aren't you?" Herbert wanted to know.

"Something like that," Frederick conceded.

"You've read too much poetry, Freddy," Herbert said. "Besides, what did Blake know about clouds?" He hung up the phone.

"Wordsworth," Frederick said to no one.

All his life Frederick Stone had believed that everything he did could be chalked up to experience. No action would be wasted, for it would be an education in itself. This philosophy in mind, he considered, briefly, a career as *The Failed Man*. He, too, could make his rounds of the talk-show circuit. Oprah, in her infinite wisdom, would discourage an all-female audience from openly spitting on him. "Let's learn from this creature," Oprah would beseech the enraged crowd. "There aren't many of this species in existence." They would pass him about. He would go bleeding, his entrails growing shorter and shorter as pieces were ripped away, from Oprah to Sally Jessy and Dr. Ruth and Vicki and Jenny Jones and Faith Daniels and Jane Whitney and Whoopi. In the end, no woman would want him again. Perhaps he could go on the road with a seedy circus, turn up at county fairs. For a modest fee, women could hurl softballs at the mechanism that would plunge him into a barrel of cold water. COME DUNK THE MALE ASSHOLE, the sign above his head would read. Small children would wear T-shirts bearing his face, covered by a huge black *X*. *The Failed Man*. Eventually, Chevy Chase would do a movie about his life.

Frederick sat before his computer without turning it on. Its large black eye, the eye of a cyclops, stared at him, silent, foreboding, the dark face of God, maybe. He couldn't abandon it forever, couldn't ignore the significance it would play in the future of the world. Computerized man was on the cusp of discoveries that he had only dreamed of in the past. Would Leonardo da Vinci—Herbert's tie person—probably the world's greatest genius, have walked away from the idea of the computer chip? What would the perfect Renaissance man have created, sitting before the latest 66-megahertz 486DX machine? And no doubt about it, Leonardo was of a dual spirit, man and nature coexisting in one body, Chandra's kind of man. Leonardo had refused to eat meat. "I believe the day will come when we look upon the murder of animals as we look upon the murder of men." Leonardo had said that, five hundred years ago. Maybe he had learned something, some universal secret, while sketching all those muscles and sinews and tendons of humans *and* animals. Maybe he had seen a connection, a brotherhood, a sameness that most people miss. A beating heart, after all, is a beating heart. And he would be the sort of man to bring the two worlds together: the world of nature and the world of technology. If Leonardo da Vinci was President of the United States—running on an independent ticket, of course—maybe he would pass a law stating that all poets must learn computers. And those young businessmen and -women, that Let's-Make-a-Buck crowd, would all be required to study mythology, poetry, music, art. *Study,* not simply take as college requirements and then cast aside. Because, if the two worlds—Chandra's world and Frederick's world—*didn't* learn to function together, there might be no world left when they flew apart.

Frederick thumbed through his file of programs. He felt as though he were an initiate upon the road to some discovery, a journey of the self, a regular Gilgamesh. And he must take the proper gear to aid him on this quest. So what would today's Gilgamesh, a man who has everything, need on his voyage? One matter was apparent: He would require some new software. He had been using the *Marriage* software. He would need to reprogram. From now on, he would need the *Lonely as a Cloud* software.

Seventeen

"Nobody, not even the rain, has such small hands."

—*E. E. CUMMINGS*

This girl was a child
Existing in a playground of stone.
Then one night her life was changed
Her hopes and dreams were rearranged
And she would never be the same again.
This girl is a woman now.

—*GARY PUCKETT & THE UNION GAP*

O n Saturday afternoon, Eddy Walsh called to say that the bank had approved the loan for his prospective buyers. Within the month that nice young couple would become the new owners of the lovely Victorian house at the end of the cul-de-sac on Ellsboro Street, the only house left in that neighborhood with the old-fashioned, screened-in front porch. Frederick and Chandra had bought it for seventy-five thousand, fifteen years earlier, because she had fallen in love with just the sight of it. Now, after paying off the remaining mortgage and deducting Eddy's percentage, they would be left with ninety thousand dollars to split, forty-five thousand each. Not a bad investment. Except that, at least to Frederick, there seemed a great sadness in the notion that a man from the bank could hand him a slip of paper, *Pay to the order of,* and it would represent all those years of his married life.

After hanging up the phone from giving Eddy the final go-ahead, he filled his cup with fresh coffee and went out to the front porch. It being Saturday, his neighbors were about, raking leaves into piles, stacking firewood in their backyards, putting up the occasional bird feeder, inserting bulbs into the ground for spring blooms. He could see Home Depot marigolds, wilted now in some of the lazier yards up and down the street. A few of the punctual homeowners had already replaced their dead marigolds with fresh Home Depot pansies, perfect colors for fall. Smoke was now corkscrewing out of a chimney here and there, the first fireplace fires of autumn. Even the Mullers had stoked their hearth. Frederick saw a wisp of gray ghost rising into the air over their house, followed by that fresh forest smell of hardwood. No doubt about it, it was another apparent metaphor: Autumn was putting summer out of its misery. He wondered if there was a poem in that notion. He could find himself a shoe box lid and jot it down, the way Tom Wingfield did in *The Glass Menagerie*. But Frederick had already decided that poetry was not his strength. Just as he was getting rid of the Victorian house, a painful memory of his past, he had decided to abandon his literary dreams as well. He was no poet. He was a man who had once studied English literature but now had a degree in accounting, the possessor of a damn good business mind. That was all. And it was enough. Besides, *Kenny Perkins: Tales of a New England Vet* would be published the following year. One author in the family would be sufficient.

It was to be his Saturday off from Cain's Corner Grocery, but now he was walking his usual walk to the store, and dreading his arrival. He would be obliged on this day to tell Mr. Cain that he would not be coming back to work. He whistled as he walked, the way he had done as a child on dark nights, frightened to be strolling home from choir practice, frightened of leaves in the wind, noises dribbling from back alleys, shadowy shapes in the graveyard, frightened of his own mortality. Yet what did he have to fear now, in the glorious afternoon sunshine of late September, with that marvel of ocean spilling before him, the gulls' little white petals fluttering above the surface? He had nothing to fear but the rest of his life. He had nothing to fear but that same old mortality.

Mr. Cain was most upset to learn the news.

"You can't be serious," he protested. But Frederick was as serious as a receding hairline. How could he tell the old man that there was something in Chandra's having found him there behind the cash register, having *exposed* him, as though he were the rotting throb of a bad tooth, that had spoiled the place for him? He hadn't been ready to be rooted out when he was. Now, like David Janssen in "The Fugitive," like David Carradine in "Kung Fu," he would need to travel on, to drift, rove, wander, glide into some other scenario.

"Things were just starting to pick up," Mr. Cain insisted sadly. He rubbed dust from a bottle of sweet pickles. Frederick nodded.

"And they'll continue to do so, Mr. Cain. You just wait and see." It was a good thing Mr. Cain had not computerized yet, as Frederick had been urging him to do. He would have to add COMPUTER EXPERIENCE NECESSARY on his Help Wanted sign, thus narrowing the body of applicants.

"Do you really have to leave?" the old man wondered. Again, Frederick nodded. Was that a moistness he saw in Mr. Cain's eyes? People were so reluctant to let go of their heroes, weren't they? And heroes had a hard time staying put. That's what sunsets were for. "It used to be that a good supply of flour, sugar, milk, bread, butter, and an assortment of candy was all you needed to do well in the grocery business," Mr. Cain went on. "But how am I supposed to know about things made out of sheep shit?" He waved a package of tofu hot dogs in emphasis.

Frederick smiled. He canted his head to one side, what Chandra had called his birdlike stance. *Hubris, Freddy.* He could almost hear her voice rising from the spaces between the canned vegetables, from atop the bags of wheat flour. *Unadulterated hubris.* Good. He was glad he still possessed a little pride, after all he'd been through.

"I'll come back now and then," he promised Mr. Cain. "Just to check up on you. And now that your grandson will be graduating from college, well, you'll be in fine hands." He patted Mr. Cain's shoulder. He would miss the old man and his rickety little store.

"How the hell am I supposed to recognize coffee beans from South America?" Mr. Cain demanded to know. "I was selling jars of instant until you came along."

"I've printed you up a chart," Frederick said. He produced a manila envelope. "Just hang it up in the back. You can choose a special blend each week. And I've written down a few more items you should order." Mr. Cain accepted the list with great trepidation.

"Is that home pregnancy test on here?" he wondered. "You know my wife won't let me order that contraption."

"No home pregnancy tests," Frederick promised. He didn't feel too terribly bad about not giving any notice. After all, Mr. Cain himself had stated often how the Help Wanted sign had been in the window only ten minutes before Frederick Stone had walked in, his eyes red with gin and grief, and ripped the notice down. Frederick shook his hand firmly, a good substantial shake. He turned to leave.

"Freddy?" said Mr. Cain. Frederick stopped, turned, waited. "You should get a haircut, son," the old man advised. "You're starting to look like one of the Andrews sisters."

It would take him half an hour, but he would walk to Panama Red's. He was meeting Herbert and Maggie there for dinner at seven. They had decided, at Maggie's insistence, to live together this time around, at least for a while, just to see what lessons had been learned. He would miss Herbert's company in the long stretch of autumn evenings that lay ahead, but then, that was a part of learning to live alone. And Maggie, he hardly knew Maggie at all. Maybe now he would be given the chance.

The sun had already sunk and now the slight chill of autumn, the first tremor, had moved in upon Portland. Leaves floated down like brown boats, some knocking against tree trunks, others sailing in the pure blue sea of open air. As Frederick walked, he noticed that neighbors, the Saturday cicadas, were finishing chores in their yards. He could hear their excited buzz of conversation, drifting from lawn to lawn. He thought about his own neighbors, back on Ellsboro Street. He would miss the Mullers in a strange kind of way. He wondered if he would ever take part in the notion of *neighbors* again, or if he was destined to become some kind of hermit. An Austin friar, perhaps. Maybe he would end up in a monkish cell, Caedmon's monastery, overlooking the ragged English sea. He could go off into the green mass of some immense forest—he knew there were still a few left—and take on a job as a watchtower person, the way Kerouac had done. Or perhaps he would become a lighthouse keeper on some tiny island, giving out paternal streams of light, drawing ships to him, steering them safely away from the jagged teeth of the rocks, offering up the occasional wave of hand to pleasure boats passing in the distance. After a period of years, they would refer to him—affectionately, of course—as The Old Light Keeper. And the stories of legend would grow up around him. Years after his death, they would keep him alive by telling of ghostly sightings: *It looked like a lantern, near the abandoned lighthouse, swinging all by itself, as though Freddy, the old light keeper, was still carrying it.* He would eventually *belong* to the community. Every Halloween folks would swear that the beacon of the abandoned lighthouse had blazed forth just at the stroke of midnight, its ragged fingers searching out the ships that have been lost at sea. There were worse ways to be memorialized. Communities had a way of remembering only horse thieves. And Frederick would rather be renowned as a midnight phantom than as the purloiner of Old Paint.

He had curled the newspaper open to the want ads, and as he walked, he read. Not a great deal of opportunity for a well-educated man, not in a state that had recently declared bankruptcy, as Maine had. But he didn't really have to work, at least not for a time. He wasn't a poor man, after all, not really. He had the money from the house, and his share of several thousand more dollars from the joint savings account. And he would inherit fifty percent of his mother's estate. Maybe he would bounce around Europe for a while, spend a summer in Vienna as he'd always planned, walk through the musty reminders of Franz Kafka's old room. You could do things like that when you had money. You could do lots of things.

In an instant, he decided that he would buy Herb and Maggie their dinner. Later, he would drop by The China Boat and toss a free round of drinks down the bar. Maybe he would even invite Marta, the bartending geisha, out to dinner sometime. They could drink a Dirty Mother or two, talk about the sadness that had engulfed their early lives. This was the stuff great literature was built on, after all. This was the stuff that had brought down both kings and paupers, this talk about families, this longing for love, this battle against mortality. Countries had risen and fallen for less.

He knew one thing for sure in regards to his money. He wanted to buy Polly's kids something nice, send it down to Connecticut by UPS. Maybe a collector's doll of some kind for the niece. But he had no idea at all what to buy the nephews, those young men.

A baseball bat? Michael Jackson's latest CD? A disease-free prostitute with a gross of condoms clutched in her fist? In a week or two, he would phone them up and talk to them one at a time.

He stopped at the little park overlooking Casco Bay to slip the aging pictures from his wallet. The two boys resembled their father, Percy Hillstrip, at least from what Frederick could remember of his brother-in-law. But the little girl looked so much like Polly that he felt enormous grief just gazing at the photo, grief followed by a monstrous surge of guilt. Frederick was aware, suddenly, of a sense of duty to Polly, a sense of retribution brought on by the dream he had dreamed the night of the animal-rights march, when she had risen up, flesh and blood, to speak to him. Who else did these children have to tell them things about their mother, to recall the stories of her youth? He would make up what he hadn't bothered to notice about his sister during all those years of growing up together. Here was a way in which he could put his writing talents to some fine work. Polly had been in demand all over Portland by only the best bachelors. She had been so swamped with offers to take her to the senior prom that she had hidden in the musty attic all day, just to avoid the phone calls. The flowers being delivered nonstop to her door had nearly asphyxiated her. She had been a genius at the piano, mesmerizing relatives and friends with her nimble fingers. She had been beautiful beyond words, her skin like a fine white silk. Pity, the only pictures left behind had shown her as dumpy and plain; but then, she had never been photogenic. And yet, in the midst of all this beauty, this talent, she had chosen wifedom and motherhood, chosen to bear three little children rather than play the piano across Europe, sip Dom Perignon with the jet set. The children's lives had been precious to her. She had held each of them, at birth, in her hands as gently as if holding snowflakes. And he would tell them that, soon. Maybe at Christmas he would catch a bus down their way just to meet them. He would be Uncle Fred. And they had an Uncle Herbert, an Aunt Maggie. People shouldn't drift apart, families shouldn't.

Several herring gulls, thinking he held food in his hands, swooped in at his feet, their loud noises *hiyak hiyah* jarring him away from the pinwheel of Polly's dear children. He put the pictures back into his wallet—such sweet young streamers—wiped his eyes, cleared his throat. He wasn't such a bad guy, not really.

So why, then, did it seem that he had had the lion's share of reparation? He wished Mr. Bator would say a little something. As soon as Frederick was settled somewhere, he would hire a private detective to find Mr. Bator, find that tiny spot in the world where his old biology teacher had crept to. And maybe he would even throw a suitcase into the trunk of his car one weekend, drive all the way down to Washington, to the Vietnam Veterans' Memorial. *Ten* boys from his senior class, the class of 'sixty-six. He might even do his own rubbing of Richard Hamel's name, as Gene Nelson had done. The truth was that he still hated the sleazy bastard, even if he *had* died a hero's death. Once a mumblety-peg cheat, always a mumblety-peg cheat. But there was nothing wrong in rounding up everyone you had once known, was there? There was nothing wrong with a little safety in numbers.

He heard the Toyota before he saw it, recognized the sputter of the muffler. It pulled into the small crushed rock drive next to the picnic tables and sat there, idling. In the oncoming waves of evening, with the pole light just beginning to flicker on, the car was a reddish-orange. Then the engine suddenly died, and Frederick heard the door creak open, slam, footprints stepping on the crushed rock, coming closer.

"If it isn't Little Red Riding Hood," Frederick said, without glancing up.

"And if it isn't the big bad wolf," he heard Chandra say. "Just who I'm looking for." She sat beside him on the bench. He could smell woodsmoke on her sweater and wondered if she had a fireplace in her new home. He knew the real address this time—7 Sir Pelias Terrace—but he had not bothered to drive by, not once, not even in those long stretches of evening when he sat out on the screened-in porch and listened to the heart of Ellsboro Street beating all about him. Their respective lawyers, on the other hand, had been keeping in close touch with each other over the sale of the house.

"How'd you know where to find me?" he asked.

"Well, it began with my driving by the house and seeing the For Sale sign gone," Chandra said. "Then I went on to Cain's Grocery to discover that you'd quit your job and gone off walking. I assumed you'd take the scenic route, and here you are."

"Why were you driving past the house to begin with?" he asked. "It's in a cul-de-sac."

"Nostalgia," Chandra answered. "I love that house. Moving out wasn't easy for me, you know."

"*Staying* wasn't a picnic," Frederick reminded her, and then he looked at her for the first time. There seemed to be more gray hairs about the sides of her face, or was he merely hoping this, praying that she had come out of the storm a bit weathered herself?

"It's been sold?" she asked. He nodded.

"Hasn't your lawyer told you yet?"

"She's gone away for the weekend with *your* lawyer," Chandra said. "He's taking her to Cape Cod." They sat quietly, thinking about this great irony. When Chandra laughed aloud, her lilting, happy laugh, Frederick was able to laugh with her. "Do you think we're obligated by law to buy them a wedding gift, if they should decide to take the plunge?" she wondered. "Maybe they'll ask us to stand up for them at the ceremony. After all, we brought them together."

"For every action there's a reaction," said Frederick. "I suppose that goes for divorces, too. You'll need to sign papers so that we can divide up the booty."

"Who bought it?" she wanted to know.

"A nice young couple just starting out," he told her. "A nice young couple madly in love, the way we were when we first moved in. How long do you think *their* fairy tale will last?" She merely shrugged.

Gulls had discovered the new arrival and now they gathered unctuously around her feet, thinking surely she had something for them. Frederick watched for a few seconds, realizing that he'd been a bit like them at one time. But Chandra didn't seem to have any bread crumbs to give the gulls, either. Poor buggers. He knew how they felt. He'd been there.

"How's what's his name?" he couldn't help but ask. The tip of her nose was beginning to turn reddish with the evening chill. She had buried her hands deep into her sweater, clutching it to herself. She thought for a moment before she answered.

"Ted?"

"Mr. EPA." Frederick nodded. "The man with a natural forest of hair."

"That was a mutual interest that just fizzled out," Chandra answered.

"I'm sorry to hear that," said Frederick. He thought he heard her snort softly, one of those little disbelieving snorts for which she was well known. He decided to ignore it. They sat quietly, the sound of traffic bleating away softly in the background, the screeching gulls at their feet, the bay unfurling before them in the gathering dusk. He wondered what it would be like to touch her, this stranger sitting next to him, this newly established entity: *a divorced woman*. He had never even dated a divorced woman before—although he had dallied with a married one, the ubiquitous Doris Bowen—and now he wondered what divorced women were like. More experienced? More understanding? A wiser creature than before? He'd even pulled *divorce* up, on his *American Heritage Dictionary III, Software Edition*—310,000 words at his computer fingertips—and discovered that it came from the Latin *divortium, to turn different ways.*

"Back in our courting days," Chandra said suddenly, "I always knew that you hadn't written those poems you sent me in letters. Even at Woodstock, that very first night. I always knew." Frederick spotted the Peak's Island ferry, crossing Casco Bay, a well-lit little country moving toward shore, a tiny universe, the Enterprise, even. He could make out the silhouettes of people aboard, tiny blips of humanity. She was in the wrong line of work, his ex-wife was, if she was that well-versed in the poets of the twentieth century, not to mention those easily forgotten poets laureate. But then, what else could psychology majors partake in, while they were waiting to turn their counseling skills loose on an unsuspecting world, but plenty of English courses at the 100 level?

"I see," he said. "And you went ahead and married me anyway. So much for your ability to judge character." She giggled her little giggle, the kind of thing that one might refer to as a *cackle,* after forty, fifty years of marriage. To Frederick's ears right then, however, it still sounded sweet and innocent. If asked about this innocence, his computer thesaurus would probably suggest that Frederick refer to Chandra's laughter as *guileless.*

"I always thought it was charming of you," she said. He nodded, appreciatively. There was little else he could do. Many times, during those long lonely nights in the Victorian house on Ellsboro Street, when he had lain on his back in their marriage bed, or on the hellish settee, and contemplated the greenish numbers on the clock, waiting for time to carry him toward another day, on those nights of crucifixion, nights of impalement, nights of self-flagellation, he had found comfort in the only constant in his maimed life: At least she thought him an excellent poet. Well, it was good this knowledge had come to him at the last, and not the beginning. He wondered, genuinely, why it had come to him at all, wondered what she was doing there. Granted, she had reason to be concerned about the disappearing For Sale sign, reason to wonder when her share of the money would materialize. She did, after all, have bills to pay in her new life as a divorced woman, a woman who has *turned a different way*. But it was more likely that she'd come back simply to tell him about the poems, to unmask his plagiarizing ways, to expose his last shred of human dignity to the cool evening air. Well, he had *turned a different way* himself in these many declining weeks, these days rushing past as though he were on a fast-moving train, staring helplessly from behind a passenger window.

Frederick stood, brushed the seat of his jeans as a safety measure. He had dropped down onto seagull shit more than once in his current life as a bench person.

"I've got a dinner invitation from Herbert and Maggie," he told his ex-wife. "I'd better be running."

"Herbert and *Maggie?*" Chandra was sincerely shocked. "I'll be damned," she added. Yes, well, let her be damned. Not all the male Stones had been skipped out to sea, flat, useless rocks, never to be retrieved by the sirens who had tossed them there. Some were worth the saving, although why *Herbert Stone* was among the salvageable was still a mystery to Frederick.

"It was nice seeing you again," he said, and warmly, he thought. "If our lawyers ever surface, I suspect they'll have some money for us." He turned away to follow his well-worn trail along the strand of bay.

"Freddy?" There seemed to be wind in her voice, lifting the word, a youthful vitality that the years could never diminish. What had he thought of her, that first night after they'd made love, when she stood before the window of his old Boston apartment and watched the rain beating itself to death on the pane? He had wondered then if he could ever hold on to something so free, so ephemeral, so like the rain as this illusive, fanciful creature.

"Yes?" He stopped, turned again to face her.

"Tell Maggie and Herbert hello." Frederick nodded. He felt a crisis emerging and was horrified to be tested so soon, so close to his having arisen like a Phoenix from the ashes of his marriage. But a crisis was winging close to his lips and he felt them tremble, quiver with the question they longed to ask: *Would you like to join us for dinner? Oh, please, join us for dinner. Join us forever.* He could almost see the pinwheel starting up again, the streamers turning slowly, then faster and faster until they were a colorful blur. He nodded once more, then turned back along the path.

"And Freddy?" she called out. He stopped, waited for her words to reach him. "I need to tell you that I'm sorry, from the bottom of my heart, sorry that the fairy tale didn't last. And I hope that we can at least be friends." He didn't bother to turn this time, too afraid he'd surrender, too afraid he'd squander all his painful lessons in one fell swoop.

"I wrote two of those poems myself," he shouted back at her.

"I know," he heard her say. " 'Ode to Woodstock' was one of them." The gulls rose up at the noise of her words, their wings full of wind, floating above his head now like old metaphors. She was right. "Ode to Woodstock" had been one of them: *Here on this bounteous field, we reap the first harvest of our youth.* Or had it been the *last* harvest? They were reaping *something,* was all he could remember now. He looked back to see her hair rising in strands with the wind, her baggy sweater hiding those breasts he had touched so many times in his career as her husband, the skirt hiding her graceful thighs. Would he ever touch her again? Maybe if he agreed to become her friend? After all, they had started as friends, that night at Woodstock, when she had looked up at him with eyes that held a thousand protests in their pupils. *Chandra,* she had told him. *It's Sanskrit for moonlike.*

"What was the other poem I wrote?" he asked. Was he so easily read, even by his wife? It was important for him to know this.

"That one you wrote about me the first night we made love," she answered him. "You know, the one that begins 'Nobody, not even the rain, has such small hands.' See? I knew all along." He heard her sweet, natural laughter rising above the strident cry of the shore birds. So he could still make her laugh, could he? That was a poetic art in itself.

"You nailed me," he told her. "I should've known I couldn't

fool *you*." He turned back down the beach, felt his feet moving beneath him, eating into the sand, taking him away from her. Poor e. e. cummings! Poor uncapitalized bastard! Well, it was no skin off his nose now, was it, if *frederick stone* got credit for the poem? Frederick wondered where the poet's ghost was hovering at that very moment. Maybe e. e. had gone to some kind of Sesame Street hell, where all the letters of the alphabet were huge capitals, poking at him with red-hot tridents.

He heard the Toyota start up, the muffler giving itself away again—he had planned to take her car in to be fixed the very day she had packed up and left him—and then she was gone in a tiny swirl of pebbles. He stopped to watch her taillights disappear into the deep blue of evening. Seagulls came in quickly and lit upon the gravel where the Toyota had been, scratched among the grit, certain there had been a gift in her having been there.

The lights on Peak's Island were just blinking on. He paused at the edge of the strand and stared across at that swell of land emerging from the ocean, as though some huge sleeping creature had allowed a few people to live on one of its humps. Maybe he would write a children's book. He would call it *The Mystery of Dragon Island,* about a prehistoric creature who fell asleep for a million years, only to waken and find that people are now living on one of its exposed humps. They have built houses, a school, a church. They are very, very serious about their little knoll of land. Now the dragon cannot move beneath the sea because moving would wash the island people away. So he floats, his limbs growing weak and stiff, his scales crystallizing. But no one on the island suspects the truth. No one knows of his Great Sacrifice. Or is it a sacrifice? Frederick decided that the dragon did the selfless act because he had been lonely before his enormous nap. Now he can feel the scuffle of feet across his back, the soft caress of picnics, the tickle of baseball games. Every now and then he is stung by the pinprick of someone's dying, the puncture of the spade, the scraping coffin. But he is not alone. He is never alone.

Frederick picked up an abandoned conch shell that lay at his feet. It was not just on Ellsboro Street that homes were being left behind. He put the shell to his ear, and there it was: the sound of his blood rushing to and fro, the sound of his heart curled up safely in his ear. His life, beating away by seconds. He tossed the shell far up into the night sky, saw it rotate nicely in midair, a little universe spinning, Triton's horn airborne. He could move to an island. There was something clean about the people who lived on islands, people who kept themselves at a pristine distance. From shore, no one could peer into their windows with cameras. Their entire lives appeared to be lights flickering on the horizon, flags waving. Their unabridged language, the foghorns one hears in the gray mist of dawn. To people who are landlocked, even the screams of islanders sound like the sweet songs of dolphins. They sound like fairy songs to those people who have pressed their ears to the sea. *Come away, O Human child, to the waters and the wild.* Maybe he *would* live on an island. Maybe a daily ferryboat ride, a Sea Change per diem, would help fill up the empty spaces. There would be so many new things to learn. He would be up all night tearing down misconceptions about island life. Maybe he would find himself a single room at some boarding house, a room with a private bath, one that would offer the safe perimeters of his old college room. *Because he had felt safer in those days,* with four walls, with Webster's dictionary on his desk, a radio, a clock, and a teakettle that worked. The world wasn't such a big place then. The world was something that could be taken on, if a young man had such inclinations. He would find a boarding house run by a big, robust woman with a swaying bosom, who whipped up home-cooked meals and dished out folksy advice. It wasn't just the Yuppies, Frederick decided, who were looking for Norman Rockwell. He would live at a place called Emma's Boarding House, and Emma would keep a watchful eye on the type of women he dated. The muscles of Emma's large bare arms would tremble as she weeded her summer garden. She would scold him about his shirts not being freshly ironed, the ponytail inching down his back. He would cut all her firewood, because he wasn't a bad guy, not really. Chandra would tell him that he was seeking out a mother figure in all women, but then, Chandra wouldn't know he was living on an island. Chandra wouldn't know where in the world he had gone. In the early evenings, he would take his dinner at Will's Restaurant, commenting now and then on how fast little Will was growing. He would spend late nights in the parlor of Emma's Boarding House, sipping Pernod before a raging fire, listening to the old fishermen tell stories of vessels wrecked at sea, of gold coins swirling in underwater currents, of silver goblets being sucked up by whales. He would politely oblige the unscrewing of a wooden leg in order to gape at where the real leg had once lived. During the day, he would sit before his computer up at the single window in his room, the window overlooking the ocean, the window looking back to landlocked shore. All he'd ever really wanted was a job he could do from the privacy of his own home. He used to think that writing poems would be one way, but there was no money in poesy, not unless one wrote badly enough to hit a public nerve. The only other way he had, or so it seemed, had been through his accounting degree and his beloved computer. Was that so wrong? He wished now that he'd asked Chandra that very question. His eyes teared unexpectedly, and he felt a genuine surprise that they did. He dug a Kleenex out of his pants pocket, the little plastic packet such as they sold at Cain's, and blew his nose. And then, there it was! Above the play of the waves, an old familiar voice, barely audible now.

"Listen, Freddy," Mr. Bator whispered. "Stop the whining. Nobody likes a loser. Nice guys finish last because they can't bear to hang out with the assholes who finish first. This isn't Auschwitz, son. This isn't Dachau. Pull your chin up and point it at the future." Frederick smiled, stuffing the Kleenex back into his jacket pocket. That was the speech Mr. Bator had given him the day Frederick knew he'd never play football for Portland High.

"The chin, Mr. Bator," Frederick recited, "is the lower part of the jaw that is below the lips." He put his hands into his pants pockets, for they were growing numb. Down the stretch of beach the melancholy silhouettes of late-feeding gulls rose, then dipped above the surface of water. A few boats bobbed against the skyline. He thought of other ships, other gulls beseeching food from those original tourists. The first had been Norsemen, probably as early as the eleventh century, not exactly an Alan Alda crowd, those boys. Then one day the Cabots appeared on Portland's horizon, around 1498. What did they want, these seafarers? What drove them? Surely, it was something more than land, than conquest, than riches. Did they suffer the same wild seed that drove poets onward? Chandra would say that the Cabots, Columbus, Magellan, Balboa, Cortez, the whole lot of them were wading around up to their armpits in pure testosterone. Not to mention all that politically incorrect shit they were stepping in. And maybe that would be true. But they had all left behind what they knew best, what they must have loved best: hearth, friends, country. Had they dreamt of their wives, all those bobbing, bouncing nights at sea? Was it the fear of *ubi sunt,* that old fraternity dare of *carpe diem,* that pushed them to such discovery, and destruction, in the New World? Could he take lessons from them, these brothers, his kinsmen?

Unlike them, he would start out slowly. He would wait for spring before he launched out to new spheres—what *had* those Pilgrims been thinking of? Portland was, after all, a *wintering* place. Winter Harbor, they had called it. He would wait until the birds of spring came winging back up the coast, until he saw black specks of migrating hawks from his car window. Until the trees were green again with leaves, as though all the neighborhood men had gone out into their yards and stapled the leaves back on with Home Depot staple guns. He thought of Herbert, waiting for him at Panama Red's, his brother, his family. And Maggie's pretty face rising above a glass of white wine. He felt the immediate need to be with them, to be close to them, to share with them the aging photos of Polly's children. He speeded up his pace, walking past the statue of Henry Wadsworth Longfellow, walking past the stop sign where he'd received his very first traffic violation, walking toward the cluster of lights he knew to be Panama Red's. He would begin by moving out of the house on Ellsboro Street and finding a new place to live, *a room of one's own.* He would look under the "Rents Available" on island after island until he ferreted out the perfect place to put down anchor. Maybe he would discover that he didn't want to travel as he thought. After all, with a home computer, the world was at his fingertips. He could order special coffee beans via his modem. He could purchase home appliances, flowers, airplane tickets. He could rent motel rooms and automobiles without ever leaving his comfortable chair. He could communicate with lonely people in all fifty states through private or public notes. He could discuss houseplants with specialists, model trains, photography, shortwave radio, country music, ear mites in dogs. Would Leonardo da Vinci have walked away from all that? Leonardo would have *loved* tofu hot dogs.

Frederick would revive Stone Accounting immediately. *Dear*

Client. It is my sincere pleasure to inform you that after a brief interruption of daily business procedure Stone Accounting and Consultation is now reopening its doors. As he crested the top of Fickamore Street, he paused. Below him, Panama Red's was blinking like a newly landed spaceship. He saw the forms of men and women filtering in from whatever lives they had chosen to lead, cuneiform creatures trickling from their jobs, their homes, their automobiles, their lovers, coming to join the other humans for a rendezvous with unintelligible time. Their voices rose up to him, excited, happy timbres. He wondered if, in an idle, careless second, he had dreamed them all up, had invented them simply to amuse himself while he floated, like his crystallized dragon, in an ocean of time. And had he perhaps imagined a woman named Chandra Kimball, a woman whose eyes seemed to hold all humanity, whose cheekbones were smooth chalky cliffs? It wasn't a question of whether or not he could live life without her. He knew now that he could. The question, instead, was *how* he would do it.

He began the quick descent down Fickamore Street, toward the flashing crimson lights of the Panama Red's sign, for his toes were growing numb, *crystallizing,* perhaps. Or maybe they were oxidizing. "We're rusting, Freddy," is what Herbert had said. "That's really what happens as one ages." He paused on the corner of Fickamore and Beech as a city bus rumbled past. He wondered if it was Tommy Viorikic, hurrying home to his 1953 Chevy. At least Tommy had a plan. And Frederick himself was not without plans. First, he would fend off the cold with a quick scotch, and then he would beseech Herbert to tell the old college story about how the human leg ended up in the veterinarian lab. Second, he would find an island on which to live.

The faces standing under the door to the restaurant were young and fresh, ready to go off and find continents, even if it meant falling from the very face of the earth, falling over the edge of the world. Frederick stopped before them, a young man, an even younger woman. Beneath the flickering Panama Red's sign their faces were on fire with reflected light, moving, shimmering, as though they were faces submerged in a lava lamp, faces from Frederick's personal history, faces from the sixties. *The Ghosts of Woodstock Past.* He would live on an island.

"To hell with John Donne," Frederick muttered to the youngsters before him, and felt quite satisfied to hear them laugh deri-sively. It was now his job, as a rusting, sputtering middle-aged man, to irritate the young. He would live on an island. He would receive visits from Herbert, Maggie, his niece, his nephews by blood, and Mr. Bator, should the fine teacher ever emerge one day from the brine of early high-school wishes and dreams. He would find a homey boarding house, and from his single room over-looking the sea he would keep a constant eye on the mainland. He really wasn't such a bad guy, and maybe one day Chandra would realize that. In the meantime, like a kind, benevolent lighthouse, he would keep a watchful eye on Portland. And maybe, after a time, it would no longer seem as if he'd left something there.